NO WEAPON FORGED

RON HADDOW

NO WEAPON FORGED

RON HADDOW

SERENDIPITY

Disclaimer

This is a work of fiction, albeit with a basis of biblical prophecy. While, as in all fiction, the literary perceptions are based on experience, all characters are either the products of the author's imagination or are used fictitiously. No reference to any real person is intended or should be inferred.

Copyright © Ron Haddow 2006

First published in 2006 by

Serendipity
First Floor
37 / 39 Victoria Road
Darlington
DL1 5SF

All rights reserved
Unauthorised duplication
contravenes existing laws
British Library Cataloguing-in-Publication data
A catalogue record for this book is available from the British Library

ISBN 1-84394-191-0

Printed and bound by CPI Antony Rowe, Eastbourne

A debt of gratitude is owed to my family, as, like so many servicemen, I spent much time away from them, spread over so many years. Unexpectedly, a similar pattern followed as a civilian. However, it was during these latter times that the opportunity came to gather added and even unique experiences that have formed the authentic background on which this novel is based. Although the text was often assembled piecemeal, in various parts of the world, my wife Dorothy has borne the brunt of the time I have often spent reviewing and revising. It is with grateful thanks that I dedicate the following to 'Dorit' and to Israel.

contents

PROLOGUE

The need for this book was perceived over the last ten years. The author had spent most of his life immersed in defence matters, world situations, threats, and in researching and analysing the technologies, essential for both civil and armed forces requirements. Apart from spending many years in the military, flying, lecturing, designing, testing and travelling extensively, a turning point occurred in 1975, when a new appointment required lectures to be given on the Arab-Israel conflicts. It was soon realised that, when examined in detail, certain peculiarities in the results of these wars did not accord with normal military analysis. The niggling suspicion that something beyond normal comprehension had repeatedly taken place, refused to go away. This, therefore, is a war story with a difference.

What is the significance of the small State of Israel and its capital city Jerusalem? Why is it so regularly featured as headline news? What is likely to happen next?

This book, written as a novel, not only covers the key aspects of this scenario, in which so many nations seem to be involved, but is based around a key aspect that affects us all in our daily lives - OIL! More importantly, it also takes the reader into a journey about the future events in the Middle East.

Novels usually rely heavily on the imagination of the author. However, the content of the initial chapters here are based on actual events. As the story unfolds, they are seen to be the essential background that will shape a future conflict. It will be seen by the reader how these, apparently diverse contributions, like pieces of a jigsaw puzzle come together. It is assessed that within years rather than decades, for those who can see, there will be a major war in the Middle East. The future scenario that is forecast here can be fairly accurately based, as the technologies required, a description of much of the action and the protagonists already exist. Currently, they are in various states of capability and preparedness.

The passage of time is, of course, inseparable from history. It moves inevitably forward, in only one direction. We cannot return to it even a moment after it has passed. Many scientists now believe that history does have a fixed end point, or destination. While literally millions of events occur daily world wide, some appear to cluster together and evolve into what can be clearly identified, indeed can be classified, as 'milestone' events. Do these occur by accident, or are they in some way designed?

Who will have the last word on the Middle East? The reader is left to judge for him or herself!

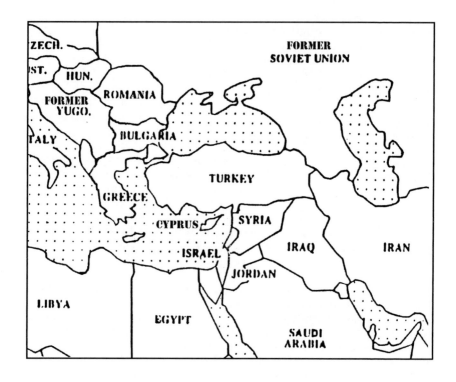

The Players

CHANCE ENCOUNTER

Keith increased his pace and, fleetingly, risked looking round. It was early evening, after a very hot and dusty day. Clearly, a young lad, perhaps as young as 12 years old, was following him. Keith suddenly stopped and took a great interest in the wares of the nearest vendor in the souk. The store contained rolls of suiting material stacked to the ceiling. Spotting his apparent interest, the berobed store owner authoritatively clapped his hands. An assistant shot out from behind a curtain, carrying a stool. His master implored Keith to enter, sit and watch; no doubt sensing a possible sale to this relatively pale and most certainly rich Westerner. A made to measure suit was not on Keith's agenda and he quickly stepped back into the milling crowd before the sales pitch started. The boy was still there and had stopped. Their eyes met briefly. Why was he following?

In the Shah's Persia, in the late 1950s, since renamed Iran, perhaps the boy was just trying to sell something. In this part of the world this might be anything from 'dirty' postcards to something more physical. Things may be even more serious. Was he working for someone unseen? Had he been lurking there right from the hotel? Keith reminded himself that British soil - the British Embassy - was but a few hundred yards away. A robbery would certainly not net much for this lad. Keith was down to his last few hundred rials. Robbery, he decided, was fairly unlikely while both crowds and daylight remained. He must hurry onwards.

The huge arched entrance to Teheran's covered main bazaar, with its intriguing merchandise and multitude of pervasive smells, many of dubious origins, now loomed just yards ahead. The inevitable beggars were clustered near the entrance. He could no longer see the boy. The place was crowded. Maybe it was just coincidence? He glanced again. The boy reappeared, yet again, this time only feet away across the narrowing souk. There was no doubt that he was intent on following. But why?

Keith stopped and examined some leather goods. The crowds jostled. They were also in a hurry. From a distant muezzin the call to evening prayers had started.

In the gloom, under the vaulted roof of the bazaar, the boy was slightly ahead, waiting just beyond a barrow piled high with flat round bread-loaves. Keith moved onwards again, as much as one could in the increasing swirl of humanity. He turned sharply into the jewellers. Here were the best bargains in filigree silver, spotted only the day before.

In the Western sense, to describe the establishment as a jewellers was a considerable overstatement. The jewellery was individually produced on the spot, by two craftsmen who sat, cross-legged, on the floor. There was much filing and scraping, some grunting and an occasional burst of gas flame, as some intricate piece was silver or gold-soldered. Very few examples of their work were displayed, most objects being made to order. A very small counter boasted a very rudimentary set of jeweller's scales.

When Keith arrived a rich-looking local customer was leaning over the counter. He was talking very loudly and brandishing a golden ring in one hand, while occasionally hitting the counter emphatically with the other. Perhaps this was not Keith's best time to haggle with the proprietor! However, it was probably Keith's last chance to buy, before flying home. He waited.

With a final flourish the owner broke off his presumed disagreement with his customer, who hustled out. No doubt the owner had recognised Keith, as one who had haggled less than 24 hours before. Here was his chance of a killing! He gave a loud shout! The inevitable low stool was produced. Keith sat. Lemonade arrived in a few seconds in a dripping wet bottle, accompanied by a small glass. A drinking vessel that was so filthy that he would have not used it for a domestic animal back home. Keith declined the glass and wiped the neck of the cold bottle, before tipping it up. Strange people - Westerners - thought the proprietor. The last one hadn't wanted a glass either.

The boy, Keith's unwanted shadow, who had been standing watching in the doorway, also entered the shop. He joined Keith, grinning as he sat down close-by, on the floor. The proprietor did not seem in the least worried by this unexpected intrusion.

Not speaking Farsi, but hoping that the boy might understand his annoyance, Keith turned and spoke to him quite sharply. 'Why are you following me?' The immediate reply was a surprise. 'Only because I wanted to speak to you in English. I am Ahmed Pavli and I want to speak to people in English,' he said. 'You are American?' 'No' replied Keith, in some surprise. 'English!' 'Real English?' said the boy, grinning broadly, in delight. 'I only wanted to try English,' he continued. 'When I grow up the Shah will be gone and I will be famous, so I shall need to speak English,' he said.

Keith was somewhat amused by this statement, as he had recently met the Shah, on one of his rare private visits to England. It was difficult to imagine the demise of the Peacock Throne - especially when spoken by a mere boy!

In those (now distant) Cold War days, Keith and other electronics specialists like him, often visited Iran on duty. This was well known to the Shah, who had given permission for his territory to be used both as a listening base and for overflight facilities. This was an absolute monarchy and the Shah was in total command. The perceived threat to his huge country was from the Soviet North. Little did the Shah, or indeed anyone else at the time, realise that a potent, and much more imminent threat was an invisible and spiritual one. This was being fomented and developed both from factions within his own country and from France. A radical Muslim Cleric, known as Ayatollah Homeini was waiting out his exile, in Paris. Was this mere boy a follower of the extremists who wished to overthrow the Shah? Were Keith and his fellow crew members under some sort of surveillance? Could the boy possibly be in the pay of the Russians? At least it was clear that he had nothing to do with *Savak*, the Shah's secret police.

Keith had just completed his last special radar 'calibration' flight. Possibly he shouldn't have come out alone. He said nothing and turned from the boy to the proprietor. Several samples of filigree silver were brought out from an ancient safe, hidden under a blanket in the corner. They were spread out for inspection on a shabby cloth, draped over another stool.

An item of silver was eventually selected and a bargain was struck after haggling, despite frequent interruptions by the boy - both in Farsi and English. Keith had gained an unwanted interpreter, but this was not necessarily a good thing. From past experience in the Middle East he had discovered that some prudent language 'misunderstandings' were always useful during haggling. There were also times during haggling when one, in feigned puzzlement - indeed in disgust, needed to turn away - as if to leave. However, the wily shopkeepers often knew all these tricks. Indeed, sometimes one did go away and returned later. This was not always successful - as this usually indicated particular interest in some specific item. Thereafter, only a small reduction in price could usually be achieved. On the contrary, it often paid to turn away and appear to lose interest by taking interest in another - or even several - of the wares on show, rather than departing. This was often a good ploy to get a further reduction. Indeed, to become adept at haggling took experience. Ahmed kept interrupting. Perhaps the boy was a 'plant' and in the employ of a whole lot of similar shopkeepers?

Keith's overseas allowances were actually far less than the store owner could have imagined, and considerably less than the American servicemen - or the British Civil Servants, serving in the region. In those days the British tax-payer got 'full value' from all servicemen on 'temporary duty overseas'. First, their daily food allowance was cancelled when they left home; even for just a day or two. It was replaced with what was known as 'local overseas allowance'. This often amounted to much less, and was supposedly based on the cost of living in the country concerned.

The result of all this was that, foremost on Keith's mind was that he had lost six shillings a day (seventy two pence in 'old' money), in coming to Persia. By some quirk of government calculation it was replaced by just five and seven pence - a daily reduction of five pence! This was not to be dismissed as trivial, when one was only paid just £15 a week, including flying pay. Clearly remembered were some locations, where the daily allowance would only buy one good meal a day.

On reflection, perhaps things could be worse, as the coalminers back home were currently striking for sixpence more a week!

As an aside, the question of the meagre allowance had been a point of regret on his previous visit to the Middle East. It had been to Sharjah, in the Persian Gulf, where, in an extravagant fling of an entire day's allowance, he had haggled in an Arab souk over a metal carpenter's set-square. Keith had been bent on replacing a wooden one, made at school carpentry classes. In retrospect he had realised that the Arab hadn't haggled overmuch, because, when the next DIY task came along, the marvellous new set-square turned out to be less than square! Such was life. The incident had considerably amused Keith's eldest son at the time. However, the errant set-square, (after suitable adjustment), remains serviceable to this day. One indeed needs to learn by experience!

Moving back towards the hotel, the boy continued alongside. He kept talking. Although dressed in a well-smudged T shirt and long baggy shorts, Ahmed's face was bright and with a quick smile. His clear olive skin, shiny hair and well-nourished appearance, showed that either he was from a relatively well-off family, or he fended for himself very well on the streets. He had not attempted to beg, which pointed to the former. In quite good English, he spoke of his considerable ambitions. Soon, he said, he intended to go to university. One day he would lead the country! A laudible ambition indeed. However, Keith noticed that when he spoke seriously there was a fixed tension in his gaze. Almost the sort of fanatical look one normally associated, at the time, with nuclear 'disarmers', anti-fluoride-in-tap-water freaks and certain political or 'human rights' activists, when interviewed on TV. A bit worrying really. But only a boy!

Keith hurried on. What a strange land this was. As the sun sank down behind the mountains, huge shadows were thrown. The haunting sound of the muezzin gave the final call upon the faithful to prayer. Quite suddenly the street had rapidly emptied, but others bowed to the ground where they were. The boy followed, right up to the hotel steps. However, the door-keeper gave him a stern glare and said something rapidly in Farsi. Ahmed turned away and was last seen looking back over his shoulder, before finally waving goodbye. Now a sudden silence. All traffic and pedestrians had stopped for prayers.

A chance encounter? Keith had seen so many sights and strands of humanity on his world-wide travels. Some of it was appalling, in Western terms. Live TV news-gathering had yet to bring the 'world village' theme to everyone's living room. In those days he had been quite privileged to have had the diversity of so many experiences at first-hand, especially, as was the saying in the Armed Services, - it was 'at HM The Queen's expense'!

Within the high-rise modern hotel - one of only a handful in the city - a buzz could be heard coming from the direction of the bar. Alcohol was permitted in such establishments, but only under very strict control. The majority of the hotel guests were businessmen, engineers or geologists, mainly concerned with various major building projects and the oil industry.

Not wishing to join the relatively overpaid and boisterous Australians, who were up from the Shah's rich oil-fields to unload their cash, Keith called the lift. Alcohol, forbidden to the Muslim population at large, seemed to be the Australian oil prospectors' main concern. Keith supposed that the effect of two or three months at a time, oil prospecting in the scorching desert, drove one to these extremes. In an hour or two the 'Aussies' would probably be at a floor show, 'full of eastern promise'. He entered the lift, the hotel sounds faded. In his high-rise room the roar of traffic had re-commenced, indicating that prayers were noticeably over!

Just two nights ago Keith had received a phone call from a distraught member of his squadron. Three crew members were being held in a cramped police cage, together with two of the Australians and several other locals. Could he please come at once and explain to the Shah's police that there had been a misunderstanding? Keith finally arrived at the precinct police station after haggling with the only taxi driver to be found at that unsociable hour.

The picture gradually became clear. His colleagues or, more likely, the inebriated Aussies, had apparently tried, to get 'Green Shield' stamps from a night club proprietor. Green Shield stamps, as a method of obtaining rewards for shopping, had not reached this part of the world. The man, believing that they were after his green banknotes, had called the police, who had ruthlessly searched their pockets. Their British Servicemen's ID Cards were seen. Unfortunately, the British Embassy had then been informed. A member of the diplomatic staff arrived at the same time as Keith. The 'miscreants' could be seen, looking miserable in their cage. It took much diplomacy to get them released. Daylight came, just a few hours later, at which point they were arraigned, in disgrace, on the Defence Attaché's carpet!

Keith paused briefly on the landing to gaze over the skyline. The sun, now reduced to a dull red glow, outlined the dramatic mountain range that surround the city of Teheran. It was a salutary reminder of the meticulous descending flight profile one had to follow, when approaching the Shah's fairly new show-piece - Mehrabad airport.

Beyond those mountains, lurked the Russian Bear. Indeed, not far away were located the Soviet missile testing grounds. Between here and there Keith knew that bandits roamed and wolves were widespread. It was a mainly mountainous wasteland. Not much chance if one came down in that area, he thought. The Attaché had been talking about carrying bribery money, when motoring up to visit the British-built radar station, located at Babul Sar, much further to the north.

However, Keith and his fellow crew members carried no such funds. Neither did they have small arms for self protection, or suicide pills; as did Gary Powers, the unfortunate U2 pilot, and his other US colleagues.

Apart from the U2 aircraft on overflights we flew just as close to the same hostile borders, as did the US crews, during the same period of the Cold War! The British public, unaware of these activities, unless something went wrong, got more than their money's worth. None of Keith's colleagues had been lost on these special missions. The USA had not been as fortunate. In those days the Russians deliberately interfered with Western navigational aids, deliberately attempting to lure the unwary crews to cross their borders, by duplicating friendly beacons. US aircrews had sometimes been less than diligent in their navigation checks and several aircraft were either shot down or crashed into the enormous mountain peaks just over the Persian-Soviet and Turkish-Soviet borders.

The sun had set but the temperature remained high. With no air conditioning the window was ajar. Nine floors below, several lanes of traffic thundered relentlessly towards nearby traffic lights. One could believe that there were only three options - full throttle, full brakes or sharp ninety-degree turns! Keith's environment for much of the night, would be punctuated by car horns and squealing brakes and tyres. Every time the lights changed, there were measured periods of hush, followed by a crescendo of revving and roaring engines, as the eager drivers sped away at the very instant that the lights changed. Occasionally, the smell of brakes, rubber and exhaust fumes penetrated the room.

He withdrew from the window. The sound level fell abruptly, allowing very faint piano playing to be heard from the reception atrium and filtering up the central lift well. Keith noticed, with some irony, that the hotel's adept pianist was playing 'Moscow Nights'.

Keith was grateful for the comparative luxury in here, having seen the poor lot of so many, in this city of contrasts. He had seen their hovels that lined the old airport road, until finally the crew transport sped along the final extravagance of a new, prestigious, flag-lined dual carriageway.

All cars were imported and not many British cars could be seen. The quality of the few was poor. 'Red Robbo', controlling the Trade Unions, was already busy back in England's car factories! The start of Britain's decline - or just its continuation? Many believed that this decline had started in 1948. Well, Keith reasoned, at least if we couldn't sell them cars the Shah was friendly to Great Britain and the Persians would surely continue to sell us oil. Wouldn't they? But who would have guessed that, within a few years, a series of dictators in various parts of the world, including Persia's Ayotollah, would cock a snook, indeed many snooks, at the West. Britain and the USA would come under pressure and condemnation from the Middle and Far East, as well as from the Soviet Union. This behaviour would include that of the new, extremist, rulers of Iran. The price of oil would rocket.

Keith sat on his bed and counted his remaining rials, wondering - was there really a listening device in the telephone by the bed? Possibly. They had all been warned! Only a few rials were left! In those days the premium for an illegal bottle of spirits was high. Keith had already illegally disposed of a bottle of spirits to the hotel barman, purchased outbound, on the Malta stop-over. Of course it was strictly 'for his own personal consumption'. The duty free cost was just seven shillings and sixpence. A handsome profit had been made - enough to buy toys for the children and the filigree jewellery for his wife.

Strange how one could quietly and legally buy alcohol in the hotels of some of these Islamic nations. In contrast, one risked all sorts of retribution, including the possibility of lashings at dawn (and worse) if one was caught buying, selling or drinking the stuff beyond the hotel door. Nevertheless, the Air Force would take a very dim view - even a Courts Martial - if they found out! It was a sad fact that no one would dream of bringing alcohol to sell if the British government had been paying their servicemen properly. It was indeed a point of discontent that everything was done on a shoestring, when compared with the pay and conditions of the US and Canadian servicemen; and even of the British Civil Servants, with whom we frequently had to live and operate.

Of course, our complaints were as nothing compared with the miserable existence of many Persians in those days. The 'Shah of Shahs' was still on the throne. He ruled at the sufferance of the Ayatollahs of the Ulema - the Shi'ite Religious Council. Before long, the Shah would try to change things too quickly. In many ways he had not perceived the underlying trends in his country, trends that he should have considered before the haste to modernise.

There were extreme elements in the country. It was even likely that Ahmed, Keith's evening shadow, might, one day, be prepared to die for his cause. Most probably he would be encouraged to take this line by his elders - maybe for fear of not getting to Paradise in the future. Unknown to Keith at the time, Ahmed's father, an influential Mullah, and many others, had insisted that there had been far too much Western influence in Iran. They wanted all traces of the West to be removed and a pure Islamic state. They wanted the eventual destruction of anyone that they designated as an enemy. It would not be long before Ahmed was leading Iran's version of a student committee - a local 'revolutionary komiteh'. In just a few years, at the age of 16, Ahmed, my friendly and unexpected brief acquaintance, would be just one of many thousands shouting for the overthrow of the Peacock Throne. By the age of 19 he would start political studies at Teheran University. Ahmed was clearly privileged and intellectual. Nevertheless, in the future he would become the worst type of political animal, coloured by Islamic extremism. However, the world would not hear of such extremes for some time.

When the time came to leave Teheran, Keith was more than ready. He had seen quite enough of this semi-hostile environment. When compared with the relatively comfortable and stable life of the West it was another world. As Teheran's Mehrabad Airport fell away below, they rapidly climbed above the forbidding Alborz Mountains and headed for a one night stop-over in Cyprus, then home. For many years Keith would thankfully forget Persia, as it was still known at the time.

Despite the Shah's efforts to introduce the benefits of modernisation to his country, in order to promote the growing prosperity, Ahmed and his contemporaries were hostile. They were not interested in prosperity, only in spiritual control. They were unable to stand the secular pace of change, so far removed from their Sharia culture. In their minds surely The Shah would fall!

In the two decades immediately following Keith's visit, the national income of Iran dramatically increased, indeed rocketed, from 5 billion dollars in 1973, to about 19 billion by 1974. A dynamic boom ensued for those in the oil business and wealth for only a limited section of the population. No doubt many of Iran's citizens felt aggrieved that they had not benefited from the enormous oil wealth. Indeed for the majority time had stood still for centuries. Women still wore the 'chador', the veil, long after some other, more liberal, Islamic nations had changed. When the strict fundamentalist rulers took over, the news media showed many other practices that had amazed the Western World. Some of the future TV footage shown, including that of the Ayatollah's funeral, ten years later, would be almost unbelievable.

Iran, however, was not the only oil-rich nation in the area. It was common knowledge that, while the Iranian oil reserves were then estimated to be about 50 billion barrels, just across the Persian Gulf, (now the Gulf of Iran), the Saudi Arabians were estimated to be sitting on three times that amount.

The Saudi economy was also booming and they would also be key players in the coming nightmare scenario.

Soon, the world would hear of the Shah's expulsion and, eventually, of his death in exile. The fall from power of the Peacock Throne was a milestone with significant consequences that soon became evident. However, there would be even more dramatic events to follow, soon after the beginning of the third millenium.

It would be over 40 years after Keith's visit to Persia when the name 'Ahmed Pavli', quite unexpectedly, alerted Keith once again.

DELEGATES & DOODLEBUGS

The Third Steering Committee of 1997 had gone on all day. Keith Alexander Perham quietly eased back his chair and wandered off to the rear of the long conference room. The afternoon's ample supply of sticky cakes, biscuits and bottled soft drinks had by now been severely depleted. It had been a hard preparation day and the next few days promised to be even harder. However, during the more boring periods it was only too easy to let one's thoughts wander. How, he asked himself, had he possibly reached this point? Where had it all started?

It must have been influenced in the far off days of World War 2, when Keith's home was situated some forty miles to the north of London. Located within easy cycling distance, for keen aircraft spotters, were several Royal Air Force and American Air Force airfields. But it was not until many years later that Keith had discovered that the nearest airfield had supported one of the most interesting clandestine activities in the war. For it was from here that many brave agents were flown, usually under the cover of darkness, to parachute into enemy-occupied parts of Europe. The proximity of these airfields had undoubtedly influenced Keith's future ambitions for adventure and to fly with the Royal Air Force. In retrospect this was despite the fact that the young mother, lodging next door, had lost her airman husband on one of these perilous missions, dropping Resistance volunteers, into German-occupied France. Now, over five decades later, Keith reflected, we were all supposed to be friends together in Europe.

There had been many other influences as far back as he could remember. The whole area surrounding his home town had visibly and inextricably been linked with the war effort. Apart from the airfields, which had, of necessity, been constructed on the flat areas - almost the edge of the fens, there were densely wooded hilly areas. These provided cover for extensive ammunition dumps. Sadly, for reasons of safety and security, while the many aircraft which droned almost continuously overhead were an aircraft spotter's dream, the wooded areas, with their mysterious camouflaged huts, were officially out of bounds. Initially, this was a disappointment - as several woods were temptingly just at the end of the road. However, ways could be found.......! Additionally there were a good number of books for air enthusiasts, such as the Biggles adventures and authors like Neville Shute and others. There was no public library but books were available from a newly-opened local phenomenon - a 'house-library'. These were undoubtedly a strong influence in setting the scene for Keith's later life.

As he sipped some apple juice today's meeting continued. Keith allowed his thoughts to drift on, picturing his home town as it had been almost fifty years before - complete with Park House by the river and several large country estates, owned by the local gentry, complete with gardeners, cooks butlers and chauffeurs. Now this small country town had rapidly grown. Under the government's London overspill scheme, it had become a town of many thousands. It seemed hard to realise that in those now far-off wartime days there were almost as many servicemen to be seen in the streets as locals, and certainly more military vehicles than civilian ones. Uniforms were seen at every turn, coupled with unusual accents that included those of the evacuees, from the big cities - principally from London.

What was much later to be dubbed 'Dad's Army' - the local Home Guard - provided a certain amount of amusement. They were often to be seen on the Market Square or 'falling in' outside the barber's shop, for, in our neck of the woods hairdressers had not been invented so far!. There were not enough guns to go round and they took them in turns. Young boys watched these antics which always seemed to comprise much unintelligible shouting and thumping of black-booted feet. Little had Keith realised what the future held - almost thirty years in the RAF!

Apart from all this activity and the occasional aircraft crash in the locality, the only sign of real enemy action, was the frequent air-raid sirens but, mercifully, only a few attacks. One night an isolated stick of bombs, probably dropped by accident rather than design, fell across the local fields. Of major concern to boy footballers, the explosions also stitched a row of large holes right across the town's only football pitch. The airfields or perhaps the ammunition dumps were the probable targets, but the enemy had missed these by anything up to three miles.

Keith clearly remembered the evening when a V1 'Doodlebug' flying bomb came by. A crude 'Cruise Missile' of its era. After passing overhead at low altitude, making its characteristic pulsing sound, the unmanned device came down near a village some fifteen miles to the North. By this time it had missed its intended target - London - by almost sixty miles! Despite the air raid warning and his worried mother's exhortations not to go outside, the distinctive sound of its engine was just too much of an event for a keen young aircraft spotter to miss - even with his heart in his mouth in case the engine suddenly stopped. A real missile had been spotted. Something to tell his school pals the next day. At that time Keith would have been very surprised to find that missiles and air defence would be one of his specialities in the then distant future.

Fatherless since the age of three, the war had ended when Keith was just nine and a half years old. At that age there was little opportunity of really understanding the wider implications of what had been going on. Even to a young boy at that time many events closer to home indicated all was not well. The few privately-owned vehicles remained in their garages, apart from those able to get 'black market' fuel. There was a shortage of most commodities such as food, fruit sweets and clothes. None of the family was well-off and rationing was in force and coupons were required for most purchases. Excitement reigned at school when free chocolate powder was placed in brown paper bags 'to take home for family cooking'. Little arrived intact, as the bags tended to 'leak' - especially when poked into with licked and grubby fingers! Night time brought the black-out.

World War Two ended and the troops, whose presence had been so pervasive, went home to their families. The evacuees returned to their homes in a battered London. Strangely, at the time when the London evacuees were leaving London for the country, some very distant relatives had opted to stay there throughout the blitz. They had an extremely lucky escape, when a flying bomb literally went through the bathroom while they were in bed, and had woken up sharply to an unexpected outside view. To be born at that time, followed by many years exposure to the coming 'Cold War' would affect the lives of thousands of young men for years to come.

Keith's wandering thoughts were sharply interrupted and attention was drawn back to the Chairman and the rest of the Committee - who had suddenly all turned to look down the room intently towards him. A response was needed. Rapidly he moved back nearer to his place at the table and made a few appropriate comments. The moment of embarrassment passed. He really must try and stay in tune with the meeting - however hard his chair had become! He was not only representing Britain but also was leading the threat assessment team. The reality was that lots of talking was done but the bulk of the work would be done by just a handful of the nations represented. However, we must all be most diplomatic!

Today's meeting promised to go on for some time yet. Then there would be the individual assignments - jokingly called the 'homework'. Today it would be early evening before the delegates dispersed, only for most to meet up again within the hour in the appointed hotel. The trouble with these international working parties was that only the national host was in his own nation, usually with his home close-by. The rest had travelled from the diverse nations that formed the International Alliance. Looming ahead were another four similar week-long sessions before the year-long study was completed, and agreed deliberations produced in a multi-volume report.

For several years NATO had been considering it's future role, following the collapse of the former Soviet Empire. To many it seemed that the reason for the existence of NATO had disappeared. Some even believed it might become an armed force for the United Nations Organisation. Others thought there would be no further world threats. Keith knew differently.

His boyhood interest in aircraft and later, electronics, had continued. Later he had flown with the Royal Air Force and, still later, specialised in Radars, Computers, Air Defences and Guided Missiles and finally as a civilian Chief Scientist. This explained his current position on this NATO Air Defence Study Group Steering Committee.

The meeting laboured on. To assuage national pride everyone had to have their say, even if they had said nothing useful by the time they sat down! The comments of each of the nations present, at only three or four minutes each - on even the most mundane of topics, plus the Chairman's comments, would consume almost an hour. Often it took even longer before they could move to the next item. Only the most skilled of chairmen could stem the flow of some delegates, once they got started. Most of them had some hidden agenda to conduct on behalf of their national interests - even though this was, officially, strictly forbidden.

Keith resolved to try and pay more attention for the rest of the session. After all, the topic for this year was by no means trivial, because all previous studies on this topic had resulted in little international or national action. This, despite a clear message that weapons of mass destruction and the means to deliver them were spreading and there seemed to be little that could be done to stop them.

The terms of reference of the group were daunting - they were to recommend how to protect the alliance members against attack by ballistic and cruise missiles. One day these deliberations might mean life or death to perhaps thousands of the citizens of one or more of the nations represented - yet their governments had done little but dither for years. One could easily become discouraged! Keith resolved that his team would make the strongest possible recommendations, before it was too late.

Apart from the possibility of threats from several unfriendly nations - and there were plenty of unstable and cunning dictators about - there had been a particular proliferation of the 'poor man's' nuclear weapons; the worrying chemical and biological options. Although by the mid 1990s the International Convention on the Development, Production, Stockpiling and Use of Chemical Weapons had persuaded 157 nations to sign-up, many others had refused. This convention called for the destruction of existing chemical weapons and prohibited both weapon transfer or retention. Apart from those that would not sign, there remained suspicions about several who had signed but might decide to ignore their promises when it so suited them.

Still thirsty, Keith turned once again to the refreshment table. Half way through pouring out the remaining fruit juice, the German delegate sprang up and started to speak. A balding and imposing character with a very loud voice, Herr Doktor Johann Woolf spoke excellent English - as all delegates were required to do in open forum. 'My government do not see any need for missile defence', he said. 'The threat from the East has gone away from Germany.'

As the threat team leader it was Keith's immediate reaction to speak up in reply. However, as two other nations had already indicated to speak - and anyway as he was not in his seat, it would have to wait. He had identified a glaring flaw in the German statement. Didn't they know about the new 'Out of Area' operations which a change in the German Law now allowed? If they were asked to help by the United Nations in some dreadful place, it would be too late for German troops if they had no air defences. Perhaps they would be facing some cunning dictator bordering on the unstable or even a madman - whose people would blindly follow his irrational instructions. Were the Germans expecting someone else to provide their troops with air defence cover - surely not?

Germany had been fortunate thus far. Since World War Two, German Laws had prevented their participation in any external military activities outside their national boundaries, other than in routine training exercises. Other nations had borne the brunt of Germany's defence for forty years, involving heavy costs, loss of lives during exercises and training and occasionally losses due to sporadic Soviet action. Keith felt strongly about this, as some of his aircrew colleagues had been shot at, even killed. The victorious nations of World War Two had unceasingly poured-in money into Germany, until the economy got on its feet - and even to a level well beyond.

The communists had eventually been faced down and withdrew. Keith, when flying overhead in the early fifties, had observed the destruction, still evident ten years after the war. He had seen at first hand the subsequent huge re-construction effort and the rapid rise in Germany's living standards.

However, it had not been until 1994, after the rising cost of UN protection activities elsewhere in the world and with much encouragement from the USA, that the German Court at Karlsruhr had finally changed the rules - Germany's armed forces could finally operate overseas.

Defence against ballistic missile attack was going to be expensive. Surely it was incumbent upon all present to share in the cost of these new missile defences? Mobile defences were needed that could be deployed either on one's own soil or to protect a nation's or a coalition's force should they be required elsewhere.

A new generation had arrived and now one was expected to be diplomatic and accommodating! The German standard of living had exceeded that of several of the victorious allies, certainly of Britain, and we were still wondering where we had gone wrong! Even today, Keith had felt let down to find that all his opposite numbers in Germany's industries were swanning around in company-provided Mercedes! Now they had the neck to complain about the high cost of re-unification with the East and the need to work a four day fortnight! Memories seemed to be getting even shorter. Who had caused World War Two in the first place and hence led to the division of their land anyway?

Keith was old enough to remember and still couldn't forget that Germany had never been on the end of a missile attack - Britain had! Further, in the recent past, several German companies, albeit some from the former East Germany, had supplied certain materials to the very Middle Eastern nations of current concern. These included Libya and Iraq - just two of the group of nations which were quite likely to cause problems in the future.

Meanwhile, the voluble Doktor forged forcefully ever onwards. Inevitably, several other delegates also sought refuge at the refreshment table!

Keith recalled that more than ten thousand of the 'V1', or 'Doodlebug' attacks on London and the South East had been followed up by over 1000 'V2' ballistic terror missiles. These supersonic missiles could not be heard coming - which was just as well for their unsuspecting and unfortunate victims. The USA, by then participants in World War II, were immune, because neither the V1 air-breathing missiles or the V2 rockets had the range to reach the USA from Germany.

Since that first use of ballistic missiles in World War Two, the world's news media had reported the eight year long 'SCUD' missile 'war of the cities' between Iran and Iraq, which ended in 1988. Then had followed the first Gulf War in 1991, when Iraq fired dozens of 'SCUD' missiles against both Saudi Arabia and Israel.

Keith's team would have the problem of determining the technical details of all the current and projected threats, before the other teams could decide how best to counter them.

Returning to his seat, he made a note and looked up. The Spanish delegate had interrupted the German speech to say that his country were concerned. Spain, he pointed out, is located much closer to some unstable characters in Northern Africa and hence to the shorter ranged ballistic missiles which could reach Spanish territory. Briefly noting the strength of the Spanish argument, Keith's mind again drifted back to his mother's fireside.

He briefly recalled those days - glad that the Doodlebug's motor had puttered on. There was no radio at home. Television, having just been invented, had been suspended for the duration of the war. Mother would not have a newspaper. It was a case of relying on books - of which there were few new ones to be seen. As a result it had been some years before Keith grasped what had been going on in the wider world - a world from which he had been, in many ways, insulated.

Now Germany was re-united and one of his best West German team members had left to join another team to investigate the military materials, much of Russian origin, left in the former Eastern Germany, the GDR. Who could guess at what they might find?

In 1989, one of the Chief Guests in the GDR had been Yasser Arafat of the PLO. He linked with the GDR's 'Stasi', secret service to set up security and intelligence with some Islamic nations. Following which, based at the Springsee/ Beeskow complex, outside Berlin, the Stasi reportedly provided training in weapons, explosives and even nuclear devices. What else had the former E.

Germany supplied? Keith suspected that the supplies included chemical weapon and missile know-how.

He glanced down at his latest information. During the Second World War only one nation had been capable of waging ballistic missile warfare, now, almost six decades on, within a few years probably twenty nations would have the capability to do so.

Literally dozens of nations had the capability to fire at least some sort of air-breathing stand-off missile and nineteen of these could be described as possessing a crude cruise missile. The reach of these weapons varied, from about 50 to 2000 miles. Unfortunately, for many years, during the Cold War, while the opposing East-West factions had each been busy developing cruise missiles, they had not taken much note of the consequences that might follow if this type of weapon proliferated. Now, in 1997, the inevitable had happened and was co-incident with the recipes (even being given on the internet!) on how to make both nuclear and chemical warheads for these vehicles to carry All this would have to be succinctly reported by his team.

At this point yet another 'comfort break' was called!

DEFEND OR DIE?

A sudden change of accent! Spain had finished and the Italian delegate was speaking, but his topic was of little interest.

Keith allowed himself one last thought, as it was nearly his turn to speak again. Times had significantly changed since those German V2 rockets had reached Great Britain. His place at the table bore the initials 'UK'. What had become known as 'The West' had lived through the constant threat of nuclear-tipped Soviet missiles - and yet - almost unbelievably, there had been no counter to these missiles in all this time. The 1968 Nuclear Non-proliferation Treaty had since expired, and the nations could not agree on the way ahead. Smaller nations argued that as the larger ones already had their nuclear deterrents - so why should not they be allowed to have theirs too?

For most of the 1980s Keith had been busy with research that had been dubbed by the media, 'Star Wars'. It was because, originally, it was thought that the incoming ballistic missiles could only be intercepted in space. The topic had since been studied for so long that the name had been changed. Next it was either called Ballistic Missile Defence, or BMD for short, then 'Theatre Missile Defence', and, for the US element, 'National Missile Defence', or NMD. Although just the same problem, now, as in 1997, the current study title this time was to be 'Extended Air Defence'.

Since the first days of the 'Star Wars' research, many had seen the devastating effects of ballistic and cruise missile attacks during the Gulf War, broadcast nightly right into people's living rooms. Of the nations that owned ballistic missiles, thankfully thus far, only seven had nuclear weapons - but it would only be a matter of time before even these were more widespread. However, others already had chemical and biological weapons.

Surely the meeting was almost over? Now it was Turkey's turn. Keith had some sympathy for the dusky pro-Western, friendly, Turkish delegate. Turkey, although a nominally secular state, and the only member of the study group with a predominantly Islamic population, had recently elected an Islamic government. Inevitably there had been speculation on what might happen if, in the future, the population were called upon by their spiritual leaders to confront NATO over some issue or other.

Meantime, the Turkish-Greece stand-off was still on-going. Despite strenuous efforts to get a form of wording which was acceptable to Turkey in the team's previous year's report, there were complaints. These concerned the possible repercussions of the re-distribution of water from Turkey's massive south eastern Anatolia Dam. There was even dissatisfaction because the Kurds and the PKK had been mentioned.

For the moment, it certainly suited Turkey to remain a member within the defensive alliance. They had the most to gain as continued members, should things start to go wrong in neighbouring Iran, Syria and Iraq! Meantime, with both Greece and Turkey present, the words Rhodes, Limnos and Cyprus were 'hot potatoes' and not to be mentioned in the final report!

Keith stole another glance at his watch and jogged the nearby Study Rapporteur's arm. 'How long can we stand him going on about it?'

'He must have his say', said the Rapporteur, while ignoring the tirade and calmly continuing to write up the first part of the meeting report.

The Turkish delegate, having expounded on everything from Kurds to dams, finally sat down, puffing, and probably realising that his huge country was near indefensible. Who, Keith wondered, would want to take over large areas of it anyway? Possibly someone with an eye to oil? Trouble of some kind was usually brewing in this part of the world, anyway. Within the nations immediately to Turkey's East, Keith surmised that the lid could only be kept on the pot for so long - then rampant fundamentalism would, almost certainly, boil over - with disastrous effects.

Keith, on behalf of Britain, eventually said his piece, keeping it brief. He reiterated that Turkey was not being accused by anybody present of mistreating the Kurds or interfering with anyone's water supply. Privately he reflected that however diplomatically it may be put, and however one looked at the situation, one could not doubt the purpose of a dam. As everyone knows, it is undoubtedly designed to prevent water flowing away, to hold it back, and then to divert it somewhere else! Keith was more than aware that water would be a key factor in fomenting future trouble in this region.

He was also more aware than many of those present, from personal experience in the Middle East, that black could be described as white and vice versa - to the bafflement of all who were listening!

The whole problem of assessing where the world threat was going had been dumped in his lap when leading the 'Threat and Geopolitics' team for several of the previous studies. This was always a veritable minefield of possibilities and probabilities! There was also the difficulty of trying to get his team of experts to agree and write down their findings and submit them for the report. Not the least of the problems was to attempt to predict what would be happening at that geographical cross-roads - where the NATO West meets the mainly unpredictable East. Indeed, part of Turkey lies in Europe and the rest is in Asia! Keith reflected, with some satisfaction, that his 1990/91 team had correctly predicted the fall of Russia's Gorbachev, with NATO plaudits all round.

The experiences of the team were neccessarily varied, with age playing an important part. All needed to be aware of the diverse alliances some of the potentially hostile nations had made in the past.

Soon the specialist technical teams would start their deliberations and they would rely upon Keith's Threat Team to correctly assess the coming world situation. The final assessment should leave no one in any doubt that each of the armed forces of the Alliance Nations should be entitled to defence against missile attack wherever they served. Missile defence was also essential for their homelands.

Finally, the much heralded peaceful 'New World Order' would soon turn into a scenario of 'defend or die'. Could the politicians in these nations not realise that they would be to blame if they failed to provide adequate air defences? Could any of the nations present now fail to see that action was essential?

RUSHING WATERS

The jovial, laid-back American Chairman valiantly tried to sum-up the discussion so far. In his summary he chose to ignore the Turkish remarks - which had gone completely clear of the mark. There would always be another day! The Chairman was bound to be smartly accosted by the Turkish delegate directly the meeting ended anyway. For the moment he compromised by calling a very short 'comfort break'. The sun had noticeably fallen another notch and the glorious mountains of Norway were beginning to cast their deep evening shadows. At this rate it would be dark by the time they got outside. Keith was getting ready to leave, not realising it was but a short recess, when the Chairman restarted the meeting!

He felt restless today. It had been both pleasant and tempting to gaze longingly out of the windows, the crystalline clarity of the fresh green countryside sharply outlined in the crisp air in this valley. Above the interminable 'mush' of the air conditioning could be heard the faint but insistent sound of the largest of several nearby waterfalls. A beautiful spot and very remote from the problems of defence against ballistic missiles! Were we dreaming all this?

In 1993 this unlikely Norwegian setting had also been the location for the long-awaited leap forward of the Middle East Peace Settlement. It had been a surprise - because, quite undeservedly, no one had cast the Norwegians in the testing role of peace-brokers. However, it had transpired that the agreements made would not stand the test of time.

Keith also remembered his many visits, years before, to the far northern parts of Norway, flying from Andoya, in the Lofoten Islands and Bodo. In those days everything seemed to smell of fish - even the loos! Fish eyes floating in the soup! Memories flooded back. The midnight sun. The Aurora Borealis, or 'Northern Lights'. The heaped snow beside the runways. The freezing outside air temperatures of minus 76 degrees when he was flying at fifty thousand feet and the Red Bear - the mighty USSR - pointing their probing radar beams menacingly in his direction. He was fortunate indeed to be here today.

Once again a speaker rose. Surely this must be the last session of the day. The French delegate was on his feet - speaking perfect English. The French delegates always spoke French, when possible. This meant importing interpreters, but this time he had no option. A point of order had arisen. Although the French representation as a whole was already larger than that of any other participating nation, they still wanted another team leader position. Eventually, after much discussion and even more hand-waving and emotional expressions, Monsieur Michelle Le Broq was approved as the Future Technology Team Leader.

'L'honour de France' was saved! Haw He Haw! The nominee, a corporate figure with a glowing red face, closely cropped white hair and a stance reminiscent of a silent French film comedy actor of Keith's youth, had secured his place. Admittedly his experience of things 'militaire' was extensive, having started as a boy in 'Le Resistaaa......ance'. How, Keith wondered, did he rate the Germans and Italians now? His selection for this task, as would be soon revealed, would turn out to be a disaster. We would be stuck with him for a year and, amazingly, his appointment later resulted in fisticuffs in the Rome meeting. Happy days!

It was getting dark outside. The session had lasted many hours and at six-thirty the Chairman was finally recapping and busy deciding on assignments. These would inevitably be carried out by the delegates from perhaps six or seven conscientious nations. It would be their words that would eventually reach the Alliance Defence Staffs at HQ, in Brussels and the Defence Ministers of the Alliance Nations. In reality the Alliance would be a shambles without certain key players. If one was honest, the rest of the nations attended and just made the right noises. Despite all the efforts the carefully worded Executive Summaries would likely be further shortened by their staff officers before reaching the Ministers' desks, hopefully without loss of meaning. Would there be real action this time?

The report would undoubtedly be finished on time and the recommendations would detail how the Alliance should proceed. Starting from its vulnerable position of having little defence against cruise missiles and no defence at all against ballistic missiles, an affordable rolling programme must be set up. It must include system design, trials, manufacture and, eventually, deployment. The final system would be partially adjusted by the individual nations, who, like the Spaniards, may have specific national concerns to address, because of their closer proximity to unstable parts of the world. Collectively it could be achieved. Would the politicians of the respective governments finally listen? The lack of this collective insurance could have devastating consequences - and perhaps much sooner than expected by the uninformed.

Keith observed, that since the 'Iron Curtain' had come down, the world had, in reality, become a much more unstable place. A fact which the general public and their political masters were slow to grasp - as they had immediately imposed massive defence cuts! With the demise of the mighty Soviet Union, by the late 1990s any additional expenditure on defence had just gone out of fashion.

Other factors were also changing. Keith's team had regularly warned of the demographic changes that would affect the likelihood of young people coming forward to join the armed forces. As so often the warnings would be ignored. By the early years of the next millennium the predicted recruiting crisis would indeed occur.

The 'homework' had been set! They had reached the end of the session. He hurriedly grabbed his briefcase and left the building. Outside it was good to inhale the crisp evening air. A mother was urgently herding her two children into the back of a car, holding the door against the slope of the road and a cool wind. All three were well-coated and scarfed. It was already frosty.

Keith was reminded of his own grand-children several hundred miles away across the North Sea. He glanced at his watch. Was there a time- shift or were we on the same time now? What might they be doing? Maybe he would ring them from the hotel. Habits from the Cold War days died hard. In those days when he was flying from an undisclosed location, no phone calls home were permitted, for very good reasons. Perhaps he would send a postcard to each tomorrow. What was he doing here anyway?

Work would start in earnest tomorrow with the arrival of some forty international expert members, to form the teams. Some would probably arrive in the hotel later tonight. Keith knew that from then on he would have his time fully occupied. He would be issuing the work plan for his team, co-ordinating the requirements, 'arguing' in the best traditions of diplomacy - especially with the Turkish and Greek delegates - and making endless radar and missile intercept calculations.

Literally dozens of scientific 'working papers' would be produced. Similar working meetings would be held in other NATO Nations. In between meetings computer modelling would take place. The proposals would be analysed, reorganised, argued over and re-written several times. Then, the results would be presented in open forum in the next few months. Finally, a consensus would be reached and written up for the several volumes that would comprise the final report. Then they would all meet again, probably in Brussels, to present the detail of the report to a NATO Air Defence Committee.

The pavement surface was quite slippery. 'We struggled today,' - a voice from behind. He turned to find Lieutenant Colonel Phil Narvik, one of the two military observers, approaching up the steep path. He was attached to the group to provide operational advice. The only problem was that no one apart from a few Americans at Dhahran and the Israelis, in the Gulf War, had any recent operational experience of defence against rockets plunging from the sky at several times the speed of sound. 'Don't know how you put up with it,' remarked Phil, when he caught up. 'Slow going today,' he said. 'Good job most of these others were not in the Falklands - or you would still be fighting the Argies now!' They walked on, the cold air catching their throats. The hotel welcomed them with a blast of hot air.

There would be just time to clean up and catch the hotel evening meal. Otherwise it would mean searching this small unfamiliar town for a restaurant. He crossed the room and observed the few vehicles parked outside, including the safe presence of his hire car, now sparkling with frost. Keith gazed in the bathroom mirror. Bit thin on top these days, he thought. At that moment it seemed that all the past training and experience had come together for the imminent task. However, it seemed that most of his contemporaries were unaware and even unbelieving of the coming world scenario - and how the coming events had all been forecast so many years ago. Keith had no doubts that various events were slotting into place, piece by piece, and, at the appointed time they would all be in place. He drew the curtains, switched on the television, flopped onto the bed and stared at the ceiling. It looked much like any other!

The hotel room was warm and cosy. The nearby waterfall gushed unceasingly. He stood before the Steering Committee, who were all shouting at him in their diverse languages in a cacophony of sound. His report was no good! His scenarios for the future were all wrong. The Turkish delegate was standing up and gesticulating and the Frenchmen were gesticulating back at at least twice the rate. The German was rapidly stuffing his papers into a briefcase, while blaming Keith for the enormous cost of Germany's re-unification several years before and for the shortened working week. Everyone was in the process of adjourning to another room downstairs. Keith was in disgrace. He was not believed. Herr Doktor Woolf's final guttural words, resounded above all others. The Turk, sporting a fez, strode out of the room with a roll of carpet under one arm. The US Chairman departed, puffing a big cigar. Keith hurried in vain to catch up and explain. In desperation he called the lift. Why did it take so long to come? After an interminable wait, although the bell rang and he looked through the little window, the lift had not arrived. With a jerk his hand fell off the side of the bed. It was 10.30pm. The television was sounding off loudly - in Norwegian, and the hotel telephone was ringing insistently no more than a foot from his head.

'Peter Saunders here. Didn't see you in the restaurant! Have you done the assignment - the 'homework'? In a daze Keith asked for thirty minutes to finish it off. He badly needed something to eat and drink but it was too late. The evening meal would now comprise a coffee and some biscuits, provided on the customary hotel plastic tray. Why was everything was wrapped in those infernal plastic packets? What lurked in the bottom of the small electric kettle? He boiled it first as a precaution and found his briefcase. Now - what and where was the task that he had been set?

With a groan he realised that, in his haste to leave, all his vital notes had been left in a pile on the table in the meeting room. It was almost a mile away and the place would have been locked-up for hours, with no further access. Outdoors the unceasing waters thundered relentlessly onwards. He returned to his bed in disgust, rang Peter to sheepishly apologise and booked an early call. In minutes the waterfall lullaby had resumed its soporific effect.

As he drifted off he could see that the key players were being prepared and that the stage was being increasingly set for the world's nightmare scenario. However, he had no idea that one of the prime participants would be a little known Russian scientist, presently living just a few hundred miles to the east of Norway. In contrast, but unknown to Keith at this time, the scenario would have another major player, then only a boy, whom he had met very briefly in Persia, now Iran, in the early 1960s.

FRENZY!

Teheran's city walls had been covered with slogans as early as the 1970s. The daubing proclaimed 'death to The Shah' and 'extermination' to almost everyone in the West, especially the USA, Great Britain and, of course, Israel. At that time the USSR, the mighty Soviet Union, on Iran's northern border, was also considered to be an enemy. However, eighteen years, after Keith's brief encounter in Teheran, the inevitable Iranian revolution came. The Shah went in October 1978, firstly to the USA and then to die later, in exile, after spending time in Egypt.

Ayatollah Khomeini eventually took power in 1979, in accordance with his long-planned intentions, on returning from his own exile in France. The Imams declared that it was 'God's own government' and 'the first lawful government in the country for 1200 years'. Within two years he had roused the population to an even greater hatred of the 'Big Satan', the description applied to America.

Martyrs - 'shahids', were welcomed and it was clear that Khomeini, the fundamentalist Islamic theologian, had returned from exile in triumph. the West had great difficulty in trying to understand the mentality of what was going on. Extremist's activities were a new phenomenon to those living a cosy existence in Europe or the USA. Ayotollah Khomeini was known as 'The Master', and his 'pasdaran' - or, 'forces of the Lord', took control.

Ahmed Pavli, Keith's unwanted, youthful, Teheran shopping shadow, back in 1960, had lost none of his fire. He vowed to leave university, continue into government and to faithfully follow the great Imam's edicts. He would obey the words and orders of the Mullahs and also of his 'Khatib' - his local prayer leader - whatever they might be.

Soon, the USA suffered the indignity of her Teheran Embassy staff being taken as hostages, followed by catastrophic consequences, when US forces failed to rescue them. Release only came later, when the shamed incumbent of the US White House, President Carter, handed over to his successor.

Ahmed appeared briefly on the world's TV screens some years later, although Keith would not have recognised him among the masses. He was holding a position of importance, at the frenzied funeral of Ayotollah Homeini. As a member of the government he joined with the second rank of mourning Mullahs, lesser Ayotollahs and the few visiting dignitaries. Those trying to prevent or at least to contain the turbulent behaviour at the funeral were unsuccessful. That evening's television news, viewed the world over, showed scenes of almost demonic fervour. Ahmed had been delighted. This surely showed the world the unswerving faithfulness of Iran's population for the new rule of Islam and the

27

continuation of the policies of the now deceased Ayatollah. The hatred of the West, especially of the USA, would live on. This same hatred was also on the rise elsewhere in the Middle East. In the 1990s, in Keith's study group, in deference to the Turkish delegate, this type of activity would be politely accorded the title 'Politicised Islam'!

Few in the West realised the long term significance of what they were observing. To the more thoughtful, a decidedly evil undertone to the events could be discerned. To so many others it was just another crowd of wild and extreme religious enthusiasts and of no real concern in their own 'civilised' Western world. 'Religion' again! said the scoffers, and turned their backs. If it had not been for his tasks in assessing threats at the time, Keith would probably have agreed with them. After all, to the man in the street, Iran seemed a long way away and did not much concern everyday life in Britain - unless of course oil prices rose!

Iran's eventual economic collapse would not come about until the next millennium, when the number of unemployed approached no less than 50 million. During the 1990s the Iranian government, as well as obtaining new air defence equipment and many other armaments, had continued to berate the West. Their nuclear programme had continued, with Russian help. The International Atomic Energy Authority attempted to negotiate to reduce the possibility of nuclear weapon proliferation. Iran's cash mountain, was available to the world's military and naval equipment salesmen, and Iran started to re-build its forces after the eight year long war with Iraq - provided they could get round certain embargoes. Western nations mainly agreed with the USA's embargo on military trade with Iran. The inevitable result was that China, North Korea and the former nations of the USSR would soon became Iran's main suppliers.

The aircraft flown by the Iraqi Air Force to Iran, during the first Gulf War, had earlier been absorbed into the Iranian Air Force. Right through the decade western Defence Journals had reported increasing Chinese and Russian weapons deliveries to Iran. Eventually, the Presidents of the USA and the Russian Republic had come to a tacit, though doubtful agreement, to try and limit Russian arms reaching Iran. No doubt some reductions were achieved by using the leverage of American bribes, both in aid and in hard currency. Nevertheless, quite a lot of naval equipment did find its way to Iran, including some ex-Soviet Kilo class submarines. This arms deal could have caused a significant problem, had delivery occurred before or during the first Gulf War.

At the start of the new millennium, Iraq was still under an embargo, with the exception of the 'oil for medicine' arrangement, and Saddam Hussein was still in power. He had ignored the United Nations resolutions concerning weapons of mass destruction, while regularly and vehemently denouncing Israel and the West, especially the USA. His demise would come!

Meantime things were stirring in Iran. By the start of the new millennium, having been a strong influence in Iran for several years, Ahmed's final step to real power would coincide with the need to divert the people's attention from their economic problems. By the year 2002 many of the population had seen enough of the rule of the Mullahs. Student demonstration led to bloodshed. Exiled Iranians, broadcasting by satellite television, from the USA, implored the students forward on a 'Free Iran' platform, but they were not strong enough.

Meanwhile, Ahmed was cunningly planning a number of military preparations in case they were needed. In particular, he was carefully studying his near and far Islamic neighbours. He decided that it was time someone took control of the Islamic world. Nasser of Egypt had unsuccessfully tried. A little later Kassem of Iraq had similar ambitions. Then Saddam Hussein, claiming to be the 'New Nebuchadnezzar', had failed in the first Gulf War. He would be ousted by coalition military action, in the second war, in 2003.

In just a few years, Ahmed Pavli, would be embroiled in a completely unforeseen world crisis situation. On behalf of the new rulers of Iran, boasting that he would show their enemies, especially Israel, exactly what Iran stood for! Then the rest, including all the Arab nations would surely follow him! Unknown to Keith, like a jigsaw piece, another personality, essential to the coming scenario, had moved into place. Others were also moving into position, in another Mid-Eastern State.

DESERT STORY

Talal Aziz was very proud of his five children and of his Saudi Arabian ancestry. Four of the children were sitting before him, on the roof terrace. They were always eager to learn about their father's latest travels, to receive their presents and to hear the stories of their inheritance once again. A computer game for young Omar, who was fast becoming a young man, and a new dress each for the girls. A junior-size football for little Abdul.

A servant brought in their cool drinks. Although the day's sun had lost its searing heat, it was now being given up by the stone of the city buildings; acting like a huge storage heater. Today, it had topped thirty-six degrees in the shade in Ryadh, the capital city of the Kingdom of Saudi Arabia. Now, it was a time to relax, although the news was disturbing. Regular terror attacks on foreign nationals working on the country's infrastructure had recently started. The West were aware that one Ben Laden also had Saudi ancestry and that he was most likely to be behind the latest outrages. It was the year 2002.

Omar was keen to try out his new computer game - but, in respect to his father, that must wait until tomorrow. The girls kept their eyes on the new presents. Abdul played quietly in the corner with his new ball.

It was time now to settle down on the well-stuffed settees and listen. They knew that Father would not stand any nonsense when he started to tell his stories. Iyad, Talal's eldest son, of whom he was especially proud, was not present. He would not be home on leave from the army until next week. Iyad knew the inheritance stories by heart. He had heard them many times while growing up. However, neither Talal or Iyad realised the critical part that Iyad would soon play in world affairs in a few years time.

Apart from general anecdotes, Talal had decided to say very little about the purpose of his visit to Venezuela. This had been to attend the Oil Ministers Meeting. The children would not yet understand such complex issues. However, their own history was a different thing, for this must be repeated over and over so that they knew it well enough to pass on, when he had gone to Paradise.

Talal sipped his iced drink and started. There was always something a little different - a little embroidering, here and there! Several other family members arrived to welcome Talal back home. Talal's audience caught the thin breeze. They would also listen and dream.

During his long flight home Talal had decided that it was time to tell them about the sequence of family events that had led to his present exalted position. Inevitably he would, once again, explain the ongoing conflict that characterised the Middle East.

'The family story started,' said Talal, 'at the end of the last century, when my own grandfather, your great grandfather, had been a desert warrior with Abdul Aziz. Of course you can all be very proud, as many of the warriors were our relatives.' Little Abdul, too young to understand this kind of detail, dropped his ball with a thump, giggled and grinned proudly, as he always did when his name was mentioned.

Talal continued, ignoring the interruption. He told them that their great grandfather had been one of the reputed select band of perhaps three dozen or so of Aziz's warriors, who, according to the story passed down, captured the fort at Misurak.

Talal paused. He had particular reason to remember this story of his proud heritage, because he had been regularly reminded in just the same way, first as a young boy and later as a youth. In those days the family had sat near their tents, in the desert starlight. For although Abdul Aziz had been the first major player in the new country's history, many of the extended family had continued to live in tents for some years. Indeed, even as he spoke, the wandering desert tribes, renowned for their hospitality, still lived in much the same way.

Next he told the children how the exploits of their ancestors to control the area had later succeeded, when the tribes all followed great grandfather Abdul Aziz. And, how Aziz had welcomed the British into the area as a counter against the feared Turks, the huge Ottoman Empire, which still occupied many lands in this part of the world in 1902. He did not mention much of the detail at this stage. For example, that Britain had been helpful in those early days and a key part of the evolution of what was later to become the Kingdom of Saudi Arabia. In those early times nations boundaries were either ill-defined or not really defined at all. The Turks were a threat. As it would turn out, they would withdraw in 1906, little realising the enormous but undiscovered wealth that they were leaving behind. The unrelenting desert, the wandering tribes and the Bedouin would remain.

Talal, took another sip of his drink, flicked away a persistent fly and again reminded his children that, even today, this cruel desert was an enemy of all who travelled in her.

Even when traversing the desert all those years before, as a youth, Talal had dreamt of power and honour for his family. Later, as a young man, the occasional visits made back to his roots were relished for the freedom, the sand and the open skies. Now, he was spoilt as an air-conditioned city dweller! A times he almost forgot that he had been brought up to withstand the unrelenting mid-forties temperatures, and the sudden wind-blown stinging sand. In but a few years one could get used to luxury!

Next, he told the children how the travellers slowly wended their way between the grazing areas of the Bedouin tribes. Tribes that had been regularly warring, for as long as anyone could remember, long before the nation was formed. Talal also explained how the small towns on the trade routes were so interesting to a young boy. Everyday aspects of life had been the same for centuries. Goods and animals were bartered. The meetings were the chance to sample the rice and cardamom coffee, while talking well into the night. Treasure was bartered in the form of pearls from the distant Persian Gulf, where divers by the score had risked an early grave. There was ivory from Africa. From the children's faces Talal knew that they loved to hear about treasure. Even Abdul turned again to hear father and watched his face and expressive hands with wide brown eyes, his new football forgotten - for the moment.

Talal then vividly re-told the tales of his father's own part in raids on hostile tribes. In the north the infidels had come on the water. He told of the British, with their strange religion, and who, for many years, ruled the sea routes around his country, controlling the pirates, a feature of the Gulf area. The British had an Empire which had fed off treasures and goods of all descriptions that had flowed along this, the key route to India and beyond. They took the goods back to the seat of Imperial Power of which the desert dwellers knew nothing. At that time they had known nothing either, about a far greater treasure. It was hidden beneath their very feet.

Talal recalled that in those days it was often a bare existence for all. Even in the coastal regions, where, for example, fishermen along the Red Sea coast had also struggled to exist. This Spartan existence was accepted as the will of Allah.

The older of Talal's children, as did their ancestors and millions of their fellow-citizens, daily consigned their fate and destiny to Allah. They revered Allah at the appointed five times each waking day. Talal's children were well aware of this as their daily culture dictated. Their inheritance - although there were no real tribal boundaries drawn on any agreed map - included the Al Hasa region, where the dark rich amber-coloured dates were relied upon by the tribesmen. To a large extent they had been contented, for they knew no other life, apart from that of the desert.

Next Talal explained how this huge area had evolved, with the suppression of more and more tribes, into what would soon become the Saudi Empire. This, Talal told the children, can be traced as commencing at the beginning of the 19th Century. The changes, he said, had extended from Syria in the North to the Yemen in the South, and from the Red Sea in the West to the Persian Gulf. By 1914 Britain had recognised the facts and the importance of the key person who had made this possible, the children's own grandfather - Abdul Aziz. Little Abdul, almost asleep already, raised his head from the carpet. The moment passed and he drifted off.

Talal explained that the 'Great Power' depended on their Royal Navy, a Navy that needed oil, having taken the decision to convert from coal fired ships just two years earlier. Hence, by 1916 Britain were struggling with the Turks for control of the wider Middle East.

Talal told his keen listeners how, in 1916, Britain had sent out an army officer - Captain Lawrence; later to be known as Lawrence of Arabia. Lawrence, on Britain's behalf, had supported Shareef Husain Ibn Ali, who had proclaimed the Arab Revolt. British aid was provided for an attack on the dreaded Turks, following the British-Saudi Friendship Agreement. By 1918 Abdul Aziz had realised that the Saudi-British Agreement was of little consequence, as Britain clearly had her main eye on the trade routes, via the Suez Canal to the West and the Persian Gulf to the North.

All this was complicated for the children to remember but they would certainly hear it repeated again and again. Talal stopped speaking and looked around, adjusting his robes. Abdul's interest was gone and, with the onset of tiredness, his little head was resting on the ball. Omar and the girls, being a little older, were still almost attentive. The ever-present buzzing flies were suddenly either quiet or resting.

He dug deeper into his memory. He explained how Great Britain had decided that her policy would be best-served by controlling the Middle East from the Eastern end of the Mediterranean Sea. Talal related how Britain's promises and collaboration with Arabia - soon to be recognised officially around the world as 'Saudi Arabia' - would falter and fail. Abdul Aziz had vowed to regain any territory lost when the time came.

A major milestone had occurred when, in 1932, King Abdul Aziz announced the unification of the dual kingdoms of Nedj and Hijaz into a single Kingdom of Saudi Arabia. As it turned out, the acquisition of a greater Saudi armed force would be many years ahead.

America was always being mentioned in the family and on their TV, so Talal went on to tell them that Venezuela, where he had just been, was in South America. The United States of America would also come into his story soon. In the meantime he told them how Britain and France had divided up the rest of their area - the Middle East.

At this point he decided that, further detail could wait until next time. This would include an explanation of the huge geographical extent of Saudi Arabia, about the size of Europe. Further that its inhabitants had, mainly, continued to follow the Wahhabi mould of Islam. Within this largely desert area the children's ancestors who were Sheikhs and Sultans had ruled. Heavily veiled womenfolk cooked the flat bread, produced the sweet coffee to entertain the occasional visitor, and were owned as vassals and chattels. This was the way of things. Talal understood. His ancestors had known no other code to live by and they believed in it absolutely. For generations they had not questioned their lot in life. They were pleased to wrap around the coarse camel hair blankets in the cold winter nights, resigned to their lot. While resting on the sandy and stony ground, they and their rulers were unaware of the presence of what was to become later thought of by most a freak of geology. There was oil-bearing porous limestone, far beneath their heads.

Abruptly Talal stood up. Everyone was suddenly alert. Even young Abdul, who had long since dozed off. The dates and melon slices were being passed round, but Talal had not quite finished. He would do so tomorrow night. Young Abdul was taken off to his bedroom and the others left the room. Some of Talal's tale would be remembered this time. He looked forward to the next evening.

From the Western viewpoint it had taken some fourteen hundred years, since the Prophet had come to the area that had shaped their lives into a strange and apparently permanent world. However, a new scenario, far removed from Talal's permanence would soon be played out.

SHIFTING SANDS - DOLLARS FOR MULLAHS

The following evening it was cooler for Talal's continuing narrative. As the National Oil Minister he knew the next sequence of events so well, as he related them to his young but attentive listeners. He proceeded first to give them a general outline of the next events. In 1922, their ancestors were still poor desert wanderers and unaware of explorations taking place in the area of Bahrain, far to the North, near the Persian Gulf. An oily scum-like material had appeared on the surface, near where some oil prospectors had been searching. It was a milestone occurrence - oil had been found under their land.

The children were proud of their father and, apart from young Abdul, understood what 'Oil Minister' meant. Their father was clearly very important! Talal turned aside to take a drink, thinking about the next phase of his narrative.

Until then no oil had been found on the Arab side of the Persian Gulf. Later it transpired that the eventual oil finds on the peninsular at Bahrain, would miss the far greater oil discoveries on the Arabian mainland. These were to come later. In fact, during the world depression of 1929, like everyone else, Abdul Aziz needed money. The revenue from the pilgrims to Mecca was not enough.

A British adviser - who would be later suspected of fomenting intrigue in the Middle East in particular, and in a way which would deliberately not turn out the best for Great Britain, reportedly told Abdul Aziz that he was 'like a man sleeping on top of buried treasure'. But Abdul was not so sure. Many years later it would be shown that the British adviser, one St John Philby, also known as Jack Philby, had been much of the influence behind putting the House of Sa'ud on the throne, as the King of a new nation.

Nevertheless, although Abdul Aziz was pro-British at the time, the American offer of gold sovereigns for the oil prospecting concessions won the day. In many ways it set the scenario for much of the future. Gold was a commodity Abdul Aziz understood. Britain had thrown away its chance, including the really big break, in 1938, when oil was struck at Dhahran. Coincidentally, the RAF were based in Dhahran in 1991, to defend Saudi Arabia, in the first Gulf War. As Talal's narrative was being told in 2002, the point in history had not been reached where Saddam Hussein, ruling Iraq since 1979, would eventually be toppled from power, in 2003.

Talal started to speak again, continuing the epic after the 1938 oil find. After their own ancestor King Abdul Aziz, there had been King Sa'ud. Then King Feisal took over from King Sa'ud, to handle the everyday running of the increasing complexity of modern life, then later still, King Khalid. Talal paused again momentarily. Of course the children would soon learn about the various kings at school.

Western-educated, in Texas, Talal could go on. He remembered how many of the family had thought that his contact with Western infidels would corrupt his upbringing and alienate him from his roots. However, every college holiday he had always returned home to be refreshed in his people's culture, before the Westernising influence became too great on his life. Regularly he talked to his children, as he did this night.

As far back as he could remember Talal was aware that the saga of Palestine had been present. He would come to that in a moment. He decided against telling the children certain other facts. For example, how Arab-Nazi contacts had started in the 1930s when the Arab National Movement had close ties with Haj Amin el Husseini, the Grand Mufti of Jerusalem, Husseini had offered to foment a rebellion behind Allied lines. At the time there was also a significant pro-German movement in other lands nearby, including among the younger Egyptian Army Officers. Also, German-supplied weapons flowed to the Arabs in Palestine, via Saudi Arabia, but Abdul Aziz was seen as sitting on the fence. Later, during the Cold War, very soon after World War 2, German armament specialists had left East Germany, by then in the Communist Camp. They were not allowed to design and manufacture arms in East Germany - so they went to King Farouk's Egypt instead. Talal hesitated. In his own thoughts Talal was getting ahead of himself. Time was getting on - he must return to his narrative as things were in 1939.

Despite the late hour Omar, Talal's sixteen year old son, had remained completely attentive. The girls, however, tended to nod off to sleep, aided by the balmy atmosphere. Several male cousins, who joined them were also struggling to keep awake. One day, they would have to tell this story to their own offspring. For Talal the events described were coming up to date and perhaps for that reason the information was becoming more interesting to Omar, as these later topics were sometimes spoken of by his schoolteachers.

Talal, realising his diminishing audience would not last much longer, called for more drinks, sweetmeats and dates. He quickly told how the King had protested against Britain's Peel Report, that had recommended the partitioning of a British Protectorate, immediately to their North. The area had been known as Palestine, ever since the Roman occupation 2000 years before.

Because he just did not realise the true facts - or refused to face them - Talal did not mention that their King, like all his subjects and many, even in the West, had been erroneously led to believe that the Jews wanted the whole of the Middle East. A belief with no foundation whatsoever, but one which amazingly persisted in the Middle East, even at the highest levels of government.

More cool drinks arrived. Perhaps, in the light of recent peace initiatives, reasoned Talal, as he paused to sip his drink, the people had been over-suspicious. But he nevertheless recalled the day that his elderly father had related the tale of the Hashemites and Trans-Jordan.

As his father had stopped speaking. Omar, now restless stood up. However, Talal continued almost at once. So Omar quickly sat down again. Talal was about to come to the really important part of his story.

King Aziz had been suspicious that Abdullah of Transjordan - leader of an artificial kingdom generated by the British - might have plans to integrate the wider Palestine into the Hashemite Kingdom. Relations with Britain had become more difficult. Action was needed.

'What happened next?' Omar asked his father, suddenly. Talal then pointed out that the decision was taken to send Saudi Arabian arms and moral support to the Arabs in Palestine. It was thought that this would surely help to frustrate Hashemite ambitions. At the same time it would upset both the Jews and the British.

Talal's thoughts came quickly to more recent history. To the North of Saudi Arabia a shattering event had occurred in 1948. An event as incomprehensible to Talal as to those in the rest of the Islamic world. Contrary to all expectations a new nation had been born virtually overnight. Could it really be true? Of course not - it must only be temporary quirk of history!

The people that had done this, the Jews, had earlier been offered a slice of Uganda. This they had rejected. His audience reacted with incredulity, when they were told that the Jews had even been offered parts of their own land, now the Kingdom of Saudi Arabia. It was the part where those luscious Al Hasa dates grew. However, the Jews had not wanted that either!

Talal explained how he, as a boy, had considered how strange it was that other peoples in other lands should even consider interfering with his land. But, of course, they were strong and his land was weak. Abdul Aziz had the vision but not the strength. How, as time went on it would it be otherwise - it was surely the will of Allah. Talal could not even bring himself to say the name of this new state to the north.

The older children knew, from their teachers that it was the land which the infidels called Israel and the Zionists called Eretz Israel (The Land of Israel).

Talal's considerable insight into this phase of his country's history was evident. Undoubtedly it had been embroidered by the telling and re-telling. The tale was at a point where any doubtful statements became 'set in concrete'. The given facts - even if they had been proved wrong, would still have remained in their original form!

Having studied the world oil history in some detail, Talal was conscious that, during World War 2, the USA forces had consumed, together with her allies, a larger proportion of the USA's own oil reserves than originally envisaged. Hence,

Talal was well-aware that it was, with gratitude, that the USA found it could help develop the oil-fields and spend dollars on Saudi Arabian oil. Diverting for a moment from his historical sequence, he just mentioned briefly that, in 1991, it was largely under the influence of the USA that the advance of Saddam Hussein beyond Kuwait - even possibly into Saudi Arabia itself, had been stopped.

It was time for Talal to mention money. In the 1990s the King was grateful for the continued revenues, both from the USA and many other nations who bought the oil. By then, the Mecca pilgrim revenues were growing again - albeit slowly. The peculiar situation was that the USA, while befriending Saudi Arabia, were also, from its beginnings, good friends of the new State of Israel.

Talal reminded his audience that the majority of the Arab nations did not recognise the existence of Israel. He told them, how, in the early days, the Arab delegates walked out of the United Nations Assembly when the members reached the point of discussing Israel. How could you discuss a topic if it didn't exist, he asked them? They all nodded.

Next he related how, first in 1948, and then again in 1967 and yet again in 1973 the impossible would happen. The mighty Arab forces would each time fight with the Israelis but, almost beyond belief, Israel would still be there. Talal omitted to say that this had caused a considerable wound to Arab dignity. Nevertheless, he said, 'The Arab nations still have the oil and Israel have none.' There would be another day!

Talal was silent for a minute. He decided to continue with a painful phase in their history. To Talal's family, many others in their Kingdom, and in the brother Arab States, it seemed that Britain was also a supporter of Israel. None of them could understand this. He paused and recalled to mind that everything in their upbringing and very nature told him that all was in the will of Allah! Without saying anything he mused for a moment. Surely something must have gone wrong here? Could Allah have made a mistake? This must be the case and most certainly it would soon be rectified - and Israel would somehow disappear. He spoke again and told his audience how their King had considered joining the King of Jordan, in the 1948 war against Israel. However, Saudi Arabia did not do so, because The King was fearful of being an indirect cause of helping the Hashemites in their quest for more land. Soon, in 1950, King Sa'ud would take over. In the meantime King Abdul Aziz would survive another three years before his death and King Feisal would be assassinated by one of the Saudi Princes. Talal sighed and sat down again. Speaking of Israel had always been painful and now, in the year 2002, Israel was still there - it was incredible!

The listeners were fighting sleep in the soporific atmosphere. Talal decided he would continue the story tomorrow just with the children. They were roused and taken off to bed, each clutching their gifts. A few minutes of general conversation followed. The older relatives remained.

Talal stood up, gathering his robes, and went to the balcony. He continued thinking while surveying the distant lights of the city, the stars overhead and the closer lights of the traffic.

There were things that he really knew were true but simply could not bear to say out loud. After all, his children might repeat them at school. In 1956 he knew that King Sa'ud, had listened to the President of Egypt. President Nasser's proposal, that 'all Arabs should unite to defeat Israel', had indeed been appealing. Nevertheless the King had not gone to war with the others, but instead had retaliated by stopping the flow of oil to both Britain and France. The closure of the Suez Canal had cost Saudi Arabia some forty per cent of oil revenues. This, just when the income from pilgrims was at a low, and the King was getting heavily in debt.

Of course, Nasser had claimed a victory over the Imperialists. To Talal's father it had probably seemed like a victory - and yet Europe went on and prospered. The USA prospered even more. Worst of all Israel had survived and flourished, despite their heavy defence spending. Talal never stopped to consider why he opposed Israel - who had never done any harm to his nation and neither was a rival in the oil stakes.

The mainly US-run Saudi-based oil companies had made vast huge profits. Talal's father had told him that an oil cartel had been formed in 1960. It included Venezuela, Kuwait, Iran Saudi Arabia and Iraq and the initials 'OPEC' were soon known world-wide. It was now forty years later and Talal had just returned from the same cartel today. It was so good to be home and back with his family.

He turned from the slight breeze that was now creeping over the balcony and faced his remaining audience. They fell silent. The older ones would understand the implications of what he was about to say.

He explained that, although the nation had enjoyed peace at that time, some minor troubles had erupted closer to home. For example, when the Yemeni Royal Family was removed, with Egypt's support, some southern Saudi towns had come under Egyptian bombing. This was because Saudi Arabia's King Sa'ud, had supported Yemen. The Yemeni King, by 1969, deposed, had died in exile in Athens.

Talal, as he had told it so many times before, explained that his father, after the Six Day Arab-Israeli War of 1967, had been, like all Arabs, deeply suspicious of the West. It was, Talal reasoned, that the West must surely be holding the Arabs back! Why not turn again to the Communist Bloc for armaments - why not indeed. At the time the Communists needed oil. Saudi Arabia itself would not itself require the arms, but they realised that an ample supply of Saudi money could be used by the other Arab states to purchase them. It was a crafty scheme because, they could then use Saudi money in confrontation of Israel, while acting only to payroll those doing the dirty work! However, every new nation had an airforce, as well as an army - so the time had come to expand theirs, just in case they needed them in the future. Perhaps Israel might attack them! So Saudi Arabia had first purchased a number of Lightning fighter aircraft, and other equipment from Great Britain. The Lightning aircraft was complex at the time, and much of the maintenance was done by British contractors. Following-on, they had bought American aircraft and now they had purchased the Tornado from Great Britain, under a huge oil deal, known as the Al Yamama programme.

He remembered a crisis at the time. A summit had been rapidly called by the King, following a new outrage in Jerusalem. Surely it must have been the Israelis who had deliberately allowed a deranged visiting Australian Christian tourist to set fire to the Holy Mosque of El Asqua? Although Talal had never been to Jerusalem he spent some time explaining the departure of the prophet - praise be to his name - on his winged horse from Mount Moriah. Talal said that, one day, the city and indeed the whole site would be reclaimed for Islam. The elders listening, who had rarely spoken while the children were present, now wholeheartedly voiced their agreement.

He reminded his listeners that after the 1973 Arab-Israeli War, the world's population became increasingly aware that most of the world's black gold was beneath the sands of Saudi Arabia and several other, mainly Arab, nations. This was power indeed. They could afford to pay many infidels to come and build up their nation. Although they were getting into debt they could expand their armed forces even further. The infidels possessed skills that they did not have themselves at the time. Meantime they could send many men overseas to receive technology training. Surely a time would come when they could operate alone? Talal did not say so, but he realised that it was taking many years indeed to reach this point

Strangely, nearby Israel, did not seem to have any of this precious oil. This must surely be the will of Allah. His listeners all nodded in agreement. The rulers of yesterday had decided that all who had supported Israel in their Yom Kippur War, which Talal, and his listeners naturally called the War of Ramadan, would therefore pay dearly. An oil embargo would be imposed starting on the 20th October 1973. No European nation would risk any US aircraft, en route in support of Israel, to land for refuelling.

Although selectively embellishing his story, Talal through his frequent contacts on his world-wide travels, knew much more about the reality of the situation. Oil 'the Product' had, almost overnight, become oil, 'the Weapon'. The Shah of Iran, who had been an oil-supplying friend to the West and to Israel, was gone. The Ayatollahs had taken power and Iran had refused to sell any more oil to Israel. When the Saudi oil embargo took place, the USA, the world's largest consumer, were, fortuitously, importing less than five per cent of their daily oil consumption from Saudi Arabia. Most nations imposed oil rationing and, in time, the embargo came to nothing. King Feisal had announced a Jihad - a Holy War - against Israel. At the time all the Arab countries, except Iraq and Libya, had joined in the oil embargo.

Now, even Omar had almost dozed off. He awoke, kissed his father and went off to bed, carrying the instruction book for his new computer game. The moon high and luminous, was casting shadows ever more intensely. The temperature fell sharply. The Oil Minister looked out over his city with some satisfaction. His relatives departed to their homes.

He had omitted to say that he knew that Saudi Arabia's contribution to Yasser Arafat's PLO terrorists was probably well over a billion dollars since the 1973 war. Enough had been said for yet another evening. Talal had decided, that if the information was repeated sufficient times, his family would surely follow in his own ways and thoughts. Allah did not make mistakes!

Talal was not aware that a member of his family would play a terrible role in a conflict for which the key elements were gradually coming together. The clock was ticking - but few heard it!

DESERT TRAINING

At breakfast the next morning, Omar said 'What happened next, Father?' Talal, again promised, that he would continue that very same evening. Omar could not wait for the evening to come.

His Father started earlier than usual and explained how a turning point had occurred in the world economy. He related how the price of oil, as an essential energy source, had suddenly rocketed. It had resulted in a transfer of wealth across the world, that would be unequalled in world history. Oil power soon resulted in major deliberations in the United Nations. As the main oil producing area, the Middle East was at the forefront of world news.

Talal knew that there were other reasons why the Middle East was important, but said nothing. He knew that the political importance of the Middle East was such that the Palestine Liberation Organisation had been allowed into the UN, even though they were not a nation state. Talal whispered to himself 'Bismallah Al rachman Al raheem' - in the name of God the Compassionate, the Merciful. There were many other facts that he could relate but he did not say more on this topic, for the moment.

For the next few moments he mused on the next part of his story. Saudi Arabia, together with Iran, Iraq and Kuwait to the North, became rich on oil. In fact, Talal's predecessors would have been amazed to know that the country would become so rich. Such power was surely granted by Allah. However, the reality was different. Despite the apparent wealth, credit had been necessary and a considerable debt had built up. For example, by 1996, there had been thirteen successive years of budget deficits. While they lacked an understanding of the real state of the nation, thousands had wished to oust the monarchy and dispense with the dozens of spendthrift princes of the Sa'ud Royal Family.

Until this oil treasure had so unexpectedly arrived, Saudi Arabia had relied heavily upon the income from the great pilgrimages. Talal knew that Omar understood about these, as he saw the many thousands that passed through the Capital city, en route to Mecca. Talal did not mention that, although slavery had supposedly ended in 1962, Muslim Africans coming to Mecca for the Haj, would still sell their children to pay for the journey home!

Talal's story was rapidly coming towards the 1990s, but he decided that a few more key points should be mentioned. Another great oil price rise had added to Saudi Arabia's enormous exchequer in 1979. Ironically this had followed the Iranian revolution, in which Saudi Arabia had played no part. This occurred because Iranian oil production had suddenly plummeted by several million barrels a day. The price of oil had doubled again. Money simply poured in - as fast as oil poured out. This was the second huge price rise in the 1970s. Furthermore, Saudi Arabia still had oil in the ground, in plenty. It was probably better than having money in the bank! A new world economic order had arrived. Saudi Arabia could buy anything it wanted. It was at this time that all Talal's family, uncles, cousins - the lot - had moved into permanent accommodation. They left only a distant arm of the family in the desert; an enormous contrast from Talal's new existence, in the luxury of the expanding new capital.

Talal came to the important part, in his eyes. He told his audience that, despite all this unexpected wealth and ownership of a vast land area, things were not right. Like so many citizens of the Middle East, including their leaders, Talal had been brought up to believe that Israel and the Jews were the cause of all their troubles. Talal did not mention that Israel, occupying a small land area, and with no oil, were clearly never a competitor for oil trade on the world stage.

In contrast, Saudi Arabia's income was assured. They had an excess of land and, at that time, no one was really interested in attacking them. Located on the fringes of the country were just a few rebellious tribes, of no real consequence. Talal explained that, in the cities, they just had to sit back and let the oil flow and pay for anything they required. This included large numbers of foreigners, recruited to do the essential tasks and provide the technology and services of a growing modern infrastructure. Talal stopped for a moment to let these key points sink in. Although he had not spoken out all his thoughts, he was sure that Omar had grasped all the main points. During the evening his other children had occasionally put in an appearance. They would hear it all again, another time.

Talal continued. Pilgrims could now afford to come in by air. If the oil did eventually run out, then there was plenty of natural gas, to follow. He reminded his listeners that it was one of their own relatives, also educated in the West, that had realised that it was possible to capture the excess gas. This was a significant advantage, rather than waste it by burning off, as they had done for so many years before.

By this time Talal's government had become adept at accounting for a web of complex relationships between Saudi Arabia and her neighbours. Many of the nearby nations had become military powers to some extent. Not able to manufacture arms, they had purchased them from a variety of sources, obtained foreign military training and also employed well-paid mercenaries.

He had reached the inevitable topic once again. Talal had always imagined a world where his Palestinian 'brothers' were 'free' - so the fight must go on! He did not mention any alternatives to his son. Neither did he mention that the Israeli-Arabs (the 'Palestinians') were the only Arabs that had the vote in the Middle East.

Had Keith been present to speak to Omar he could have told him that, like most of his race and indeed most in the West, Talal seemed to be unaware of many of the facts of history. For example, just one day's oil revenues, from the Saudi coffers, would have rapidly re-settled all the refugees, many years previously. The problem would have been over at a stroke. Today's refugees were descendants of those 600,000 who originally fled in 1948, even though many did not need to. At the time they were urged to do so by the then Mufti of Jerusalem. It was said to be a 'temporary measure', while the victorious Arab Armies exterminated the Jews. It turned out differently - much to everyone's surprise. The situation had nevertheless been orchestrated by the Mufti, who had been a supporter of Hitler during World War 2. It had become a convenient cause to use against Israel and remained so, ever since.

Of course, Omar did not receive this information. Neither was he told that Saudi Arabia were funding the PLO, while other nations in the area, including Iran, were funding the Hesbollah, Hamas, Islamic Jihad, and several other terrorist groups. For some reason his father and so many others had not grasped the inescapable fact that, despite the billions of Saudi dollars given to the PLO, over many years, there seemed to be no difference to the plight of the people they thought they were helping! Only impoverished Jordan had tried hard to give them shelter. Where had all this money gone?

The Mufti, who had acted as a trigger, had, of course, long since vanished from the scene! Jordan was friendly with the West. After all, Great Britain and France had divided up the land, so as to create Transjordan in the first place! Talal had also omitted to say that the PLO had caused so much trouble in the country that King Hussein of Jordan had thrown them out.

The information was almost up to date. After very briefly covering the Palestinian situation, Talal moved on and explained that Saudi Arabia had never got far with the Soviet Union. When the mighty Soviet Union collapsed, Russia had become one of the new states that had supported the international action against Saddam Hussein in the first Gulf War. When the vote was taken, late in 2002, Russia had also supported the UN Security Council again, for action to be taken against Saddam Hussein. As he spoke Talal did not know that, when the Council would be called upon to vote again, at the beginning of 2003, Russia and France would vote against action.

At the time Russia possessed only limited muscle, and was nursing her own steadily dwindling oil reserves, hoping to bolster supplies from Iraq, once the crisis was resolved. France could see her somewhat undercover oil agreement with Iraq collapsing and could also see the US gaining more control in the oil rich area.

Talal explained to his son how the scope for the development of instability in the region was very far ranging. For example, in 1981 Iraq had the intention of developing a nuclear weapon. Talal told how Israel had attacked and destroyed the Iraqi nuclear reactor.

Iran had been at loggerheads with most of the world, since the fall of the Shah, especially with the USA. With the Ayatollah in power the USA had undergone the indignity of the failed rescue attempt for the US embassy staff, held hostage in Teheran. Finally, he also related how Saudi Arabia had boycotted Egypt, following the visit by President Sadat to Israel.

Talal finally brought his family tale to an end and the gathering broke up to pursue other interests but Omar still remained, talking to his father.

'What shall I do?' questioned Omar. 'You must keep studying my son and go to university and then, like your brother Iyad, join the Army,' replied his father, sitting back with a contented expression. 'We have oil and gas to last all your lifetime.' He did not mention that, unless more was found, at the current rate of world consumption, the known oil reserves would only last for a few decades. In fact, the Russians were clearly planning their strategy for long term oil supplies now. Without doubt others would come knocking on the door for an even greater supply of Saudi oil. Whoever they turned out to be - they might not knock gently! Therefore, the Saudi Arabian armed forces would be a good career for Omar.

Talal decided that Omar was old enough to be told a little more. As his country's Oil Minister, Talal had progressed into a position of power, centred in the Saudi Arabian offices of OPEC, in Ryadh. Early in the decade, a change of government had occurred in the Jewish State and peace talks had surprisingly and suddenly started in Norway. These had progressed to more talks nearer home - in Egypt - and now his Arab brothers in the PLO, had apparently taken the first steps towards peace and a Palestinian State. To do this they had no option but to recognise the State of Israel and talk to its leaders.

Like all Arabs, but somehow not seen by the gullible West, Talal knew that this was in reality only their first step in ridding the area completely of this 'False State'. It seemed that Allah, in His wisdom, had temporarily placed the Jews in command of the Holy Place - Al Quds - Jerusalem. Talal said that the guardian of this holy place should be Saudi Arabia and certainly not the Hashemite King of Jordan. Surely, he thought, Allah would soon act.

Of course Talal had been unaware of the PLO's intention to reject all the peace plans, but instead to start another intafada in the year 2000. This had resulted in a very hard time for the Palestinians, with much bloodshed on both sides. It was still going on every day. The peace talks had collapsed and they had gained nothing.

Talal's last promotion was to chair the deliberations of the all-powerful oil cartel. The position allowed a seat at the King's council as the number one adviser on oil matters - the major source of the kingdom's revenue. This, he frequently told his older sons, was their inheritance.

Talal was not to know that, within a few years, yet another major national milestone, leading to international repercussions, would occur. The continued Saudi Arabian co-operation with the West would lead to fundamentalist and radical Arab elements in the surrounding nations to call for an excuse for the 'punishment' of the Saudi Royal Family. By that time the Royal Family would have spent massive sums to build forces to deter anyone in the area with designs on their land or wealth. Just as in Iran, the majority of ordinary citizens had received very little. Both internal and external forces were already at work, planning for the coming take over of Saudi Arabia, by the Mullahs.

Already, in September 2001, Islamic terrorists, some of Saudi Arabian origin, had carried out attacks on the two towers of the World Trade Centre buildings in New York. The West then assembled a coalition of forces to attack the Al Queda stronghold, located in the Taliban fundamentalist-controlled nation of Afghanistan. Even as Talal had been speaking a wide search was on for Ben Laden, the Saudi leader of Al Qaeda.

Now, in 2002, the United Nations Organisation had reports that, despite his denials, the Iraqi leader, Saddam Hussein, was either developing or obtaining weapons of mass destruction. The UN voted unanimously that Weapons Inspectors should return to Iraq to resume their checks; from which they had been expelled several years earlier.

Talal told his son that it had seemed that Iraq, armed with new weapons, might seize an opportunity to topple the Saudi regime, control the oil and greatly reduce the influence of the West in the area. Other states nearby, Arab or otherwise, were also very wary of Saddam's ambitions. All attempts to limit arms transfers in the area had little effect. A number of states, with no interest in arms limitations, had obtained biological and chemical weapons. Many nations in the area had benefited from the training they had received in the West and in the Former Soviet Union. Some were ready to act. Saddam might even act as soon as his weapons were ready, primarily against Israel. Further, he might pass on these weapons to anyone who would use them against the USA, Europe and Israel.

Having described the main points, it was Omar's bedtime. Talal had some papers to attend to before he turned in. Only two more days to the weekend!

In the coming months Talal had continued as Oil Minister and Omar had enthusiastically resolved to study hard and follow his big brother Iyad, just as his father had suggested.

Back in Britain Keith continued to monitor the scenario. As ever, tensions had continued in the area. Several foreign experts were killed in terrorist raids on their living compounds in Saudi cities. After Saddam Hussein's overthrow, in 2003, there were democratic elections in Iraq, in 2005, and there were even more efforts to prevent the spread of weapons of mass destruction.

Chairman Arafat, leader of the PLO, had died in 2004, but not much had really changed in the conflict, despite negotiation attempts together by the new Palestinian leadership and Israel. By 2005, the main problem in negotiations was in providing adequate security for Israel. Israel had agreed to leave certain areas that they had been forced to police for their own protection. In addition the Knesset passed plans to withdraw settlements from land that the Palestinians claimed was theirs. This all at considerable cost to Israel.

Concerted efforts were still being made to prevent the spread of weapons of mass destruction in the area. The USA were even suggesting that Israel should destroy her nuclear weapons. A new government was elected in Iraq, opposed by terrorist action backed by Al Queda and others. Within a few years, across the Gulf of Iran, the seeds of far-reaching events were already germinating.

In Ryadh, in 2008, Talal thought nothing of possible forthcoming world shattering events. He was looking forward to seeing Iyad, his fine Army son, who was planning to be home at the weekend. It was a bitter disappointment when Talal arrived home from work, to find a brief message from Iyad. Iyad had apparently been ordered on a deep desert training exercise for a few weeks and a letter was on its way. He rang the barracks in the hope that he might have a word before Iyad departed on exercise. Iyad, it seemed, had already left!

At the weekend, when the letter arrived, Talal was naturally inquisitive. Surely, he thought, this seemed to be an unforeseen exercise. Why couldn't the exercise have waited until after the weekend? The letter didn't say a lot - but Iyad rarely said much about his work - after all he was a Battery Commander on the unit that trained with Saudi Arabia's latest ballistic missiles, recently acquired from China. Perhaps something unusual was afoot. However, he had heard nothing unusual from his normal sources. Further, he would soon be away for another OPEC meeting.

However, events were fast approaching that Talal and the majority of the world would find astonishing. Further, the world had yet to hear of the activities of a Russian Jewish émigré to Israel, named Isador Zaritski!

EXODUS - AGAIN!

Isador Zaritski had much to consider on his departure day. Most of it came to mind just after the aircraft took off from Moscow's dismal airport. It was a day that he would not have considered possible, just a few years before. This was an adventure into a new world indeed! The past was behind, changed forever since the unprecedented events of the early 1990s - events that seemed to have been triggered by the actions of a single man - Mikael Gorbachev. Gorbachev had expected to improve the efficiency of industry and thus the lot of the ordinary citizen, but he had also expected that the Soviet political order would take a few reforms and otherwise remain more or less unchanged.

Despite all exhortations and the efforts of millions of Soviet citizens, Gorbachev had found that the resources of his empire could no longer support a viable internal system. Even less could it continue to support a world-wide military and ideological confrontational attitude. The West had faced up to numerous and frequently repeated threats by a series of Soviet Leaders, who had intended to spread communism across the world, by any means possible. Their ambitions had led to an expensive, 40 year long, armed forces East-West confrontation, following World War 2. Now, during the exciting journey just beginning, it was inevitable that Isador would spend some time considering his family's past, because soon they would all be starting a new life. Further, unbeknown to Isador his future actions would change the world.

Isador's life in Russia had been tolerable only because of his position as a scientist. However, both his father and his grandparents had suffered persecution and deprivation, in the days of the Czar and even afterwards, in the 'glorious Soviet Union'. They had been born in this alien land, and, like so many other Jews in the Diaspora, had come to expect no different. The lives of many relatives and most of the family records had been lost in one or other of the pogroms, the regular attacks on the Jews. It was miraculous indeed that his family had survived. Now, the Zaritski family were being allowed to leave Russia. As the aircraft taxied he could glimpse the nearby forests of his youth. The aircraft was about to take-off.

As they climbed steeply, Isador's keen thoughts were elsewhere. In his mind he recalled the day that the big change to all their lives had started. A change that was clearly unstoppable. Afterwards Gorbachev had said, 'We had reached the limit, we were heading for disaster. Something had to happen.' Indeed, a point had been reached where the USSR could barely feed its own population. In 1985, some five years before the final collapse, Gorbachev, while speaking to the US President of the day, had said 'The USSR has never intended to fight the USA and does not have such intentions now. There have never been such madmen within the Soviet leadership and there are none now.' Clearly a world milestone had been reached that would have eventual repercussions, far beyond most citizens wildest expectations. Isador was thankful that the milestone had been reached in his lifetime - but was it inevitable - or if not, why had it happened now?

Isador clearly remembered the time when Gorbachev had become the 8th Soviet Leader. It had been the culmination of a sequence of quite surprising events. Of course, the general population were not privy to much that went on within the confines of the Politburo. Indeed, most were unaware of the intriguing means of Gorbachev's rise to power.

Firstly, Gorbachev's peasant family had successfully survived the 1930, 1932, and 1933 famines. Young Mikael Gorbachev had been just 8 years old when one, Suslov, came to power. Their paths were to cross when Suslov became Gorbachev's mentor decades later. Isador was too young to remember the all the horrors of the intervening years, although his parents had often mentioned those most difficult of days.

In 1991, the huge land-mass containing millions of citizens, collectively known as the Soviet Union for most of the century, was still in the process of reforming as Independent States. Isador sensed that, with Gorbachev, change was coming. It came faster than they could scarcely believe. Of course, the twin factors of geography and climate would not change but they had been especially critical influences when his country was under communist domination. Both factors had been particularly relevant when such a huge area was run as a vast collective agricultural farm, under central control. Whoever was in government, there would always be a limited 'time-slot' available in which to gather in the harvest, even when a good harvest is available. Success or failure was frequently dictated by the weather, but was also dependent upon the gross inefficiency of the Soviet system.

For a large and isolated country, that had attempted to be self-sufficient, the importance of a successful harvest cannot be over-estimated. However, during the decades of communist rule, the masses in their Moscow tenements only heard of harvest catastrophes by word of mouth. The real truth was never revealed in their newspapers or on their national television, or radio. Radio broadcasts beamed from ' The Capitalist West' were deliberately jammed by the authorities, to prevent the ordinary citizen being 'corrupted'. Only the great achievements of the Soviet people were shown on the media, never the problems. Anyone who spoke out, as a dissident, very rapidly found they had a non-return ticket to a labour camp. It might be to Perm, Potma, or worse. Isador knew that the failure of agriculture, and hence food supplies, had been an important part of the changes taking place. He also suspected that trying to face up to the West, particularly to the USA, had cost the nation dearly - even to the point of collapse.

The aircraft's engine noise reduced. As they circled and headed westward, the airport runways could be glimpsed for a last time. The link with the country that had been their homeland for so many years had been broken. Isador knew the history only too well, as they had often struggled to survive.

Although it was now 1999, he had reason to remember the events that occurred in 1959, 40 years earlier. The new Soviet Leader Kruschev had sacked the Agriculture Secretary, following a poor harvest. It was an unforgettable year because Isador's wedding to dear Sarah had taken place. The same year, at the unprecedented age of just 29, Mikael Gorbachev had been promoted. However, Isador, like most of the Soviet population, had known nothing of Gorbachev in those far-off days. Nevertheless, it was the start of a sequence that would affect the world.

Only 4 years after reading law at university, Mikael Gorbachev had been made responsible for agriculture, for his entire home area. Although this was unprecedented, it hadn't made news in Isador's circle of friends, in far away Moscow. Neither had the situation three years later, when good weather brought a bumper harvest and Gorbachev was promoted again. By 1968, after completing a correspondence course in agriculture, he had become Second Secretary for his local area. This was achieved by skipping the position of Third Secretary, despite the availability of much better-qualified people. Quite an achievement!

Most ordinary citizens knew little of the manoeuvrings for power among their leaders. They were told only the bare minimum. Information often became known later, by unofficial word of mouth, or 'officially', if the party deemed it suitable, appropriately timed; and advantageous to their cause.

The aircraft's engine note changed again, as the pilot set the plane onto a steady climb. However, Isador's thoughts still remained far away. Amazingly, in 1970, after a very poor harvest, Gorbachev was appointed as a Deputy to the Supreme Soviet. Isador also remembered this event, because it happened to coincide with the seventh birthday of his first son. It was also to be especially remembered because the very next year there followed yet another poor harvest. Times had been hard. Nevertheless, having just taken-over his tasks, Deputy Gorbachev had fortuitously survived. Then there followed a good harvest. This consolidated his position. However, in 1975, there was yet another harvest failure. Although irrational, a scapegoat was surely needed!

This was the way the ruthless Soviet Union conducted its affairs, as Isador had come to know so well. Surprisingly, Gorbachev, who normally would have been held responsible, survived again. Instead, another man, Polyansky, was blamed and banished as Ambassador to Japan, as a punishment! Several good harvests followed. Gorbachev had not yet reached the top, but he was well on his way. For the time being other repressive leaders had been in power. Meanwhile, nearing the top of the aircraft's climb, Isador briefly remembered the time when Nikita Kruschev had suddenly gone and another leader, Leonid Breshnev, had taken command.

Soon after Isador's university studies were completed he had obtained work on the purely scientific aspects of the physical properties of matter. Few Jews were allowed to work on overtly military projects. Nevertheless, Isador knew that his work must have had some military applications, in common with most research within the Soviet Union. His discoveries had merely been passed on to another department. Isador hardly ever heard the final outcome. All anyone heard was Breshnev's constant urging for his population to make even greater achievements. Once the Americans had reached the moon first, the space-race had slowed. Now, Mother Russia wanted something new.

Breshnev's expected successor was Kulakov - but his heart stopped suddenly. In the interim struggles of prospective leaders Mikael Gorbachev had been moved to a post in Moscow. The saga of communism - inevitably spending much of its time striving to meet the minimum requirements to feed the people - had continued. The next two harvests were poor overall. Only the harvest, back in Gorbachev's home area, was good! Doubtless his Politburo masters considered that this must have been due to the organisation that Gorbachev had put in place, in the past. Hence, having conveniently been in Moscow, once again he did not incur the Politburo's wrath. Neither was he held to blame for the widespread crop failures elsewhere. The weather that directly affects harvests is, of course, beyond man's control. Not that this fact figured in the thinking of the men in the Kremlin!

The situation was serious and the USSR had been forced to buy grain from abroad. However, the following year, the United States imposed a grain sales embargo on the USSR. As a result, the implementation of the '1981-91 Ten Year Soviet Grain Plan', became Gorbachev's task. By then, he was promoted as the youngest member of the Politburo, his advance seemingly have taken place against all obstacles! However, there was surely even more underlying factors at work, as Isador continued to muse.

Sitting near the window, as their journey progressed the aircraft had flown across vast fields, only intermittently visible, but far below. Some looked like grain. Isador suddenly realised that the underlying reasons for the 1980 grain imports had been hidden from the citizens. Only now did he realise that, incredibly, Gorbachev's position had not been affected - because he had been promoted again. Isador remembered that yet another poor harvest had come along again, in 1981. However, once again, Gorbachev had remained in his job. This time, and not of his doing - the situation had coincided with the

USA's decision to lift their grain embargo. For Gorbachev no less than a saga of survival each time!

Coincidentally, Isador also well remembered the day in 1982 when Suslov died, although he did not know that Suslov was one of Gorbachev's supporters. Nevertheless, it was a time of rejoicing in the small Jewish community where Isador had lived at the time - Bar-Mitzvah time for his second son. There was trouble with the harvest yet again. Andropov, a powerful figure in the Politburo - and soon to take over from Breshnev – blamed the poor harvest on corruption and lack of discipline. Another scapegoat was required. Surely Gorbachev was definitely in line for the 'axe' this time?

On this occasion the official naming of the scapegoat had been delayed until the celebrations marking the Jubilee Year of the Soviet Union were completed. Most of the Soviet leaders looked miserable and Breshnev certainly so, as he took his place on the Kremlin Wall for the annual Red Square military parade. He died suddenly afterwards and the need for a scapegoat was forgotten, and, amazingly Gorbachev had survived yet again! The pace of change was about to quicken.

Andropov had taken office next. Within months he fell seriously ill. In 1983 the harvest improved and Gorbachev was praised. In 1984, Andropov died and Chernenko took over. Another disastrous harvest followed. Chernenko was taken to hospital. In an unprecedented move, the first of its kind since 1957, not Gorbachev but the Chief of Staff, Marshal Orgakov, was dismissed.

The aircraft droned on, crossing into Germany. Isador remembered that he had briefly met Orgakov on an official visit to Isador's laboratory. Much later the citizens realised that Gorbachev must have come very close to dismissal later in 1984, but had escaped again. Nevertheless, Gorbachev had been left off an official photograph. He was finally blamed, but survived in office once again.

In December that year, things suddenly changed for Deputy Leader Gorbachev during a most successful, but short-lived, visit to the United Kingdom. The day after the television news reported how successful his visit was progressing, Gorbachev suddenly left for home, amidst a national leadership crisis. He returned to attend Politburo Member, Marshal Ustinov's funeral.

The aircraft turned once again, now climbing much more slowly. Isador momentarily looked out of the window. There was nothing now, but dense white cloud. He gave a sigh of relief, realising that they had definitely left this unforgiving land behind. He realised that, in the last minutes he had summarised most of the key influences on his family's past existence.

Isador's total world was now in this airliner cabin. It was somehow cosy. It reminded him of the Russian winter whiteness outside and the contrast of a welcome home comfort, with the family. It also recalled the amazing events, starting in December 1984, that had finally brought Gorbachev to power.

Chernenko, the latest leader at that time, had been seriously ill - and died within about ten weeks of taking power. Later assessments concluded, that had Chernenko survived to vote until the Party Congress, then Gorbachev would not have stood a chance as his successor. Being second in command in the Soviet Union had never been a guarantee of succession to the leadership!

Chernenko's death rated black borders on the official photograph, but they were only half the width of those three years earlier, for Brezhnev and, just the previous year, for Andropov. These, seemingly trivial, facets of the Soviet system signalled, to those in the know, including Isador, some significant facts about Chernenko's standing in the Politburo - or rather the lack of it - and the fact that events were occurring almost too quickly for the people to understand the imminent consequences.

The Soviet people were soon to discover that a hurried Politburo meeting had been held. It was possibly only three hours after Chernenko's death, and was not fully attended. Coincidentally, three members - none friendly to Gorbachev, happened to be absent overseas. Nevertheless, the much reduced Politburo had convened and had made a momentous decision. Any five dissenting members could have blocked Gorbachev's nomination. With three members overseas and the others on duty at great distances across the vast Soviet Empire, all those who would have opposed him were well out of reach of Moscow. As a result of this unique set of circumstances Gorbachev's appointment was approved. He took over as Leader of the Soviet Union on the same day, March 10th, 1985. Within five years the outcome would be recognised as a major milestone in world history.

As the aircraft flew steadily onwards to freedom, Isador again mused over the exceptional sequence of events that had run through his mind in but just a few minutes. It had been an amazing sequence indeed, without which Isador would not have been sitting above the clouds at this time. Firstly, when Andropov died there had been no less than five poor harvests and yet Gorbachev, as Chairman for Agriculture, had somehow survived in office. This outcome had been even more remarkable, as, in 1984, Marshal Ustinov, Gorbachev's strongest supporter, died suddenly from 'a cold'. Next, had all the Politburo members been in the country on 10th March, Gorbachev would not have succeeded Chernenko. Sackings usually followed failed harvests. However, despite the fact that Gorbachev was officially responsible for the department concerned, dismissal - surprisingly - always happened to someone else. Thus, Gorbachev had been promoted, again and again and again. Significantly, a succession of Soviet Leaders had died at opportune moments and Gorbachev was suddenly in power, co-incident with unprecedented economic pressures.

Isador perceived that the scenario had indeed been set for major world changes. As a scientist he also knew that the natural statistical probability of the occurrence of the sequence of events, that he had just turned over in his mind, was extremely low. His enquiring mind realised that the sequence that he had just recalled was unique. Who could be behind such a sequence of events and why had they happened? How would the changes across the former Soviet Empire, be manifested in the wider world?

For Isador, the national dramas had brought about his freedom this very day. Given foresight, he would have realised that these events would soon trigger changes to millions of lives, across the world. The demise of the former 'Evil Empire', as President Regan had called the Soviet Union in 1983, would first interact in one Soviet-controlled country after another. Those first to feel the effect would be the citizens of Eastern Europe.

Later, the demise of this oppressive empire would trigger a whole series of ethnic and other conflicts. There would be repercussions in Western Industry, in China and the Middle and Far East. It would affect every family in hitherto divided Germany. Isador could not predict the future, but inevitably he wondered what would become of the country he had lived in for so long and yet which was not really his home. He knew that some of his contemporaries, now unexpectedly free from complete control and domination of their lives, would not be capable of handling the new situation.

There had been seventy years of overall state control. Soviet citizens were not used to buying and selling in the manner of the free economies of the West. Nevertheless, they had yearned for the day, indeed expected, that their standards of living would rise overnight. He reflected that most probably, before long, whole areas might disintegrate into ethnic and religious division, crime and strife. He was soon to be proved correct. He would be thankful that he had left there on this momentous day.

From his family's perspective a life-changing milestone had also been reached. Isador, a Jew, was free to leave the Former Soviet Union with his family and emigrate to Israel. In fact, he was free for the first time to go anywhere that would have him! However, something, or someone, was pulling him to Israel - yet it was a place he had never been in his life. Why was this?

Considering the recent situation at work, it had been a correct decision to leave. The funding for Isador's laboratory had been dramatically reduced. Soon afterwards, the free perks - a sign of the status of a scientist - had declined. For some months he had not been paid at all. The family had to survive by selling a few personal possessions, for hard currency. Seventy years of communism had been exposed as a complete and cruel failure. What with the Czars and the Communists the Jews had probably suffered more than the other citizens.

Just before Gorbachev had come to office, Isador's father, Isaac, had grown very frail. Like so many Jews before, Isaac had hoped for a new beginning and that promises would be fulfilled. It was therefore a terrific blow, during the previous cruel winter in St Petersburg, just as things started to change a little, that Isador's father had died. He never lived to see Gorbachev struggling to keep the country going. He did not see the lifting of the 'Iron Curtain', as The West had named it - the barrier that had detained him for a lifetime.

Isaac had looked forward so much to leaving St Petersburg and joining his other son, Yuri. Yuri had been so very fortunate to obtain an exit visa to Israel, but it had taken a wait of more than two years. The windows of opportunity to leave had opened and closed several times. Yuri had left in the 1970s, just before further emigration of Jews had been stopped, once again. Unable to obtain an exit visa, Isador had not seen his brother since.

Isador's closest laboratory colleagues Jossi and Boris, came to mind. Now left increasingly far below and behind. How would they fare in the new Republic of Russia in the future? Of course, Isador realised that some of his neighbours and associates still believed that the Soviet experiment had been a success, especially as they could not yet see any advantage in what had followed. They longed to return to the stability of communism. At their level communism had provided a job, food and a roof, for most of the time.

Hardships had been increasing for so many citizens. In the months before his family had boarded this aircraft today, Isador had heard of problems in many cities. So much of industry had relied on the production of armaments. These activities had now ground almost to a halt. Factories making tanks were now making wheelbarrows. Some top electronics craftsmen were now making jewellery. Even when funding from the new government was promised, it was uncertain and few were receiving regular pay for their work. Now, there would be a new and hopeful future for all his family.

He looked round at them and smiled. 'You were totally lost in your thoughts for so long,' said Sarah, who grasped his hand, trembling with joy. 'Soon we shall see your brother, Yuri,' she said. Their two children, now quite grown up, were smiling at them both, from across the aisle.

Sarah was sadly aware that they were leaving with another family member missing. Several months previously, Isador's mother, Deborah, had not been at all confident about leaving. It was the only country she had ever known. Now, quite suddenly, her son wanted to take them all out, into an unknown world. At her age Deborah was bound to be suspicious. She was well aware that so many Jews had been scattered, often forcibly, in the past. However, Isador had not been worried, and in contrast with the older generation, he had always been quite self-assured. As a well-qualified mathematician and physicist, he reasoned that he could surely get a stable job in the USA, or in Israel. Everything pointed towards taking the opportunity to leave, in case conditions worsened again. With his father gone, Isador had yearned to take everyone together. But it was not to be.

Isador recalled the conditions that he had discussed with his colleagues when four years had passed after the collapse of the regime. They had agreed that industrial production must have fallen by about two thirds. The signs had been ominous, but there was little they could do about their coming plight. Eventually, as they had suspected, there was not enough currency movement to buy the promised consumer goods, in the new market economy.

What was plentiful for the first time was world news. Isador had been an avid reader and listener because it was news of a quality that the citizens of the Soviet Union had never been privileged to see and hear before. It was never ending and Isador not only took an interest in everything, but was fast becoming able to interpret the deeper meaning of what was happening around the world.

Just as they left, the latest surprising news was that Russia would probably sign up to the 18-signatory Partnership for Peace programme with the NATO Alliance. Perhaps this would bring some stability! Nevertheless, for the Jews, in their subconscious, they knew that whatever happened in Mother Russia in the future, they should really be living elsewhere. In Israel!

Supposedly, Russia's avowed future would be non-confrontational, defensive and deterrent in nature. Promises had been made and assurances given, but Isador had simply not been prepared to wait and see what the future would bring, whatever the promises! Another new development, just announced, was that Gorbachev's new Russia would be collaborative with Turkey who shared common borders with unstable former Southern Soviets, now known as Independent Republics. Turkey had oil!

While Isador had been busy making his plans and applications to leave, unprecedented international moves had occurred. China had come back into the fold of co-operation both with Russia and with the USA. Russian co-operation with the new regime in Iran was considered beneficial, especially in view of future supplies of Iranian Oil! Isador wondered how long would it be before the fundamentalist's pressure exploded in Iran again? Possibly it might re-appear in an even more virulent form than before. Also, any new regime might be influenced by events in the Southern Republics of the former USSR and Afghanistan. Already Isador had heard that Chetznya had been causing lots of trouble.

As their aircraft changed course once again, Isador considered whether Iraq, still in the hands of an unpredictable dictator, would affect their coming lives in Israel. He was not to know that the Iraqi dictator would only remain as the Iraqi leader until the year 2003. It was only in recent months that Isador had realised how little he knew of the total world picture. So much awareness of world events had been lost through censorship in the Soviet system.

Isador's train of thought was briefly interrupted, as the stewardess brought some tea. His musings then drifted to a remembrance of his mother-in-law, Deborah. Deborah's resistance to the thought of moving, had caused him much soul-searching. The quandary had been solved unexpectedly. when Sarah had returned home, after a day's hard work as an interpreter. She had found the shared apartment strangely quiet. Deborah had not risen from her bed that morning. She would not, after all, be emigrating to Israel. She had gone. They had all been devastated at the suddenness of her sudden but natural death.

However, the event had given them an added impetus for the move. They all badly needed a fresh start. At the time Gorbachev had gone and Yeltsin was in charge - when he stayed off the vodka. At the time there were already those backing a new figure. One who had no time for the remaining Jews in Russia. Although himself with some Jewish ancestry, Zironovsky, an anti-Semite might win an election. In addition, there was a rumour that one Vladimir Putin, an ex-KGB operative, now politician, might take over the new nation one day. Indeed, this latter rumour was eventually to be correct.

This recall of recent events reinforced the determination to leave before another wall descended! A commercial Mafia seemed to have come from nowhere. Most of the big cities were already dangerous places after dark - and some even in daylight. Roubles had little value. Hard foreign currency was required to buy almost anything.

Fortunately, the family's exit visas had come through more quickly than expected. Flight arrangements were hastily made. There were surprisingly few delays and Isador, with his wife Sarah and their children were now finally on their way. Although one or two of their friends had made this journey recently, they were not aware that they were just a part of a mini-exodus. In the early 1990s this peaked to an incredible 11,000 Jewish emigrants travelling to Israel every month. Many had travelled overland to the Black Sea and thence by sea from Odessa to Haifa. Today's air journey, first to Paris, would be followed by an onwards flight to Tel Aviv, by El Al jumbo jet. Isador did not realise, as he journeyed, that some seven hundred others were also converging on Israel that very day. They had departed from Russia, the USA, Britain, South Africa and Argentina. Similar numbers would be en route again next month. Isador sipped his tea gratefully and savoured his good fortune.

The aircraft had left the vastness of the Former Soviet Union, crossed Poland and entered German and then French airspace. Not long to go now. Isador finally reflected on his past work and postulated on his future. His had been a world of theoretical physics. However, because of his ethnic background, his career had been limited. He knew as much as anyone about nuclear magnetic particle movement, magnetic resonance and neutron moments. Of late he had worked on the devices for optical detection of these microscopic effects. Now it was over, and he would probably never work in his own laboratory again. After all, he was fifty four years old. Perhaps it was time to teach?

Surely, he reasoned, teaching would be a requirement in Israel. However, he knew from Yuri's letters, that certain formalities would come first. The whole family would be placed into the immigrant absorption process, a well-developed system that ensured all new arrivals in Israel entered into a smooth integration process. This land of their ancestors had been re-formed as a modern State, in a little more than fifty years. He had heard that their first step would be to attend the 'Ulpan', the modern Hebrew language course. For generations his family had only used Hebrew sparingly. After all, the Jews living in the USSR had been banned from learning or teaching Hebrew. They could only send a proportion of their children to school by a quota system. Hebrew was reserved for studying their religious book, the Torah. Many still used Yiddish when with their kin-folk, but most of the time Russian was both spoken and written.

Although Hebrew would be essential, Isador's family would find that there would be no shortage of Russian speakers in Israel. Many thousands of the migrants to Israel who arrived every month in the early nineties, had come from the former Soviet countries. In fact, the first migrants one hundred years previously, moving to what was then known as Palestine, under Ottoman domination, had also come from Russia.

The pilot announced that they would be landing in Paris in thirty minutes. Isador smiled at Sarah and then returned to his thoughts. It had been almost as though his previous life had flashed before him. In many ways Isador had undergone an isolated childhood. It had been a mixture of ethnic isolation and poverty. As a boy he remembered many occasions when the family were forced to hide, in fear of their lives. There had been little or no warning when a pogrom - ethnic slaughter - occurred nearby. In the early days Jews hoped to escape compulsory service in the Czar's Army, where they could even find themselves rubbing shoulders with those that had taken part in pogroms. He had heard of the bribes, taken by the Czarist Police. Known as the 'Black Hundreds', they sometimes accepted money bribes to by-pass a particular village. Surely it was a fear that few in the West, where they were about to land, could barely comprehend.

Isador pondered why this miserable lot had come to his race - the Jews. He could still vividly recall the horror in some of his mother's stories, which she did not tell very often - the memory was too painful. It usually started with the so-called Christian Festivals, the approach of which was a time for dread. For some reason that was not clear to him as a boy, the Christians imagined that the Jews used the blood of Christian children as part of the Jewish Passover Festival. It was total nonsense - but sufficient to trigger real trouble, whenever a non-Jewish child went missing. When she could be persuaded to talk about those dreadful days, Mother often described the big horses. Her tales of the stallions, the swords, the spurs, the noise, the burning and the rape and death, had indeed been frightening. Almost anything seemed to trigger an excuse to persecute the Jews!

In the days of Russia's Czars, even the Cossacks couldn't be trusted. During times of relative peace, they had acted as spies for the Russian Army. Isador's ancestors had certainly endured many frightening times.

So many, mother would frequently say, had simply 'fled to Poland'. Stories abounded about the area known as the 'Pale of Settlement'. This was an area set aside, to which thousands of Jews had forcibly gone. Isador knew that, just minutes ago, they had just flown over Polish soil!

The persecutions had been mirrored elsewhere in Europe, for hundreds of years. There had been the Spanish Inquisition, the Crusades, and many other anti-semitic attacks. In the USSR even their religion had been attacked. The orthodox synagogue that Isador had known as a boy had, long since, been put to the torch. After that, together with the other poor boys, he had been sent, clandestinely, to Torah Hebrew classes in a cramped basement flat, now demolished.

Now, as he soared in security above the clouds, he wondered for a brief moment who would be moving into his drab, third floor, government apartment, vacated but a few hours ago.

After Isador had grown up, studied hard and qualified, his family had fared better than many. Of course, the apartments in the Soviet Union's large housing 'show blocks', where they had first lived as a family, were quite small, even cramped. Less than the twenty five square metres designated in some communist states. In the early days it meant a shared kitchen and bathroom with other families. Luxury increased with promotion, leading to larger apartment blocks, but with only half the roads made-up. The resulting battle against mud had lasted for most of the year. Failing mud, the battle was against mosquitoes, which the authorities did little to control. For most of the time and most memorable, there was the all-pervasive cold, lasting months at a time until the mosquitoes came back again. Temperatures reached over thirty degrees centigrade, during the brief respite of summer.

The aircraft turned, presumably having reached some beacon or other. The key points in Isador's life were still passing through his mind. So much had happened since poring over his first studies. It was said by others that a brilliant scholar had emerged. Before returning to the Institute at St Petersburg to research and teach, Isador had spent many years researching at the secretive, closed, scientific city of Gorky; but he had rarely been told what the end-product would be.

Even further back, at the age of thirteen years, Isador remembered the celebration of his arrival at the age of responsibility. The simple Bar-Mitzvah ceremony had been held in a make-shift synagogue. The ancient bearded Rabbi's ministrations were soon over. Somewhat irreverently, he still remembered more of the accompanying celebration feast, which his parents had somehow managed to get together. It had been the highlight of the day, rather than the ceremony itself. Now there were new horizons.

The lot of the Jew had often been grim indeed. Earlier, Isador had also been aware that the aircraft, had successively passed through the airspace of the lands where his race had suffered in the extermination camps of Auschwitz, Dachau and others. Names of horror that were indelibly impressed into the minds of Jews for ever. He had been told by his mother, a long time afterwards, that some of their more distant relatives had perished in these places. What had possessed Germany's leaders to such excesses? This had never been satisfactorily explained in a nation that had seemed to have everything - such fine art, music, culture and science.

Although excited, Isador was always rational. Lost in his thoughts and the steady note of the aircraft's progress, he had held Sarah's hand. Shortly, the cabin crew asked for seat belts to be fastened. The announcement had said that there would be a two hour stopover at Charles de Gaulle airport, Paris.

The transfer and departure occurred according to plan. Turning to Sarah he remarked 'that perhaps things always happened like this in the West'. Glancing round at the family, they all looked happy. Airborne once again, he settled contentedly to read the El Al flight magazine, finding, on the first page, a prayer in Hebrew. Isador was an inveterate reader but it had been many years before books, other than 'party approved' publications and scientific textbooks and technical papers, came his way. He marvelled at the quality of the printing, the clarity of the colours, and even the quality of the paper itself, in the simple flight magazine he held. Rarely had he seen this quality of paper or printing before. This was greatly encouraging, as was the apparent happiness of the cabin crew. Soon they were cheerfully clearing up, after an excellent meal. No dry sandwiches here! He could not wait to get to Israel to see what the future held.

Isador glanced at his family. Understandably the children were excited. To all intents they were on Israeli soil - even though they were still on 'eagles wings'. Sarah's earlier excitement had finally turned to sleep. The time spent on the ground before leaving Charles de Gaulle airport, Paris, had been one of wonder for them all. Never had they seen such luxurious goods as those in the airport shops. Sarah had said that they might be able to buy such things one day - perhaps even in Israel!

Having settled in peace, there were still unwanted interruptions to intrude on Isador's thoughts. Regularly there were announcements about films or someone wanting to form a group of ten, a *minyan* for prayers. Otherwise it was a dream come true, as the jet winged its way unerringly down the Adriatic, passing to the south of Rhodes and ever onwards across the Mediterranean, towards the Holy Land.

Isador nodded off. He dreamt of being a student again. He was on the compulsory chemistry section of the course. Given a small sample of material he was engaged in qualitative analysis - finding out what it was made of. Strangely, although valuable results could be seen, the techniques did not appeal to him any longer. He dreamt on, considering the physical options, perhaps for changing the nature of the material - even transmuting it into something else.

After university, he had originally tried to get a job in a chemical laboratory. His colleagues were obtaining interesting research positions but, as a Jew, he had been passed over several times. At the time he had decided that perhaps he had better stick to the study of the structure of matter, from the physicists' viewpoint. Physicists studied matter from within, whereas chemists tended to study matter from without. His shallow slumbers ended suddenly when the aircraft captain made another announcement. After fully waking and looking across at the others, he remembered the dream.

He was struck by a sudden thought. Perhaps in Israel he could study matter this way? A decision was needed - to change from his former specialisation into his first love - the science of physical chemistry. On the other hand there may be nothing for him to do. How did one start in a new and strange land? Soon they would be at their destination.

Within a few minutes the aircraft started to descend. Sarah was crying with tears of joy, as she looked into his eyes. The children were still glued to the dying moments of the in-flight film. They had learned enough English at school. The co-pilot announced that they were approaching the coast of the Holy Land. The film had finished. It was replaced with aerial views of Israel. Next, 'Hatikvah' - 'The Hope', Israel's National Anthem, could be heard over the aircraft's loudspeakers and in the earphones. An air of great expectation came over the passengers as the coastline and the twinkling lights of Tel Aviv and Jaffa suddenly approached and then swept swiftly past. In five minutes they were down and everyone on board, even the returning Israelis, pilgrims and holiday-makers, clapped their hands excitedly. This had only been their second flight and no one had clapped on the Aeroflot flight when they had landed in Paris. Perhaps, thought Isador, people always clapped on all other airlines?

For Isador and the family this was surely the start of something really new. Little did he realise the enormity of what lay ahead, especially his personal part in coming events that would soon change the world.

The stage was gradually being set for an enormous confrontation. A fact that most of the world's citizens were completely unaware. The build-up had depended upon some of the key players, the events that had taken place in the former Soviet Empire and the rise of fundamentalism in the Middle East. The foundation events included many of the circumstances that Isador had reflected upon, just a few hours ago. A world-shattering climax would be reached, just a few years hence. Amazingly, Isador's own discoveries would be the predestined trigger!

HATIKVAH

Despite being early evening, directly the aircraft door opened there was a rush of warm air. A contrast with Moscow! The long immigration queue seemed interminable. They were eager to move on. At last they moved towards the customs channels, dodging hurrying luggage trolleys that sniped at their ankles. They converged with the excited passengers from the other channels, leading to a narrow exit door. Beyond, they reached another covered area. It contained hundreds of people.

Several aircraft must have arrived at the same time. They had never seen so much luggage and so many people together in their lives, or heard so many languages. Isador was beginning to despair of their next move as they were carried along. He needn't have worried, for he heard a shout in Yiddish. Then, much louder in Russian.

'Isador! Sarah!'

The calls emanated from several rows back behind the barrier, where a short man was standing on a luggage trolley. The stranger wore a grubby tee-shirt. In the evening humidity, it was stuck to his chest. Isador gathered the family together and, by a roundabout route, approached the man - who immediately beamed his welcome. 'My name is Moshe,' he said, clearly pleased that he had found the new arrivals. 'There is some processing to get through tomorrow. Meanwhile, I have been sent to meet you by the Faculty of Physics at the Technical University in Haifa - The Technion. Professor Haim Bar Erev would like to have a chat with you at the earliest opportunity.'

Isador was slightly concerned, as he could recall no-one of this name. Before he could reply, Moshe went on, 'The professor has changed his name since coming to Israel, but I am not going to spoil the surprise you will have when you meet him tomorrow morning.'

Clearly, their new friend was very enthusiastic with the task he had been given. After hugging them all, he said, 'We were contacted by your brother Yuri and he has arranged some temporary accommodation on a Kibbutz near a place called Netanya, not all that far from Haifa. Right away we have a car journey of about 40 kilometres to make. Yuri and his family will be there to greet you.' This was indeed a surprise, compared with the beaurocracy he had expected to encounter.

Scenes of family greeting and re-union were going on all around. Isador and the family had little time to grasp it all before they were steered outside and loading their baggage into a very large estate wagon. They set off, soon leaving the airport avenues of palm trees and joining the dual carriageway of the Jerusalem-Tel Aviv highway. They had expected nothing like this, and they hadn't gone far before, dimly seen in the car and road lights, was a brand new railway, running right alongside the road. Moshe kept up a running commentary on what was happening in Israel.

Soon, they swung North at an interchange, picking up the main route towards Haifa. On the way they saw signs to both new and very old places - Hertzlia and Ceasarea. To either side, were vast fruit orchards and new building sites everywhere.

Isador considered the situation thus far. Apart from the successes of financiers, doctors, musicians, entertainers and Jewish mathematicians, he knew that engineers and scientists had also done particularly well in the Diaspora. They had been awarded many Nobel Prizes in the course of their dispersion to some eighty countries. In fact, Jews had been awarded more of these prizes than any other nationality on earth, in proportion to their numbers. In the days of the USSR the practitioners of engineering and science had been among the favoured classes, largely free from political interference. Isador had seen this preference changed before he left. Towards the end, any money available had barely met their salaries - and then most intermittently. The funds for a plentiful supply of scientific equipment had ceased. In the last two years even the funding for attendance at scientific conferences had become impossible. Their standards had become ones of bare survival. They were no longer considered to be an elite group. Of course, the ordinary citizen was generally even worse off. Freedom from communism had not brought instant comfort! Isador knew that his family would also be comparing everything, with the life they had left behind.

From Russia, and elsewhere, many Jews had now returned to this, their country of inheritance. The nation was prospering as never before - an amazing, indeed incredible situation, as less than a century ago most of this land had been virtually barren, for thousands of years. Most importantly, Isador felt as though he had come home - a feeling that he could not explain. This, despite the fact that he had also come to a land that had been in conflict ever since the United Nations had voted for its renewed existence, back in 1948. Nevertheless, Isador sat back in the car, somewhat apprehensive of what the future might hold for his new country.

Back in Great Britain one of Keith's tasks was to keep up to date on all world aspects where threats to his own nation and to the nations comprising the NATO Alliance might develop. Despite opposition by a section of Israel's own population, peace talks had taken place with Arab leaders. There had always been a craving for peace in Israel, but it had not been possible. Now, the enormous expenditure on defence had been reduced and money was increasingly spent on the country's infrastructure. This had to provide accommodation for the vast influx of Jews who were entitled to live in Israel, under the Law of Return.

These huge building programmes also provided a large proportion of employment for the Arab citizens of Israel - the Arab-Israelis. In addition, thousands of Arabs, from Gaza and other areas that were wholly or partially under Palestinian control, travelled daily into Israel to work. The achievement of higher living standards had soon become the envy of the surrounding populations and many Arabs and other nationalities had come to obtain employment. Nevertheless, Israel had to continuously watch her security position, because there were potential enemies all around. Little did anyone realise that a new 'intafada' would start in just a few years, or how near the region was to a major conflict.

On the scientific 'grapevine' Isador had heard about Iraq's ill-fated Super Gun. After reaching the design and production stage in various parts of the world, the gun's final assembly had been thwarted, not long before the 1991 Gulf War started. Not to be outdone, Iraq had launched SCUD ballistic missile attacks, against Saudi Arabia and Israel. As a result, Israel had embarked on a programme to build an anti-ballistic missile system, should it be required for the future. Most had hoped that at least a relative peace would come before too long. Meanwhile, despite careful cost reductions, they were still having to spend valuable resources on defence. Sporadic terrorist attacks occurred at regular intervals across all Israel's borders.

Many in Israel had disputed the wisdom of the defence reductions. Most citizens knew that several of the more extreme elements in the area, and among Islamists within the country, were still violently opposed - even to the existence of Israel. However, peace talks continued under the auspices of the United Nations, the European Union, with strong political backing from the USA.

This situation was also of interest to many Jews who were also US citizens. Most were aware that the standard of living in Israel was high, and, coupled with the inexplicable draw to their land, thousands of American Jews had left to take up their right of return. With a peace agreement, the US politicians might see this as an opportunity to cut US aid to Israel.

Throughout the 1990s there was a rise in anti-semitism in the world. Soon, even Jews with long family residence in the USA and Europe, would find it less comfortable to remain. Anyway, as their numbers diminished in the USA, their voices would probably be much less heeded by any political party.

Jewish migration from the USA had mainly depleted the Jewish younger voters for both parties, in the Senate and Congress. This had already reduced the necessity for representatives to satisfy Jewish voters, in supporting Israel.

Since the collapse of the Soviet Empire Isador had seen most of Russia's own nuclear deterrent signed away, after a concerted effort by the Leaders of the 'New World Order'. Elsewhere, many found it progressively harder to see the rationale for Israel's retention of their nuclear option, if a peace deal was accepted. Even China, they imagined, might sign theirs away! The leverage was immense. The 'Islamic Bomb', it was promised, would be destroyed - but only if Israel also destroyed hers! Israel, they said, was a serious obstacle to real world peace. Pakistan, already a nuclear power, refused to sign on this basis and Iran were said to be busy developing their own atomic bomb.

In the weeks leading up to the family departure, Isador had made an effort to improve his knowledge of Israel, by listening to the Voice of Israel Russian language evening broadcasts. He was aware that, if the projected peace deal was put in place, the ever growing population of Israel would be concentrated in a relatively small land area. Already many of the areas that Israel held after the 1967 and 1973 wars were almost completely given to Egypt and the 'Palestinians'. This would have many impacts on life.

With the loss of many land areas that contained the water supply aquifers, various ingenious schemes devised by the country's engineers had kept the water supply, though not over-abundant, at least in balance. Isador had heard reports of water shortages, due to irregular rain patterns. The situation had deteriorated to the point that plans to import water from Turkey had been approved. Approval was also given to built a number of desalination plants along the Mediterranean coastline.

Other problems were imminent, though of course not yet apparent, at the time of Isador's arrival. Within a year or Isador's arrival a further Palestinian uprising would occur and in 2005, in Southern Lebanon, the Hizbollah would inflict a further blow. In total opposition even to the existence of Israel, they would divert river water, thus preventing an important freshwater source to the Galilee. But no one was aware of these problems yet, or of the fact that, before then, there would be another Gulf War in Iraq in the year 2003. Isador would soon learn much more about Israel's position.

For example, the main disadvantage of the loss of any land inevitably impacted on defence. Military strategists were aware that, should anything go wrong with the peace guarantees, it would be difficult to defend a nation that was just minutes flying time from potential enemies. The land of Israel was now only about forty to fifty miles in width for much of its East-West extent, and much less, about 15 miles, at its narrowest. There was no longer adequate defensive depth to prevent the nation being cut in two, if a serious armoured war occurred.

The nation's early settlers had turned this once swampy and arid land into a verdant land of agricultural and horticultural prosperity. Malaria was rife in the early days and life was hard. To achieve all this many had died defending their kibbutzim. There had been no less than five wars. In between, there had also been a considerable toll in death and injuries in literally thousands of terrorist attacks. Nevertheless, it was still their land - the only land they could call their own - 'Eretz Israel'. Isador would soon learn much more about the land and the hostile attitude of so much of the world. At last he would be free now to see unlimited news and other data from around the world.

After the second Gulf War a concerted effort was made to impose a peace, at almost any cost. Israel was continuously pressed, even almost forced, to give up land and make all sorts of concessions. The security of the nation was uppermost in the mind of the Prime Minister, but he was reluctantly giving away land for peace. Soon Israel would withdraw from many areas predominantly Arab in population. Jewish settlers in many areas would be forced to re-locate, albeit with some compensation. A peace of sorts would appear to be possible. However, there would always be some extremists.

In the world economies, Israel's exports of quality goods and their agricultural expertise had soon been recognised. With only a few fundamentalist exceptions, the nations had removed their embargoes on dealing with Israel. Agricultural and horticultural exports were flourishing as never before, as was the export of revolutionary irrigation methods. Tourism would dip alarmingly after the year 2000. Economic investment was difficult. The Jewish bankers of the Diaspora were experts in the world money markets, but the economy of Israel had always seemed to lag.

With an excellent health and education system coupled to the other successes, including high ratings at the Olympic Games, in sporting excellence it was not surprising that some were beginning to get quite envious of Israel's position. Ominously there were still those that wanted every Jew and the State of Israel itself, eliminated!

The underlying capabilities of the Jewish nation were formidable. They had excelled in science. Isador knew that, back in the 1930s, science in the West, had significantly advanced, due to an influx of Jewish scientists. In particular the work done by the theoretical physicists who escaped from Europe before World War Two. They laid down much of the foundation of chemical, physical and even atomic theory. While the British scientists, like Chadwick, with his discovery of the neutron in 1932, and Cockroft and Walton with their proton accelerator, had been able to proceed with their discoveries, the Jewish scientists in Germany had either to flee or pay a terrible price. A very large number of these world class experts were gratefully received in the USA. Isador had heard that many of them had since left the USA, to live in Israel. No doubt he would meet some of them soon. He could not wait to get to work.

Meanwhile, back in Britain, Keith was, once again pondering the current world situation. Of course, he was unaware of the existence of Isador or of the arrival of Isador's family in Israel, or indeed that Isador's chosen research would soon have far reaching effects. Keith regularly monitored the short wave newscasts from this small country. It was essential to obtain a balanced view, because most other national and international news services often distorted or biased the Israeli news coverage to an amazing extent.

Relative to the centuries of development in other nations, none could dispute that Israel had achieved a huge amount in just a few years. It had taken sheer expertise and hard work and had been achieved without the luxury of possessing any of that key resource - oil. At one point, per head of population, more than five times as many engineers and scientists were engaged in research and development in Israel than in Britain; and at least twice as many as in the USA.

Now, in the new millennium of the Western Calendar, the nations had concentrated on the defeat of terrorism. However, the leaders of those who called themselves Palestinians, had given only lip service. They were unable to control their more extreme elements. Throughout the 1990s, Israel had made enormous concessions to obtain a limited peace, but to no avail. Eventually, it would not come to pass in 2004, when, mainly in exasperation, they would give up expecting a reliable 'peace partner', since all previous promises had come to nothing.

The world regularly heard of regular attacks on Israelis. Israel's population, indeed Jews everywhere, had to recognise that security was a daily, indeed hourly concern; at home, during travel and at work. It was already thought that only after the removal or death of Chairman Arafat would some sort of negotiated peace be possible. No one could know possibly that this would not occur until the year 2005. It would only be a fragile and patchy cessation of violence even then.

Keith was aware that many of Israel's surrounding nations had improved and modernised their armaments. They had done this mainly through the purchase of Chinese, N Korean and Russian equipment. There was no shortage of manpower - it was overwhelming when compared to Israel's small population. Keith was also aware that if a new State of Palestine ever came about that they would soon convince the world that they also needed armaments of all types. At that point, the United Nations, with a built-in anti-Israeli majority, were bound to come to an agreement that would adversely affect Israel. Armaments, offensive in nature, rather than purely defensive, would surely be approved. In the longer term it would probably become impossible to prevent proliferation anyway. As the new millennium dawned Jerusalem was the key! So far, each time it came up on the agenda the solution had been postponed. Keith sensed very serious trouble ahead.

Large amounts of oil money - most of it obtained from oil sales to the West - was also fuelling the armament purchases in the those neighbouring oil-producing Arab countries, and in Iran. For some time it had become clear that, not only had Saudi Arabia been bankrolling the PLO for years, but most probably for many other arms deals and some other terrorism as well.

Israel had struggled with her own governmental 'doves'. They had questioned the necessity of maintaining an adequate level of conventional armaments. Certain members of the Knesset had wanted peace at almost any price. They could no longer see the need for defences of any sort, except policemen. Some imagined that the peace would be guaranteed by the United Nations! As a threat analyst, Keith knew better.

Israel had the nuclear weapon, probably in limited numbers - for many years kept as an ultimate deterrent. This weapon was now becoming old. Since France's nuclear test programme in the Pacific, in the late 1990s, there had been an embargo on development or testing. Both India and Pakistan had made underground tests. The spread of nuclear weapons had largely, though not entirely, been limited by the efforts of the United Nations Atomic Energy Control Commission. They had also spent time policing the spread of weapons of mass destruction within Iraq at the start of the new millennium. They had been forced to leave in 1997. Inspections by a UN team would not restart until 2002 and would be withdrawn before the start of the second Gulf War.

Elsewhere, the Islamic nuclear bomb, developed in Pakistan, was a fact - although no firm evidence had been recorded that a live atmospheric test had ever been carried out. Underground tests had been detected in Asia. Both Pakistan and India were involved in atomic activities. There were also suspicions that one or more weapons may have been acquired by someone else hostile to Israel; possibly from old Soviet stocks. Meantime, it was suspected that uranium was being mined, refined and delivered to at least one nation potentially hostile to Israel and the West, Iran.

The older, more cautious, of Israel's citizens, still remembered the tense days of June 1981, when Israel had attacked Iraq's first nuclear site. This was to stop her most likely antagonist at the time, from obtaining the ultimate weapon. The day after they had destroyed the Iraqi nuclear reactor at Osiraq, near Tuwaitha, Israel had said, 'On no account shall we permit an enemy to develop weapons of mass destruction against the people of Israel.' Nevertheless, in the 1980s, there had been plenty of others willing to supply nuclear, biological and chemical materials, with expertise, to certain countries in the Middle East.

The situation had, once again, come to a head by the time of the 1991 Gulf War. At that time Saddam Hussein was probably on the verge of producing some sort of crude nuclear device, even if not a viable nuclear delivery capability. Indeed, the West had been horrified to find how close Saddam Hussein had been to obtaining a nuclear device. About the same time there had been wild speculation in the world press about a mysterious material, known as 'Red Mercury'. This was possibly a reference to uranium. Nevertheless, in 2003 Israel said given cast iron treaties, with her neighbours, she would be prepared to come to a point where nuclear and other weapons could be destroyed.

As the car journey continued, mostly in darkness, many thoughts passed through Isador's mind. He was well aware that Israel was vulnerable to both conventional, chemical, biological and nuclear attack. Based on the 20th Century history of the Jewish people, they had very serious reasons to fear gas attacks. How would these terrible weapons be delivered? For this reason, Israel had succeeded in obtaining significant US financial backing for an Israeli-designed version of 'Star Wars'. This system comprised a very long ranged radar to detect incoming ballistic missiles and an interceptor missile to shoot them down. Starting in 1988, the USA had directly funded about three quarters of the cost of the 'Arrow' interceptor. Known as 'Chetz' in Hebrew, it had been successfully tested and entered service well ahead of the USA's own systems. The USA had most probably, though indirectly, also funded the associated complex target tracking radar. Isador was aware of this type of system, because he had heard that the Soviet Union had two Surface to Air systems that could intercept some types of ballistic missile. He just hoped that the family would be safer here than back in Russia!

For some years it was clear that the leaders of some Middle Eastern nations, despite their common Muslim heritage, were fearful of being toppled. The area was always in flux. The Middle East contained the most of the world's known oil reserves, and would remain so even if Britain opened-up both the South and Eastern Atlantic oil fields. To Israel's north, following elections, Turkey, a member of NATO, had not yet achieved membership of the European Union. They had significantly strengthened their friendship with certain, mainly Islamic, southern republics of the former Soviet Empire. Close links were developed with the Russian Republic, with whom commercial and military agreements had been signed. Also various commercial activities in Turkey, for example in the aerospace industry, and for fresh water, were still contracted with Israel.

The earlier analysis by Keith's future threat team had identified several situations that seemed to be likely, even essential, contributors to a coming scenario that would befall the world at some point fairly early in the new millennium. These had been reported, even though governments seemed to take little notice. It had seemed that the coincidence of a number of these would impact together with a final event would act as a trigger for conflict. Some examples came into Keith's mind as possible or probable factors.

Fuel and energy destabilisation would remain a key concern. Another Chernobyl-type radiation disaster could not be ruled out. Following such a disaster would inevitably be a period of massive world condemnation. Despite the huge investment in safe nuclear power production, a second major civil atomic calamity could surely cause, by common United Nations pressure, the final decommissioning of nuclear power in many nations. As a result energy would become much more expensive. Oil and gas would therefore be the prime energy sources for industrial and domestic power generation, and continue unchallenged for transport. Coal would take second place.

The availability of fresh water would become a key factor, and even a bargaining tool in some areas. Fuel and water together, could well be triggers for conflict, combined with ethnic and religious differences.

Natural conditions must also be considered. An evaluation of weather and earthquake statistics has showed undeniable evidence that not only are the world weather patterns changing but earthquake frequency and intensity is increasing at a remarkable rate. Hurricanes and tornadoes are demonstrably on the increase. While the predicted major earthquake under California had not yet materialised, there were measurable increases in quake activity both under land and sea. The latter could well give rise to tidal waves more devastating than the 1946 Pacific Ocean, or the 2004 Indian Ocean waves that could affect populations so tragically. Apart from the local economic cost of these calamities there was also the tragic loss of life and the affect on economies far removed from the scene.

Because of the wild fluctuations in the world's money markets and stock markets, commencing at the start of the 21st century, a new world-wide system of centralised economic control would probably be established. In the future a lack of confidence, evidenced by the September 2001 attacks on the USA, could lead to a reluctance to entrust monetary dealings exclusively to centralised electronic control. It would clearly take several years to obtain total confidence and fraud protection, but a co-ordinated physical attack on several financial centres, even on data-carrying satellites, could cause world chaos.

The Eurozone common currency would be widely in use and would gradually gain acceptance in Eastern Europe. Indeed the Euro could become a dominant currency over the dollar, unless the USA remained strong. However, for the short and mid-term the key to the underlying prosperity of the world would seem to be rooted in liquid gold, in the form of oil and gas, rather than in solid gold as in the past. Research, might well allow the transformation of most precious metals from others, using the newly acquired techniques of the physical chemists. The make up of most materials, biological tissues and DNA could be manipulated - and this capability would accelerate. Even diamonds had been made by the end of the 20th century. If gold could synthesised in some way it would reduce in usefulness as a currency. Gold reserves were already being sold off by governments. Even the United Kingdom had sold much of its gold reserves by the late 1990s.

National security had become a major world issue as the millennium came to a close. Terror attacks, hostage-taking and suicide bombings had become a way of life in much of the Middle East, eventually spilling over into both the West and the Far East by the 1990s. Keith's Team Report had warned of the likelihood of attacks on the West by extremist regimes, networks and even those using individuals, for whom the value of life held little meaning. Further, the report had warned that the concept of deterrence means nothing to such ideologies or regimes. Not until the year 2001 did the penny drop! A new 'multi-polar threat scenario' was indeed being revealed. It was not President George Bush's hoped-for scenario of world peace. A number of steps were already occurring so that a 'New World Order' was coming into place, piece by piece. Soon it would be the case that systems would be put in place that could eventually control almost everyone's lives. But so many were still failing to recognise exactly what was happening.

Just before leaving the aircraft Isador had recalled some new ideas which he been thinking about. He had been under pressure in Russia to complete several research tasks before he left. There had been no chance to spend time on his personal ideas in the past. He would have no chance of getting backing for research of a type that was not carried out in his own Institute. Now, perhaps Israel would give him the opportunity?

Now, the more Isador thought about it, as they headed for their temporary Kibbutz accommodation, the more his sudden new ideas became feasible. During the two air-flights, totalling about six hours on the way to Israel, he had probably achieved almost six hours of an uninterrupted review of the past, mixed in with some brain-storming. Given the opportunity, he could not wait to try out the new ideas which had been germinating during the flight. He had arrived in the Land of Hope.

Lights twinkled to the left. The car was turning off the road. Yuri, who they hadn't seen for many years, could be seen waiting by the buildings just ahead. It was a very special time.

A few days later Isador and both families, motored down to Tel Aviv, to complete some of their arrival documentation. At dusk, the heat of the day spent and most of the formalities in order, Isador relaxed and gazed over the city from the public viewing platform of one of the tallest structures in the Middle East - the Shalom Tower. Despite the promise of peace - real peace, Tel-Aviv's residents still had to be vigilant. From the conversations since arriving, he was optimistic that the latest rumoured peace talks might even reach a final break-through. Nevertheless, the family were reminded of the need for vigilance. Yet another reminder, Sarah's handbag had just been searched once more, as they entered the huge tower block. Isador and the children went through the electronic checker. In the Russian Republic, he had not been subject to random bombing and shooting - yet he knew his decision to leave and come home to Israel had been the right one.

As they ascended in the lift, Yuri said that from this tower, on a clear day, one could sometimes just see Jerusalem, the Holy City. Today's visibility was sharply reduced by a layer of haze. Isador had never seen anything like this before. It seemed to be suspended over the city, like a fluffy brown-yellow duvet. The upwards view towards the reddening sky was clear, as was the view to seawards, but the horizontal view over the rooftops looking inland, and over the entire city, was heavily obscured. Pollution!

This view confirmed Isador's thoughts, in which he had been immersed at every spare moment since his arrival. Isador had his answer! He would use the idea he had on the aircraft to crack the problem of traffic pollution! Surely everyone would welcome such a move?

He descended in the lift, hardly noticing the eager tourists or indeed his own family. They knew he had something on his mind. They were used to periods when he said little and lived in his 'scientific world'. As they pushed forward to leave the building others were jostling to reach the lift, eager to take in the panorama and to watch the fast approaching sunset. This evening they would only see the sun through what amounted to a big dirty yellow filter!

The family turned left, drawn towards the gently murmuring sea. Within minutes they entered the Charles Clore park, on the sea-front. Conveniently, a family had just vacated a bench, for a sunset stroll. Isador gazed out to a calm sea. In their previous existence Isador's family had only seen the Baltic Sea, twice. This was just marvellous. They could come any day!

They were already enjoying their 'Aliyah' - or 'going up', to Israel. Now the beach could also be visited daily. Within minutes the sun descended smoothly over the sea. It touched the surface, gloriously splashing its golden light towards them. Even as they watched, it could be seen moving. It finally vanished from view. He realised that, at this latitude, darkness came very quickly. The inevitability of the daily cycle was perhaps more clearly felt by many residents in these latitudes, because so many lived to a strict daily religious ritual. As the sun sank, the calls from a nearby mosque quite near the sea-front, were once again calling the Muslims to prayer. Isador's Hebrew and English were improving, but the urgent voice from the Muezzin was, of course, in Arabic.

Unbeknown to Isador, within just a few years, the world would plunge towards a combination of apparently unstoppable serious economic and other de-stabilising events. The nations did not wait in anticipation, as they were unaware of their imminent pre-destination. Few would hear of Isador's coming contribution, until it arrived. It would be the critical de-stabilising trigger for disaster, rather than the triumph for which he had hoped. Like so many of man's developments, Isador's invention would be too late to 'un-invent'.

Tomorrow Isador and the family would have even more to celebrate, The confirmation of his appointment to the staff of the Technion. The renamed 'Professor Haim Bar Erev', mentioned by Moshe at the airport, had turned turn out to no be less than Vidal Osipov. Vidal had been his most respected and closest colleague, in what were now fast-receding memories of those days in the Former Soviet Union. Vidal had been overjoyed to see Sarah and Isador again. This was going to be a good life!

THE PREVARICATORS

Keith had reviewed the team's findings for the last time for the final report back in 1997. What would really be driving the world for the next fifteen years? His team had done their best, based on all available evidence. Inevitably there were a number of 'what ifs' involved. The most recent clear warnings and stark lessons were seen during the 1991 Gulf War. Only time would tell whether these had been understood.

Unfortunately, NATO and the West had usually been slow to act. Study had followed study on what should be done. Keith suspected that it would be years before the nations approved the substantial collective expenditure that the team had deemed necessary to provide both their citizens and armies with a shield against ballistic missile and cruise missile attack. They had merely picked at the problem in the past - and were likely, despite very clear recommendations from several of their advisory teams, to do so again in the future. Apart from the USA, only Russia and Israel had achieved any sort of experimental designs. The possibility of delivery of Weapons of Mass Destruction was so awful that it was no longer an option to do nothing. The politicians must act, for it would be far more than a political disgrace, and far too late when unprotected nations came under attack.

At the beginning of the 21st Century a crude rolling programme had eventually been approved. Too late, in the view of the advisers. They had studied the future threat projections in detail. Now certain unstable regimes, within range of NATO territory, were already flexing their ballistic and cruise missile 'muscles'. Others were clearly obtaining 'weapons of mass destruction'. These could be carried by missiles, by aircraft, and even by terrorists in a car or on foot.

Even in 1997, to the more perceptive citizens, the 'thinking minority', it must have been clear that a threat from ballistic missiles was very real. In fact, it was fast proliferating, perhaps no more than five years away. Yet, there was still no reliable fixed anti-missile air defence system in place, either at home - to protect the nation - or in a mobile form that could be used to protect soldiers, sailors or airmen, whenever they might be called to operate outside the boundaries of NATO's own nations. Ever since the 'Iron Curtain' had come down, 'Out of Area' operations seemed to be on the increase. Had no one noticed that the USA had suffered its first ballistic missile casualties, at Dharan, during the 1991 Gulf War?

The Cold War, 'bipolar', confrontation - Communist East versus Capitalist West - had been swept away almost overnight. Gorbachev's leadership had been the turning point. But, had this man alone been the trigger?

Keith believed that a number of other factors, commencing in the 1980s and extending into the 1990s, had finally tipped the economic balance in the Soviet camp. These additional factors probably started in 1979, when the Soviet Army invaded Afghanistan. Within years some 120,000 combat troops of the Soviet 40th Army were battling what amounted to a group of haphazardly controlled 'mujahideen', armed at the start with the most crude light weapons - ancient rifles! There was little cohesion. For years disparate Afghan tribes had, more or less, been continuously been at war with each other. They were hardly a nation or a people, but tenacious in battle. The hallmark of their fighting activities was torture and cruel deaths.

The American Central Intelligence Agency, realised that they could hurt the USSR, by providing modern mobile weapons to the tribesmen of Afghanistan. By using Pakistan as a surrogate go-between for the supply and transfer of the weapons, added pressure could be kept on Moscow in addition to the 90 divisions that the Red Army maintained facing NATO in Europe.

Meanwhile, in 1980, the USA had suffered the horror of fifty US Embassy Staff being taken hostage in Teheran. Next, they instigated operation 'Eagle Claw' and suffered eight fatalities during a failed rescue attempt.

Despite this separate Islamic hostage-taking event, it probably seemed a good idea at the time to cultivate Islamic friends, especially as it was a method of preventing the Russians expanding southwards, towards the Iranian, Iraq and Saudi oilfields. It would also check any designs that the Russians might have on reaching the Gulf of Iran - and thereby future access to warm-water ports. In effect, the Afghanis would be fighting the spread of communism on the USA's behalf. In fact, unbeknown to the tribesmen, they were participants in a US-sponsored 'jihad' - a word that was increasingly to be heard on the world news coverage.

To aid the effort the USA even persuaded Saudi Arabia to share the cost - dollar for dollar with the US contribution. Before long, both the Chinese and the Egyptians and, reportedly, several other Muslim nations, also donated funds. What the USA was actually doing was aiding Muslim fighters. Taliban rule in Afghanistan, a US invasion and all that would follow in the global terrorism saga would be some years ahead. Of course all this was unforeseen at the time.

It worked! Inevitably it took a few years. The mujahideen's major problem was the Russian helicopter, nicknamed HIND by NATO. Initially, none of the tribesmen's weapons could bring down the armoured HIND. Their bullets just bounced off! After some time the Russian's own Surface to Air Missile, known as SA-7 in NATO, or 'Strela', found its roundabout Middle East route into the hands of tribesmen. Even the British Blowpipe missile was used. The former was ineffective and the latter more difficult to use. The weapon really needed was the US 'Stinger'. Eventually, in 1986, the US agreed to supply the Stingers that the

Russian HIND pilots feared.

Pakistan was crucial to the CIA activities in Afghanistan. Russia soon realised this and reportedly confronted the Pakistani President at Brezhnev's funeral in Moscow. Soon after, Pakistan were again confronted, this time by Gorbachev, on the occasion of Chernenko's funeral. Pakistan denied the facts. Apparently it was permissible to 'lie for Islam'. Further, also denied, was Pakistan's nuclear weapon programme. They sought nuclear triggers from the West as early as 1985. It became Soviet policy that the Afghan war did not exist - it was just some Soviet Advisers that were trying to help 'suppress bandits'.

By winter 1986, the Soviets could not sustain the effort without massive escalation - and this would be an admission that there was a war, after all! Keith recalled that, early on in the war, Southern Soviet State forces had involved Muslim fighting Muslim. Soon the Russians had been forced to withdraw their soldiers that were Muslims. The total Russian withdrawal took some time. It was the start of 1988 before the Geneva Accords for withdrawal were completed and February 1989 eventually saw the last Russian depart.

Soon the withdrawal would trigger a series of world changes, as the Soviet Union collapsed and knock-on repercussions occurred that lasted for several years before some sort of stability was achieved - for example, in the Former Yugoslavia. However, one of the most important factors that is often overlooked is that the Afghan adventure had awoken an implacable foe. From the Islamic viewpoint it appeared that the Afghani jihad had defeated an occupying army and accelerated the fall of a superpower! If this was possible with the help of Allah - then surely the USA could be next!

Almost simultaneously, several other small conflicts had commenced. Most of these could be traced back to Soviet activities or legacies. Many were fuelled by population discontent and aided by large quantities of arms, left behind in various countries, when the 'Evil Empire' collapsed. Together, territorial, nationalistic, ethnic and religious animosities were suddenly turning out to be a deadly cocktail.

Millions of innocent humans had been caught up in these 'low intensity' conflicts. NATO and several other nations had been drawn in to help the United Nations Organisation. As well as 'peacekeeping' duties, this 'aid' amounted to handling everything from earthquakes to disease and famines. United Nations sponsored forces were placed into areas where there were violent clashes between peoples who had, hitherto, lived forcibly in peace, mainly under the unforgiving 'thumb' of communism. In these difficult operations, other problems, such as horrific atrocities, were thrown in for good measure.

The remit of Keith's team was to study threats from any source. Clearly those potentially hostile nations along NATO's borders or those within missile reach were the main concern. However, the current status of nations in the Far East and their potential future developments were also closely examined. In mid

1997, during Keith's final report assessment, the colony of Hong Kong was handed back to China - a nation containing about one fifth of humanity! With the overall regional population numbering over three billion, there was reason to be concerned in the longer term.

Marxism and Maoism was coming to an end in China, but the communist leaders, frightened of being toppled because of communism's failure, were intent on holding onto power. They were already turning to capitalism - and very cleverly exploiting both markets and technologies of the West. While it was clear that the 'yellow hordes of the East' were not yet a threat, as it were, in person, both China and North Korea had already exported military equipment. Chinese ballistic missiles were deployed in Saudi Arabia and N.Korea had sold guided missiles to Pakistan and Iran. The ballistic missiles were of concern as they could reach the easternmost NATO nations and also threaten the fragile stability of the Middle East. China had also developed an atomic bomb and a space capability.

Rapidly changing scenarios close to Europe would soon be taking place. The communists had been overthrown in Poland. At this point few realised that within a short time, Poland and several other nations, previously under the USSR's control, would become members of the European Union. Just nine months after the Russians left Afghanistan, the Berlin Wall came down. Within a short time the Chernobyl nuclear power station exploded and the USA carried out an attack on Colonel Gadaffi's Libya.

As the second millennium had drawn to a close, large weapon surpluses were sold-off by the Former Soviet Union across Africa, in the Middle East and elsewhere. Even the arms embargo imposed against Syria had been lifted or circumvented. Russia's new Commonwealth of Independent States, especially the Russian Republic, needed to get their hard currency from somewhere!

Nevertheless, many of Russia's military professionals still hankered after the 'old order'. Russia was desperately trying to find its feet in the New World. They suffered a military debacle in Chetzniya, to be followed some years later by Chetznyan terrorism in the centre of Moscow.

While all this was going on, apart from Israel, the USA seemed to be the only nation to take both the ballistic missile and growing terrorism threat seriously. The United Kingdom just made the right noises and carried out studies. They continued to man the Iraqi 'no fly zones' for more than ten years after the first Gulf War. The UK also volunteered for all sorts of peacekeeping duties but increasingly became hard pressed to meet their minimum commitments, in manpower, equipment and cost. Regular cuts were being made in the size of the UK armed forces.

Nevertheless, what were known in the military as 'low level conflicts' continued to erupt, often for ethnic reasons. With some dismay Keith remembered that, of the world's 170 or so nations, only about one tenth were ethnically and religiously homogenous. There were many recipes for inevitable friction around the world. UN-sponsored forces of several nations had suffered humiliation and the inevitable tragedies of soldiers killed or airmen shot at - or shot down during these ethnic conflicts. Their task were usually to keep belligerents apart, to guard demarcation lines, to protect food convoys and to provide vital supplies, such as medical supplies and water. The expense in sheer effort, in humans and materials, was enormous.

The cost in aviation fuel alone was staggering. It was an energy cost that could never be recovered, as it involved the permanent depletion of the earth's oil resources. Thousands of vehicles and aircraft criss-crossed the air, land and sea routes in support of these diverse peacekeeping and 'humanitarian' operations. Citizens, keen to keep their own transport running, mainly counted the monetary cost, rather than that of the permanent loss of fossil fuel. Many of these low-intensity conflicts were in poor countries. Fortunately, so far, these skirmishes neither involved ballistic missiles or even the use of sophisticated air-power. Had they done so the necessary air defences would not have been in place. Nevertheless, they dragged on for months, often years.

It was understandable that the ordinary man in the street, who was paying through his taxes, was frequently heard to say that 'the West and the UN should not stick its nose into other people's business. 'Let them get on with their own war if all they want to do is to fight each other!' It was, however, a fact that many conflicts would otherwise escalate, spread and spill-over into even more critical areas, if they were not contained. Mankind was in a permanent struggle to try and solve one problem after another.

Right at the beginning of the new millennium the price of fuel soared to an unprecedented $50 per barrel. Fuel price rises occurred right across the already highly taxed areas of Europe. Eventually, governments brought pressure onto the oil producers' consortium to pump more oil, but not before hardship was caused to millions of businesses. National leaders often treated these events as short-term problems. They did not seriously take note that the major oil producers, predominantly Islamic nations, though greedy for the money, could cause major crises at any time they wished.

Meanwhile, other bombastic, ambitious and often unstable nations, were preparing for even more aggressive activities. In a few areas UN embargoes were enforced. Policing patrols were carried out both by ships and aircraft, as well as armies on the ground. Vast quantities of food and medical aid was delivered to stricken areas. Poverty, particularly in Africa, continued, despite all the aid poured in for decades. Meanwhile, the environmental lobby continued to complain about global warming, while another group was busy demonstrating against global trade. Nevertheless, embargoed materials always got through to those who had oil money to pay.

Despite Israel's attempts to obtain viable peace agreements, the nation suffered almost continual and horrific terrorist outrages. In contrast to NATO Europe, Israel had finally perfected and deployed their anti-missile air defence system. When in position, although not publicised, Israel's first system would probably not be able to handle simultaneous multiple missile attacks from diverse directions. The USA's 'Patriot' missile batteries were the only other, shorter ranged back-up system, that Israel had at the time of the second Gulf War with Iraq. Israel had stayed out of this war. Unlike the previous occasion, Saddam's forces did not manage to launch missiles at Israel.

Now, the USA had threatened funding cuts for the improved phase of the Israeli missile defence programme. Support for the system had started back in President Regan's time of 'Star Wars'. The US had probably used the lever of possible funding cuts to encourage Israel to continue peace negotiations, despite the obvious dangers.

Israel had also continued her own space programme and launched sensor-carrying satellites, specifically to maintain reconnaissance in the area. Despite the concerted efforts of the USA and Europe to encourage peace, Israel sensibly remained very wary of her neighbours. After all, the Israelis had suffered almost 50 years of war before this 'New Age' had arrived. Israel had hoped for peace as a reward for actually withdrawing from territories that were historically and rightfully hers anyway. Next, almost unbelievably, the Palestinian Authority had demanded monetary compensation for Israel's 'occupation'! Keith had seen such irrational behaviour several times during his studies of world affairs, especially in the Middle East.

In Europe, even in the year 2000, NATO had acknowledged that there was a ballistic missile threat that could not be defended against with the current systems. Europe's only air defence system, with limited capability against ballistic missiles, comprised a few US 'Patriot', Medium Range, Surface to Air Systems. The plan was that others would be rushed across the Atlantic if trouble started. They might handle a few sporadic short ranged ballistic missiles - but not a properly co-ordinated attack.

There were also certain other reasons why some aspects of NATO readiness was in doubt. Put more starkly, some NATO nations had purchased equipment which was nowhere near sufficient to do the job - the 'rolling programme' planned had indeed rolled - to a stop. It was a matter of cost. Other government programmes took precedence over defence spending. Even if they had the basic equipment, the few heavy airlift aircraft available were woefully inadequate in numbers, to provide a rapid response.

Keith cast his mind back further. Back in the 1980s several European nations had taken part in the US-funded 'Star Wars' programme. Billions of US dollars had been spent on this programme, following President Regan's surprise announcement. The USA would provide a ballistic missile shield - by implication, mainly in space - to prevent Russian ballistic missiles reaching the USA - or her Allies! The problems were gradually understood and the technologies developed. At the time a world recession was soon biting at all expenditure, particularly any military expenditure that did not seem to have an immediate application or pay-off. It was already costing quite enough to fund these, seemingly unending United Nation calls for 'reaction forces', for peace-keeping, and policing.

Until the 'Star Wars' programme was announced it had been argued that, following any Soviet nuclear attack, survival by even a small percentage of the West's retaliatory nuclear deterrent was possible. Therefore, it was sufficient to rely on deterrence alone. It was argued that the Russians were surely logical and rational people. A 'Red telephone' link was set up between Washington and Moscow, to prevent accidental conflict. Because of the certainty of retaliation, the leaders who controlled Russia and her Union of Soviet Socialist Republics would surely not be the first to attack - unless it was one hundred per cent certain of success? Others argued that the chances of a high percentage of success would be reduced if the West had at least some form of ballistic missile defence.

The first 'Star Wars' studies - later re-named ballistic missile defence (or BMD), had taken place in the days of nuclear deterrence. Even then, it was soon realised by the participating engineers and scientists that to make a completely 'leak-proof' ballistic missile shield, implied by the incumbent US President of the day, was a completely unrealistic dream. They were being asked to achieve an almost impossible goal. It would take many years to develop even a basic missile shield. So, as the Cold War confrontation continued, the concept of a nuclear balance, or, Mutually Assured Destruction, remained as a form of deterrence. As some would say, it was very appropriately abbreviated to the acronym 'MAD'. Then the Cold War came to an end - but, in reality, the threats had not all gone away!

Surely the World War Two V2 and later, the Middle East SCUD experiences in the Iran-Iraq 'War of the Cities', were a sufficient forewarning of what might emanate from unstable regimes in the future? The West were painfully slow to realise that, if these weapons proliferated, a day would come when they might have to deal with an irrational foe. Previously NATO had expected to deal with an enemy that thought logically. One that valued the lives of their own citizens and armed forces.

However, another horrific activity was noted at this time. One that should have further alerted the West to future probabilities. In the Iran-Iraq war many thousands of young men had died because they carried out suicidal military campaigns under the instruction of the Ayatollah. They were reportedly carrying plastic keys that would grant them access to paradise! They carried out totally irrational actions.

Satisfied with the Cold War fall-back position of deterrence, many academics and political strategists argued that ballistic missile defence was unnecessary. Others claimed that the dubious threat of a pre-emptive attack on Russia's nuclear weapon bases might be considered an adequate deterrent. Together, the mainly economic arguments and some technological barriers claimed by the detractors won the day. As it turned out perhaps deterrence was enough, but only when faced with a rational foe. However, little consideration had been given to the proliferation of nuclear weapons, with biological and chemical weapons of mass destruction not far behind. Perhaps those that had opposed the development of ballistic missile and effective cruise missile air defences would have adjusted their stance on 17th January, 1991 - the day of the first Gulf War ballistic missile attacks. That is, if they had been living at the receiving end of a SCUD attack, instead of the unfortunate residents of Dhahran or Tel Aviv! Six years later, Keith and his team had done their best to highlight the problem in simple terms. Would the governments act now?

In the first wave, seven SCUD missiles, carrying conventional high explosive warheads, had hit Tel Aviv and Haifa at three o'clock in the morning. Almost 1600 buildings were damaged and nearly 50 citizens injured. Almost 4000 were homeless, about 40 SCUDs and 40 days later the attacks ceased. Only three citizens had died - due to heart attacks. Overall this was a miraculously low rate of fatalities and destruction. All involved were grateful that warheads of mass destruction were not used. Would it be the same in London, Manchester or Paris? When ten years had passed, Keith still found it incredible that very little action had been taken in Europe.

Because of 'MAD', it was argued that the Russians had held-off during the Cold War. Leaders who had never served in the armed forces were now in power in most European nations. Some had decided that they neither needed deterrence nor protection! They would have a hard lesson to learn as the new millennium commenced and a terrorist threat, hitherto only really experienced by Israel and to some lesser extent in a few other nations, would really bite home. Proliferation of terrorism was exposing even more nations to threats of this type from the Middle East, North Africa and the Far East.

During the Cold War it was assumed that all ballistically-delivered Soviet weapons would be carrying nuclear warheads. The launch of any ballistic missile against the West would have therefore would have triggered nuclear retaliation - by the Polaris or, later, Trident - submarine launched missiles, by cruise missiles or even by manned bombers.

After so many years of deterrence, the Western nations seemed to have forgotten that ballistic missiles could also deliver all the other unpleasant types of payload. These include the chemicals and biological nasties, and of course, the so called, 'conventional' high explosives, carried to London by the fourteen-ton

V2 rockets, so many year before.

Further, quite apart from the spectre of chemicals, viruses, or plain high explosives, it had been postulated to NATO that a ruthless regime might use quite new methods of attack. It was not necessary to possess an actual nuclear bomb, just find an enemy with a nuclear power station! Alternatively, an unstable regime might be pre-disposed, in a moment of sheer madness, to dispose of their unwanted (or otherwise acquired) nuclear waste material, by deliberately firing it at, or dropping it upon, their enemies! To achieve similar effects the same regime might consider crashing an aircraft or missile into a nation's nuclear power stations!

Development of chemicals as weapons probably takes less time than the complex research needed for biological devices. Not until 1992 had President Yeltsin finally admitted to a Soviet biological weapon programme. Although he signed a decree to end the programme, reliable sources two years later said that it was still in place. What had happened to this material? Who might have some of this material now? NATO needed to be cautious!

Even after observing the human and economic consequences of conventionally-armed ballistic missile attack on the populations of Iran, Israel, Saudi Arabia and Afghanistan and the chemical action against the Kurds, the NATO nations dithered. Finding and destroying hidden launchers, before missile launch, was another, largely unsolved, problem. A disproportionate amount of the Allies first Gulf War air and space reconnaissance effort had been put into the detection of the mobile SCUD missile launchers. Once missiles were fired, the only option left was some sort of air defence to intercept them in flight, and stop them reaching their targets. Even if a viable air defence is in place, with SCUD missiles closing their targets at a speed of up to 2 km per second, there are only a few minutes available to intercept them, before impact.

By the late 1990s, after several abortive test firings of their own interceptors in the USA, the US-funded Arrow interceptor missile had been perfected separately in Israel. Despite the peace accords with her neighbours, Israel had, in the end, been well ahead of NATO in deploying a purpose-designed anti-ballistic missile system.

Israel's, or indeed anyone's right to deploy their own air defences, could hardly be denied. Fortunately, in a small and compact land, fewer systems are required. Unlike the NATO nations, Israeli Forces would not expect to operate overseas, so system mobility was not a major problem. If an attack came, Israel would have to defend itself - as Israel had found out too often and nearly too late in the past! The Patriot system provided during the first Gulf War, to keep Israel out of the offensive war, was not a complete defence. Now it had been retained as a complementary 'inner defensive layer', operating together with the Arrow.

By the year 2005 NATO had finally made some effort to stretch their existing air defence systems, so as to provide a semblance of air defence against missile attack. Most of the technical problems had been understood for at least ten years. A large quantity of new equipment was essential. It would cost billions of dollars. The token programme had started with the introduction of new early-warning systems. These were very long range, ground based radars and ballistic missile launch-alerting sensors located on space-satellites.

France was particularly worried about her southern Mediterranean coast and exposure to possible future trouble from North Africa. They also went ahead first on sensors, and were rapidly catching up with defensive missiles, with some Russian collaboration. As the French delegate remarked, 'If we have the sensors first - at least we shall know who has fired at us, even if we cannot intercept them for a few years!' Presumably the French imagined that they would survive any weapons of mass destruction that came their way, until they had time to develop some interceptors!

Meanwhile, the US Navy had developed a new high altitude, outer layer, air defence interceptor and placed this on some ships. The theory was that these ships could be sent to areas of possible conflict to provide a defensive umbrella. They would shoot down the ballistic missiles as they climbed, soon after launch! Provided, of course, that the nation launching the offensive missiles was conveniently placed close to the sea, and provided that the ships could get there in time! The USA had also received permission to place a new long range sensor, on the Yorkshire Moors, in Britain.

Looking at things realistically, by the start of the new millennium, most of the European NATO countries were still unwilling, or unable, to spend sufficient money. It was clear that Europe would be largely unprepared and defenceless against ballistic missiles. Yet they might be called upon to help out in a conflict area or even to protect their own homelands. They were also too late in trying to address the terrorist threat, having ignored the warning signs for ten years.

Sadly, Keith noted that, apparently willing to risk the awful consequences of an attack by weapons of mass destruction, from any direction, NATO had now become an alliance of prevaricators. Israel, in contrast had, at least, made some prudent provision! Israel had been countering terrorism since 1948. The USA had also made some provision. Russia, together with some nations they had supplied, could do no better than the, now ageing, SAM 10 and SAM 12 systems.

By 2005, there were Western demands that the Arab States should embrace Western-type democracy. However, it is clear that these, apparently reasonable, ideas do not take into account the Koranic culture. If the Koran is revered and Koranic Law is enforced, then only a theocracy can exist. Therefore, is the current Islamic stance to be - 'peace with your enemy now, until you are in a position to defeat him?'

Muslim nations still remember the date of the re-formation of Israel as the

'Day of Catastrophe', based on the Koranic view that, once territory has been included into the House of Islam, it must forever remain so. The UN is remarkably silent about the PLO Charter, still containing calls for the extermination of Israel, and about the hate education against Jews going on in Palestinian schools. From every aspect of analysis, Israel, albeit with an insignificant land area, about the size of Wales, with its capital city, Jerusalem, is clearly the key to future major world events.

Such was the world situation, in Keith's assessment, as the next part of the jigsaw fell into place. His overall assessment was that it would be an interesting, though frightening, next few years. He estimated that it would probably be around the year 2007, or 2008 when the balloon would really go up.

THE FALSE PEACE

The USA will be a prime recipient in the foreseeable future of all the more expectable forms of 'blowback'; particularly terrorist attacks against Americans in and out of the armed forces, anywhere on earth, including the USA.'

'*Blowback*' Chalmers Johnson, ISBN 0316854867 year 2000.

World-wide celebrations had taken place in the year 2000. It had been both a momentous final century and final decade for its citizens. Even those with little interest in world affairs must have been aware that 'peace' was suddenly in fashion! It was almost ten years since the long-standing 'Iron Curtain' between East and West had finally opened up. The 'Berlin Wall' had come down. Even North and South Korea had agreed to meet and talk. China was again trading with the USA and a sort of peace had eventually prevailed in the former Yugoslavia, in Northern Ireland and between India and Pakistan.

The lives of millions of the world's citizens had been changed. Many for the good - but some considered that they were worse off than before. This, mainly in the former Communist nations, who felt that they had not benefited from the market economies that had unexpectedly been thrust upon them. In both the former Eastern Bloc and in the West the 'blessing' was inevitably marred by huge job-losses in the defence industries. Indeed, many in Europe believed that there were no further threats to worry about.

The Middle East first saw peace 'break out' seriously in 1995. Pictures were seen around the world of smiles and handshakes on the White House lawn, between the PLO Leader Yasser Arafat and Prime Minister Rabin, of Israel. At first sight this looked like a good thing to the majority. There had been trouble for as long as most could remember in the Middle East, especially if one's own fuel supplies were adversely affected. However, by October 2000, the PLO and other groups commenced a new 'intafada' against Israel.

Back in 1996, few could fail to notice that the Balkans also enjoyed the start of a brokered peace. One former leader, Milosovic, was in the dock in the International Court of Justice, but others were still at large.

These peace efforts looked good to the man in the street. However, since the end of the, so-called 'Cold War', with the Soviet Union, the unpalatable underlying fact was that the world had actually become a much more unstable place. For some reason this was not evident to many in Europe. In reality, minor conflicts were still widespread and several had the potential to expand into really serious problems. Long after the first Gulf War, the name of Iraq's leader, Saddam Hussein, must have been known to most of the world. There had also been glimmers of hope. Saddam's time would come!

The first Middle East peace initiative with Israel had been triggered way back in October 1973, by President Sadat of Egypt. Others continued to oppose Israel. It was twenty years later, after the 1993 September Accord with the Palestinian Liberation Organisation, that things moved forward again. It was not all plain sailing. There had been a surge in Islamic Fundamentalism in the 1990s, coincident with adverse economic conditions in many Arab countries, making the peace task that much more difficult. Egypt, for example, had suffered a terrorist outrage that had killed more than 40 innocent tourists, visiting Luxor.

A series of events took place. Israel attempted to stop cross-border Katusha rocket attacks against their northern territory. The Prime Minister of Israel, Yitzhak Rabin, was assassinated. There had been subsequent elections, firstly of a right wing and then a left wing Israeli government. Talks were finally commenced to address the most difficult of problems - the future of Jerusalem itself. Nevertheless, by the year 2000, the talks had got nowhere. Prime Minister Barak's Labour government was defeated and Ariel Sharon had been elected Prime Minister. It would be his task to confront the new phase of terror. Many factors were at work in this part of the world.

Keith and his analyst colleagues watched all this at home in peaceful Europe. Here, in contrast, the major hassle was the European Community'ss insistence on the shape of bananas, the colour of tomatoes, or some new human right!

Meanwhile, Isador in Israel, Talal in Saudi Arabia and Ahmed in Iran were much closer to the reality of what was soon to affect the entire world. Keith had made an 'end of millennium' summary report on the current world situation and a future assessment of where the next conflict might be. He would have the task of updating the scenario again as the year 2006 dawned.

As it was unnecessary to repeat his earlier findings, he started, early in 2006, by summarising the main factors leading up to the year 2000.

By 2000, it had come as a surprise to many to discover that oil-rich Saudi Arabia had been in debt for over 30 years. Indeed, by the mid 1990s the Saudi kingdom had suffered the worst economic problems since the oil price collapse, in the mid-1980s. It was partly the result of the enormous multi-million dollar debt for the 1991 Gulf War. Saudi Arabia's state spending had been cut by a fifth, but this had the effect of extinguishing economic growth. Unrest about royal spending had followed. Iraq and Iran had seized on the militant reaction within Saudi Arabia and supported calls for the overthrow of the regime.

A virulently anti-Western fundamentalist, Ben Laden, whose family had earlier made a fortune in the Saudi Arabian booming construction industry, was busy planning world-wide terrorism. At this time it was thought that he may well have been responsible for some embassy bombings, but little could be proved. At this time Ben Laden still lived in Saudi Arabia. He had money in the bank. The nation had reserves, principally oil for the future.

By the time of the momentous events in the USA, on 11th September 2001, Ben Laden had been running his training camps in Afghanistan. It was here that he hid immediately after the attacks on the New York twin World Trade Centre Towers and the Pentagon in Washington DC.

The multitude of princes of the Saudi Royal Family had continued to build expensive palaces, while there was a call to increase internal petrol prices from the ridiculously low few cents per gallon. This was not popular with Saudi citizens, who felt they should have a greater share in the oil wealth. There was unrest in 2004, but the Monarchy had held on and instituted firm policing. Several terrorists were captured and others killed

The Saudi Royal Family would undoubtedly have to flee to safe havens abroad, if the fundamentalists ever took control. Those who did not manage to escape would surely face public punishment. In this part of the world it would be execution, by beheading. Further, if the Mullahs took control the application of Sharia Law would apply, and many foreign workers would be expelled.

Increasingly, Egypt, Algeria and others were subjected to growing internal fundamentalist influences. Despite the so-called peace agreements, Iran was openly supporting Islamic groups carrying out attacks both within Israel - and on external Israeli targets, such as embassies around the world. Egypt had suffering severe economic problems, despite assistance from the USA. Egypt's rise in unemployment was compounded by uncontrolled population growth. In the meantime, on the African continent, the Sudan was used as a training ground for extremist terrorists.

Despite the economic difficulties, in order to replace the vast quantity of arms expended during the Gulf Wars, arms spending across the Middle East had continued. The armed forces of Saudi Arabia had been expanded and were now approaching double their size, compared with the time of the Gulf War. Would sufficient of this force remain loyal to the King, to ensure his survival? It was becoming clearer that the combined forces of all those nations opposed to Israel could soon cause trouble. A charismatic leader with a persuasive personality would be necessary. With Saddam Hussein gone, in 2003, who would lead an assault on Israel now?

However, some states in the area were happy to keep out of the actual hostilities. They were happy to sit back and draw substantial oil revenues. Paid mercenaries, in the Hamas and Hesbollah, harassed Israel, on their behalf. Some leaders in the area were becoming increasingly concerned about the possibility of an Iranian nuclear weapon threat.

After the Arab-Israel peace talks, it had been thought that the main threat in the Middle East would diminish to the possibility, rather than the probability, of low intensity conflicts. For 40 years the Israeli bomb had been the ultimate deterrent in the area. As a last resort, there was little doubt that this devastating weapon would still be used, if the actual existence of the major cities of Israel, or the survival of the nation itself, were ever threatened.

When Keith examined the statistics it became clear, in hindsight, that the end of the Cold War had been the start of waning US support for Israel. Only about six per cent of the US population were Jewish. This was assessed as amounting to less than one per cent, in about eighty per cent of America's voting constituencies. This percentage was no longer adequate to change the balance of a US government or ensure financial help for Israel, in the form of foreign aid. Loans might still be possible. By the end of the millennium more Jews than ever had moved to Israel. Part of the reason for more Jews emigrating was that they perceived a real likelihood of imminent anti-Semitism. By the start of the year 2003, the Jewish population of Israel exceeded the Jewish population of the USA, for the first time.

The USA still needed an Eastern Mediterranean base which, in emergency, could be used to confront hostile activity in the area. Russia was no longer a threatening world power! Oil was still flowing from the Middle East. The USA could always fall back, temporarily, on Venezuelan oil, until the next Mid-East blip was sorted out!

By late 2005, Israel had transferred security coverage of the so called 'occupied territories' either fully or partially, to the Palestinian Authority. They knew it might be necessary to enter these areas if trouble occurred. Under much pressure, in exchange for 'peace', they had gradually ceded the control of thousands of square kilometres of territory.

President Assad of neighbouring Syria had unexpectedly lived a long life. It was hoped that Assad might take a more moderate tone, but he had died with no final agreement on the very militarily significant area, known as the Golan Heights. He was followed, as leader, by his Western-educated son. Disappointingly, nothing really changed. Syria maintained about fifteen thousand troops in the Lebanon until 2005, despite attempts within Lebanese society to get them to leave.

The fanatical opposition of the extreme Islamic fundamentalists to the PLO's agreement with Israel had continued, with random attacks on Israel's military and civilian population, until the year 2000. At one point the instability was demonstrated when the world was treated to the unlikely TV news spectacle, of Arab fighting Arab. This occurred in Gaza and in other PLO-controlled territories. Clearly, Chairman Arafat could not control his more unruly elements. Soon it was obvious that the PLO 'security forces', who had even been armed by Israel as peace keepers, were taking part in shootings against Israel and doing little to stop the atrocities against Israel.

Israel had tried various methods of control, such as periodically closing the daily access points to the many thousands of Palestinian workers. Once these closures became longer and more permanent, the economic pressures built up within the Palestinian populations, reaching desperate levels. It was indeed amazing that the peaceful Palestinian population did little to stop the terrorists, who were living among them, but causing them severe hardship.

Despite many offers of peace and cease-fire settlements, the demands of the PLO reached a peak in the year 2000. They wanted sovereignty over Jerusalem with no compromise. No limits on airspace or armaments were acceptable. They then threatened to declare a Palestinian State.

Keith realised that what they really wanted was the total destruction of the Jewish State. For some reason no Western leader was prepared to come out and say that this was the truth of the matter. For four hundred years, until 1917, the Ottoman Empire had ruled over the area. Most world leaders have not grasped the point that it is a tenet of Islam that a land once ruled by Islam, is always to be so controlled. In their eyes this applied to Jerusalem more than any other!

In the West, the USA, the only remaining superpower, had reduced her armed forces by a significant amount. The United Kingdom had also carried out swingeing cuts, including cutting the Royal Air Force by a half. It had been stated that a repeat Gulf War would severely stretch the remaining resources. Nevertheless, a further Gulf War did occur in 2003.

However, it became clear that UK defence cuts would mean that simultaneous involvement in more than two regional low intensity conflicts would be impossible. The outcome was that economic and political, rather than military power, was dominating Western thinking and strategy. This, despite clear and ominous warnings that a resurgence of Russia's armed power could take place. Further, the Islamic nations were arming way beyond what was needed for defence. Rather, by 2004, many were clearly planning on offence rather than defence in the near future.

Large quantities of uranium were, reportedly, unaccounted for - heralding an almost certain clandestine attempt by someone to become a member of the 'nuclear club'. Those who could not get their hands on this vital material legally, attempted to do so by other means. The other option was through the medium of civil nuclear power generation. Back in 1968 Iraq had purchased and installed a small thermal research reactor at Tuwaitha. It had more than doubled its power capability, using enriched uranium, ten years later. Two years earlier Iraq's project 'Osiris' - the 'Osirak' project - was started. The intention was to produce weapon grade plutonium. This was also known as 'Project Tammuz 17'. Tammuz, at 70 megawatts would have made the earlier reactors, at just 14% of that value seem small indeed.

In the diverse ways of the Middle East, things went wrong. The reactor cores, under construction in a French factory near Toulon, suffered the attention of unknown saboteurs resulting in catastrophic explosions at three o'clock one morning! The Iranians attacked Tuwaitha - and, of course, the Israelis later attacked Osirak.

The main bulwark of deterrence and hence peace in Europe for so long, had been NATO. There were still potential threats from the South, although Libya had become less threatening, when Colonel Gadaffi dropped his weapons programmes.

After the Soviet Union collapsed, the possibility of terror attacks had rapidly become more important than the erstwhile Central European threat. The new enemy was not necessarily visible. He could strike at any time and any point. In a nutshell - the stability, underwritten by the NATO Alliance for more than 40 years, was no longer assured. The old, bipolar, threat orientation had turned into a multipolar set of uncertainties.

Meanwhile, Israel's agricultural expertise continued to make the desert bloom. Indeed, this had become even more essential to feed the expanding Israeli population. The economy had expanded at a phenomenal rate. In contrast, despite the wealth that oil should have brought to the populations of Israel's oil-rich neighbour nations, the ordinary Arab or Iranian citizen was often struggling for his or her existence. It was clear that, when the oil finally ran out, or, if a new, hitherto-unknown replacement energy source was discovered, then there would be a major crisis in the Middle East. One that no government would be able to handle.

The inhabitants of these hapless nations had always imagined that a large amount of the world's non-oil wealth was owned or controlled by Jews. Therefore a spirit of anti-Semitism once again crept across the world's more ignorant and gullible populations.

In Russia several transformations had occurred since the Gorbachev era. Yeltsin had gone and before the new Millennium began, a new name was in control - Mr Putin. Within a few years, Russia, almost a dormant token force for some ten years, having either sold or scrapped their older equipment, was again emerging as a significant non-conscript force. They were building defences equipped with the latest tanks, missiles, aircraft, ships and nuclear warheads. Few of the Southern States of the Former Soviet Union had prospered as independent republics.

There were major population changes in the 1990s. Well over a million of the Jewish inhabitants of the former Goliath states had left in an almighty and unprecedented Aliyah to Israel. As an example, some 23,000 came from Belarus, alone. These Jews were the descendants of those that had been scattered for

2000 years, all of whom were entitled to live in Israel. The lands of the former Soviet Union had lost a great human asset. It included hundreds of medical doctors, musicians, teachers, mathematicians, engineers and scientists. After the enormous problem of settling all the immigrants was solved, Israel's economy boomed; doubling the economy in just five or six years.

Large water and communications infrastructure programmes were well on course, and the Mount Carmel road tunnel project was near completion. It had been necessary to build water desalination plants along the coast to balance the loss of water. This was caused, both by a new Syrian reservoir on the Golan, which reduces the inflow to Galilee and the loss of control of aquifers on the former West Bank. Some drinking water was also being imported from Turkey. The United Nations had passed a Resolution approving control of natural resources by the Palestinian Authority, including the resources of Jerusalem, by an amazing 143 votes to 3. Only the Marshall Islands, Israel and the USA voted against. Israel had few real friends.

The southern-most of the former Soviet States had signed military agreements with Russia. The Ukraine held flawed elections and then re-elections. To overcome the south's instability problems Russian and Ukrainian troops were, once again, stationed in various parts of the Russian Commonwealth of Independent States. The Ukraine continued independently with limited help from the West, mainly from such organisations as the World Bank and the IMF. Most Western nations came under continuous pressure to cancel all Third World debt, irrespective of whether moneys borrowed had been spent wisely or squandered. More former Eastern European nations joined the European Community. the West had their own economic problems. To make matters worse there had been a series of natural and man-made environmental disasters around the world.

The worst of these, occurred almost immediately after a period of supposed improvements to one of Chernobyl's remaining nuclear reactors. Another overheating catastrophe had occurred and just short of a melt-down the safety systems had shut it down again. This had happened more or less just as an extremely cold spell of weather came along. However, the loss of power to a large area around Kiev was as nothing compared to the unseen damage done to the reactor core and base. It was several weeks before the symptoms of animals and humans led to an investigation. It was discovered that the reactor was leaking radioactivity into the nearby river. Large numbers of the population who had remained or returned to the area, following the first Chernobyl disaster, had been rapidly evacuated, but it would be too late for many.

Starting in the mid-decade a series of major events were reported by the news media. Few had the common sense to interrelate them, because they appeared as separate items, spread over a few months. Firstly, Saudi Arabia procured even more Chinese ballistic missiles. Russia was building up as an anti-Western state again. Pakistan and India obtained, through indigenous development, ballistic missiles and, as both had become nuclear-capable, could therefore deliver warheads of mass destruction. Iran had become increasingly militant, was re-arming, almost certainly developing a nuclear weapon and increased the price of oil yet again. With an impending fuel shortage, Russia had made an agreement to extract oil from the Caspian Sea. They also signed a contract to take oil urgently from Iraq, following the freeing of that nation from Saddam Hussein's rule.

Turkey, the 'Cross-Road of Europe', had strengthened ties with the Turkic former Soviet States of Azerbajan, Turkmenistan, Uzbekistan, Kazakhistan and Kirghizistan; all of which were mainly Islamic. These states, populated by 17 million, many with fundamentalist views, were becoming increasingly militant. Turkey was caught in between. She had enough troubles already along her Eastern and Southern Borders.

Turkey's leaders had pondered on which way to go, influenced from within, as well as by their surrounding Islamic neighbours. Would Turkey, as a member of NATO for so many years, a prospective member of the expanding Western European Union, expect any protection if things went wrong? What would happen if her neighbours turned awkward and advanced simultaneously on multiple fronts? Tajikistan, in this group, though not Turkic linguistically or ethnically was also Muslim.

Turkey itself might well become largely de-coupled from her membership of NATO if a militant party was elected. Turkey had suffered terrorist attacks and, as in Egypt, there had been a creeping rise in fundamentalism. This looked like becoming an unstoppable force. Turkey's apparent trend towards liberalisation and constitutionalism, aimed at solving the area's many problems, could well be dashed for the foreseeable future. While the problems in Cyprus came nearer to solution in 2003 but they continued to irritate Greek-Turkish relationships - both members of the NATO Alliance.

Syria had continued to play the waiting game, deliberately delaying any agreement until the pressure on Israel to close the final link, to accept 'peace', became unbearable. Under considerable pressure from the USA and the European 'Quartet', Israel looked like conceding the final step in Syria's basic terms - to agree to quit the Golan Heights to Syria in their entirety. This only in the agreed absence of any Syrian nuclear capability. An assurance was required over Israel's nuclear capability and on the condition of further peace talks to move towards an eventual nuclear-free zone in the Middle East. The latter might possibly be reluctantly agreed-to by other Islamic nations.

Having given up trying to reach a peace agreement with Palestinian representatives, the Prime Minister of Israel rejected Arafat as a negotiating peace partner. By the start of 2005 Arafat had gone and talks could commence with the new Palestinian leaders. Talks often had to be tailored to match the timing of the replacement of a Middle East leader. The election or even the death of a President or King, or the appointment of an acceptable 'peace broker', could delay any agreements. In the background were those who still wanted Israel wiped off the map.

Unfortunately, the mainly Western-inspired Nuclear Non-proliferation Treaty had failed to prevent nuclear proliferation. Both Iraq and Libya had been signatories to various agreements, when it suited their purpose. However, because of Israel's nuclear weapons, Arab leaders had ignored their obligations. The UN International Atomic Energy Commission's safeguards were flouted, once the embargoes were lifted. Iraq's nuclear programme came to a halt in 2003. Iran, also a signatory, had been not only attempting to develop an indigenous nuclear capability but had possibly been busy procuring a basic nuclear device from a Far Eastern supplier. They had frequently threatened to withdraw from the Treaty, due to what they saw as inaction against Israel. Not that their rhetoric mattered to most people in the West an awful lot, anyway. Most did not know or care what went on, as long as their petrol was available! However, the time was coming when they would have to sit up and take notice.

Keith had frequently pondered on how much these treaty signatures really meant. Mostly, he had concluded, they were a means of making a political point and a delaying tactic. He remembered that all sorts of threatening postures were taken back in the 1990s. In the attempts to get non-proliferation signatures, statements were unhelpful. Typically, 'we will not sign, if Israel does not sign'.

Israel had long taken the view that ownership of their ultimate weapon, the so called 'Samson Option', had for many years offset and balanced the threats of their neighbours, who frequently threatened to use biological and chemical weapons against Israel. Israel had always been ambiguous about the status and numbers of her nuclear weapons and this had most probably been a stabilising influence - the uncertainty persuading their many enemies not to attack.

The extreme fundamentalists groups, Hamas and Hesbollah, despite the peace accords, still opposed Jews anywhere. They even claimed that World Jewry were somehow 'plotting to overthrow both Islam and Christianity'. This, they claim, using rhetoric and false information, is according to the Torah, the Jewish scriptures. These extremists also claimed that 'They, (the Jews) want to destroy the world, Britain, and US and French society'. The fundamentalists said that - 'Israel will be destroyed by the Muslims'. Saddam Hussein, had used much of the same rhetoric, before he was defeated. The age-long antagonisms seemed to go on for ever!

Before his final defeat, Saddam, like the Grand Old Duke Of York, had marched his men towards Kuwait again and marched them back again, towards Turkey, towards, Syria and towards Jordan - and back again. He had even apologised to Kuwait in December 2002. This was at the time the UN Weapons

Inspectors returned on a quest to find Iraqi weapons of mass destruction. They tried to persuade Saddam to explain what had become of the materials intended for these weapons that they had recorded as being present just four years earlier. Saddam had not explained to the satisfaction of the USA and others, and this had led to the second Gulf War in a little over ten years. Democracy was introduced to Iraq, among much terrorist bloodshed, while the nation was under the temporary control of stabilising forces, mainly from the USA and Britain.

Was this to be the future form the world was to take in general - a sort of imposed 'false but unreal peace'? How many times could the United Nations request nations to send their young men and women to quell trouble spots? By late 2003, many items in the US-inspired 'Road Map' for the Middle East, were in place, but the violence against Israel had not ceased. Some Palestinians were probably ready to declare a state. After Arafat's demise, from Israel's perspective it really was looking like peace might be possible at last, after so many years of turmoil. There was finally an opportunity to open their borders Jordan, Egypt and Lebanon, and on occasions, with Syria.

Although many factors were pointing to some type of impending disaster, who, among those living within safe borders in Israel, could fail to rejoice in their new-found peace? They had spent so many years in persecution. What would the next few years bring?

However, by 2005, even more testing times occured in Israel, when their government announced the intention to withdraw from several areas populated by Jewish settlers. The withdrawal date, eventually in August 2005, had been opposed by many, who saw this, not as a step towards lasting peace, but as a victory for terrorism. It was also particularly worrying that, in the late spring of 2005, Syria had carried out ballistic missile test firings, including tests of the improved SCUD, known as SCUD 'D', with a reported range of 700 miles.

It was clear that the scenario was being set for a crisis - apparently with 'Oil' at its centre. A combination of oil, together with the other factors of territory and religion, could unleash a conflict of forces far greater than one caused by oil alone. This clash could not be very far ahead. One in which the world might well see the second use of nuclear weapons. Who would be the main nations and the driving personalities?

In submitting his report Keith decided that the government could surely draw its own conclusions - but would it grasp the fact that this scenario was clearly going towards a phoney 'peace'.

GENESIS OF A POLITICIAN

Reuben Harel was born on a kibbutz in 1946. As he was born in the land and not an immigrant, like so many of his friends, he was a known as a 'Sabra'. His parents, Avi and Yael Harel, had crossed Europe from Lithuania in 1938. They had travelled hundreds of miles on foot. No mean feat as the turmoil built up the year before the Second World War. When they arrived the land was administered by Great Britain, under the United Nations Mandate of Palestine. Britain had tried to keep law and order in this turbulent area, since 1917. There was no State of Israel in those days.

The re-birth of the State of Israel was some three decades ahead. It would literally happen overnight in a dramatic declaration by Ben Gurion, himself a migrant from Russia. He would be the first Prime Minister.

In the year they arrived, Reuben's parents had been but two of a very small quota of Jews that Britain had allowed in to the land. Under Arab pressure stringent entry quotas had been imposed. On the other hand Britain had a need for land and air bases, convenient ports and passage for trade through the Suez Canal, to the far-flung British Empire. To Britain's shame, Jewish immigration was deliberately hindered by the anti-Semitic and wilful influence of certain British administrators. There had been Lawrence of Arabia and the influence, among others, of Britain's diplomat and spy, Jack St John Philby, in the aftermath of the First World War. Oil had supplanted coal to propel the ships of the Royal Navy. The British Empire had an over-arching need to be located in geographical positions of influence. It was in Britain's interest to have bases near those countries that could supply both Britain's merchant and naval fleets with oil. The nation would thus be able to protect her maritime and trade interests, in keeping vital sea lanes open.

It has since been shown that even the officially declared policy of an allowed quota of returnees to what was still called Palestine, suffered the indifference of many of Britain's Government servants. They often took it into their own hands to apply local 'rules', as they saw fit. Many such influential people were Arabists, aligned with Ibn Saud, the ruler of the new nation of Saudi Arabia. By 1921 Philby was moved from his advisory post to King Saud. He was made responsible, from his new position in Jordan, for the control of the whole area that came under the British Palestine Mandate. The extent of his sympathies for the Arab cause was evidenced by a personal 'conversion' to Islam. By 1930, Jack Philby was transformed into 'Abdullah' Philby. Certain US businessmen, from major oil companies operating in the Arabian Peninsular at the time, were definitely anti-Semitic. Later some became senior US politicians. They clearly had an undue adverse influence, albeit indirectly, on the lives of Reuben's parents and on all Jews who had already arrived or were attempting to enter the land.

The early migrants to the land soon learned more of its history from first hand accounts. Of course, there was no such thing as the State of Palestine. The land did not have any government, other than that imposed from outside. Mark Twain's description of the land, during a visit in the late 19th century, clearly shows that it was more or less barren and sparsely inhabited. It was an area that had been re-named during the occupation by the Roman Empire. The root of the name was 'Phillistia', a coastal area, where the Phillistians lived, who were enemies of the Jews in antiquity. The Ottoman rule was to last for four hundred years, until Britain took over.

In the early 1920s Philby had worked for the creation of the Arab Legion, the first Arab force organised and trained under British Officers. The Mandate was a purely administrative arrangement. It was mandated to Britain, until such time as a better solution could be found to handle the warring factions. There was certainly no formal state or national government in place.

If the name Philby seems familiar, many years later, Philby's infamous son, Kim, would also come to the public's notice. He fled to Moscow from the Lebanese capital, Beirut, to join other British traitors. For years he had been a dangerous Cold War spy for the USSR and would die there.

Reuben's Harel's parents had lived through so much. The Arabs had sided with the Nazis during World War 2. During this time there were Saudi arms deals with the Nazi regime from 1939 onwards. This resulted in a flow of weapons for Arabs to fight Jews. As always, there had been repeated calls for 'Jihad' - Holy War from the fundamentalists. It would be anything but Holy for those trying to live in peace.

After World War 2 the Harel family had welcomed the Holocaust refugees arriving from Eastern Europe, many of them having barely survived British attempts to prevent entry to their own land. It had been oil and oil again, that had indirectly controlled their lives.

Earlier, during World War II, the USA had bribed Saudi Arabia, in order to prevent further oil reaching the Nazis. However, even more could have been done at the time, as the Harel family would hear that the USA and Great Britain, well aware of what was going on, had refused to bomb Hitler's gas chambers in order to save lives.

There had been great joy in Reuben's household as the family had hung on every word when the United Nations voted for the partitioning of the mandated area. On 14 May 1948, this had led to the declaration and re-birth of Israel, as a sovereign State. The USA supported this unique action and recognised Israel eleven minutes later! At this time they had probably acted to prevent the possibility of the whole area falling under the dominance of the Soviet Union.

The US foreign policy makers had clearly decided that this might lead to Soviet dominance of the larger proportion of the world's oil resources. In contrast, the USA had not supported Britain, who sided with Israel, eight years later, during the 1956 Suez Crisis.

Now Reuben was in a position to assess for himself the perilous position that Israel faced. It was there again - oil, oil and oil again, affecting so many decisions and ruling so many people's lives. Why was it that Israel had virtually no oil of their own? 'If only Moses had turned right instead of left', they joked. Reuben wondered why this was the case - was it just coincidence? It seemed ironic that they were surrounded by unfriendly oil-producing nations, but had to import all their fuel oil. As a result they even had to go out and buy the stuff from the other side of the world!

By the time of the enormous oil boom of the 1970s, Reuben and his family had survived three wars and countless terror incursions into their land. The Saudis had financed anyone who would oppose the Jews, but had cleverly arranged for others to do their fighting. From time to time there had been news of frustrated attempts by the Palestine Liberation Organisation to obtain whole shiploads of arms for their terrorist fighters.

At the time when there had been a large influx of Sephardic Jews - Jews from Morocco, the 'Black September' terrorist threat had spread across Europe and the Middle East. The most despicable attack, among the many that took place, was on the 1976 Israeli Olympic Team in Munich. Eleven of the Israeli Olympic team members were murdered. Another shattering blow for the nation. This, just three days before the Jewish New Year.

The world news often reported yet another killing of Jews by this same organisation, either in Israel or somewhere in the world. There were a number of such terror organisations equally opposed to Israel. Whether Jews were in ships, aircraft, airport lounges, shopping streets or buses, markets or embassies, they have all been targets. There were even attacks on schoolchildren in their schools and homes. The devastation was usually very briefly reported, before some other newsworthy event occurred.

Other nations had suffered terror, from the IRA, the Red Brigades or the Basque Eta Group. However, none had suffered like Israel, as a proportion of their population. Aircraft hi-jacking probably claimed the greatest publicity. These were soon forgotten by those not accustomed to using airports. In contrast, frequent air travellers were thereafter constantly reminded of the need for vigilance, baggage checks, delays and expense. A pattern that was to intensify even more in the future. Reuben and his people suffered these atrocities while trying to carry on with their lives. Little did they realise what was still ahead.

Many of the young people were not aware that their fledgling nation had been helped by Czechoslovakia in the pre-Warsaw Pact days. Military equipment was provided through plans significantly orchestrated by an obscure Czech Jew. He was named Lev Hoch

In those first critical days Lev Hoch had been busy. He ensured that, starting from a weak position with little defensive equipment, the new State of Israel would receive thousands of rifles, hundreds of machine guns and a dozen Messerschmitt 109 aircraft. These were initially delivered in bits and assembled clandestinely. An estimated 20 Spitfires were flown in and even some ageing Beaufighters and Flying Fortresses. The Czechs gave flying instruction and, as time went-on, the Israeli underground (the 'Haganah') apparently controlled a Czech airfield. It was from this airfield, under the most hazardous of conditions, that supplies were flown directly to their new State. Other supplies arrived by running shipping under the noses of those bent on destroying Israel before it became established.

Reuben had heard of all these activities from first hand knowledge, at home. His father was proud to have been an unloader of these clandestine supplies, usually in the dead of night. He was a founding member of the underground organisation, known as the Haganah. They bravely sought to protect their largely farming population against repeated Arab hit and run attacks. Almost daily attacks had started directly after the new State was announced. The Haganah helped and protected those newly arrived in the land, often under extreme conditions of hardship and endurance by sea.

Many years later Lev Hoch would come to world prominence, as Robert Maxwell, the newspaper magnate. Under bizarre circumstances, many years later, he apparently took his own life. It then came to light that he had allegedly been 'misdirecting' huge sums of money within his world-wide publishing empire. Eventually he had run to unprecedented levels of financial manipulation and debt. Reuben realised that Lev Hoch had probably done a lot more to help Israel than will come to light for some years. He was surely entitled to his final resting place on the Mount of Olives in Jerusalem, after his untimely death.

Reuben was right in assessing that his family future would be one of even more turbulence than his father could have possibly imagined. At the age of three Reuben had survived an attack on the children's house within the kibbutz. It had been shelled from the Golan Heights, across the nearby border with Jordan. Before some had time to reach the shelters, several infant fatalities had occurred. Those who lived through this period would later recall the '1948 War of Independence' as the first of a succession of wars that Israel would be forced to fight, in order to survive as a nation.

Most families suffered bereavement of their own or close friends. One dark night Rueben's father was killed by an Arab sniper, while taking his turn on night guard, at the kibbutz perimeter defences. By the late 1950s it was clear to Reuben that peace was not likely. As a very young man it had dawned on Reuben that he would personally have to fight. There would be no option. It was necessary to ensure his family's and country's continued existence. In Europe, the USA and Canada, trained men might have a four or eight year liability for reservist call-up. In contrast, Reuben's and Yuri's military service would effectively be for life. They would always be 'reservists'.

In the aftermath of World War 2, many young men, citizens of the victorious Allies, would find that the prospect of war had not gone away either. However, in Europe they would not have to think daily about possible acts of terror. In contrast, Jewish citizens of Israel had to consider their security every day of their lives. Isador's brother Yuri, like most of the youth in Israel, found themselves conscripted into the national defence forces, for a period of two years 'national service'. Later it would also include the girls.

Reuben had just heard that Egypt was working on a long range rocket - a ballistic missile. Ex-Nazi scientists, leaving from Eastern Germany, behind the 'Iron Curtain', were now working in Egypt. It was a worrying situation. Perhaps hundreds of rockets would be built. Up to that point in world history, Reuben knew that only Great Britain had suffered at the hands of ballistic terror weapons. There had been no defence against them - other than attacking the launch sites in advance. Finding the sites was a major problem. If England hadn't achieved this by the mid-20th Century to protect London, then it was clear to Reuben that Israel could not presently do so either. It would be many years before Israel developed a defence against this menace.

Many of Israel's citizens, still mindful of their recent survival from the holocaust, began to worry whether, as rumoured, this might mean nerve gas attacks. Their fears were well-founded at the time. It was soon reported that Egypt were using a mustard or bacteriological type of crude weapon against civilians in the Yemen. It could be Israel's turn next! Was it possible to use missiles to carry this murderous material?

As Reuben grew up the other Arab nations nearby were in the process of being armed, mainly by the Soviet Union. Some also received armaments from the West during this period. Reuben learned that, to counter the proliferation of weapons of mass destruction, his own government had plans. His leaders had been far-sighted enough to start to research on their own nuclear weapon and the 'Jericho' ballistic missile programme. Everyone hoped that neither of these weapons would ever be needed.

For the time being, there would be no defence against ballistic missiles, should any of Israel's enemies procure them - as they undoubtedly would one day. Throughout the 1960s and 70s, the big powers, Russia and the USA, continued to be engaged in their 'Cold War' intercontinental ballistic missile 'race'. In Israel, it was the lesser-ranged missiles, right on their doorstep, that people were beginning to be concerned about. Reuben shuddered to think what might happen to their small nation, should their near-neighbours use them, even with high explosives.

As a true 'Sabra', Reuben had grown up to take pioneering and hard work in his stride. In 1965, at the age of 19, he easily passed through military training. Excelling at sport, he had received encouragement from his kibbutz ruling council and became an accomplished athlete. In June 1967, Reuben's expectation of completing his military service and then moving to the reserves, was abruptly curtailed. For the first time, he found himself in action, in the later-named 'Six Day Arab- Israeli War'.

Again he excelled and ended the war as an officer. It had been an amazing victory for Israel. They had gained territory, but at the cost of many lives. The most significant outcome was that Jerusalem, the City of Reuben's distant ancestor, King David, came once again under Jewish rule. This after almost 2000 years of foreign domination, the Jews having been scattered all over the world for that period of time. It was an unprecedented occurrence, both in World and Military History - and Reuben had taken part in it!

Few in the West noticed, or even cared that, even after this important milestone, the nation's name - Israel - did not appear on Arab maps. It was the start of a hugely successful propaganda coup by the mainly Arab, Islamic nations. Despite the vote of the United Nations, that Israel should be a homeland for the Jews, most of the world was hoodwinked into believing that the Jews should not be there at all!

Instead of returning to the kibbutz, where his ageing mother still lived, Reuben moved on to Technical University. Thereafter his army career progressed splendidly. He made an enormous contribution to the winning of yet another Arab-Israeli war - the 1973 Yom Kippur War. By this time King Faisal had taken over from King Saud in Saudi Arabia and had the same hatred for the Jews as his father. 'Is there to be no peace Reuben?' his exasperated mother would ask.

Even though they had not directly taken part, as a retribution for the Arab forces losing the war, Saudi Arabia imposed an oil embargo on all of Israel's friends. There were not many friends but they represented some of the world's largest oil consumers. Oil as a weapon of diplomatic and economic leverage had become a fact of life! European nations suffered fuel shortages.

Quite apart from the problems of having hostile neighbours, Reuben also heard more and more of the West's grudging acceptance of Israel. On the one hand, many of the West's military forces, particularly NATO's, were full of admiration for the amazing victories that such a small force had won, against seemingly impossible odds.

On the other hand some very disturbing events occurred, because later it would come to light that, during the 1970s, British mercenaries had even supplied the Palestine Liberation Organisation with a limited number of weapons. It was claimed that this was to enable British penetration of terrorist ranks! However, it was believed, with good reason, that the infiltrators had often known in advance of intended terrorist action, but had failed to warn Israel.

Then, during the actual fighting, a British arms embargo was placed on Israel. Urgently required spare parts, needed for British-supplied tanks, were denied to Israel. This disgraceful action was ordered by Prime Minister Heath's government of the day. Britain had appeased Israel's enemies once again. This 1973 embargo, imposed by Britain, was not finally lifted for another 20 years, until after the PLO-Israeli Peace Accord in 1994. Fortunately for Israel, the USA and France did not follow Britain's poor example. Meanwhile Soviet arms continued to flood into the area. Factories in the former Soviet Republics continued to refurbish and supply Soviet equipment to the Arab nations.

This lack of support for Israel was nothing new. During the time when Anthony Eden was British Foreign Secretary and even in the times of John Foster Dulles, the US Foreign Secretary, the USA was suspected of going behind Israel's back. Most probably, they were driven by the interests of major oil companies. Both of these influential politicians were suspected of being strongly anti-Semitic.

The answer, Reuben knew, was for Israel to be independent, as far as possible. Certainly they needed to be self-sufficient in critical weapons. Her few friends could not be trusted when it came to choosing between oil and Israel. A true friend, in the Israeli sense, actually means one who would actually lay his life on the line. It seemed that there were none of these friends to be found - if the choice also involved oil! The 1973 war had been an especially hard time. Israel had lost no less than 500 tanks in the war. They had just seven days spare parts left, before help arrived. The Soviets had encouraged the Arabs to inflict a final blow. Iraq bolstered the Arab forces by supplying some 1200 more fighting vehicles, comprising two Tank Divisions. They failed! Amazingly, by any standards of military analysis, Israel had survived once again.

Israel also suffered serious attacks in the north, in 1982. This led to the 'Peace for Galilee' operation. The US embassy in Beirut was attacked by a suicide bomber, with serious loss of life. This was just as the era of Mid East aircraft hi-jacking and hostage-taking of foreign nationals reached a peak. Beirut was in ruins. This city had been previously described as the 'Paris of the Orient'. It was renowned for its markets of beautiful rose, iris and gladiolus blooms and gracious living for those who prospered. Indeed, peace seemed a long way away - but there was always hope.

The day finally came when it was realised that two thirds of the known oil supplies in the world could suddenly come under the control of a single nation. The nations had finally woken up to this possibly when Saddam Hussein invaded Kuwait, late in 1990. It was also realised that Saudi Arabia was probably in his sights once Kuwait was subjugated. The United Nations coalition forces had ejected Iraqi forces from Kuwait. A series of UN embargoes and weapon inspections were imposed on Iraq, before Saddam Hussein was finally removed from power, in 2003. No actual biological or chemical weapons could be found when searches were carried out after the war. Had they really been destroyed? Had they been cleverly hidden in this huge land area? Had they been spirited to an ally, across a nearby border? Following Saddam's removal from power, an Iraqi government was finally elected, while the country suffered considerably from terror attacks - believed mainly to be carried out by insurgents into Iraq from various extremist forces, such as Al Qaeda.

During his varied career Reuben had gained considerable experience, both militarily and politically. He was aware of all the hardships, the terror attacks and the hostilities from surrounding neighbours - and from much of the world. He had both served and widely travelled overseas, and completed training as a pilot in the USA. Later he returned to the USA to be appointed as his nation's Scientific Attaché in Washington.

On leaving the Israel Defence Force, as a Colonel, Reuben's entry into politics was successful. He had soon become a Minister in the right wing government of 1992. However, he had seen only brief periods of relative peace, despite the major negotiations of the 1993 Oslo Accord, the US-inspired 'Road Map to peace' and other attempts. At the start of the new millennium Reuben was his nation's Senior Adviser to the Minister Of Defence. His - and the nation's greatest trial - would soon occur, commencing, as so often during the two thousand years of his nation's dispersion, with little warning!

The Trigger

FUEL FOR CONFIICT

Already, several of the predictions made by Keith's NATO Team ten years ago, had been fulfilled. These had ranged from the fall of Chairman Gorbachev, to the correct prediction of locations of several 'low intensity' conflicts that had since taken place around the world. Of major concern then and now was the Middle East. Keith mulled over the situation again, while mowing his lawn.

The need for United Nations operations supported by NATO and other non-NATO members, had, as forecast, increased dramatically. The UN had virtually ignored the appalling ethnic cleansing situation in the Sudan. Noises were made but little or no corrrective action had taken place. Turmoil continued - there was never total peace. Terrorism, also forecast in the study report, had increased. As expected, it was largely centred and controlled from the Middle East.

In stricken areas, it was sometimes possible to get food or medical aid through. Not unsurprisingly, outsiders could only have limited influence in settling the underlying political or other causes of the disputes. By the time action was taken skirmishes had often escalated into small wars. Somalia had been a case in question and the UN had finally pulled out in 1995, after the US and other forces, acting on behalf of the world's nations, had run into dangerous confrontations. UN participant nations lost many of their troops in skirmishes with the unpredictable belligerents, who were self-styled local 'War Lords'. Political, economic and ethnic upheaval had followed in some form or other in most of the nations that had been earmarked as the most likely protagonists in Keith's earlier team reports. Despite the predictions, indeed, almost the certainties, no one seemed able to nip these in the bud before they reached a level of bloodshed.

Most had realised that a major milestone in world history had occurred, when the Soviet Union and the Eastern Communist Bloc collapsed. Now, approaching two decades later, another milestone seemed likely to break on an unsuspecting world. This time, it would be at the Eastern end of the Mediterranean.

As Keith continued his mowing, he was completely unaware of a former Russian scientist named Isador Zaritski. Isador was currently busy in his laboratory, far away - at the Eastern end of the Mediterranean. He had just sat back, with considerable satisfaction. The block of material on the bench before him looked like solidified chicken soup. He could just about press his thumb-nail into it. Yet, under the right conditions it would change its form at a controlled rate, from a solid, into a combustible gas. A gas that could be used as energy. In the laboratory, just next door, were several experimental blocks of the same substance. Beyond them could be glimpsed the experimental material production apparatus, with its mixers and presses.

Isador had encountered many set-backs while researching his dream material. He had explored the processes using solid naphtha, aluminium chloride and several other materials. To the layman colloidal and combustion chemistry were but mysteries. He had first considered working on fuel cells that took fuel and oxygen from an oxygen-rich source. These would act in a sort of electro-chemical combustion and then generate electricity directly. They could be made to produce water and heat as side products, or natural gases - no pollution. However, his present ideas were for 'solid gas', which would be simpler and cheaper. His invention permitted the modification, rather than replacement, of what the world already had in their millions - internal combustion engines. He reasoned that a new and safe method of mobile gas production was all that was needed. The internal combustion engine could then continue as the main form of surface propulsion, in the absence of gasoline.

The gas that each fuel block produced was fuel-rich and combustible. Today he had just completed the final design and testing of a sensing probe. Now he could completely control his process. The probe transferred the gas-producing technique to a second block automatically, when the first was consumed; thus continuing the combustion process. Conversely, he had also perfected a system to quench the process and stop gas production on demand; and to accelerate or decelerate the process. It was also now possible to replenish the fuel blocks, just by loading another one in - and so on, as required. The gas produced was temporarily piped into a storage vessel and then passed under precise control through injectors and into the combustion chambers. Here it burned with a pure flame.

In the engineering laboratory of the Technion - Israel's Technical University - a similar apparatus was not producing flames, at least not visibly. It was driving a smoothly-running standard automobile engine. Isador had made the breakthrough - he had invented a clean, almost pollution-free, vehicle engine. Spare blocks could, he surmised, be quite safely carried in a car boot. They could only be ignited by the intense heat produced by a pulsed laser. The laser power was derived from the power of the sun by day and continued by a sun-charged battery, that took over after dark. Only enough solid material was burnt to keep the gas reservoir full, so the burning was taking place in pulses, according to the required vehicle speed and load.

Engines had run on gas before. Liquid petroleum gas, 'LPG', had been available for vehicles for many years. Compressed natural gas, or 'CNG', had also been the subject of experiments and looked promising. The cost of removal of the carbon monoxide pollutant in the latter, using a catalytic converter, was only one third of the former and about one fifth of that for normal petroleum. However, Isador had even moved further. He had invented a new process for vehicles, the 'solid gas generator'. Previously, this method of mobile gas production had lasted but for seconds, by burning solid rocket fuel. It had only been achieved to produce thrust for guided missile rocket engines, in the now defunct mighty Soviet arms factories. In contrast, Isador had perfected full control over the gas conversion and a method of throttling its entry to the familiar internal combustion vehicle engine.

Isador could list the benefits. There would be no hazards of inflammable liquids or gases under high pressure - so dangerous in auto accidents. No special handling equipment at fuel stations. Apart from normal engine lubrication, no oil would be required. Fuel would be just another, safely-packaged, solid item, sitting on the supermarket shelf! Like buying soap powder, he thought! The recipe was a cocktail of readily available chemicals, some of which could be synthesised from certain common plants. These grew in the semi-desert and they would soon be grown in vast commercial quantities.

Not realising the wider implications of what he had done, Isador hastened to fetch the Laboratory Director to demonstrate his achievement. He had precisely accomplished the task embarked upon almost two years before - the control of pollution. He paused in the corridor, reflecting that he could afford to indulge for just a minute. He looked out over the city of Haifa. Below, on Mount Carmel's slopes his family house was among those clustered among the trees. Sarah would be preparing the evening meal. His youngest son, now 20, was away for a while, completing his compulsory military service. Everyone hoped this could soon be ended for so many of Israel's young people. Israel had recently reduced the commitment for military service for young women.

Isador suddenly remembered that it must have been but a short distance from here, on Mount Carmel, that Elijah the prophet had defied the evil forces of Baal, with God's miraculous fire. Would Isador's miraculous fire have the same effect on this and the succeeding generations? Would Isador Zaritski be remembered in the same way as biblical Elijah, in another three thousand years time? Probably not, he thought!

The days-end shadows were lengthening, as indeed did his stride, as he proudly carried the good news to the Director.

Isador was glad he had left Russia. It was almost as though he had never been there. He realised that his work and his invention was just one of the many that were being made by scientist émigrés to Israel, from the Former Soviet Union. It had meant a lot to Isador that he could carry on working. This was certainly more exciting than the teaching job that he might have hoped for. Remembering where his inspiration began, atop the Shalom Tower, Isador hoped to see clean air soon, over a pollution-free Tel-Aviv skyline. Even better, on a clear day perhaps he would now be able to see the eternal city - Jerusalem - high on the distant mountains.

The Director was delighted and immediately accompanied Isador back to the demonstration laboratory. 'So many exciting developments these days,' the Director remarked, with a sigh. He would be retiring soon. Leaving these brilliant colleagues to go on to even greater things.

After the successful demonstration, Isador counted it as a very satisfactory day. He decided to leave early, to tell Sarah. It wasn't until Isador was on his way home, that the wider implications of the invention suddenly began to niggle.

The sunset to the west of Mount Carmel was glorious indeed as he turned into his drive. After chatting briefly to Sarah, as was his routine, Isador scanned the Jerusalem Post and then the Hebrew newspapers. Although there was a Russian TV channel and Russian language newspapers, both his Hebrew and spoken English had improved dramatically.

He now had access to more information and up to date news on the world and local situations than he had seen in a lifetime in his former existence. Like all Jews in Israel he was beginning to form views on what the future might hold, if a proper peace process was completed. He also considered what might happen, if the peace failed. He hadn't been particularly interested in politics in the Soviet Union - after all no one expected choice in those days - there had been no options to vote for! The news today was about the same as yesterday. The newly erected protective security fence, built to separate Israeli and Palestinian territory, had been damaged again by an explosion. He sighed. Nothing really changed. They really did need a stronger leader!

It was almost dark when his meal ended. He went out into the garden to look for the first star, not realising that this very day his actions would trigger one of the biggest news stories of all time. The view over Haifa, its port and the sea were always a fascinating sight as the sun set.

Far to the West, Keith Perham was also taking a late evening stroll, his mowing completed. His stars were also shining brightly. How far ahead would the next world milestone be? He could not predict the time - only the inevitable chronology. Undoubtedly a new era would soon dawn. He knew that it would be one that few wished to see.

The imminence of major events would not leave his mind the next morning so Keith used the opportunity of the hour-long train journey into London to review the current world situation, the 'big picture', and to make some reference notes. It involved a series of events that appeared to lead towards a frightening scenario. If his estimates were correct the scenario would confront planet Earth's citizens in as little as eight to ten years time. All the key ingredients were rapidly coming into confluence. His next report was due in just a few days - but he always worked best under pressure. He considered the key players, the history, the technology, the weapons and the probable intentions. Above all, he considered the geographical area where trouble was most likely to occur.

From all the information analysed it was becoming clear that militant and political Islamic fundamentalism had resulted in pockets of tension and violence. These were presently combining under someone's master plan. The events were spreading around a huge area, centred on the Mediterranean, the Gulf of Iran, to the North of the Black Sea and towards the East. The people were either in rebellion against entrenched regimes or lived in lands where fundamentalists had already taken over and imposed their strict, undemocratic, beliefs. Underpinning these regimes were the 'Party of God' - Hezbollah, 'Holy War' - Al Jihad and the 'Army of God' - Jund Allah and several others. An Islamic population was now in the majority in more than 40 nations - many of them located in this area. This amounted to about one fifth of the world's population - almost the same as China's.

Little had changed in some nations. They had already been applying the 1300 year old code known as 'The Sharia' - the 'straight path'. This code was applied to everything and everyone. It was largely designed to protect their mode of society, rather than the rights of the individual. As a result, court trials with a defence lawyer were almost unheard of. Executions were the norm. Even the King of Saudi Arabia was condemned in 1991, and again in 2003, because of the presence of Western coalition troops. The USA largely withdrew from the Dahran airbase in 2003. Within weeks terrorists struck at a compound housing western workers in Ryadh, with huge loss of life.

These US troops, who went to the aid of Kuwait, had been initially based in Saudi Arabia for the duration of the first Gulf War. In the eyes of the fundamentalists the troops had violated the Sharia Law, by stepping onto Islamic soil! The fact that the troops had also been protecting Saudi Arabia, as Saddam Hussein had remained in power for another twelve years, seemed to have completely escaped their attention.

To the Islamic faithful, the system of government in the West had failed, as in Eastern Europe had Marxism, ten or more years previously. The answer, they believed, was an exact interpretation Islam. The imposition of the Islamic religion as a way of life, is in contrast to what so many other religions had become in the West - personal beliefs, often barely held, and no more.

Islam was at diverse stages in many less-developed nations. Those which had become semi-secular were blamed by the others as accepting 'decadent' Western influence. There had been severe reactions among the population, in the form of dramatic Sharia revival. It was realised that some of the leaders were often hiding behind a cloak of Islam, while in the pursuit of their extreme actions. This had happened over recent years in Iraq, Iran, Egypt, Libya and Pakistan.

However, in Egypt a nominal Islamic Government was not moving far enough or fast enough for the oldest fundamentalist group - the Muslim Brotherhood. On occasions they had been ruthlessly suppressed by the authorities, over nearly forty years. In their view it was increasingly time for real action.

Not the least of the causes of unrest in the Middle East was engendered by the periodic calls from leaders and militants alike, in a number of Muslim nations, for the complete 'liberation of Baytulmaqdes' - or Holy Jerusalem.

So called 'peace talks' had really been unacceptable to the fundamentalists. Many of these lived in nations that were trapped in a mixture of socialism, poverty and political Islam. They were ripe for exploitation and manipulation. They were frequently reminded, by their very vocal leaders, that Israel's presence was a blight in the area - despite the weak peace agreements.

The humiliations of the Arab military adventures against Israel during the past four decades had not been forgotten. Of course, it was all blamed on The West. Several times a 'Great Jihad' against Western imperialism had been called for. Clearly much pre-planning was taking place behind the scenes, especially by one faction, led by Ben Laden. No one needed reminding that, in September 2001 this had culminated in the aircraft attack on the World Trade Centre buildings in New York and on the Pentagon, in Washington. This attack, above all others that had already occurred over many years, on US interests overseas, had focused the US President on the threat, as never before.

Ironically, all these nations, who increasingly nurtured terrorists, needed to sell their oil to the very nations that they claimed to have caused their present problems! In the Middle East things were rarely what they seemed.

It was the nature of the weapons that several of these militant nations had recently acquired that Keith considered to be the most worrying factor. Back in the early 1990s the US Counter Proliferation Initiative had been started. This comprised both diplomatic and military activity to deny the unstable nations any access to weapons of mass destruction. It had a limited effect at best. Military force was still a political instrument - but had also become a religious instrument. It was, in short, impossible to prevent the spread of specialist weapon knowledge. It was even claimed that one could find the basics of bomb-making - both conventional and nuclear   on the world-wide Internet! The inevitable happened - a new nuclear threat had dawned.

Meanwhile, and particularly since the mid-1990s, efforts had been made by the United Nations to curb international trade in conventional arms. At the very least it was agreed that the signatories would declare their sales and purchases. Of the 185 nations only 84 had actually revealed their purchases. Major expenditure, by four nations who were unwilling to disclose their transactions, had totalled no less than 25 billion dollars over a few years. These were Saudi Arabia, Egypt, Syria and Iran. No friends of Israel! By the year 2003, it was assessed that Iran could have a nuclear weapon within 2 to 3 years, and a new missile to carry it.

As his early morning train drew into the bustle of Liverpool Street Station, Keith knew that it could not be long before a really serious confrontation would occur. He passed a news-vendor's stall outside the tube station, it proclaimed two stark words - ' Iraq Unrest'. This despite The West's attempts to introduce - some said impose - democracy. There was no doubt that the lead players were being cast and the stage for the scenario was being well set! The key question now was - 'what would be the timing'?

PRELUDE TO CONFlICT

As the year 2005 commenced, Keith reconsidered the apparent crisis situation, so as to confirm the underlying causes and main players, because tensions seemed to be rising in several places. Half way through the eventful last decade it had been forecast that an internal Russian revolution might occur, which, as it turned out, did not occur. Nevertheless, President Yeltsin's poor health did result in a change in the Russian government. It did not appear to bring a militarist or expansionist one in its place. Now it was time, not only to focus upon political and internal economics, but to consider the energy situation, in a free economy. The changes in the economies of all the former Soviet states had noticeably increased their dependence on oil. For many years it had been assessed that any new regime would be necessarily - first and foremost - tied to a struggle for internal survival. Now it seemed certain that Russia would soon be looking outward for oil within a few years. Keith doubted that the current regime, were making sufficient progress - and there was always the possibility that new leaders, would seek a diversion sooner rather than later - if they failed to bring the nation's fortunes to an acceptable level.

The demise of the Soviet Union as a major world power had been just one major milestone which had affected the Middle East. The other had been internal change within the Middle East itself, following the peace impetus. Within recent years most of the world had realised that the international economic situation was also balanced in a precarious way - as evidenced by major money market fluctuations. No one had forecast these events. However, apart from the escalated fears of international terrorism, it had now become clear that part of the instability was due to the sudden increase in the world-wide use of electronic transactions. This method of money transfer, now available to a large proportion of the developed world's citizens, was also a ready vehicle for money laundering. There was an increasing fear that things could easily go out of control.

At national levels, those with money - never formerly able to obtain the latest in technology, were now able to buy and buy. It had become easier to disguise the end users of military technology. Meantime, French companies and others had flocked to Baghdad to sell. Oil prices had soared, at one point exceeding 60 dollars per barrel. Another world economic milestone had been reached. The military balance was threatened and the economic balance would never be the same again!

Early in 2006 a sudden change in oil prices had forced the world's developed nations to re-assess their economic strategies. Within a month new oil controls, in the form of quotas, were placed on importers of the cheap oil. Although much to the annoyance of the ordinary motorist, who were already highly taxed on top of the real cost, this action, demanded by the United Nations, had once again brought home to the oil-greedy West just how critical oil had become as a world resource and its interaction with the world's economic balance. Adding to the gloom were the ever-vocal environmentalists, who wanted even more fuel tax to reduce global warming. Governments seeking re-election had an increasing number of diverse views to accommodate.

Extremists were waiting in the wings in Syria and Jordan. Relatively recently the leadership of both had been changed, with the succession to power of, inexperienced men. Jordan's wings would indeed be clipped forever if the PLO joined with the other fundamentalists in the area. Keith could imagine the area without Jordan - a re-combination of the territory, that for so many years had been delineated by the artificially drawn straight lines, so foolishly put in place by Britain and France.

Back in 1991 King Hussein of Jordan had upset his long-standing friends in The West and supported the Iraqis in the Gulf War. Although, before his demise, he had a change of heart, this only led to suspicions that the same thing might happen again. Admittedly, located in an impoverished buffer position, between Israel and Iraq, the King had few choices at the time - all of them unpopular with someone! Although his son, King Abdullah, had settled down well, he still had to walk a precarious tightrope. Keith realised that it would be easy for determined radical groups to topple the rulers in both Syria and Jordan, join forces with the Palestinians scattered among these various locations and form a power bloc with certain other nations against Israel.

Perhaps, he mused, at that stage Jordan might become Palestine proper - which it probably should have done in the first place, had it not been for the European meddling with the none-too distinct borders in the first place. Jordan had been made aware of the real state of affairs in Iraq, in the immediate post Gulf-War years, by the defection of some of Saddam Hussein's most trusted personalities - including family members. Some of the defectors had been foolish enough to return - at which point they faced Saddam's usual summary executions.

Strangely, history shows that King Hussein of Jordan was the deputy monarch of Iraq at the time of the 1958 revolution. Now, in the year 2006, things had come full circle and soon an Iraqi-Jordanian-Saudi Arabian Alliance could be possible. Another factor was that the demise of Jordan as a separate entity, would surely not displease the new fundamentalist rulers of Saudi Arabia. No great love having been lost - it was the founding of Saudi Arabia that came about when Ibn Saud captured the Red Sea coastal plain from King Hussein's father! The continuance of the succession of rule in Saudi Arabia could by no means be totally assured. A proliferation of Royal Princes in the ruling family and their spendthrift ways had done nothing to encourage support by the population in general. For example, if a hitherto semi-dormant militant group of the Wahhabi creed rose up - the Royals might have to flee for their lives. In the event, presumably they will have salted away enough to live-on comfortably elsewhere in the world!

A revolution could be fuelled by the large numbers of students, greatly influenced by strong religious teaching. A teaching that had often equated any sort of democracy as 'an enemy'. They would undoubtedly call for social, political and economic factors decided by Islamic Law - nothing else would do. Such discontent, festering for years, could come to a climax with little warning. The same was likely to happen in other countries in the area before long. Turkey, having elected an Islamic parliament, could easily waver.

Fortunately, of late, much more foreign currency had been exacted from Saudi Arabia's pilgrim industry - The Haj - which had suddenly suffered an upsurge due to the world-wide increase in the followers of Islam; many from The West. This was most welcome, as it had been necessary to be much more prudent with government spending.

Over the years the scope of Keith's threat studies were necessarily wide. They were regularly reviewed and updated. Currently, he felt more certain than before that things could well come to a head sooner than later.

In military terms the world had become a much smaller place since unmanned aircraft - cruise missiles and especially ballistic missiles, carrying weapons of mass destruction, could be sent a thousand or more kilometres in a matter of tens of minutes. This form of threat had exposed Britain's and NATO's populations. Cruise missiles, in the hands of friends, had been used in the Gulf War. Now others had developed or easily purchased the same worrying capability. Keith noted the background and current status of other nations who were within range of the Eastern Mediterranean, and who might either cause conflict, aggravate or contribute to a conflict there. He decided that the main players at a future time of conflict would be those summarised here.

Firstly, much further away to the East, there were regular and ominous rumblings in Pakistan, who, like China and India, were busy manufacturing ballistic missiles and their payloads.

An Islamic Separatist movement had been rampant in Kashmir, and on the Pakistani-Indian borders, confrontations of varying intensity were regular events. Ever since India's first nuclear device, tested in 1974, Pakistan had also pursued an urgent nuclear programme, reportedly based on a Chinese weapon design. This continued, despite the termination of valuable military and economic assistance from the USA, in protest. Once Pakistan had acquired and tested the bomb underground, they had relied on deterrence in the form of free-fall aircraft delivery using their US-supplied F16 aircraft. In answer to India's longer ranged ballistic missile programme, the indigenously made Pakistani 'Hatf 3' was only managing a range of 600 kilometres. Keith assessed that, most probably,

Pakistani nuclear technology had not reached a level of sophistication to enable it to be packaged into Hatf 3. Not that these were likely to be an immediate threat to Britain or NATO's interests, unless these items were moved further westward as part of arms deals. The only sign of peace progress in the region had been some rudimentary agreements over the position of Kashmir.

Iran, meanwhile, had had serious diplomatic clashes with Russia over the cost and method of payment for their recent huge arms and nuclear deals. However, Iran already had the arms. Now, oil supplies to Russia - the agreed trade offset for the arms had been changed because Iran was, alternatively, shipping much of her oil to the Far East, where the still flourishing nations of the Pacific Rim were able to pay more. This trade was being seriously affected, now that Iraq's new democratic government, no friend of Iran, had overcome the oil control quotas that had been imposed during Saddam Hussein's rule.

Meantime, Iran was thankful that Chinese and North Korean arms had already bolstered her already substantial armoury. For some years Iran had deployed several hundred SCUD missiles with ranges up to 500 km. Forty five of the N Korean NODONG type 1 ballistic missiles, capable of carrying warheads of mass destruction - chemical, biological or even nuclear, for a thousand kilometres - were also in Iran's inventory. Some had forecast that Iran would eventually have both the advanced NODONG, capable of flying 300 km further, and nuclear warheads for them both.

Keith had suspected that several of the former Soviet Republics, still struggling in their new market economies, were also helping the Middle East States and Iran with arms supplies and upgrading existing equipment. NATO were understandably interested - indeed alarmed, as others, in addition to Turkey - the only NATO member hitherto in ballistic missile range - were now coming under the ballistic missile threat.

Of particular relevance, from 1995 onwards, Iran had persuaded Russia - with the aid of a 800 million dollar deal - to complete the Iranian nuclear reactor at Bushehr, originally started back in 1976. The two German-designed pressurised water reactors were almost two thirds completed when work was abandoned when the 1979 Iranian revolution occurred. As early as 1995, (fortunately an incorrect assessment), the United States intelligence agencies had predicted that Iran would have a nuclear weapon within five years - a prediction that caused concerns and fears in the West. In 2005 it was confirmed that Russian help for the Iranian nuclear reactor would go ahead, despite the misgivings of the USA. It was also stated that fuel rod delivery would allow the Iranian atomic pile to operate by 2006/07. Few had questioned the need for Iran, a major oil producer, to have a need for nuclear power generation. Iran continued to claim that this was only a civil requirement.

This was not all! By courting the N Koreans and Chinese for some years and despite enormous efforts by the West to prevent nuclear weapon proliferation, it was possible that, by 2007-08, Iran would acquire a limited number of ready-to-use tactical nuclear warheads.

Initially, the delivery of these weapons onto their targets would be made by small unmanned aircraft, that Iran were suspected of developing, relying on navigation from simple and cheap satellite navigation systems, of the type used by yachtsmen. With ballistic missiles from N Korea and the more recent purchase of Russian SS-25 missiles, in exchange for oil, it was certain that Iran now had more than one method of delivery of these weapons of mass destruction. the West was also aware that, when the Cold War ended, the USSR had several hundred of the SS-25 road-mobile 'TOPAZ' missiles in service. They had soon realised that they could be sold for hard currency. Who had them now?

Although throughout the previous decade Iran had carried out a reconstruction of her own arms industry, they had spent no less than five billion dollars on arms purchasing during the first five years of the 1990s. By mid-decade Iran was well into the development of the 'Zulfiqar', a main battle tank, probably based on an original Russian design and named after the legendary sword of the Shi'ite Muslim warrior hero 'Ali'.

As the decade drew to a close, suspicions in the West had mounted that Iran may have developed a crude cruise missile. Possibly this could be linked to the development of Sarin and other chemical warfare agents, together with a likely biological capability developed at the Damghan centre. Iran's suspected cruise missile may have been an offspring of the Soviet 'Silkworm' missile, achieved with the assistance of N Korea. Few of the nations who faced Iran across the Gulf of Iran wished to publicly acknowledge the potential threat located just to their north. Many of them felt that it was too sensitive to name a potential enemy as it might make him into one!

Several other nations in the Middle East had replaced their old 300 km SCUD missiles with 500 km-ranged SCUD variant, known as SCUD C, but armed with conventional warheads, and SCUD 'D', mentioned in an earlier report. Damascus, for example, had also received the Chinese M9 ballistic missile, with a range of 600 km, armed with conventional high explosive warheads. In total Syria had an estimated 5000 tanks and probably up to 1000 ballistic missiles with several tens of launchers. Syria was strongly suspected of developing biological weapons and may well have acquired materials and assistance from Iraq at the time of Saddam's fall from power.

Despite UN assurances, Israel's citizens were very uneasy at these developments. During the Cold War Israel had been assured that the USA had been committed to help - but now they were not so sure. Threat ranges and timings were now so short. Help could be a long time coming! The promised 'New World Order', where the rich would protect the weak and there would be justice and fair play for all, did not seem at all convincing, when new arms continued to flow into the region almost daily. Further, following the latest peace agreement, it was rumoured that Russia might have agreed to supply the new Palestinian State with armoured vehicles and some other arms that were clearly not required for self-defence. During 2005 Russia had supplied sophisticated air defence missiles to Syria.

Uranium mining on five sites in Iran's Yazd province had proceeded apace and nuclear processing, near to the Saphand mine, had started. For some time Argentina had trained Iranian nuclear scientists and it was estimated that several hundred had returned to Iran with many more trained support staff. The USA had first become alarmed at these activities back in 1995 and had placed a Trade and Investment Embargo on Iran at the time - to the tune of barring over 600,000 barrels of oil a day. However, Iran, busy selling 500,000 a day to Japan, was not greatly affected! The general population of Iran remained impoverished. After 20 years they had still not fully recovered from the eight year war with Iraq.

Keith was very concerned about proliferation of nuclear materials. Even nuclear accidents could cause havoc. Chernobyl in the Ukraine had been an example. Chernobyl is situated in an area which is a water source for about nine million people. Each annual flood was still releasing radioactive contamination; and it was now about twenty years since the reactor top blew off the power station. The psychological effect was great and fish, mushrooms, soils, forests and meadows were still 'no go' areas. Care was still needed to avoid letting the contamination get airborne on the wind by stirring up the soil by ploughing, vehicles on contaminated roads or by forest fires. Keith could only imagine the consequences if this scenario was repeated in the dusty Middle East. Even worse, might be the potential for the use of nuclear radioactive waste as a terror weapon, against dense populations.

Non-nuclear Weapons of Mass Destruction had, of course, already been used in the region. Iran had encountered chemical weapons when, in 1982, their troops were caught unprepared, during Iraqi attacks. As a result they had themselves since invested heavily in chemical warfare. Now, they had chemically loaded ballistic missiles ready, in contrast to chemically-filled artillery shells, waiting to be fired.

There were other factors that could not be ignored - all building, in diverse ways, opportunities for instability in the world. The Middle East Oil States, particularly those scattered around the Gulf of Iran, had controlled oil prices through OPEC for more years than Keith could remember. The United Arab Emirates, Saudi Arabia, Oman, Bahrain and Qatar had literally held the world over a barrel for many years. The OPEC nations controlled seventy five per cent of all the world's known oil reserves, of which about sixty five per cent was buried beneath the sands of the Middle East. Early in 2006 the price of oil rose sharply. China had become an increasingly important oil consumer. Measures were taken by the OPEC countries to pump more oil, so as to stabilise the situation. Saudi Arabia still had about half the world's known oil reserves beneath her feet, accompanied by a third of the world's natural gas.

A further consideration in this turmoil was the situation of the common citizen in so many of these lands - a poverty time-bomb literally waiting to explode. While infrastructure, jobs, health and water should have been main concerns, the focus of spending was usually upon defence and security - leaving little for the ordinary man and his family.

At the end of the Second Millennium AD it was amazing that, after sixty years of oil trading, most of Iran's sixty million inhabitants were still below the recognised poverty-line. Of course, much had been squandered earlier, during the long war with Iraq.

Pakistan and China had not been without blame as international arms salesmen. The proliferation of their weapons was influencing the present scenario. Keith had also seen press reports, which there was no reason to doubt, that Syria had been quietly running a small nuclear research reactor for some years. Like the activities of North Korea, he was always suspicious of the outcome of seemingly innocuous 'peaceful research', where the word 'nuclear' was involved, especially when it was carried out by extremist regimes. Things were certainly hotting up.

The Saudi Arabian National Guard, a largely Bedouin force, responsible for internal security - and independent of the regular army, had embarked on a major re-equipment programme. Originally formed in 1916 by King Abdul Aziz, who founded modern Saudi Arabia in 1932, they had almost doubled in size, to nearly 60,000 men. For years they were considered to be the House of Saud's last resort against internal opposition. However, they would turn out to be ineffective when the inevitable revolution came. Meantime the regular army, having spent massively on armaments and contributed greatly to the national debt, had acquired long range Chinese missiles.

Israel, prudently, had expanded her Jericho II force, in accordance with the Peace Accords. Despite the 'peace', Israel - always an interminable thorn in the flesh of the Islamic Fundamentalists - had continued to suffer some terrorism at home and attacks worldwide on Jewish communities. Following Israel's year 2000 troop withdrawal from her Lebanon buffer zone, Hesbollah skirmishes on the Northern borders continued. Syria had promised to remove the terrorist military capability, provided Israel signed a peace accord. But this had proved a near-impossibility to enforce. The Hesbollah military wing, originally formed in 1983, had ample time and sponsorship to get established after Israel left The Lebanon. Syria had initially been called upon to calm a potential civil war scenario and had maintained thousands of troops there for twenty-nine years, until April 2005, when the pressure of a UN withdrawal resolution was finally successful.

Apart from those giving support from within Syria, there were plenty of anti-Israel factions remaining in the Lebanon. Lately it was suspected that Hesbollah had got hold of some American Stinger shoulder launched anti-aircraft missiles, through Afghanistan; and launched at least one against an Israeli helicopter. Fortunately, the helicopter's electronic countermeasures could defeat the missile guidance system. Although it most probably shouldn't have been the case, Keith was still amazed that this terrorist organisation was run by Shi'ite clerics and much backing from Iran's revolutionary factions - presumably claiming to be 'men of God'. Of course, after a little research one realises that they are actually 'men of Allah', which is not necessarily the same thing. Despite the increasing responsibility for control of their own areas, the authorities were still either unable or unwilling to restrain these attacks.

Since the latest Israel-PLO peace accord, Israel's security had finally been guaranteed by the United Nations. Israel, in return had reduced much of her forces and opened her borders with Jordan and the Lebanon; and continued her open borders with Egypt. Many years previously a treaty had been signed with Jordan, in October 1994. Nevertheless, it had been clear ever since then, that despite the peace accords, and Israel's withdrawal from Southern Lebanon, Gaza and much of the 'West Bank', that the 'struggle' - would not be completed, in the terrorist's eyes, until Jerusalem, the capital city of Israel, was 'liberated'.

Jordan, was, as ever in need of economic assistance, with a multi-billion dollar debt and still labouring under economic constraints imposed by the International Monetary Fund. Jordan's armour and aircraft had an ever diminishing operational capability - totally outclassed by all her near neighbours. If any of the King Abdullah's 'fraternal brothers' to the north, south or east took a fancy to Jordan's territory it would all be over in a matter of days! An earlier request for a 'twelve billion dollar aid spread over a decade', had a less than enthusiastic response from the President of the USA.

In the meantime, the Egyptian and Jordanian agreements were being threatened by a waxing and waning fundamentalist undercurrent, that threatened the possibility of a violent take-over in both countries.

Algeria, in a state of unrest, although far away, still remained a lesser player in the scenario. Algeria had apparently helped Saddam Hussein's nuclear programme both in the 1980s and the early 1990s. Located between Tunisia and Morocco, Algeria had always been plagued with fundamentalism at some level - surely spurred on originally in the 1980's by Iran's fundamentalists. This took the form of a type of Islamic Nationalism. Algeria had depended on revenues from its oil and gas exports. The fall in prices caused a major collapse and nation-wide riots had ensued in 1988. The president was assassinated, and, after three years of terrorism and eleven thousand dead, a State of Emergency had been declared.

While the Algerian fundamentalists had supposedly won a correctly and fairly-conducted election, they had been denied power. By the late 1990s the ruling - but non-elected government - had no option but to let the elected fundamentalists take control. The long forecast repercussions then swept through Morocco, Tunisia, Libya (with UN sanctions removed in 1999) and Egypt, with Sudan aided by Iran. Iran were also threatening Egypt with the help of internal fundamentalists in the country. Only a spark was needed to set the whole string of North African Islamic nations on fire. But would they take part in a future mid-east conflict, or not?

France, as a result of much unrest among her immigrant population, including ethnic Algerians - was now facing several increasingly hostile nations to her south. Some of these had just received ballistic missiles from friends in the Middle East. Even Germany, with her two million and more Islamic citizens were in a difficult position. These countries, and Britain to a lesser extent, had all suffered some internal unrest in their big cities, mostly because of rapidly occurring economic or ethnic problems, the threat of terrorist action from within and without. Soon there would be a backlash against the imposition of 'rights' for all sorts of groups, under various European Community directives. At times a knife-edge situation existed and threatened to put pressure on any foreign decisions taken by these governments which might affect their ethnic brothers and sisters. By 2005 ethnic riots would occur in France and Britain.

Despite all the Arms Limitation agreements and the scrapping of vast numbers of arms after the Cold War ended, within the flank area of Russia there remained literally thousands of tanks, armoured combat vehicles and artillery pieces.

One thing was very clear, there was no way that the United Nations or the major powers could stop the proliferation that was occurring. Several potential conflicts were being fuelled or had already been both fuelled and primed!

Keith reflected that it was still not clear whether anyone would manage to unify the Arabs, as a people, if it came to a mainly East-West showdown. The possibility that political union might instead be achieved by Islam seemed much more likely - and this would include many others, not only those located in Arabia, who were fundamentally opposed to Western values. Wherever secularisation had been seen to rise, fundamentalism had not been far behind as a reaction.

The scene, Keith feared, was being set for a major event to occur on the world stage. What would be the spark to trigger this event? Where was the number one flash-point?

Israel's Commander in Chief was by now the Commander of a much reduced force, comprising a very small standing army and large reserves. Continued national security was the government's main concern. Many actually believed the UN peace guarantees. The Commander had said earlier that his force had the capability to attack any nation in the area which introduced nuclear weapons into their armoury. To this end observers had noted that the re-equipment programme for

Israel's Air Force had included aircraft with 'longer legs'. That is, aircraft carefully selected to carry their weapon loads over greater distances. Israel were also well-aware that a potential future enemy could strike from a considerable distance using the 'poor man's weapons' - the ballistic missile or cheap cruise missile. Therefore, they had to be in a position to make longer range pre-emptive attacks, should the occasion arise. A fact they remembered and had found to their considerable cost during the first Gulf War. Weapons that, so easily, could have contained warheads of mass destruction, had wrought havoc with the nation's daily life for forty days, fortunately with more structural than human damage.

On the other hand, Israel's citizens had hoped so much for peace since 1948, and finally appeared to have achieved a measure of peace and goodwill from many of the world's nations. As early as the mid-90s, no less than 46 of the world's nations had renewed relations with her since the peace treaty with the PLO, six Gulf States had lifted arms embargoes and Israel had signed co-operation agreements with Russia, Turkey, France, The Ukraine, South Africa, Singapore and India. Estonia, Romania, Hungary, New Zealand, Thailand, Malaysia, Singapore and South Korea were all among those receiving Israeli military equipment. For example, Keith mentally noted that in the design and operation of small unmanned reconnaissance vehicles, Israel had led the world for many years.

The mini-unmanned Heron long endurance air-vehicle made by the Silver Arrow Company was ideal for carrying out operations over the battlefield - spying while loitering for up to fifty hours at an altitude of thirty-five thousand feet. Several nations had also purchased the ground control system to handle the perambulations of these natty reconnaissance craft. Israel's necessity to watch what her neighbours were doing was, of course, borne of hard experience.

It was therefore - after studying threats for so many years of his life and with considerable foreboding of a major conflict soon - probably in the Middle East - that Keith had just completed his latest scenario report for his current Government 'customers'.

Was the world finally entering the expected new phase? Keith had reason to estimate that this might well occur late in 2006. In the Jewish calendar, the year 5766. Once again, he reminded himself of an inescapable fact at the start of the 21st Century. Whoever controls the oil will be in position to control the oil-dependent world - unless, of course, a replacement for oil was discovered!

In fact, a new method of fuelling combustion engines had been invented in Israel. The oil-producers would certainly not allow this. Conflict would not be long in coming. However, first there would be a short period when the world was not aware of the invention and the world's strongest nation would have to make major decisions!

THE DEADLINE

*'If we have to use force, it is because we are America. We are the indispensable
nation. We stand tall. We see further into the future.'*

(US Secretary of State, February, 1998)

Captain Hank Keen, the Squadron Attack Weapon Specialist and planning
officer, switched on his computer and called up the spreadsheets for planning
a conventional weapon attack on a group of typical ballistic missile launch
sites. It was one of the planning options he often ran through, in preparation for
armaments exercises. The squadrons always seemed to be flying these lately.
In retrospect, Hank recalled that these exercises had all increased in frequency
recently. He was well aware that the Alliance Forces spent an excessive amount
of time and effort on searching and destroying ballistic missile sites in the desert,
during the Gulf War - Desert Storm. The intelligence agencies had to find out
somehow where these sites were located, before they could be attacked. It was
not his squadron's task to find - only to destroy.

The 'Sleek' weapons, carried on the new Quicksilver aircraft were ideal for
this target. They would provide direct hits by guiding the weapon to within three
metres of the ideal aim point. They would use data linked updates and night-time
electro-optical imaging of the target, in the weapon's terminal homing phase.
Normally, by weapon impact time, the attacking aircraft, having quickly turned
after launch, would be in comparative safety several kilometres away. It would
either be on its way back to base or moving towards another target.

Now, according to the rules for this particular exercise, there was imposed a
new requirement. Before departing the target area the crews would be required
to carry out a reconnaissance manoeuvre within camera range of the target. This
was so that confirmed proof of a raid's success - or failure, could be obtained!
In near real-time, the information would immediately be transmitted by the
aircraft's coded video satellite link. It would arrive back at base and in the USA,
long before the weary crews landed. Hank did not question this new requirement.
Crews were always trying out new concepts. It would be evaluated like all the
others in the past and then either adopted or rejected as a future tactic.

Hank re-checked his planning calculations and the aiming accuracy once
again and started to produce his presentation. At this stage he was, of course,
unaware that his work would form a part of the attack briefing for the Chief
of the Air Force of The United States of America. When Hank had taken every
factor into account, his computer would clip together all of the different planning
charts necessary to show the weapon planning cycle step by step. It culminated

in a final result that would advise the number of aircraft to be tasked to achieve the mission. This would follow an earlier calculation for the critical 'Over Target Requirement'. This is the number of aircraft that must reach the weapon release point, so as to deliver the correct number of weapons onto target, with a given degree of assurance and accuracy.

This planning exercise was unusual, he thought, since the request was asking for a very high - 99% - assurance of success.

Nothing was ever assumed in 'weaponeering'. Great care was required in the planning stage. Otherwise, the old maxim 'most of the weapons miss most of the targets most of the time' was still applicable, even with modern weapons and all the electronic aids in the world to get there.

Hank recalled his own training. The instructor had instilled in his students, at NATO's Oberammergau Weapons Training School, that a large number of things could go wrong! Hank should know! His were some of the weapons that did just that, when he participated in the raid on Colonel Gadaffi's Libya, some years before. Perhaps, he mused, his present task was a practice exercise - just in case Libya obtained more ballistic missiles. Hank knew that some years earlier the Libyans had fired one at an Italian island. Maybe intelligence expected another crisis. Maybe this was the reason that his squadron had moved suddenly from the USA to Spain? The detachment from their normal base in the United States had come as Hank was about start his leave. He had intended to visit his ageing mother on the West Coast. Now it would have to wait until his temporary duty overseas, known as 'TDY', was completed.

Once again Hank re-calculated the most likely along-track and cross-track weapon-aiming errors, carefully comparing the Commander's requirement against the values achieved recently by the squadron pilots on their weapon practice camps. The crews had flown the new aircraft type for only a few months. Although they were fast improving, they were not 'combat stars' - yet. Better degrade those values slightly to allow for the real world, he told himself. The boss had said that training was starting a new phase. Everything must be done, from now on, as if it was for the real thing. So Hank was obeying orders to the letter!

Could he - dare he - plan for more than one attack on each target? This procedure, of 'going round again', was now considered 'bold pilot, typical of John Wayne bravado'. Stuff of the old-time movies! Definitely not. A single-pass attack was recommended - in order to survive. These days it was far too dangerous to hang around. Nevertheless, he still had to plan the escape manoeuvre so as to get those photographs. Hank did not like these extra reconnaissance passes that were sometimes practised. So what level of attrition should he use? How dense would the air defences be? Would the enemy be able to detect the Quicksilver aircraft en route? Were the enemy likely to spring any technical surprises? Always a difficult one to judge!

All squadron members were aware that, one day, like Libya, it would again be 'for real'. In the meantime, as much realism as possible was maintained during real flying practice, and in the simulator. He could not bear to think of the possibility of aircrew losses - if they ever had to do this 'for real' again. These crews were his friends, and he had lost several friends in the first Gulf War. It was only through a freak of the appointments office that he had come to this desk-planning job and was not flying on the new Quicksilver squadron himself. Someone had to do planning - he reluctantly admitted - preferably someone else! He was told that it had been a 'career move'. Perhaps his chance would come to fly again if they formed another Quicksilver squadron?

Back to the task! He had better use all the right figures - the Chief was bound to check out all his results, if things were being taken that seriously. Hank methodically went through a list of questions that he must resolve, if possible.

What 'kill probability' were intelligence giving for the latest Surface-to-Air Missile defences so recently sold to so many nations by Russia and China? What level of training would the typical SAM crews have received? If this was an automatic defensive system, what training did the crews need? Indeed, did they need much training at all, apart from switching their systems on? With automatic systems they did little but wait for the rocket motors to fire. Weapon guidance towards the target also occurred automatically, with the operator acting only in a monitoring role. Were the air defence missiles deployed in the optimum position to defend the ballistic missile silos? Did they accompany the mobile ballistic missiles all the time, or did the ballistic missile launchers operate independently, or covertly? What was the probability of the defences engaging the stealthy Quicksilver? In a real war Hank knew that some of these facts would not be available until the final electronic reconnaissance just before the attack. Who knew where a fully-mobile surface-to-air defensive system might have moved to? Especially if it kept quiet and did not transmit? Did the enemy have any fighter aircraft to engage the Quicksilvers, even before they got near their targets?

He called on the probability calculations yet again and decided, with careful route planning, that attrition (that is, one's own assessed losses on the way to the target) might reasonably be assessed as 5%. Subtracting this from one hundred, he divided the 'over target requirement' by 0.92, after making an extra adjustment for possible aircraft unserviceability while taxi-ing before take-off, after take off or aborted sorties en-route. He allowed 8% in all.

The land-based variant of Quicksilver, a product of the heavily cut and depleted US defence industry's Lockheed Skunk Works, had been in service for over a year. It was currently achieving good reliability and excellent weapon delivery figures.

Finally, Hank, having decided that each aircraft would carry two weapons, pressed the 'enter' instruction again on his machine.

Despite all the planning, a lot could go wrong. His computer hard disc murmured and the spread sheet came up with the first answers. It told him that six aircraft would not be adequate to carry out the raid and kill all the ballistic missile launchers, with the degree of assurance demanded by his chief. Another adjustment. The chief could either have 90% assurance of achieving the required damage level, using six aircraft or 99% assurance, using eight. No one dare say 100% in war!

Hank took a swig of coffee and sat back with a sigh, as the last part of his activity turned from thought to action. Hank instructed the computer to select the graphs and source values, piece them together to form his attack weapon briefing and then finally transfer them onto his briefing disc. These took the sequence of the standard weapons briefing 'slides', the projected images which would be first seen and approved by his immediate Line Chief. Then, the next day, the flight crews would receive this information in their pre-flight briefing, together with details of their simulated target.

Simulated targets located along the low flying practice routes were used. Typically they would take some suitable route or other to Corsica or perhaps to Germany or Britain and use a bridge over a stream or a barn as the simulated target. The crew would have to bring back photographic evidence that they had found the target and positioned the aircraft correctly for a single pass attack.

Hank stopped. He had suddenly realised a peculiarity of the process of weapon planning. It is that the weapon planning process concentrates on getting the required minimum payload accurately onto the target. It was not his role to decide the safest outbound and return routes that would be flown. That would be the task of navigation and electronic warfare experts. This was, of course, less relevant if the defences themselves were to be attacked - but in this case they were not. Unless a co-ordinated raid was made by 'defence suppression' aircraft and carefully timed just before the surgical attack on the selected ballistic missile site, the air defences would still be in place. Nevertheless, these aircraft had special homing weapons to physically attack radars and jammers to confuse them. Hank thought perhaps his opposite number in some other place on another squadron, experienced in 'defence suppression', was currently planning another part of the same exercise. He would soon know, once they all came together for the main briefing.

If these suppression attacks were part of the overall plan they would have to be carefully timed so that the stealth aircraft's part in the practice raid would not be compromised. The exercise referees and monitors were very hot on this aspect of planning and execution. Pre-emptive defence suppression had the disadvantage of alerting the enemy that an attack on a nearby important site was imminent. The slightest indication of jamming of their radars or communications would inevitably warn the enemy of an impending attack. This strategy was often ruled out, particularly where stealth aircraft were involved. The stealthy aircraft would prefer to be on their own. Stealthiness was the order of the day! He flagged this option up on the display. Better mention all the options now, rather than have to do it later, he thought.

Finally, Hank despatched the results as a priority message, addressed to the Chief's mailing number on the secure internal electronic mail system, just a floor above. If he was in his office this would fire his on-screen 'attention-getter'. No doubt Hank would soon be hearing more, especially if his boss decided there was anything amiss with his planning.

Another routine task had been completed. No doubt there would be more of the same during this detachment!

He left the planning trailer and walked to the Officer's Club for a coffee and a spot of Spanish afternoon sun, reflecting that he hadn't seen much of Spain so far. Five minutes later Hank was called back. Some sealed orders had been delivered by messenger. He read, 'Pack up the mobile planning trailer and lock it up. Take all your planning results, documents, and the portable computer and report to the airfield immediately. Your flight will depart in two hours. Report to the Station Operations Block when you get there. Finally, tell no-one. Your move is TOP SECRET. Your mobile planning trailer will be following by Hercules within hours. You are going to Cyprus!'

Four hours later, Hank set up his portable computer in the temporary office provided in the Royal Air Force's Akrotiri Operations Block, located in the Sovereign British Area on the Southern Coast of Cyprus. His jet transport aircraft had landed only briefly, before flying on to Turkey. The Duty Officer had conveyed him through minimum formalities and provided him secure storage facilities until his trailer arrived. He wondered what he was doing there. He was still unaware of the drama in which the station and a Quicksilver squadron was about to take a critical part. The Comcen had not received any signals for him. He had expected to hear from his Chief - but so far - nothing. His orders were that no messages were to be sent back to Spain.

The recreational beach at Fisherman's Cove, Akrotiri, was within the Base Area. When nothing came back within the hour he locked everything up in the office safe, left a note of his whereabouts in the Ops Room, and went to enjoy a swim before sunset. As he left, passing through the outer operations room, he saw that the news event monitor was repeating yet more dire threats against nearby Israel - this time, from several nations. Perhaps they really mean it this time, he thought. He was just about to comment on the situation to a Corporal who was busy updating the aircraft movements tote board, when he suddenly remembered that it would not be wise to draw undue attention to his presence.

Hank left the building discreetly, still wondering why he had been rushed to

Cyprus. There seemed to be no other US service personnel about.

As the intense red sun lowered progressively further and finally kissed the sea, the temperature began to fall noticeably and the wind direction changed. The swim had been invigorating. Hank reluctantly turned back towards the airfield and began the trek back up the rocky path to the hill-top. This area near the beach was of molten rock. It was covered with small holes and prickly to the feet. He imagined it must be like the rocky surface of the moon. Yet there were good beaches here. Across the bay and the salt flats, could be seen the still shimmering mirage-like outline of the holiday resort of Limassol, as the street and vehicle lights came on. Just ahead the airfield lay spread out before him.

Forty years ago this had been a busy base and a major staging post to the Far East. It was one of the Royal Air Force's largest installations, with thousands of staff and dozens of aircraft. Britain had built a large military hospital here in the days of the Cold War. In those days, and even as recent as two decades ago, British Forces had still been garrisoned all over the world - but the British Empire had continued to decline. In those days many thousands of families had stopped off in Cyprus to re-fuel while en route to, or from, some exotic posting. Others, had found themselves destined for less exotic climes. These were usually unaccompanied soldiers, sailors or airmen who would endure six months, without their families, at some far-flung outpost, deemed essential at the time to Britain's interests. Others had the good fortune to remain in Cyprus for two or three years. A permanent summer holiday!

The Sovereign British Areas had been set up in the south, after the island had been divided between the Greek and Turkish Cypriots. This followed the 1950's Turkish invasion. Ever since, there had remained a stalemate with the Turkish Cypriot zone in the North, the Greek Cypriot zone in the South. The United Nations were still located on the 'green line', in between the opposing sides. Dusk was falling rapidly now.

As Hank plodded on, weary after the day's events, he caught a faint humming sound on the warm breeze. Almost simultaneously he spotted the silhouettes of several aircraft in loose formation approaching from the west. It was a surprise when an entire squadron of Quicksilver aircraft appeared. They landed in quick succession. His dilemma was suddenly clarified. It looked as if this incoming squadron would be carrying out the weapons exercise that he had planned, from this base. Nevertheless, it was a mystery why this training should be classified as Top Secret. The steep path levelled and he lengthened his stride. As he came over the brow of the hill, close to the fast-darkening airfield, he could see two Hercules support aircraft and their ground-crews rapidly marshalling the taxi-ing Quicksilvers into dispersals. The big tactical transports must have approached from the other direction while he was on the beach.

President Sheaffer had decided to keep a low profile following his last communiqué. Surely this madman of the Middle East would back down and not press the nuclear button to bring chaos to the world in the next two days? The world's media were getting restless, sensing that something - as yet not clear - was going on. It was still difficult to decide how much output from Iran was rhetoric and how much was real intent. The Press could not quite understand why Iran had taken this turn, just when things seemed to have quietened down a little in the region.

The President's Chief of Staff would be arriving in Washington in the next few minutes, to provide another update briefing. He would be accompanied by the one Star General from NATO Southern Region HQ. However, on this occasion the General would be wearing his US Air Force 'Hat', as this was not to be a NATO mission. The final decision to 'go' would be the President's. The UK government had readily agreed that the mission could be mounted from Cyprus, so at least he had overcome that hurdle.

Turkey would not be informed until the attack aircraft were actually on their way, as they would not be happy about the over-flights on a live mission. If things became awkward the US would be able to claim that Turkey knew nothing of the activity in their airspace. The stealthy aircraft would probably not be seen on Turkish radars, anyway. Hence Turkey, in ignorance of the mission, would not necessarily be implicated in any repercussions.

President Al Shaeffer's advisers were well aware of Britain's situation. Despite a vigorous environmental lobby, the nation still relied very heavily on oil. The four billion barrels, estimated in the newer Atlantic Foinaven oilfield, just to the North West of Britain, was not yet fully on stream. Also, despite the newly opened Falklands Islands oilfields, the UK still depended heavily on Arab and Iranian oil - at least for the present. The British were well acquainted with the economic problems brought about by fluctuating oil prices, having once suffered a cut in value from almost 40 dollars a barrel to just over 17 dollars when the oil market collapsed back in 1986. Now, the price of oil had climbed to over $80 per barrel. The British Government's only limitation, in agreeing to the US use of their Cyprus airbase, was that no Iranian civilians should be attacked, or religious sites damaged.

Once again the President and his aides went through a full examination of the current situation. The weather had deteriorated in the target area, and, as a result, the loss of visibility had severely degraded the capability of satellite-borne reconnaissance sensors. Only four of the six target sites had been clearly imaged in the last available time-slots. The satellites had whizzed overhead, at several hundred kilometres altitude and travelling at a speed of several thousand metres a second. An unimaginable capability in the minds of most of the millions of the citizens in Third World nations! That the Iranian missiles were almost ready to launch was confirmed by the deep wheel ruts seen on some imagery. These made by the heavy refuelling tankers moving around the missiles, already loaded onto their mobile launchers.

The other two targets were totally obscured - even from the infra-red weather penetrating sensors. The analyst assigned to the task remarked that the cloud coverage and thickness must have been 'quite something over there - just at the time good visibility was hoped for'. It could be further assumed, from the weather forecasts, that the two sites would almost certainly remain unseen for the next two days. The attack would have to be planned on the assumption that the ballistic missile launchers on those sites would remain in position and not re-deploy to other sites, before the attack took place. If they moved the whole operation would be a disaster.

'Is there really no chance at all of getting pictures later today?' asked the President. 'Reports from the 'Met-man' are that the weather will close in even more by the weekend,' declared the Chief of Staff. He stressed, 'This would also mean very poor visibility for the aircraft crews if we delay the attack.' The President was not a forceful character, in fact the opposite - a mild mannered Southerner, complete with slow matching drawl. Was there no way around this predicament? He had one more night to sleep on the decision. Somewhat dejectedly, he went off to eat and sign some more of the inevitable government papers.

By midnight there was no change of stance of the Iranian leadership. President Sheaffer called it a day and turned-in.

As he prepared for bed the President realised that his proposed actions might well hike the price of oil again. He tossed and turned and finally fell asleep and dreamt of a whole row of 'nodding donkeys' who were relentlessly pumping oil. They stretched into the distance across a desert oilfield.

It all came down to oil stability in the end. The USA had been consuming a quarter of the world's oil, while the whole of Europe, including Russia and the Ukraine were using about a third. The Asians, from which President Shaeffer could expect support for his forthcoming actions, also needed about a quarter of the oil pumped.

At 3.30 am he was awoken by a worried aide - 'Iran has brought forward their deadline by 12 hours, Sir. The attack time-slot, for an Iranian missile attack on Israel, has now been reduced to 24 hours. It is time for an emergency meeting, Mr President.'

All stood as he entered the briefing room. All who had been summoned were there, some having flown in at just three hours notice. He sat and nodded to the Chief, who commenced the briefing.

'Gentlemen! Several will be aware of at least some of what I have to say. Others have been asked to attend so that your expertise can be drawn upon later in the meeting. Before reaching the critical part of the meeting I must spend some time setting the background scenario.'

'Just seven days ago the Prime Minister of Israel flew here on an urgent mission. He disclosed that Israel has recently developed and perfected a substitute for oil that is cheaper, safer, and easier to handle than the real thing. Without going into the technicalities of the invention, I can also disclose that the fuel is virtually pollution-free. Desirable as this sounds, I need hardly add what an impact such an invention will most certainly have on the future world economy - even on world geopolitical stability, unless handled very carefully.'

He paused to let the effect of his words, and the unique situation they portrayed, sink into the minds of his perceptive listeners.

The Chief continued, 'As you know, Israel has virtually no oil, while all the surrounding nations, most of which are hostile, have plenty. This situation, together with their continuous need for defence spending, despite the peace process, has been a critical drain on their economy for many years. Accessibilty to a new fuel is also very attractive to Israel, as they are having to purify water by desalinisation of sea water - this takes energy. The need to do this, as well as purchasing water, by tanker, from Turkey, has come about because of the peace process. Aquifers, previously under Israeli control, are now beneath Palestinian-controlled territory. Israel's economic situation has worsened, as the population has risen sharply with the large number of Jews able to leave their scattered nations and go to Israel, as a right. Included among these Jews have been many scientists and engineers of the highest calibre - principally leaving all parts of the former Soviet Union, now the Russian and other Republics. One of these eminent scientists has developed the new fuel.

'We are all aware that changing weather patterns seem to be bringing cooler winters and warmer summers - both require a greater fuel consumption for heating or cooling! Parts of the world with high oil consumption, and who now are suffering increased heat, are often subject to increased air pollution. Distant suppliers to Israel have been increasing the prices. From Israel's viewpoint the advantages of having their own fuel supply, albeit synthetic, are overwhelming. The thought of Israel selling their cheaper version around the nations, directly in the face of OPEC competition - and the resulting turmoil of sharply reduced profits which would follow - could be world-shaking.'

The Chief paused again, 'All this information was relayed to the US, just a week ago, in the greatest secrecy. Four days later Israel's Foreign Minister came to Washington with some very grim news. The secret of the existence of their new process to make cheap synthetic fuel, while not officially announced, had somehow got out, but the details of how it is actually made had not!' He referred to his notes. As the import of this revelation became clear, the audience were riveted on every word.

'Within two days the CIA had noted that an extraordinary OPEC Oil Ministers meeting had been called. Libya, Egypt, Saudi Arabia, Syria, Iraq and Iran were invited. This meeting was clearly called in emergency, with no prior notice. It was almost three weeks before their next routine meeting was scheduled. As far as can be established, this action was unprecedented in the annals of OPEC.

'The plot now thickens. Within hours, the Saudi Arabian Ambassador to the United Nations, in a cleverly contrived and casual way, engaged in conversation with our own UN Ambassador. With many others they were together at an evening reception in New York. The Saudi Ambassador speculated on what might happen if oil producers were threatened in any way. For example, if someone discovered a bonanza oil well requiring little drilling, or perhaps, a much cheaper way to crack the crude, without sharing this expertise with the other producers. He implied that it might be difficult to hold back retaliation against the originator of such an attractive source - since it would surely impact significantly on all other producers. He was clearly fishing for information.'

The Chief stopped to take a few sips of water before hurrying on. His audience were spellbound.

'Our Ambassador to the UN had not been aware of the information brought by to me by Israel's Prime Minister and, more importantly he was not aware of the Israeli Foreign Minister's follow-up visit and its immediate implication. Therefore, he did not react to what was said, other than being non-committal and wondered exactly what the Saudi Ambassador was getting at.

'However, during the evening the Iranian Ambassador to the UN also said something quite similar. As a result of these two diverse but mysterious conversations, both seemingly hinting at the same thing, he reported the exchanges to the White House, in his daily UN activities summary. At the time, it seemed to be some sort of signal he didn't understand.'

'His report ended with the question - had someone discovered a new, unannounced, oilfield somewhere? If this was so, why had he not been informed?

'Our analysis was that both nations - Saudi Arabia and Iran - had either found out independently about Israel's invention, or, more likely, the news had been shared at the Oil Ministers Meeting. Someone had obtained the information. They may also have found out that Israeli Ministers had visited Washington with no prior arrangements and either assumed or guessed that Israel had turned to the US for advice.

'The next phase, Ladies and Gentlemen, was swift and startling. Rhetoric against Israel from all the surrounding nations suddenly started to increase - although of course without mention of a reason. The broadcasters and newspaper editors were clearly ordered to step up their hostile output, presumably so as to prepare the masses for what might be coming next. Within a day or two - the precise text is here for anyone wishing to see it - Iran issued a private communiqué to the US, that they knew about the invention. It was, they emphasised, a cause for future world instability.

'Next came an ultimatum! It was addressed to the United Nations. Unless the invention was handed over to the United Nations for the good of all mankind - which really meant for the good of the oil producers who stood to lose most, then Iran would attack Israel with ballistic missiles, without warning'. 'This serious situation was immediately communicated at once to Israel's Prime Minister, in Jerusalem.'

The Chief then updated his audience on the current state of play on ballistic missile defence.

'Israel, as you may know, unlike the slower-moving US development programme, has completed the development and testing of her anti-ballistic missile programme. Of course, this has been achieved with significant US financial assistance.

'Many of you will know that our own programme of development originally commenced as part of the 'Star Wars' programme. However, because of the demise of the USSR, with the consequent expectation of a lowering of the threat, full deployment, with national multi-directional defensive coverage, has not yet taken place. Therefore, much of our equipment has been built and tested, but remained in storage.

'In contrast, since the beginning of this crisis, Israel has been working day and night. The aim is to rapidly enhance their partial system, deployed since the year 2000. They should have the extra equipment in place, in a day or two. Their long range radar is already working - so early warning would be given. The Israelis still have some Patriot missiles left since the Gulf War and have updated them in the last five years as a lower altitude layered defence. However, if an attack took place before full deployment, then some leakage of incoming missiles would be inevitable.'

As an aside, the Chief added that - 'the rhetoric from Iran, and others in the last 24 hours, had alerted the more perceptive members of Israel's population that some sort of confrontation might be coming. However, since the last peace accord, most had not believed it - or did not wish to believe it.' He went on, 'For the present, the population of Israel, are currently unaware of the synthetic fuel invention.

'As regards defences, we assess that, in theory, Israel will be in a position to fire at and intercept single, well spaced, ballistic missiles, approaching from any direction, within the next 48 hours. However, if several missiles are launched towards Israel at once, or from different directions simultaneously, they will not stand much chance of stopping them all. Any damage to the population or buildings will clearly depend on the type of warheads that they carry.

'Four more Iranian communications have since followed, each increasing the pressure. These have coincided with our reconnaissance satellite confirmation that the Iranian ballistic missile launchers have indeed been deployed to South West Iran. Clearly the intention is to get closer, so as to match their range capability to the intended targets in Israel.'

The glow of the overhead projector suddenly lit up the room, as the familiar outline maps of the Middle East were brought up. Circles indicated the range-coverage of Iran's Shahab 3 and Shahab 4 ballistic missiles. The audience could clearly see that the Shahab 3 was necessarily close to the Iraqi border, in order to reach Israeli targets. In the year 2003 it had been reported that the Shahab 3 range had been increased to more than 1300km, and that its payload was 500kg. This could certainly deliver a payload of mass destruction. The Shahab 4, reportedly with a 5000km range, could be located deeper inside Iran. The Chief mentioned that the Shahab 4, and possibly a Shahab 5 variant may not have been fully tested. Either of these was likely to be more accurate than the Shahab 3.

It was time to pause once again. This time for questions of clarification. There was silence. The stunned audience had none. The US, it seemed, had still not managed to disentangle itself from the Middle East, observed one listener to his neighbour. He did not say it loud enough for the President to hear!

THE ATTACK

Final mission planning was at an advanced stage. The President had given the order to go ahead with night-time attacks on Iran's forward-based mobile ballistic launchers. Darkness fell quickly in the Mediterranean and it was calculated that, coupled with 'stealth' operations, this would provide the greatest possible chance of surprise and hence success. Right from take-off there would be no radio transmissions until the squadron requested permission to re-join the Akrotiri air traffic pattern on their return from their sorties.

The large radar atop nearby Mount Olympus would initially monitor the flight of the Quicksilver aircraft. This would cover the period after take-off until the eight aircraft coasted in, while maintaining loose formation, at Askendrun on the South Eastern Turkish coast. Lieutenant Colonel Brett Forman, the Squadron Commander expected his crews to execute their airmanship flawlessly. Timing was critical.

After reaching the first rendezvous point they would each minimise their aircraft radar signature control successively, in a timed sequence. This would ensure that their radar echoes would gradually fade from the watching eyes of any alert microwave radar operator in the area. However, decametric, very long wave radars, would still be able to spot the aircraft - but no nations were known to operate these older radars, within the planned route. Any radar operators, including the merely curious, or any that might be potentially hostile on ships, or along the Syrian coastline, would see nothing unusual. As the Quicksilver signatures gradually vanished, they would assume that the unidentified radar contacts had descended for a low level run over the sea, and thus gone below radar coverage.

Once overland a very low radar reflectivity would be exhibited by each aircraft, in its 'stealth' mode. This would delay the detection of the Quicksilver aircraft by any hostile missile fire-control radar - where seconds would count - very difficult to detect in time to react and fire interceptor missiles. By then they hoped to be long gone! The stealth mode would also degrade the detection capability of any airborne radars, carried on hostile fighter aircraft, which may have fire control capability to guide air-to-air missiles. Stealth would also make things difficult for the two airborne early warning aircraft which Iran had recently acquired from Russia should they happen to be in the attack area, at the time.

After much discussion in the flight planning rooms, the crews had set up their individual routes. This would first position them over the sea, well to the east of Cyprus, at a regular turning point, used on training exercises. To reach this point they would make a normal climb-out from base, gradually climbing to about 10,000 feet. They would then descend to the north before making a starboard turn for a 15 kilometre run towards the Turkish coast. By the time they reached Iskenderun they would be flying in pairs and terrain-following, and at an altitude well below 1000 feet. This was all carefully planned so that they would not be spotted entering Turkish airspace by Syrian radar, based in the vicinity of the port of the Northern Syrian port of Latakyia. After that they would fly for a period up a north-south oriented, and very sparsely populated Turkish valley, before turning to the right, towards Iran.

It had been Hank's job to determine the raid weapon planning but not the survivability of the Quicksilver aircraft along their intended route. This task had been masterminded by the Squadron Navigation Officer together with the Electronic Warfare Specialist Officer. Together they had briefed the crews on the possible air defences they might encounter en route. Iran's latest Surface to Air Missile systems - SAMs - if satellite photography was to be believed, had not been deployed at any of the sites that they planned to attack. Accordingly, they concentrated on the best options to defeat the older SAMs. These could surely be expected at each site.

Calculations, even if taking the shortest routes possible, consistent with the maximum use of terrain screening, had determined that those crews tasked to reach the furthest targets would indeed need flight refuelling on the return leg. This operation was planned for the vicinity of Adana in south eastern Turkey. This process would provide plenty of fuel reserves in the event that they had to divert from Cyprus to Malta, on their return.

To achieve this exit from Turkey covertly, the returning pairs of aircraft would remain at low level from the Iranian border and then climb to 10,000 feet as they passed near Adana - as though just departing Adana airfield. Flying in loose formation, they would then race-track during the refuelling. To avoid conflict with any actual Adana aircraft, which might be flying in the vicinity, several advanced, but phoney, flight plans, showing aircraft arriving from a westerly direction, had been despatched to Adana air traffic control centre. These supposed aircraft would indeed appear on radars to coincide with the correct timing, but they would actually be Quicksilver aircraft returning from their raids. This was a critical part of the operation to de-couple any overt Turkish knowledge of the raid.

The early evening lights of Limassol town twinkled across the bay as they started engines and taxied forward from Akrotiri's dispersal 'Golf'. Within two minutes Lieutenant Colonel Brett Forman opened the throttles just a final touch and his Quicksilver rapidly responded, by lining-up on Akrotiri's runway 28. After take-off a 'rate one' left-hand climbing turn over the sea would be executed, so as to bring them round onto their initial Easterly climb-out heading, of 093 degrees.

The cockpit noise level rose as, brakes on, Brett listened and acted upon the vital actions read out by the practised voice of Hiram Erlich, his Navigator. First the pre-take-off check-list and then the take-off countdown, right to the second. Glancing to his left and behind, he spotted his wing-man Jerry Hennig in 'Tango Hotel'. Even further back, still on the taxiway, the rest of the squadron were waiting to line up for their turn in the imminent, pair-wise, take-off. Each pair would follow quickly on the lead pair and within two minutes all would be riding on the slip-stream of the pair ahead, turning and climbing effortlessly.

There was no take off call to the tower. They saw the green light. The count-down reached zero and Brett opened up the engines. Quicksilver Tango Bravo accelerated along the concrete and lifted smoothly into the night sky, his number two close to the side, taking an occasional buffeting from his leader's turbulence. As the aircraft turned, Brett could not see the rest of the squadron, as a lights-off order had been given to make the take off as covert as possible.

Eight Quicksilvers in the sky at once were still a rare sight in Cyprus and this would reduce the chances of observation while near the ground. They would, however, use navigation lights once they were away from land as they climbed out, as an aid to formation-keeping. The lights would again be dowsed at exactly 25 kilometres off the Turkish coast and night vision goggles would come into their own, for the rest of the mission. Unless close to the airfield it was always more difficult for a person on the ground to count aircraft off in the dark, when there was a lot of noise and few lights. Further, as they would be turning to the left, this would give the impression that they were going into the normal night flying routine.

They climbed away from Akrotiri for precisely six minutes. To Brett, with much on his mind, it seemed like just seconds before they reached the first way-point, indicated on the flight instruments, and turned towards the north-east. Shortly afterwards, they started their descent. At once they moved into pairs in a loose trail. As several target destinations were involved, each pair would be responsible for their own navigation once they coasted in, over Turkey, in just a few minutes time. At the appropriate point, each pair would leave the entry track and turn towards their allotted route to their individual targets

Brett had faith that the weapon effort planning had gone well. His target was the furthest to reach and he had total confidence in Hank. After all, Hank had been his Navigator/EWO in the now far-off days of the raid on Libya. Brett's aircraft turned north on the satellite navigation system command, precisely at the correct point. He glimpsed several pairs of navigation lights astern as he turned. The whole squadron was there, with no failures so far. It was time to dowse the lights.

Back to the job in hand. The plan was to turn right abeam Iskenderun. It was just coming up ahead. This was well south east of Adana, which had been a major US base in the days of the Cold War. Now it was the domain of the Turkish Air Force and Turkish Airlines, with the occasional NATO transit aircraft and training sorties. They would soon skirt the northern Syrian, and later the northern Iraqi borders for as long as possible; not wishing to alert the Turkish, Syrian or Iraqi radar operators.

For their routing the flight planners had made maximum use of the terrain screening that is obtainable in this mountainous area. All aircraft heavily relied on a combination of the satellite navigation system, accurate to about 15 metres in position and their nose-mounted individual terrain following radar equipment. Each aircraft pair would take equally well selected routes to reach their respective targets.

Quicksilver Tango Bravo would pass well to the south of the Turkish airfields at Gaziantep and Sanluifa, then to the North of the towns of Viranshir and Mardin, north of Sinak and finally turn north of Hakkan. Ahead would be their primary target - the Iranian ballistic missile prepared launch site, at Shahpur. Afterwards, they would fly on to their secondary target at Orumiyeh. Both of these launch positions had been identified by the last satellite pass before they left Cyprus, and identified as sites that were ready to launch weapons against Israel within a few hours.

Brett switched on the Radar Warning Receiver - the 'RWR', as the crews called the device. It would both visually and aurally indicate if a hostile radar capable of controlling surface-to-air or air-to-air weapons was pointed at the Quicksilver aircraft. He checked out the warning system thoroughly and asked Hiram to make a final check of the aircraft's Weapon Aiming System. Within a few seconds the serviceability of both the 'RWR' and the 'WAS' had been confirmed and he announced that the mission was 'go'. They had passed the point of no return.

The responsive jamming system was also warmed-up. This was in preparation for the unwanted, but likely expectation, that an air defence weapon control radar might be pointed at their aircraft, at some later stage during the sortie. This jammer would then respond automatically with the correct signals to jam or confuse the radar which threatened them. Assuming, of course, that the intelligence used to set up the jammer was correct! Their worst fears were that an enemy might spring a 'technical surprise', and somehow change the radar characteristics. The Quicksilver jamming equipment could thus be rendered ineffective.

Brett compared his moving map display against the Satellite Ground Positioning System values. These constantly changed on his glowing instruments as the aircraft skimmed and weaved over the mountainous terrain almost at supersonic speed. In the valleys the RT was silent as they passed through Turkish territory.

Everything looked good, although as they approached their final way-point, a thin but nevertheless annoying layer of cloud obscured the sight-line to a small lake. It was one of the few natural landmarks, in the rough wilderness below, that was suitable as a way-point in this part of the world!

Soon, they were rapidly approaching the target area. The thermal imaging display was invaluable. Even though it was pitch black outside, this British-supplied equipment, originally developed just before the Gulf War, produced a wide-angle view of the terrain ahead. The superimposed cross wires of the weapon-aiming system came up clearly. These, in turn, were bore-sighted with the laser beam that would provide the homing energy for the first 'Sleek' weapon. Hiram was head-down, concentrating on the view ahead. The navigator in the other aircraft - their wing-man - would be doing the same, also flying now at a little under three hundred and forty metres per second.

In the side-by-side seating arrangement both crew members could search the imaging display for the first sign of the key identification feature - a bridge on the precipitous mountain road, along which the ballistic missile transporter must have travelled so recently, carrying its deadly cargo. Both crew members also had night vision goggles which enabled a good view to be maintained through the cockpit windows. The advantage of imaging equipment was that it could not only see in the dark, but also magnify the field of view and zoom the display.

The moving map, image display and satellite system reports all checked out, once again. The target was about 4 kilometres ahead - not much more than 13 seconds to go! A small adjustment to the flying controls by Brett, and simultaneous call, 'Target in sight!' from Hiram, was closely followed by the call for bomb-bay open. The aiming cross-wires were placed and auto-locked on the ballistic missile that could be seen nestling ahead, on its partially erected launcher. Brett could even see figures moving about on the ground nearby - probably the missile handling and refuelling crews. The aircraft's invisible laser beam came on. The 'target acquired lamp' almost immediately announced that the laser seeker in the nose of the Sleek weapon had locked-on. Within the next four seconds the first weapon had left the aircraft. The Quicksilver shuddered briefly as the airflow was disturbed as the weapon left and the bomb-doors closed automatically. The auto-track gimbals, mounted under the nose, began their task of keeping the imaging optics laser beam pointed and locked onto the target, as the aircraft went through its escape manoeuvre. Within the indicated impact time of just a few remaining seconds they would either have a success or a total failure.

As they turned, immediately after the weapon left the aircraft, Brett caught a glimpse of his wing-man, his silent shadow for so many kilometres of low-level flight. This was accompanied by the radar warner bursting into life. Almost at once there was a blinding flash and an explosion astern. If the hostile radar lock-on had occurred earlier, the RWR would have given a warning and electronic countermeasures responded. However, because of the terrain constraints during the run in to the attack, there had been no chance to use manoeuvre earlier, to confuse the defences. They would normally have 'jinked', but this was out of the question in this rugged terrain. Almost immediately as it had triggered, the RWR fell silent again. Although the sky was dark again, both the aircraft's thermal-imaging system and the crew's night vision goggles had been momentarily overloaded by the bright flash reflected from the ground.

A surface-to-air missile - or 'SAM' - had either fused on Brett's wing-man or had been command-destructed by whoever launched it from the ground. Possibly it had been fired at Brett's aircraft in the lock-after-launch mode, and failed to catch up its target. As they turned, a towering pillar of billowing smoke could be seen. It was partially obscuring the target. There was a red pulsating glow at its root. The effects of the sideways, or 'lateral acceleration', as they turned was partly compensated by the pressure on their bodies provided by their 'g' suits. Brett had high hopes of bringing his Quicksilver home - at least he hoped so - but there were other things to do first. Their escape profile allowed a brief oblique infra-red camera shot. It was this and video of the infra-red attack phase that would be transmitted, via a satellite, orbiting several hundred kilometres overhead, for the analysts. With a second target to attack, they were not out of trouble yet!

For the moment everything seemed to be happening together. Once again the radar warning receiver signal insistently sounded, as two scanning SAM radars tried to lock onto the aircraft. This time, from abeam. They must have deployed some mobile SAMs on the road, that had not been spotted by the intelligence satellite.

In the regime of 'stealth' operations, silence was golden. This meant that in addition to the aircraft designer having reduced the Quicksilver aircraft body radar reflectivity and minimised the infra-red signature from the engines, no radio emissions were made, except the downwards emission for the terrain following, height lock, radar altimeter. In fact, apart from this unwelcome and chilling sound of enemy missile-laying radars, the background 'mush' of the radio guard channel in their headsets was all they had heard, since leaving Cyprus. Flying at low level they had been unable to receive any radio transmissions that were not in a direct sight-line to their aircraft antennas. They had been mainly valley-flying, and thus screened by the terrain from any radio traffic. They had no idea whether any hostile air defence fighters might be up above, searching for them already.

Their first attack had more than advertised their presence to the enemy, so radio silence could be briefly broken. Brett made a brief exploratory call to his wing-man. 'Tango Hotel - over.' Silence! He repeated the call once more. There was no reply from Tango Hotel.

The RWR was still receiving the pervasive and aggressive, but now thankfully fading sound of a missile fire control radar, operating in the locked-on mode. Brett hoped that his aircraft's built-in responsive aircraft jammer and expendable decoy reflectors were doing their stuff. He had no way of knowing the effectiveness of the countermeasures that were being emitted by the jamming pod. Only the enemy SAM radar operator, hunched over a radar display below and far behind, would know. Either he could see Brett's aircraft and, if within missile range, was planning to launch another missile - or the jamming on his screen would be effective and confuse the operator. Hopefully, the jamming radiated from the aircraft might even degrade an automatic system sufficiently, so as to over-rule a missile launch. It was some consolation that rear missile attacks, where a missile was flying in a 'catch-up' mode, were much less effective.

The next transmission from Brett's aircraft was the 'squash' transmission in an upward direction towards the ever-orbiting satellites. This unloaded the contents of Brett's infra-red linescan and video cameras that had been running during the attack. These would hopefully give some information on the performance of their mission to the operations centre - should they fail to return!

This was no time to catch a missile up the jet-pipe. At least two missile radars had been locked on for several seconds despite the weave which Brett was now flying in the hope of shaking them off. This evasive manoeuvre was necessarily limited in its lateral scope as they continued to flee down the valley that had been pre-planned as their escape route. Even at a speed of hundreds of miles an hour every second counted.

Would another missile be launched or a salvo of two? The further they gained ground increased the likelihood of survival. Brett prayed that the Quicksilver, with throttles well open, would win the race.

There was a possibility that either Brett's radio transmitter or his wing-man's radio receiver was not working. Brett hoped this was the case. Nevertheless, he feared the worst when there was no sign of his wing-man catching up behind. If they had been hit, wing-man Jerry and his navigator, Jim Jernigan in Tango Hotel, might have ejected. If so, they would be under extreme pressure to evade capture and survive until, hopefully, they could be extracted from this foreign and inhospitable terrain. This, provided that they had survived the thousands of high velocity tungsten fragments, propelled towards their aircraft by the explosive in the missile warhead.

Brett noted that the hostile audio warnings on the RWR had significantly faded, as he moved the aircraft around a rocky outcrop. The radar warning then abruptly ceased and they were away in the clear and fast-descending towards the relative safety of Lake Urmia; soon to turn south towards their second planned target, Orumiyeh. They could relax a little after a hectic few minutes.

Target number two was located just to the west of the lake. They were particularly watchful. They had to assume that the Orumiyeh ballistic missile launch site would have been alerted, following their attack on the first site. A very unwelcoming reception committee indeed may be waiting! At almost zero feet over the lake they had assessed that, even if the enemy had managed to scramble fighter aircraft, or even had one of their new Airborne Early Warning aircraft up, the probability of detecting their Quicksilver was very low. Further, at this very low altitude, the probability of a good enemy radar lock onto their aircraft was also reduced, by the likelihood of confusing radar reflections from the relatively smooth surface of the lake.

As Tango Bravo came abeam the small town of Orumiyeh, Brett turned towards the coastline of the lake. There was no sign of Tango Hotel. They were on their own. They could not rely on the combined effect of two jamming pods, should hostile radars be present. The next few seconds would be crucial.

The opposition they had encountered at Shahpur was not unexpected. However, it might indeed have been more effective than they had assessed during mission planning. Brett wondered how the other crews under his command were faring at the other targets. He offered up a silent prayer and wished them well. Time was passing rapidly and the coast was rapidly approaching as Brett lifted the aircraft slightly, as they flew onwards, over the almost flat calm of the large freshwater lake. Mustn't fly into the water at this stage!

Although it was quite dark, their night vision goggles provided a clear view ahead. The terrain, here in Iran, reminded Brett of a holiday spent in Turkey, much further to the west, in the tranquillity of nature. Soft breezes blowing through the pines, the myriad ripples of the lake, birds, wild flowers and the rustle of leaves, the Tahtah mountains as a backdrop, the bubble of a stream. Get a grip! He had allowed his mind to wander. This was no time for romantic thoughts!

Their next turning point was coming up fast. Hiram pointed ahead at the swathe of trees down to the water's edge. Within seconds they were back overland and refining the heading as they passed over the last way-point before the final run-in to their target. The radar warner remained silent. Visibility had improved significantly. Optically, this worked both ways round - if they could see the target, then, most probably, the target's air-defence operators could also see them! Had the Iranians procured low-light night vision television for their radar trackers? Intelligence were not sure! Hence, during planning, the worst case was assumed. Such systems were a considerable problem for Brett and his squadron, since, once they approached to within a few kilometres, they could be watched, tracked and fired-at completely passively. Therefore, in the absence of radar emissions, they would receive no indication from their radar warner. The only warning would be from their IR flash detector, at the moment when a missile motor was ignited. Flying at two or three times the speed of sound, a head-on closing missile would reach them in a few seconds.

Things were going well on this run. They picked up the final identification point almost at once. Positive target acquisition followed in quick succession. So far, their tactic in coming in from very low over the lake had apparently succeeded.

Within seconds their last weapon was released. They executed the escape manoeuvre, briefly observed the spectacular explosion, finally set course for home and transmitted their second set of recce photographs. They had successfully run the gauntlet of the defences in ingressing Iran's airspace. Now they must survive, homeward-bound. As they turned towards the first home-bound navigation way-point there was a slight shudder as the pressure wave of an explosion behind caught up with the aircraft. Most probably a surface-to air missile fired towards their rapidly receding radar profile. Thankfully, it had failed to catch them up. Most probably it had self-detonated, after failing to find its target.

There was silence apart from the normal flight sounds and the fading warbling of the enemy fire control radar, still faintly intercepted by the rearward-facing radar warning antennae. Obviously, with their infra-red signature fading with range, the enemy had switched on their radar, as a last attempt to re-launch.

Brett scanned the instruments, noting a that a small but measurable rise in jet-pipe temperature had been registered - a sign that all was not one hundred per cent with the aircraft's propulsion system. Possibly a sign of minor jet-pipe damage. Everything else was fine - but one did not, as in the old days, get a stiffening of flying controls if anything was partially damaged.

Mechanical linkages for flight control had long gone. Everything these days was done by 'fly-by-wire' electronics - with only a fibre-optic cable carrying information. No more push-rods and tortuously-routed control cables that traversed the length of the aircraft body. Brett hoped that any real problems would not show-up, at least until they were back in the relative safety of Turkish airspace. He asked Hiram for a fuel calculation and was relieved to find that they had enough fuel to reach base, without the need for flight refuelling.

They turned south towards the Mediterranean - pleased that they were not, after all, in need of the pre-positioned, slowly circling, re-fuelling tanker high above. The others squadron members might need the fuel, indeed some pairs may already have used the tanker, as they progressed homewards. Now they would be behind Brett, as they took up enough fuel to reach Cyprus, with some to spare for unforeseen diversions.

Even after the long route Brett was first of the squadron back to base. He finished off his report to the Debriefing Officer in a mixture of elation and sadness. So far there was no sign of his own wing-man. The next pair were not due back for several more minutes. He drew on a mouthful of strong coffee, noticing the caricature that the, now fading, pressure of Hiram's oxygen mask had impressed onto his navigator's normally smooth skin. Back in the USA information had been down-loaded, in near real time, from the up-linked aircraft recconaisance video cameras. Nevertheless, everyone would still undergo the old-fashioned face-to-face debriefing. It had been ever the same, since World War 1. The actual recorder cassettes were being unloaded from Brett's aircraft even now. They would be meticulously scanned by the photo-interpreters. Indeed they would be essential, as the only record of the attacks, if the satellite video links had malfunctioned.

Brett waited in the operations room and heard with relief that a Quicksilver aircraft had just made its return call to the control tower. He expected that two aircraft would be cleared to land shortly. The others should follow soon afterwards.

Some ten minutes later, after the crew bus had trundled across the airfield, Brett's relief vanished. Only two, instead of four aircrew, entered the room. It was not the lead crew but that of the wing-man of the second pair.

'Where's Bill?' 'No idea,' replied Bill's wing-man, Joe Rodero. His Navigator/Electronic Warfare Officer, from Tango Alpha, nodded glumly. 'We were close up until the final way-point at the second target. It was a little misty in the valley one minute he was just ahead and then he just vanished.' 'Maybe he's landed elsewhere,' Brett said. He slumped into an arm-chair.

'We must also face the fact that I may have lost my wing-man,' said Brett. 'There was no reply when we called him after the attack and there was no sign of him on the way back either. If he had landed somewhere else en route, or even gone for refuelling, we should have heard by now.' 'Unless, of course, there's a comms failure somewhere,' added Hiram, hopefully. He lifted his gaze from the floor and turned to the others. 'Did you hit your targets?' asked Brett.

'The first was OK', Bill replied. 'We saw the leader's weapon explode, though, curiously, after our own attack, there were no secondary explosions. In fact, as we turned away after our run, there was virtually no fire at all, but we definitely hit it all right - dead centre.' 'Very odd!' Brett remarked, ' if they had hit a missile on its launcher before it was fuelled, this might have been the reason for no collateral fuel explosion.'

The standard debrief commenced, by the end of which more aircraft should have been back.

After thirty minutes Brett strode to the 'squawk box'. 'Any calls yet from Tango Whiskey ?' 'Negative,' came the rasping reply from the Duty Air Traffic Controller. 'Let me know at once if you hear,' he growled - 'Oh, and another thing. The same applies if you hear of any diversions.' He released the key switch. It sprang to the 'off' position. There was a dreadful silence.

'Still plenty of options,' said the debriefing officer cheerily, after several seconds. Brett was not so sure and asked for more coffee. Surely not, he told himself, over and over again. The others went off to get a meal.

Brett had waited in Ops for almost an hour, when the Duty Corporal snatched up the red telephone on its second ring. 'Washington. For you, sir,' turning towards Brett. Brett grasped the instrument with a trembling hand. 'Lt Col Foreman here.' 'Please hold,' an American voice said, 'The General's Aide wishes to speak.' He went on, 'Please confirm that the 'pips' are present - scrambler 'on' - then go ahead.'

He listened for the tell tale pips, while struggling to decide what to say at this stage. Scrambler pips heard! Brett stumbled through the next few minutes, pointing out the options as best he could. There was little reaction from the caller. He was probably taking briefing notes to relay to the General, who would have seen some of their satellite-linked pictures by now - and some from any of the others who had reached and attacked their individual targets.

At the back of his mind Brett feared the worst but could not bring himself to tell Washington the clear possibility - indeed likely probability of both a mission failure and loss of several Quicksilver aircraft. Of the crews, one could only hope they had parachuted to safety and were now carrying out correct survival procedures, as effectively as others had done before.

The call was not over. 'Any reaction from the target nation?' he heard himself ask. Not knowing what else to say. 'None at present,' came the reply. The line disconnected.

After a further two hours, Brett, as exhausted as the others, fell into bed, having declined the offered sleeping tablets from the Medical Officer. All involved on the ground, both hosts and the detached Quicksilver support crews, had been briefly called together and reminded of the strict 'need to know' rule which applied to the night's fateful activities. The picture might be clearer in the morning - which was now fast approaching. The fate of the others was unknown. The media were bound to have a field day when the news broke.

Follow-on activities were proceeding. The evacuation support transport aircraft had arrived, carrying relief Quicksilver crews. It looked as though they would not all be needed. Their task would be to ferry those few remaining aircraft, that had survived the operational sortie, back to Spain. They had been planned to leave within the next hour. Hank, still in Ops Centre, requested a further hour's delay, in case any more Quicksilver aircraft arrived - perhaps, he hoped, after diverting and re-fuelling. As nothing had been heard it was probably a forlorn hope. The transport support crew would meanwhile pack their aircraft, embark the ground crews, and lastly would board Brett and the others, awoken from a fitful sleep, to begin the westward flight to Spain. Cyprus would be 'clean'. The overall operation had taken longer than planned and their mates were missing.

Several thousand miles away President Al Sheaffer was plunged into yet another dilemma. Firstly, he had to inform the Prime Minister of Great Britain and agree a strategy if the news leaked. Next, should he wait or activate the pre-planned contingency - the cruise missile attack? Satellite cover was now impossible, because of the weather. Beyond the pictures taken and transmitted during the previous night's operations, there was no way of obtaining more on what had actually happened at each of the target sites. Similarly, there would be no monitoring of cruise missile performance, if they were despatched for repeat attacks.

The Quicksilver failure had unnerved the President. He opted to leave things for 24 hours and await reactions. There was just a faint possibility that the cloud might thin and allow a satellite inspection of the damage. He asked for every effort to be made to ascertain the fate of the lost crews. The listening stations close to the target area redoubled their efforts in attempts to try and intercept Iranian military messages that might indicate survival. AWACS aircraft were continually on patrol along the Iranian border, searching for emergency transmissions from the crews lifejacket beacons.

The President called for a full briefing the next day. It would be combined with a brain-storming session by selected experts, to consider the best way ahead.

That night the President of The United States of America - the strongest nation on earth - retired to bed, a humiliated man. Although no announcements would be made for some time, as if sensing a world crisis of some sort, several stock markets around the world had suffered severe falls. The pundits, knowing nothing of the night's events, just supposed that another indication of how fragile the world economic structures had become, since the start of the third millennium.

Within twenty four hours the United States of America would be castigated by other world leaders. Within days the United Nations - called to emergency assembly - would condemn the action that had been taken and had failed. With a majority of nations opposed to Israel and the West, most of the nations would have also condemned the USA anyway - even if the attack had succeeded!

Far more dramatic consequences would follow within weeks - which would not just worry, but indeed shake the nations to the core.

THE DEFEAT

Dawn was just breaking. Despite the deadening effect of the plush surroundings, hanging wall coverings, the several layers of Persian carpets and the overstuffed settees, the voice of their leader made them all jump. 'Our Swords of Islam have been attacked. Someone has bombed our ballistic missile launchers during the night.' He continued, 'It must be Israel. A Holy War - a Jihad - is surely called for!' The others assented. This was not the time to disagree. A frenzied and animated discussion began. More information was expected at any moment.

The door opened and a messenger bowed and approached the leader, bowed again and whispered briefly. A report was passed. He stared at it for a few seconds. 'Eight of our ballistic missile sites were attacked, but only two suffered real damage. Fortunately, these had commenced routine movement procedures. One was attacked as it lowered its missiles. The others had left their sites to re-deploy and had, prior to moving-on, left their decoy weapons behind. Any damage to these sites was therefore inflicted on wooden and plastic decoys!' Those present looked at each other and grinned.

There was more. 'Our glorious defences, with the new, fully automatic, Russian mobile TOR M1 SAM equipment which moved with the launchers and accompanied them on each site, shot down no less than six of the cowardly raiders!'

'From the wreckage that was visible, when daylight came, no markings could be seen. All the craft were dark grey in colour but not a type that we could recognise immediately. They may be of a new type, not seen in this region before. So far, one body of a crewman has been found and one empty crew ejection seat, near a road. We are searching the area, but it is among the mountains to the south west. They attacked all our mobile ballistic missiles that had been deployed further towards the border than normal, to enable them to reach Israel.' There was silence.

'We shall act at once for all our demands to be met. Since dawn the surviving ballistic missile launchers have almost arrived at new sites, even further shortening the range to reach Israel. The great Satan must have used satellites to find our sites in the mountains - and told Israel. We will show them! The weather is worsening in the whole area and I swear they shall not see us this time, until it is too late. Neither will the big eye in the sky be able to see that nearly all our systems are intact or even know what happened to their barbarous raid.' They all nodded.

President Al Sheaffer was gently awoken by an aide. It seemed like, as he remarked, 'he had only just gotten to sleep.' 'Time,' the aide repeated for the fourth time, 'for your meeting, Mr President.'

Within a few minutes he entered the situation room. All were present whom he had summoned, the political strategists as well as the military came to order. It was 0500 hours local time. Several had flown in at a few hours notice from across the States. He nodded to the Chief of Staff to commence the briefing. He realised that some of the audience would require repetition of much of the earlier attack briefing, including the rationale behind the original decision.

'Gentlemen - Good Morning. Several of you will already be aware of some of what I have to say. Others have been asked to attend so, that your expertise can be drawn upon later in the meeting.' He looked down at his notes. 'Firstly, I must bring you all up to date on a most serious situation which has developed in the last few days. This has been ongoing since the Prime Minister of Israel flew here on an urgent visit. He disclosed to our President that Israel had developed and perfected an oil substitute for motor vehicles that is much cheaper than oil. Further, it is virtually pollution free. Despite the apparent attractiveness of such an invention, I hardly need to tell you of the impact that it will have on the world economy, unless its introduction is carefully controlled.' He paused to let the sum effect of this unique situation penetrate the perceptive minds of his listeners.

'As you know, Israel has virtually no oil, while all the surrounding hostile nations have plenty. Added to their defence burdens, this scenario has been a critical drain on the economy of Israel for many years. Further, the situation has worsened recently, as the population has risen sharply since the arrival of many more thousands of Jews, a trend that started after the demise of the Soviet Union. It has been further strengthened by thousands more who have left the USA, Argentina and France to live in Israel. This is the right of any Jew.

'Information concerning the invention was imparted to The President under the greatest secrecy.'

The audience were spell-bound by this revelation and the following information.

'Four days later Israel's Foreign Minister, Reuben Harel, also came to the USA in extreme haste. He brought some very grim news. Knowledge of the existence of the invention, but not the actual detail of the processes involved, had been leaked. Within two days the CIA noted that an extraordinary, indeed an emergency Oil Ministers meeting was attended by Libya, Egypt, Saudi Arabia, Iraq and Iran.' He again paused for effect and looked round at the President, who was staring at his fingers as if the answer to their latest crisis would be there.

'The oil cartel had met with no prior notice. Within hours both the Iranian and Saudi Arabian Ambassadors to the United Nations - in a cleverly contrived and casual way - speculated to our own Ambassador, what might happen if oil was replaced one day and if oil producers were threatened in any way. In fact, both remarked that it might be difficult to hold back retaliation against the originator of such a source, since it would surely impact very severely on all oil producers. Gentlemen,' he continued, 'I hope that I do not need to remind you that two thirds of the world's known oil reserves are in the Middle East, and that the area is a diplomatic and military flash-point.

'This speculation, by the two Ambassadors, occurred at a diplomatic social function. At the time it seemed too much of a coincidence when it was discovered that the idea had been put forward by two different nations on the same night. On our later analysis it was decided that both nations, indeed perhaps even others, had somehow found out about the discovery. The Ambassadors were clearly sounding out the US, perhaps on the assumption that Israel had told the US.

'We soon realised that it was possible that all the nations who attended the recent, unplanned, Oil Ministers meeting might know, so a communications check was run. It revealed a sudden and unprecedented increase in contacts recently taken place between the senior figures of these nations.

'The next phase, Gentlemen, was startling. Without actually mentioning the invention, Middle East media rhetoric, against the State of Israel, was markedly increased from all the oil-producers nearby. It takes various forms, and is still ongoing, as I speak.'

He picked up a sheet of notes, then continued. 'After a few days - the text is here for anyone wishing to read it - Iran issued a private communiqué to the US. I quote verbatim, "that unless the invention was handed over to the United Nations, for the good of all mankind" - which really meant for the good of all the oil producers on which it would presumably impact - "Iran would attack Israel with ballistic missiles, without warning". We communicated this serious situation at once to Jerusalem.'

He paused. The audience were hanging on every word. 'Four more Iranian communications have since followed, each applying more pressure. It was confirmed, with US surveillance satellite confirmation, that Iran's mobile ballistic missile launchers had indeed been deployed to forward sites in South West Iran, matching their range capability to their intended targets in Israel.'

The overhead projector flashed up a map of Southern Iran, Syria, Lebanon and the North of Israel. Range circles, superimposed on the map, clearly indicated that the 1300km estimated range limits of the Iranian missiles could reach most of Israel. The missiles, the speaker said, had been assessed to have been programmed to reach Israeli targets. The lamp went off. All eyes returned to the speaker, poised intently over his notes behind the podium. The specialists in his audience noted that he had not mentioned the Shahab 3 missile, with a reported range of 3000km.

The Chief then explained how the USA had requested urgent discussions with the Iranian government and suggested that the UN Secretary General should be involved at once. There had been a negative reply.

The Chief continued. 'We could not let such an attack occur. As a result, I have to tell you Gentlemen, that you have been called here to best-advise the President of his options, in the current scenario.

'To bring you right up to date there is another major factor - the most important one.' He paused, reached under the lectern and took a long draft from the beaker of water. His listeners were not prepared for what followed, as the map once again appeared on the screen, with the addition of aircraft tracks.

'Last night, at about 0330 hours Middle Eastern Time, a further phase of the crisis took place. The President and Chiefs of Staff had decided that a confrontation was necessary, to avert an actual attack on Israel. There was corroborated and irrefutable intelligence to support our actions. We had to act in time. Events were happening at speed. It was clear that there was an intent to attack Israel, within hours. Iran had frequently threatened Israel, and the oil discovery was an ideal justification, indeed an excuse to attack. We had given Iran every opportunity to withdraw the threat and discuss the issues - but their thinking and actions had clearly gone beyond the point of no return.'

'It is a recurrence of the oil resources problem. We could not risk the possibility of a third party - Russia, who have been supplying Iran with arms - moving into the area as a result of a conflict, gaining control of Iran's oil; and perhaps, the oil of others in the area. Given the urgency of the situation there was no way of knowing, once started, how this type of conflict could be contained.'

The Chief continued, 'Israel, of course, was making some plans, but only with limited resources. This was because the various peace agreements and the economic situation, following the Al Axsa Intafada, early in the new millennium, had forced severe arms cuts. Further economic pressure had been placed on Israel as the result of the withdrawal and resettlement of thousands of Israeli citizens from land handed over to the Palestinians. Israel were therefore placed in a unenviable position. Israeli retaliation after an attack, or even an Israeli pre-emptive strike, could plunge the whole area into war. As you well know, Gentlemen, many out there have been looking for an excuse to eliminate Israel. It would have undone and set back for a generation all the peace brokering we have done, and upon which we have set so many hopes.' Many of the listeners were busy making notes.

The Speaker then reminded his listeners that, in February 2005, President Bush had clearly stated that the USA would stand by Israel in the event she was threatened. Therefore, he went on, 'A covert air attack on Iran's missile sites was authorised last night, and carried out by our Quicksilver stealth aircraft. All eight Iranian ballistic missile sites, identified earlier by our space-based sensors, were attacked. The intention was to prevent missile launch, with minimum loss of life or damage to any infrastructure that might be located nearby. The Iranians have said nothing of this yet and are clearly biding their time.'

The speaker paused again, for longer than usual. For a moment the audience wondered if he was going to continue. Indeed, he wished it was all he had to say. But there was more that had to be said. He had no option. His next words were inescapable. Perhaps the podium would act as a refuge! He grasped either side with both hands. The words were to shock his colleagues. 'It is my sad duty to inform you that this attack failed catastrophically.'

The Chief could sense the tension in the listeners' faces in the front row, in the gloom beyond the lectern. Note taking stopped and silence reigned, as they realised what this meant.

Wishing to get this phase of the briefing over as quickly as possible, he continued without a break. 'From the information we have gathered so far, of the eight sites attacked, shown by the routes and locations on this map' - Their heads swivelled towards the screen again, 'only three sites were positively hit. For this we suffered the incredible loss of six of our new, stealthy, Quicksilver aircraft. Only two aircraft returned safely and as yet we do not know what happened to the other aircraft or the fate of their crews. We suspect, from post attack imagery, that on at least one site the ballistic missile launchers had been replaced with wooden decoys and that the attack was wasted.'

'Every known countermeasure was available to our crews, who were most probably confronted by some very modern Russian-supplied mobile automatic missile air defences.'

The President shuddered at this point. He had been told this horrifying figure confidentially by an aide, just before the briefing commenced. This probably explained his cowed posture as the briefing had proceeded. He was dreading the inevitable news being confirmed. Even more so, he dreaded the fact that the American people would have to be told. Also, he privately recalled his earlier fears about the possibility of aircrew falling into foreign hands, especially in that part of the world.

When he looked up again towards the speaker he wore a worried and guilty look. How could this catastrophe have occurred? What was he to say to the nation and to the world?

The briefing continued, 'The facts are, Mr President, Gentlemen, that more of the sites may have been hit, but we cannot be sure.' The projector glowed again. 'It seems that site three was a decoy, the real launcher system having most likely departed only shortly before the attack. Most probably relocating in about an hour, under the cover of darkness. After the crews were on their way we could not confirm this movement at site three as a fact. There were only two satellite passes in the time available. Our infra-red satellite imagery had become fragmented, due to the onset of scattered thick cloud cover at the time.

'Since the attack, the weather has severely deteriorated in the area - which was the reason for bringing the attack forward in the first place. Further photographic and infra-red imagery will be denied to us, due to the weather, for an indeterminate period, possibly for days. As to what really took place, we are, as they say, almost completely in the dark.' He sipped the water hesitantly - and then summarised.

'Gentlemen, we are thrust into a damage limitation situation. Once it is discovered who carried out the attack, the US will be made to look foolish and weak, when Iran decide to break the story. Worse, the threat to Israel probably still remains - or at least perhaps as much as seventy five per cent of it does! We now await the response from Iran. Similarly, they may be awaiting our reactions. If it is not the case already, they will soon deduce that the raid was carried out by the US and not by Israel. The fact is that the mightiest nation on earth has failed with its latest technology - a grim situation and a grimmer one ahead!

'An immediate analysis has commenced on all radio traffic satellite intercepts that were received during the attack period. We may have intercepted some indications from our aircrews, if they managed to transmit, while in difficulty. Further, a concerted effort is being made to search for crew emergency beacons. Remember, all radio transmissions in the area could be screened by the high mountains and hills.

'We may face a hostage situation if any of the crews brought down have survived and been captured. Also, there is the prospect of an imminent attack on Israel, despite all our efforts. This', he paused for emphasis, 'in the most volatile region of the world.

'Mr President, Gentlemen, we must now plan our options. Firstly, we shall have no option but to prepare a statement to use either before or certainly as a response, when this bursts onto the world's news desks. Further, we have no option but to inform the families affected. They are all in the USA, as the Quicksilver squadron was detached to Spain, on temporary duty. Over to you, Gentlemen!' He slowly picked up his notes, hoping there would be no questions.

After a few searching questions from the listeners, most of which could not be answered for lack of data, the audience received copies of the slides. They departed to their syndicate rooms, each to consider the situation. The Chief flicked off the summary slide and thankfully sat down. He had only managed to fully answer just one question.

The Crisis Management Team were given two hours of brain-storming to identify and explore the options. They were then to return and place them before the President. The atmosphere was dismal. They awaited the President's departure.

The President stood up. The shocked audience got wearily to its feet. As he left he said, 'I must now inform the Prime Minister of Israel of the latest situation and the most unfortunate scenario that now faces us both.'

An Air Force General was heard to remark, 'He means the scenario that is facing Israel - it is they that are really in the front line, and have been since 1948. Not us!'

THE BALLISTIC SWORDS OF ISLAM

The Ayatollah had taken his decision. First he would attack Israel physically, then the US politically, by revealing, ridiculing, accusing and threatening before the entire world. At this point he would produce and parade the three surviving Quicksilver crew members. At this stage he would reveal 'how Israel had intended to bring down the world economy and control it'. The world would believe it because he believed it himself. Yes, he reasoned, this is all coming together rather well. The USA had played into his hands. The frenzy, especially when the Islamic World heard, would be unstoppable.

Plans were made and orders given to prepare all the ballistic missiles which had survived the American cowardly attack. They would be launched in a few hours time. The launchers would leave their hides for a minimum period - just a few minutes, necessary to erect the missiles, launch and then quickly retreat into the hides again. One set of reloads would be provided for a second follow-up attack, one hour later.

Just minutes before the attack he would inform his co-conspirators in the other nations and simultaneously go onto television, to rally his people. He considered that the dignity of Iran and of Islam were at stake. The weapons would be launched in pairs. Of the sixteen missiles originally deployed on their mobile launchers, four had been destroyed in the Quicksilver attack, and one was unserviceable.

Oh yes! he knew now that it was the Great Satan - America - who had started the aggression. What a pity his missiles couldn't reach America! This time the missiles would most certainly reach America's favourite Middle East client. So, for the first raid, he had ordered that there were to be five pairs in salvos at ten-minute intervals, followed by a final single missile against Haifa. The pairs would be aimed at the highly populated Tel-Aviv area and the industrial and technological cities nearby. Jerusalem - holy to Islam - would, of course, be spared. His missiles had not the accuracy required to wipe out the Jewish population areas of Jerusalem, without endangering the sacred buildings on Temple Mount. One day surely he would be remembered for ever - the Ayatollah who destroyed the nation of Israel. He would go to Jerusalem and rule the Islamic world from there. Surely, the USA had lost too much face to interfere again.

In the north of the country Israel's agriculture had flourished. The multiple attractions of the north were many. The beauty of the mountains, a pleasant standard of living, ski-ing, fishing in Lake Hula and in the Kinneret - Lake Galilee. The area had become an escape from the big cities near the sea. It contained many beautiful settlements, with multiplying populations. The hitherto neglected, desolate and ruined places had been re-built throughout the land - the new sympathetically merged with the old, by the careful use of local materials. Such had been the diversity of the return of the Jews to Israel, when walking in any town, as well as Hebrew, a dozen different languages could be heard.

Fields were ploughed and the rains allowed crops twice a year, the barns filled with animals, the lakes with fish and the houses with happy children. There were still a few nasty incidents. However, since the peace treaty, they were no longer under the sustained daily threat that Israelis had endured for so many years. Terror attacks across the nearby borders with their Arab neighbours were, thankfully, almost over. In a few weeks time it would be the Feast of Tabernacles.

Of late, even those Israelis who had remained suspicious and had been opposed to the imposed peace, not believing it to be genuine, had kept quiet. People wanted peace. People could get on with their lives. Now, it was reported that even the weekly Friday unholy exhortations from the muezzins had ceased.

Only Iran seemed to continue with hostile radio broadcasts, together with a few other nations who still transmitted radio programmes using various fundamentalist groups. The Palestinian elections had finally brought unexpected results but the peace initiatives had continued, aided by pressure from the USA and a four nation contact group from Europe.

Compromises had been struck regarding the 130,000 Jewish settlers, living in what had been known as the 'West Bank'. Arab autonomy had increased. Those Arabs who wished to do so had remained in Israel, as they were entitled to do, and dwelt and worshipped as they had done for centuries, once again in peace. The Christian Arabs were no longer being harassed by their non-Christian Arab brothers. Quotas had been reluctantly agreed to allow the descendants of some Arab property owners, who had fled in 1948, to receive compensation and, in some genuine cases, even to return if they wished.

Unlike those dwelling in the cities, Israel's country dwellers had moved significantly towards a simpler life. They were enjoying the glorious sunsets, singing and dancing with family and friends and living healthy and fulfilling lives. Since the peace agreements very large numbers had migrated from the various nations where they had been scattered. They were finally able to put down permanent roots in their own land.

The loss of The Golan had affected almost thirty per cent of Israel's water requirements. However, by careful planning there was plenty here for everyone, provided the early and later rains came. The land was farmed efficiently, the ponds were full of fish. Once again the sound of civil airliners bringing tourists was the main noise disturbance. There was no longer the persistent sound of fighter aircraft patrolling overhead. Peace was at hand!

It was intriguing that, while many Jews had drifted away from the Laws of

Moses and Judaism, now, they were becoming more attuned to the way of life that their forefathers had pursued for thousands of years. It was almost as though large sections of the population were becoming alive again. Now they could look ahead, instead of over their shoulders and not struggle just to exist as had their families in the past - whether it was beyond the Pale of Settlement in Europe or dreading the next pogrom in Russia. They were a nation that was justly proud of their achievements since 1948. Who else could have achieved the same within a period of not much more than fifty years?

In this idyllic state many were suddenly awoken on a Shabbat morning, right at the end of 2008. There had been several large explosions. They rushed to switch on their radios and televisions. What little was known, so far, was given repeatedly by the grim-faced newscasters. An unknown enemy, suspected at this stage to be Iran, had fired at least two ballistic missiles into Israel's airspace in the early hours. One had come down near the Israel Museum on the outskirts of Tel Aviv, the other had been intercepted by Israel's own 'Arrow' ballistic missile defence system, but many fragments had fallen on northern Israel.

The population were soon further alarmed by several more detonations. Israel's early warning radar had back-plotted the trajectories across Syria. The missiles, it was decided, were either coming from the far part of Northern Syria, or even slightly further; from Iran. It was claimed that the two missiles in the second salvo had been intercepted as they dived towards their targets, which were presumed to be Israel's major coastal cities. Not Jerusalem. There were no reports of casualties from the falling debris - some of which had forward-thrown for a considerable distance and fallen into the Mediterranean Sea.

Citizens were immediately warned not to touch wreckage of the rockets, as it was hot on impact. Quite apart from any warhead effects, rocket debris, they were told, may also contain unburned or unexploded material such as toxic fuel and possibly its chemically excitable oxidant. The type of warhead that had been carried by these weapons was yet to be established. At this stage those closest to the weapons were unclear as to whether they had heard just the explosions of impacts, the explosions of interceptor missiles sent up against them, or actual warhead explosions. This was another reason for keeping indoors and away from any debris or fumes. Nothing had been heard from any of Israel's neighbours and no warning had been given.

To avoid over-alarming the population, the news-readers had not been told that one of the high altitude intercepts had involved a huge but short-lived fireball, which was almost certainly a nuclear mis-fire - a 'fizzle' - terminology for a nuclear warhead that had been incorrectly triggered. This would have resulted in the weapon core being asymmetrically detonated and thus losing most of its power. However, those in the north were jamming the switchboards, even as the announcements were read out. In the morning sky, many had seen the largest flash in their lives, heard a rumble of sound and felt a weak momentary rush of wind a few minutes later.

Reuben, after a very busy week, as ever, was hoping for a peaceful Shabbat - a 'Shabbat Shalom'. He had celebrated the start of Shabbat the previous evening with his traditional family meal from the moment the first star appeared. It had coincided with his daughter's birthday - so in a way the weekend was a double celebration. Later, they had all planned to go to the beach at Ceasarea. The phone rang and his bleeper went off simultaneously. Within minutes he was on his way to the National Control Bunker. Reuben's family knew something very serious was happening. They rapidly started to prepare a sealed room, in case it was needed.

After a worrying fast drive along the Haifa-Tel Aviv highway Reuben arrived to hear from the Duty Officer that Israel had sent radioactivity monitoring aircraft aloft within the past few minutes. Measurements were also being made on the ground. However, the prevailing wind was from the west, as is so often the case in the morning. This would be carrying any airborne contamination away, towards northern Jordan and Iraq. Also, not disclosed to the public at this stage, he heard that the other ballistic missile on its plunging trajectory had not been intercepted, as reported earlier. It had impacted somewhere near Petah Tikvah, with no explosion reported. Teams were immediately despatched to find the site. As yet the outcome was an unknown quantity - as the debris on the surface may contain scattered nuclear waste, unexploded conventional explosive, scattered chemicals or even biological agents. Presently, a team was proceeding very cautiously towards the best estimate of the assessed impact position, which seemed to be among one of the many citrus plantations in the area.

At home, Reuben's family and most of the nation were glued to their televisions and radios. Those business visitors and holiday-makers in the nations hotels, most of whom were unable to understand Hebrew, quickly selected the CNN news channel. The news-reader continued to announce that citizens would be kept fully informed. It was likely that the gas masks, returned to storage at the end of the second Gulf War, would be re-issued - as soon as it was ascertained that it was safe to go outside. This would take several hours. Meanwhile, all householders were advised to stay under cover and to draw off and store a supply of drinking water to last for several days. Those in hotels were similarly advised. Arrangements would be made for gas masks to be issued to hotel visitors, if it became necessary.

As the news-reader spoke, the Israeli Cabinet was in emergency session, not in Jerusalem's Knesset - the Parliament building, but instead deep under the Ministry of Defence in Tel Aviv. Israel's Air Force and the other defence forces

- much reduced since the Peace Accords, had come to full alert. As a precaution, down near Yafne, the Jericho II ballistic rocket force had come to alert, ready to receive and commence loading Israel's ultimate deterrent - the nuclear weapon.

The next news bulletin followed in a few minutes, repeating all that was said before but with further information about gas masks. Even as those in the north of the country heard the radio message it was punctuated by two more distant rumbles. Citizens in the Ramallah area also saw a brilliant flash. It temporarily blinded those who happened to be looking in the direction where a nuclear warhead exploded at high altitude, over the sparsely populated area to the east.

That it was Iran's responsibility had become clear. The Cabinet reacted swiftly and a message was flashed to Iran's Leaders and copied to the US President, to the Security Council of the United Nations and to the European Union. All of whom had been instrumental in obtaining the peace agreements upon which they had, misguidedly, placed so much store. It was stated that, so far - apart from the still unknown possible effects of nuclear material, little physical damage had been done. However, unless there was an assurance that the missile attacks would stop immediately, Israel would have no alternative but to respond accordingly. It was made clear that the right was reserved to fire Jericho II, with its nuclear warhead against Iran - against which Iran had no credible defence. Israel would also launch whichever nuclear strike aircraft might be deemed necessary.

The Ayatollah, now aware that his first five missiles had failed to achieve their objective, gave the order to stop. He would re-think his strategy. Something had clearly gone wrong with his missile systems. The world was now fully alerted to what was going on, and, after a series of confusing reports, the United Nations had been called to an emergency assembly later in the day.

Curiously, within the immediate aftermath of the attack, even those nations whose citizens were likely to be adversely affected by the abortive nuclear events were drawn towards Iran's cause, rather than towards Israel's. It had always been thus, remarked Reuben to the Prime Minister.

Israel, the sole possessor of the oil substitute, was under pressure from all sides. In the past Israel had been pressed by embargoes and had to do a certain amount of careful trading to ensure that her fuel supplies were assured. For example, she imported coal to generate electricity. Nations supplying coal were likely to come under pressure from the strong oil producers. They realised that, if they were uncooperative, Israel would certainly move over to synthetic fuel, directly she could convert the power stations. Many others would follow, once Israel started to export the technology.

Oil producers came together in rapidly convened OPEC meetings, as they tried to assess exactly what this new development would mean. For decades they had held the world to ransom with their ever increasing oil prices. Now they could foresee that oil would no longer be a controlling commodity in the world! The power held over the world by the oil producers would be significantly sidelined. Perhaps finally irrelevant!

In contrast, the non-oil producing nations must decide which way to turn. Should they continue to use conventional oil supplies, or should they attempt to strike deals with Israel, and if so would Israel try to call the world's energy tune in the future? Or was there some other compromise solution?

The economies of the oil countries would surely commence a rapid decline. Strangely, despite their oil bonanzas, which were, of course, fortuitous, rather than planned, many were already in debt. The Middle East had, once again, turned the world to turmoil! There would have been an inevitable oil problem anyway before very long. Most of the world's general public had not known - or had conveniently forgotten - that, if consumption continued at the present rate, using the known resources, the world's oil reserves would be gone in a little more than three generations.

During recent wars, the general public's expectations of up to date - indeed near 'real time' television news was taken for granted. Now, 'in the sight of the nations', Israel was once again the lead topic on the news bulletins, interspersed with the views of dozens of 'experts' of all persuasions. The world was clearly shaken by this turn of events. The world's stockmarkets immediately reacted with a sharp downward fall.

Politicians had recently allowed themselves some relaxation on Middle East issues, following the implementation of the Peace Accords. They had felt it safe to concentrate, apart from a few small ethnic skirmishes, and the usual periodic crop of earthquakes, floods and hurricanes, on their own little worlds. They had been more interested on winning elections and their own national economic strategies. Some dealt, in a limited fashion, with the sporadic terrorist threats from fewer dissident groups.

Iran and her oil partners now had to consider the new situation that they faced. Despite exploding nuclear weapons, making a surprise attack on a nation almost at peace and even contaminating parts of the territories of friendly nations, they had neither been ostracised by their neighbours or by the world at large. It is an amazing fact that oil speaks louder than words or even actions!

The usual flurry of the world's professional protesters had been uncharacteristically quiet. Only a few heads of western nations, uncertain of the best line to take, were making genuine disapproving noises - and then not very loudly. It was almost as though the nations were fed up with trying to sort out the problems of Israel and Jerusalem in particular. They had tried hard for years - but their efforts now seemed to be of no avail.

Within the Ayotollah's meeting there was a mood of disbelief. They could not understand why their attack on Israel had failed. It seemed, admitted the Ayatollah, in closed session with his collaborators, that every time one or more of the Islamic nations had come against Israel, that Israel had survived and even flourished and it was time this was stopped. They had never understood these failures. Now, even these modern missiles had somehow failed. The very name of Israel stuck in their throats. Most of those present had lived through the incredible events since 1948.

First, in that year, Israel had somehow established independence - apparently against all odds. It was, they had decided, ridiculous. What other nation had been scattered in almost one hundred countries for some two thousand years, returned to their original territory, declared Statehood in a day and even restored their original language?

Then, in 1967, the unthinkable had happened. Israel had re-gained Jerusalem and proclaimed her their Capital City. How did Allah allow all this to happen? His audience all shook their bearded heads slowly in amazement, as though waiting for an answer from Allah himself. Some had taken part as young men in these earlier battles. They had witnessed some amazing scenes of battle confusion and, finally, scenes of withdrawal. Surrenders were painfully remembered, although they were never openly admitted to be failures. With their overwhelming manpower and vast amounts of Soviet-supplied weapons at the time, they could still not understand what had gone wrong. How was it possible, in 1948, that the forces of a combined Arab population of about 85 million, from five nations, had been defeated by a new nation of less than 4 million who had never had their own armed forces for nearly 2000 years? And so it had been ever since!

Next, Talal Aziz, the Oil Minister from Saudi Arabia took up the discussion. He had recently taken political control of his nation, on behalf of the Imam. He reiterated the Chairman's feelings, pointing out how even the surprise attack on Israel's most Holy Day - Yom Kippur - in 1973 had failed. Israel had survived yet again. Then in the 1980s, despite all the support for the PLO, including millions of dollars donated from those seated before him, Israel was still there. It was time, he said, for a new approach. They should, Allah forgive them, take a wider approach. He suggested that even more desperate measures were needed.

They needed, he suggested, a lead from a nation who could unite several additional nations against Israel in such a strong force that Israel would surely be overwhelmed. It was perhaps time to turn towards someone to the far north - a nuclear power - who were looking for a new role. They were a nation that would surely help. A nation to whom those present could offer, as a reward, say, 20 or even 25 years of oil - at concessionary prices. A nation whose army needed a new role but who would surely share the spoils in exchange for oil. 'The nation who could help,' he said, 'is Russia.'

He went on the explain that, once they had achieved their aim, the prize would be great, for they would control both the majority of the world's natural oil and this new 'synthetic' oil. Most importantly, Jerusalem would be theirs. The Jews would be gone for ever - driven down to the sea, as had been promised so many years ago by the Arab Mufti of Jerusalem. It would also be a turn-around for the fortunes of Russia. Their population had struggled as much, if not more, in the West's corrupt market economy; as they had under communism. They all agreed.

The meeting continued, each delegate being given tasks to do, to set this master plan in motion, while keeping it a close secret. Hard as the decision had been, they had decided that there was no other option. They needed Russia on their side.

A strongly-built, black-bearded man, but with eyes of a particular gaze, had been the final speaker. An alliance with Russia had been his idea. Had he been a 'fly-on-the-wall', Keith, many miles away in Britain, would surely still recognise him - for the eyes had not changed in almost fifty years. Ahmed Pavli was now the Iranian Foreign Minister. He had risen through the adverse conditions in his country that had characterised the lot of the lower classes during the last days of the Shah's reign. Now, he had reached a position of considerable influence as a revolutionary, having held several important posts in government, following Iran's revolution. He would indeed have the world-wide influence, as had been his stated ambition to Keith, so many year ago in the souk of Teheran.

It was Ahmed, working behind the scenes, who had master-minded the recent abortive ballistic missile attacks indirectly against the great 'Satan' - the USA's client nation - Israel. He could not think - if he ever stopped but briefly to think - of any rational reason to hate Israel. Israel had never done him any personal harm. In fact he was being driven by evil forces beyond his control. That was sufficient. Like so many in the Middle East - both Arab and non-Arab alike - he blamed the West, and Israel, for holding his nation back. This despite the fact that, like so many of the nations represented at the Ayotollah's meeting, they would not have been able even to extract this oil, or refine it, had it not been for western exploration and technology in the first place.

It was Ahmed who had received the news first, when the US raids on his ballistic missile sites had, from the USA's viewpoint, gone so disastrously wrong. Nevertheless, it would be he who would see this confrontation through to it's logical conclusion - the end of the Jews. There would be no going back now. It was surely a necessary action, once and for all, for his children and for Allah?

Talal Aziz spoke once again for Saudi Arabia. He knew the oil business inside out and the impact of any extra fuel on the markets - of whatever sort - if it competed with oil. It was their very lifestyle that was being endangered. Wasn't this, he said, why they had striven against bankers and governments for so many years to retain quota limits to keep the price up?

Talal agreed that they had to put an end to Israel. If his son Ayad had to fight - even to die - so be it. He would be following in a line of brave warriors - wasn't his ancestor the great Abdul Aziz?

The others present unanimously pledged their whole-hearted support. Much embracing and cheek kissing followed! Emissaries would go forthwith to Russia and to several other sympathetic nations, formerly part of the old Soviet Union. Their task would be to sound the Russians out and persuade their participation in the largest world coalition since the 1991 Gulf War. This time it would be the largest force ever to come against Israel. Surely they could not fail this time!

Their leader was satisfied. He rubbed his hands together, a cunning and evil scheme was being devised. They would act quickly before anyone had second thoughts, and meet in fourteen days time to review progress.

Israel, worried by one or two signs - but with no real evidence of further or imminent hostilities, appealed to the United Nations for actions against the perpetrators of the missile attacks. There was little more she could do. The UN, having gradually lost credibility and in near bankruptcy, due to a series of disasters in the last decade, did nothing of consequence, but talk. There were somewhat muted protests from the UK and US. There was little that they could do.

After all, there were a dozen other minor conflicts that involved UN peace-keeping initiatives, going on at the time. The large number of UN-imposed sanctions and policing activities, were already occupying the forces - and the purses - of several participating nations. Furthermore, this attack against Israel was fortunately over, and none of the UN peace-keeping monitors in southern Lebanon had been hurt.

It was reported that national teams in Syria and Iraq were out monitoring the outcome of the partial single nuclear air-burst explosion. Neither government would allow UN monitors to take measurements. Fortuitously, due to a series of events, rather like the 1991 Gulf War SCUD attacks from Iraq, there had been little immediate damage. More importantly, there was now a growing realisation abroad that this whole business of Israel's synthetic oil did threaten to undermine the banking and economic stability of much of the world.

The scenario was starting to play to Iran's advantage. Many members of the UN were natural oil producers, enemies of Israel, or both. A weak Security Council resolution followed, which Iran chose to ignore. Iran couldn't possibly have attacked Israel - because one could not discuss Israel. This was because Israel, in their eyes, simply did not exist. Iran had not recognised Israel - and that was an end to the matter, as far as they were concerned! The other nations, fretting about delayed nuclear effects on their citizens, from the high altitude blasts, soon gave up. The events of that Shabbat morning faded after a few weeks.

As ever, more important news occurred, in the eyes of the media. A massive earthquake in China and minor quakes in California, replaced Israel's plight, as news has a habit of doing!

Although fully informed of forthcoming military manoeuvres, under the treaty agreements, the analysts ignored the fact that, within a few weeks, Russia had suddenly decided to hold unusually large full-scale military exercises. These were clearly in conjunction with her associated Southern States. Pakistan were also carrying out exercises far to the East.

Much nearer to Israel's borders, Syria, Saudi Arabia, Iran, the Yemen and Iraq also quietly made their plans. Logistics were much less of a problem for the nations who were geographically closer to Israel, than for those of the more distant allies who would participate in the coming coalition. Libya readied her ballistic missiles, procured earlier from a South American nation. Egypt had decided not to directly participate. However, they would not prevent their citizens joining in, as the various 'victorious nations' advanced towards Israel. There would be rich pickings, once victory was within their grasp. A victory that Egypt and the others had been unable to attain in past wars.

Back in Britain, Keith was again asked to comment on the world situation. Unaware of the covert war preparations going ahead, he assessed that the USA, having suffered the ignominious loss of aircraft and their crews, would henceforth try to avoid getting embroiled in any more Middle East entanglements, unless absolutely essential. The nation and the President - who would not be re-elected - had not yet come to terms with their own disaster. It was worth noting, he suggested, that the USA itself was not under any increased direct military threat. Only the indirect economic oil threat. All nations had, however, increased their threat awareness following many terrorist atrocities around the world for several years, in most cases by Islamic extremists.

Following the debacle of the failed attack on the Iranian missile sites, it seemed likely that the USA would no longer wish to be seen as a world policeman. Humiliating defeats had been suffered. Since the 1990s there had been Somalia, the attacks on the USA and other bombings of US property, mainly embassies, hotels and ships. Earlier they had suffered the embarrassment of the attempt to rescue their embassy hostages in Iran. This latest failure was by far the worst. They did not wish the world to be reminded that they had brokered the 'peace', promised to Israel. Any surviving Quicksilver crew members that there may have been, had still not been acknowledged. Were they being held or had they all perished?

In a similar vein Keith considered that France would not presently wish to be further involved in Middle East affairs, but would 'sit on the fence' - for the sake of oil! Following the discovery of the use of the British base by the USA, for the raid on Iran's missile launch sites, Britain was still almost daily under verbal attack. These words came from the more vocal of the nations in the Middle East and Magreb. Once the US use of the British Sovereign Area, in Cyprus, had been discovered, Britain was suffering an immediate oil embargo by Iran. Several other oil suppliers had joined in, to show their solidarity.

Large scale anti-government demonstrations were a regular feature in British cities - often with violence. Fuel prices had risen sharply. British Muslims and their Mosques were inevitably being put in a difficult position, even though few had any knowledge or involvement in any of the attacks on British soil. Police leave was frequently cancelled as a precautionary measure and the armed forces had become stretched to the limit because fewer and fewer conscripts could be found. The government had resorted to a rotation of reservists, leading to the problems of a reservist sometimes policing his own local ethnic community.

Britain, Germany, Greece, Turkey, Italy and France were in a much different situation than the USA. They could not escape the worrying fact that they were daily within range of ballistic missiles recently deployed on the North African coastline, by Libya, Algeria and, more recently by Tunisia. Apart from the USA, no other members of the NATO Alliance had an indigenous defence against ballistic missiles - only sensors to see them coming! Germany and Holland had some now-ageing US-supplied Patriot air defence systems, but these could not handle the faster ballistic missiles. Further, these Patriots were rarely located for homeland defence, within these nations, as they were usually deployed elsewhere to protect various United Nations Peacekeeping forces.

As early as 1995, the US Secretary of Defence had identified the growing unrest among the nations along the Mediterranean coastline as a special problem, for NATO's Southern Flank. The expected fundamentalist take over in Algeria had finally taken place, after several years of action by the zealots. The French government were considerably worried about, even occasionally harassed, by their internal Islamic population, thousands of whom were living within French borders. Many had originated from Algeria as a product of France's history. Underlying internal friction would almost certainly surface, should France favour Israel in any potential future conflict. France was already the worst place to be for anti-Semitism. Israel did not expect any help at all from France.

On the other hand, Britain, had no serious internal problems of this sort, apart from the occasional demonstration. However, there was a growing suspicion that there might be an undetected problem, because the extent of the Al Qaeda network and their possible sympathisers had never been satisfactorily identified. Britain's politicians - Keith suggested, should therefore adopt a low profile, while the security organisations tried to keep tabs on the activities of the continuing influx of immigrants.

Meanwhile, it would not have escaped the Ayatollah's reckoning that, politically, the USA were likely to follow a similar line, leaving him a free hand in the Middle East. It was, after all, almost time for the next US Presidential election! The USA were otherwise distracted - for a time!

The USA had not thought it necessary to offer any of their newly-developed, high performance, high altitude ballistic missile defences to Israel, as Israel had her own system. Israel - as so often in the past - was on its own. Keith, had not voiced his private thoughts in his reports. However, he recalled the days in previous Mid-East Wars, when Israel was given little help once war had commenced. On other occasions help had, perhaps deliberately, arrived barely in the nick of time. Since then, Britain had gone to the aid of an Islamic community who were under threat in the Kosovo conflict and against the so-called Orthodox Christian Serbs - although few in Britain had grasped this fact at the time. Keith pondered whether Britain would do the same for the Jews when they next came under attack. From past indications it seemed very unlikely. As Keith wrote his report, none of the intelligence communities had yet discovered the plot that was being hatched against Israel.

In the days when wars lasted a few days or even a few weeks it was bad enough, but with weapons of mass destruction, Keith knew that there would be no time for help from any source, once a war of this nature and dimension started. Some nations had carried out inoculation programmes and others had gas masks. Many had done little, should an attack of this type occur. Even Britain was among those who had probably still not made adequate preparations, despite all the advice that was available.

Fortunately, the recent and unprecedented Iranian missile attack on Israel had failed. Israel had considered reprisal raids. They had decided against this action, so as to preserve the sympathy of as many nations as possible. For the moment there was little more that she could do.

The War

MOBILISE OR WAIT?

The scenario was finally becoming clearer. Deep in the control bunker under Israel's Ministry of Defence building, in the centre of Tel-Aviv, the intelligence analysts received and interpreted the latest data from Israel's Offeq 5 or Horizon 5 reconnaissance satellite. Offeq 5 was the most recently-launched and advanced of Israel's series of earth observation reconnaissance satellites. The elliptical orbit of Offeq 5 was even lower than the 228 by 452 mile high path of her earlier variants. Following the satellite's launch from the Negev desert, just a few months previously, the new orbital angle allowed all portions of the earth to be imaged between latitudes 37 degrees north and south. The critical swathe of territory that the satellite imaged contained Israel's sworn foes. Providing the weather was clear, the pictures obtained were significantly better than the few feet accuracy than had been possible from the older satellite reconnaissance systems.

For this clarity the analysts were thankful, as the latest images showed a surprising development of troop movements and army military exercises occurring simultaneously in several of the neighbouring nations. These seemed to be different from previously observed exercises. Suspicions were aroused at once, as their purpose was not clear. Also many more air force units than normal were exercising. Reuben also noticed that Saudi Arabia had been exercising, once again, with her latest Chinese-supplied mobile ballistic missiles. Simultaneously, the first sighting was seen of a new missile, suspected to be Shahab 3.

To the far South, a ballistic missile had recently been fired into the Indian Ocean, over a range of one thousand kilometres - the first ever ballistic missile launch from Saudi territory. At the time Reuben had conjectured, that the Saudis had just decided it was time to prove their Chinese training and that their expensive purchases performed correctly. Nevertheless, he still remained curious.

Reuben also interpreted traffic downloaded from the state of Israel's communications satellite - one of the 'Amos' series. It was busy eavesdropping on the latest Arab and Iranian communications networks. Nothing of obvious importance had been intercepted in the last few hours.

Israel's newest infra-red satellites, part of the future ballistic missile launch warning system were only partly deployed at present. To obtain round-the-clock coverage four satellites were needed. Only two had been put into their 600 km altitude orbits, so there were gaps in the coverage. Their task was to search for the hot spots that would be generated when missiles were fired.

Far to the west of Israel, the People's Republic of Libya had been carrying out her own logistics exercises loading and unloading large crates of general army equipment, on and off ships.

Iran, had continued to exercise her mobile ballistic missile launchers. Only two had been seen on manoeuvres, far from their base, before the cloud cover again obscured the mountainous terrain of South Western Iran. Now any movements could not be seen from space.

The Israeli analysts noted that, within a space of only two weeks, all their neighbours had recently trained and exercised their ground troops in abnormal ways. For both the armour and the infantry there had been small and large formations moving about, together with their area and point defence air-defence weapons. After exercising, many had not returned to their own depots but seemed to be in clusters, close to main roads, ports and airports. At this point Israel became increasingly alarmed and once again addressed her concerns to the United Nations, informing each member of the Security Council independently. However, the UN were currently pre-occupied with a resurgence of the dispute over the far-away Spratly Island, in the Far East. They were indifferent to Israel's worries.

Far to the north Russian terrain did not come under Israeli satellite coverage. However, the USA's satellites had also noted unusual troop movements. At the time no one realised that these diverse military preparations, taking place in Russia, a thousand kilometres or more away from the current activity in the Middle East, were in any way connected.

In Israel the western calendar month of October is a glorious one and the time of the Feast of Tabernacles. This is an eight day long feast, instituted at the time of Moses. It is to celebrate and rejoice after gathering the season's harvest of field crops, oil and wine and to remember the forty days the Hebrew Nation spent wandering in the desert, before entering the Promised Land. The Feast had been faithfully celebrated wherever Jews had been scattered, ever since.

For the Jews it had always been the case that, wherever they were in the world, their security only lasted for a time. Then some new and frightening persecution had started. Since 1948, Israelis had enjoyed very few peaceful Feasts, even after the 'wandering Jew' had returned to the land of his, or her, forefathers. They all longed for a genuine peace.

A further recent wave of migration to Israel had occurred, but many still remained in the Diaspora, principally in the USA and in several of the Republics of the Former Soviet Union. Indeed, many of Israel's new residents had left a comfortable existence in the USA, Britain, Argentina or South Africa to go to Israel. Many were often not entirely sure why they had done so. It had just seemed the right thing to do. Others had been only too pleased to move to Israel, because they had come from lands where they had been subject to years of terrorism and atrocities. These disturbing problems had been brought regularly to the world's attention, but they had not diminished.

Some of the nations where they lived had tried to control anti-Semitism in their midst, while others had not cared. After all they were just Jews! Few bothered to find out or even knew why it was that the Jews were persecuted in the first place!

Soviet Jews had journeyed to Israel in very large numbers, by land, sea and air. At one time they were coming into Israel at the rate of up to 11,000 each month. Although most had come from Russia and the Ukraine, others had come from Siberia China, India, Albania and Tadjakestan. In contrast to those who had lived in the affluent West, their lives had seen much more uncertainty and very few comforts.

Now they were home. It must have been ironic for those of Russian extraction, who were living near the Lebanese border, to find that they were being bombarded by Katusha rockets in the hands of the Hesbollah. Rockets that had been supplied by the land they had so recently left! Others had been airlifted out in the last fifty years from Iraq, Iran, the Yemen and Ethiopia.

All were aware of the forthcoming joyful festival of dancing and feasting and being together with their families as the Feast of Tabernacles, or 'Succoth', as it is also known. The children were busy helping their parents to build shelters of timber and rushes, known as 'Sukkot'. Each had the essential gaps left in the roof, to enable the night stars to be seen glinting in the heavens. These were being constructed all over Israel - in gardens, rooftops, and even on balconies. The temporary nature of the shelters would remind them of the long journey and the dangerous nights spent by their forebears, as they wandered and sojourned in the desert, so very long ago. Each family would celebrate the feast, by eating and drinking in their own sukkah in the day, and by sleeping there at night.

Meanwhile, the Israeli government were otherwise pre-occupied, as Succoth drew nearer. What should they do? Call the nation to alert or send yet another plea to the semi-deaf United Nations? They resolved to do both if any troops were seen to cross over from the more distant nations into any of the nations adjacent to Israel. In particular, they were now receiving intelligence from their own sources much further North. These reports originated from areas where US satellites had detected a concentration of forces - Russia and The Ukraine! These forces seemed to be mustering, just to the north of the Black Sea, opposite Turkey. Israel waited another night.

The following day a thick bank of cloud blanketed the Middle East from Cyprus to Iran. It obliterated not only the images the US satellite analysts were hoping for, but also denied coverage to Israel's own analysts, in Tel Aviv. They were pressed by their commanders, but, as one of the analysts remarked - they could only go over the previous images so many times and find the same results! New imagery was urgently needed.

Israel had despatched high flying aircraft and some unmanned sensor vehicles along her borders, but the range was too great for aerial reconnaissance to the far north. Few potentially hostile aircraft seemed to be airborne at high levels. If any were flying around at low altitudes, together with any vehicle or troop movements on the ground, then they were completely hidden by the abnormally thick cloud and the mountainous terrain.

The control situation was discussed again. It had become clear that something exceptional was underway. Should Israel go on alert right away, or wait? Technology could still not defeat the thickest weather. Close to home, Israel had some limited messages, received from sympathetic Bedouin friends living in the south of Lebanon, saying that a lot of troops were moving about in big machines. There was nothing more accurate to go on. The older hands remembered that, in 1973, the US - some had said deliberately - had delayed passing news of an impending Arab attack on Israel. Information had been hoped for this time - after all, the US had only recently attacked Iran largely on Israel's behalf. Surely they must have some information that could be released to Israel? Urgent requests were sent to Washington, but the US had little firm intelligence.

Although all Israel's military listening stations had been put on heightened alert for several days, reports stated that there was no perceptible change in the normal level of military communications between surface troops - even though it seemed that much more than routine exercises were being undertaken. For the moment Israel opted again - to wait.

Cloud cover lifted for a few hours the following morning. The imagery obtained, from the Offeq satellite's first daylight images, produced a shock. Overnight, large amounts of armour had crossed onto Lebanese soil from both Syria and through into Jordan, from Iraq.

Jordan supported Saddam Hussein in the Gulf War, then swung to a pro-Western stance during the Middle East Peace Accords of the mid-90s. Jordan were linked by trade to Iraq. Despite being relieved of the tyranny of Saddam Hussein, by the USA and the UK, in 2003, and with a new democratically elected government, Iraq was again in increasingly virulent opposition to both Israel and America. What price the 'peace' now? Further, several large cargo vessels were spotted between Cyprus and the Syrian coast. Clearly, they were heading for Syrian ports. Whose ships were they? Reuben was aware that Russia had a Black Sea Fleet logistic support base at Tartus. Were these Russian ships?

A huge deployment of additional ground forces had also appeared in Syria, presumably by an airlift. From where? Almost simultaneously, an urgent message came from Israel's Navy, engaged on routine patrols along the coast of Israel and off Egypt. The message said that several Libyan ships had left port and were steaming fully loaded and at full speed. Plots of their tracks indicated that it was most likely that these also could be headed for Syria.

The evidence was now overwhelming. Although it was Shabbat, Israel's Sabbath, and also the start of the Feast of Tabernacles, Israel's Prime Minister had no option but to order a full alert. This would be far from a feast celebration, but an occasion where, once again, Israel would be fighting for her very existence. As so often before, it looked as though she would be on her own. The hostile coalition had well-chosen their timing.

Mobilisation takes time, even in a small country. Some further information could come at any time. Whereas, time was also being marked off by the 95 minute period, of the orbit of the successive passes, of the Offeq surveillance satellite. The satellite, in its slightly elliptical orbit, could not provide the high imagery quality of the US systems. Nevertheless in its closest pass to the earth, a slant-range of 230 miles, many major changes of the order of battle could be determined, even without fine resolution. By lunch-time it was observed that, despite intermittent and thickening cloud, the hostile forces advancing in Lebanon had indeed been further enhanced; probably by a further airlift. Evidence continued to build. It was now clear that Israel was about to face a huge coalition of armed might that appeared to be about to invade their land; principally from the north.

This latest enemy reinforcement, of which there was evidence on several imaged airfields, was almost certainly from nations of the Former Soviet Union - now the Commonwealth of Independent States, or 'CIS'. The heavy armour must have been very rapidly unloaded from ships and the lighter vehicles from huge transport aircraft. From space it now appeared, in convoy, along the south-bound roads, like a file of monstrous insects. In the Lebanon the convoys had also started to turn southwards, towards the Israel's northern border. Simultaneously, a large drop of paratroops and equipment had clearly taken place much nearer the border.

Israel's Prime Minister, whose predecessor had so weakened the country by giving away land for peace at the start of the decade, now sat ashen-faced. Now with the haggard appearance of an old man before his time! He was reluctantly forced to give the order for Israel's doomsday nuclear weapons to be taken from their storage bunkers in Dimona, in the Negev Desert. Next they would be loaded into the Jericho ballistic missiles. Others, the free-fall nuclear weapons, would be taken to the air-bases, to be carried by Israel's manned strike aircraft. It was an essential precaution at this stage. However, it increasingly looked as though they would be needed. 'Masada' must never fall again!

The UN were alerted once again. It was hardly worth the effort!

Reuben and his colleagues remembered the advice they had given their government but a few years earlier. They had strongly called for action to destroy, or at least set back, Iran's nuclear programme, as they had done to Iraq's programme, so many years before. It had been turned down by the ruling party of the day. Now it was too late and they were about to face the consequences of inaction. It was one price to pay for democracy - when politicians were frightened of losing votes!

The Minister of Defence's dilemma was whether to wait and meet the inevitable attack head-on, directly the northern border was crossed, or to go ahead with a pre-emptive attack. But what to strike against? The opposing forces were, as far as could be established, well spread out, numerous and very mobile.

News of the build-up was now being regularly reported on CNN's World News. Israel's citizens, on full alert, were confused. Could no one stop this before it was too late? The UN were silent. Where was the UN guarantee of peace now? Would these massive forces miraculously stop at the border?

The US did little but appeal for calm, pointing out that the UN Security Council were due to meet in emergency session the following evening. Britain said a lot, but did nothing to help. Around Israel's planning table most believed that the UN meeting had been purposely delayed by certain nations. There were even those who, having already denied the Holocaust of World War 2, would be only too pleased to ensure that any UN action would be late. Plenty of statements - but, as usual, little real action! After all, Reuben reminded himself, the UN has never had forces of its own - it relied upon consensus among the nations, including those bearing down on Israel at this very moment.

The USA were well aware of the scenario, from their own intelligence resources. However, the President had declined to use his forces overseas again, so soon after the large loss of life in the aftermath of the second Iraqi war; and the even more recent debacle against the Iranian missile sites. It was also noted that several UN members, previously abstainers, had joined the media war against Israel at this very moment.

During the mid-1990s Israel had developed the 'Delilah' air vehicle. Originally designed as an aerial decoy, it had also been developed into a 400 km range conventional cruise missile. Prudent observers had noted that it probably had the capability to carry a small tactical nuclear device, suitable for attacking a hardened control bunker. However, it was not yet clear where the enemy military control centre was located. Although the Delilahs had been called to alert status during the day, they had no fixed hard targets to attack, because the hostile forces were on the move and ever approaching.   Doctrinally, the Israeli nuclear option was to be the last ditch defence and hopefully not to be used at all - despite the fact that nuclear weapons had already been, albeit unsuccessfully, used against Israel, by Iran.

Other Israeli military assets, in the form of unmanned spy aircraft, had been sent out on reconnaissance. The long endurance Heron, a fifty-four foot span, Unmanned Air Vehicle could loiter in areas of interest for more than two days. From its high altitude vantage position, pictures of troop disposition were normally transmitted back to base. The only problem at present was that the cameras could not see the ground for much of the time due to a continuing deterioration in the weather.

Reports were coming in from the monitoring services, that Iran was stepping up her broadcast rhetoric to the Arab nations and to her own citizens in even greater intensity. Other like-minded nations were joining in, clearly using scripts that had been prepared and shared in advance.

The Israeli Ambassador to the UN had meanwhile insisted on an earlier meeting of the Emergency General Assembly. He was politely listened to - but that was all. The few voices raised in his favour were swamped in a sea of dissension and disinterest and a lack of consensus on what might be done to avoid conflict. Like the human condition so many times in the past, so many could see a rush towards the brink but no one seemed to know how to stop it! Any time now, it would be too late.

Overnight, more Russian merchant shipping, also carrying heavy armour, had left the Black Sea, passed through the Bosphorous, and were steaming south of Rhodes, towards Syria. Libyan ships, reported earlier, were already docking at Syrian ports.

Although the Transcaucasian Republics had eventually obeyed the treaty that limited equipment numbers, under the Tashkent Agreement on Arms limitation, Russia had cleverly scrapped only their old armour. They had topped-up the holdings in Armenia, Azerbaijan and Georgia to the allowed limit, using almost new equipments. They had also provided 'advisers' to operate them. Thus the first airlifted modern equipment, that had appeared in the Lebanon before the oncoming heavy equipment, did not have so far to come as the Moscow-based kit - and it was modern. On arrival this was supplemented initially by older armour, already deployed in Syria.

As the coalition tanks continued to unload at the Mediterranean port of Latikya and rumbled southward across the Lebanon, cloud cover continued to intensify at all levels. Israel had no way of knowing the total armoured force that they were eventually to face, let alone the immediate front-line order of battle. As a first assessment, the opposing tank force was estimated to be many hundreds, backed by armoured personnel carriers. These certainly contained hundreds - perhaps thousands - of well-armed infantry soldiers. Undoubtedly, they would be accompanied by organic air defences - defences which were designed to give continuous protection for moving and manoeuvring land forces.

The 'Coalition of the North', comprising Syria, Iran, Russia and some of her southern Islamic Republics, with Lybia, were apparently all massed as a single force. There were so many - it could only be described as a 'great horde'! Their destruction, or at the very least the first blunting of the attack, would normally be the unenviable task of Israel's Air Force. Israel's ground defence forces meanwhile dug their armour 'hull-down', positioned along their northernmost mountain passes and hills, through which the attack must surely come. Even so, in places this front would initially be tens of kilometres wide, until the terrain funnelled and constrained the attack into several dozen narrower fronts. Israel would opt to wait until the funnelling occurred, knowing that armour and convoy 'choke points' would occur. Some older members still remembered the aircraft success against choke points in the Mitla Pass, in the Negev desert, during the clash with Egypt. Others recalled the rout of Iraqi armour, in convoy, south of Basra, during the first Gulf War. Now it was all happening again!

The Air Force Commanders were looking with increasing concern at the thick cloud aware that they could not be operationally effective at low altitude, in rough terrain, if it got much thicker.

Once the alert was ordered, right across Israel, trained soldiers joined their units by whatever method of travel was available, while the rest of the able population took all possible precautions. Vehicle, ship and aircraft maintenance staff and crews worked all night, ready for what must surely follow the next day. Extra shelters were hastily constructed and others made ready with provisions for several days.

Some could not return to the units in which they had previously served - the units had been disbanded since the 'peace' cuts. The more recent arrivals in the country, had never fought for Israel and didn't know what they should be doing. However, some had undergone military training in the former Soviet empire and were being deployed in towns and cities to allow regulars to move to the borders. Others were already beginning to wish they had remained in the Diaspora and not returned.

The Sword was primed! Ahmed was confident!

THE ROUT

At daybreak the visibility at the expected combat front was negligible, as a heavy, misty, rain engulfed the area. Israeli forward ground reconnaissance suggested that the leaders of the attacking force could be but a few kilometres away. Only limited intercepts of enemy radio traffic had been received and it was assumed that, operating under the guise of routine maintenance, well-placed extra land-lines had been laid in advance by the coalition partners in the last few days. These must have been used during the initial marshalling of the attack formations, of such a large force.

The strict radio silence, combined with the mountainous terrain and the unusually high amount of atmospheric static interference on the receivers, had together contributed the enemy success. Even Israel's airborne listening platforms were receiving almost continuous hissing and crackling, instead of any wanted signals. The weak reception was, of course, a feature of the extreme atmospheric absorption and attenuation, caused by the intense rainfall. The increasing sharp crackles indicated the onset of an intense electrical storm, before long.

Although, at the border the tanks were getting closer, because of the thick fog-like cloud, air strikes against the armour on either side were now completely out of the question. As though suddenly switched on by a mighty tap, as the first shot was fired, - tank against tank - the rain intensified to an uninterrupted deluge, hail fell, lightning flashed, and a heavy darkness descended.

'Friendly Fire', as it had become known after the Gulf Wars, or fratricide, was to be avoided at all costs. Any attempts to engage in combat by either side, by the use of infra-red night vision equipment from either air or ground forces, was useless. The infra-red signals, to produce the images, were being significantly attenuated by the intensity of the rain. Those few images presented were faint and blurred. However, Israel possessed superior imaging equipment. In theory, this should allow earlier detection and thus a first attack option. Surely this torrent couldn't go on for very long?

Israeli armour seemed to be well positioned but neither side could advance, engage, or drive the other back. The poor visibility precluded the normal procedure of calling in air support, either from helicopters or fixed wing aircraft. The Israeli Commander was loathe to call up extra tanks. Too many could be a hindrance rather than an asset in rough terrain, especially with poor identification and limited manoeuvre options.

Strange though, recalled one exasperated Tank Unit Commander, how the climate had changed in this part of the world in the last few years. Until recently,

Lake Galilee was at a very low water level and in the recent summers there had not been enough water on the national carrier for use on Israel's vital cotton, fruit and flower crops. In earlier years there had been unprecedented downpours, then recently, well over a year of near-drought. In the last few weeks they had hoped - indeed some had prayed for rain. Now the cloud-burst, just when it was not welcome! Further, it was coming at such a rate that there was no hope that the land could absorb the water, and it was just running off in ever increasing torrents, bringing down mud and stones in a sticky mess.

The rain and hail eased slightly. Cautious shelling had gone on for thirty minutes. Making little progress, the Commander of the Coalition of the North, finally decided to call forward more armour. Almost unbelievably, soon after the order was given, another sudden intense hailstorm ensued. This cut communications even further along the battle-front. Those who received the order moved forward. Others, who had failed to receive the call either stayed where they were or moved with uncertainty, not confident of having received clear orders. Some were left far behind - unaware that there had even been an order to move. The Commander was requesting all armour to report their positions. However, it was futile while the communications were so limited.

By this time, while moving forward in such a fragmentary manner, much of the rear echelon armour was bunched on the few main roads through the hills. Through no fault of their own, they had received no proper instructions for dispersal. Anyway, they could not see far enough ahead or behind to ensure adequate spacing between vehicles. Under conditions of normal visibility bunching together would have been most undesirable - indeed suicidal. Even if this crucial lesson had been learnt by the Russian forces, the lack of communications had denied correct procedures. Now they were bunched in groups, the results could be devastating, should they be attacked.

The Coalition Commanders were now urging the armour on, using the old Soviet Red-Army shock tactics. However, the only way the tanks and armoured personnel carriers could make even limited progress was on the slippery hardened roads, rather than by traversing over the quagmire of soft and slithery mud, water pools, ice and stones, that the pre-planned overland path presented.

When reports of this activity reached Israel's Operational HQ, they surmised that possibly the enemy had correctly reasoned that Israel had no means of air attack in these weather conditions. The Commanders of the coalition must have decided that an on-roads advance was an acceptable risk. They were clearly taking short cuts! Alternatively, they were incapable of flexibility and recklessly forged ahead, irrespective of conditions. Clearly they had not bargained for another, as yet unknown but imminent hazard - one beyond everyone's control.

It was at this time that the storm intensified to an alarming level and the earth literally shook under the tank tracks as they were striving to get a grip as the terrain softened. A new problem was not from the few anti-tank weapons, which Israel were sparingly firing, but from the first tremors of an earthquake. The main event and the after-shocks, in the next few hours, would soon have catastrophic consequences on the conduct and outcome of the conflict.

The main quake arrived. Around the world, the seismologists watched their instruments in disbelief, as top of the Richter scale was reached for the first ever time in the recorded history of their science. They rapidly exchanged measurements between monitoring points and soon deduced that the quake's epicentre was located at the far eastern end of the Mediterranean Sea.

None of the participants on the spot - and many had lived all their lives in earthquake zones - had experienced a quake of such intensity; or indeed a storm of such ferocity. Forty miles away from the battlefront, in Tel Aviv, tall buildings were shaking and swaying as though in a furious wind. All over the land people were running out into the streets. Many older buildings collapsed, including parts of the Old City of Jerusalem.

At the front line, those immediately in the Israeli line of fire, were actually coming under attack just as the ground beneath, the surrounding hills and the roads were heaving around them. What was happening? The assault troops, who were following the armour while huddled in the smelly semi-darkness of their claustrophobic personnel carriers, had sensed the unusual motion in addition to the normal vehicle motion.

Now they had all stopped - but even with the brakes on the vehicle was still moving! Flat ground had suddenly become precipitous. All firing had suddenly stopped. In the forward tanks it was a living hell. Their drivers could not see where to go, or their commanders who to attack. Some of the coalition tanks had been forcibly moved round to such an extent that their crews, unaware of the sudden rotation, were unknowingly firing blindly towards their own forces.

The electrical storms had severely affected the signal reception on the coalition's 'Glonass' satellite positioning equipments - the Russian equivalent to the West's 'GPS', or Global Positioning System. The vehicle standby compasses were useless, following the lightning strikes and they had no way of resetting their less accurate ground navigation systems, as they had no recognisable geographical references. They could not see far. Wherever they looked everything looked the same. Even the maps did not seem to fit the terrain that they thought they should be near. Some were not going any further anyway, as they were either tilted at crazy angles, half buried in rocks or were even upside-down.

Those still fortunate enough to be on level ground were making frantic radio calls for orders or help. They were unable to make a decision on which way to move. The accompanying air defence weapons that had been brought along, were useless, as there had been no air targets to fire at. These were much lighter vehicles. Being only lightly armoured, and less stable, many were now tipped up and blocking the way of the armour. Missiles had fallen off several and had been crushed by following vehicles. A fire had started where fuel tanks had been ruptured and solid propellant had caught fire from the damaged rockets. Finding that they could not drive the vehicles away from the fires, the crews were trying to leave their vehicles in a panic.

The atmosphere was continuously filled with heavy precipitation - water - falling either as hail or intense rain. It obliterated the targets on both radar and infra-red imaging displays with interfering echoes. The armour been fuelled early in the day and had already travelled many kilometres. Now many who were still mobile had started to be concerned. They realised that they could not reach their planned rendezvous points with their existing fuel and they could not contact their support vehicles. Most did not know even which direction should be ahead!

Armoured personnel carriers, their shaken crews each cowering twenty at a time in what seemed like steel tombs, were impotent to carry forward the attack unless the heavy armour gained ground. Hailstones the size of quails' eggs intermittently hammered on the thin hardened metal of their once-proud chariots. Not being able to see out, in a shocked and ignorant state, they imagined this to be hails of enemy bullets, warhead fragments or even cluster bomblets. They expected each moment to be their last.

In places, huge piles of hailstones were sufficient to cover entire vehicles, blinding their drivers. The hail also built up on the top of vehicles and obscured vision from the slit-like observation ports along the vehicle sides or from the drivers or commander's periscopes. Their night vision equipment was useless. Not knowing where friend or foe could be and fearing their own fire, some were totally obsessed by the likelihood of a direct hit from enemy heavy weapons, at any moment. It was a time for the strictest battle discipline, but none had experienced this scenario before. Despite all the exhortations to the contrary by the vehicle commanders, dozens had already opened the vehicle rear doors and fled. They abandoned what protection they had. Now they were on foot in the gloom. Many would never be seen alive again.

Frantic radio calls had brought little response. In many cases the extreme electrical effects of the storm had damaged both the primary and back-up radios permanently. Further, when a radio operator heard the occasional message it was usually in an unintelligible language or dialect of another coalition partner. Chaos and panic reigned. The amount of water vapour in the atmosphere was also playing havoc with more distant radio propagation conditions. Operators were receiving some freak messages from far off while, infuriatingly, not receiving those from colleagues of their own nation, who were close by. This probably also explained some of the language difficulties.

Even those drivers who could see a little way through their visors did not know which way to turn. The slippage on the tracks due to the excessive mud, even on the hard roads, had caused serious errors in the mechanical vehicle along-track recording apparatus. Hence, even the mechanically-driven land navigation equipment carried by Russian battle vehicles was of limited use. Tracks and wheels had spun to the extent that mechanical readings were in error by hundreds of metres. Some tank commanders thought they had arrived at their assigned positions when they had not, while others had travelled on past the point where they should have been. They would become exposed as sitting ducks, if the weather cleared suddenly. A few realised the problem. They referred to their navigation manual log, and then attempted dead reckoning, to establish how far they had travelled. It was, however, a futile exercise.

Most of the time the visibility remained near to zero, punctuated by either the short-lived diffusion of a flash of lightning or the flash of a nearby explosion. On occasions when they crawled forward a little, the momentary silhouette of another vehicle appeared. Even this was of limited advantage, as they could neither communicate with or identify the vehicle. Worse, the silhouette might turn and shoot at them at point blank range at any moment. A frightening prospect! Particularly worrying were those going in the wrong direction as they were bound to be mistaken as the enemy, and would certainly shoot at their friends!

Because of the urging-on of the armour from behind, and the narrowness of the remaining roads, those ahead were now finding it extremely difficult to continue, slowing down every column. Occasionally a blockage eventually cleared, by which time the impatient or foolhardy had often tried to go around. They ventured down craggy paths leading to raging torrents in the wadis or dead-end ravines, from which they could only extract themselves by reversing. Many leaving the roads found themselves with little traction, immersed in flash floods. Even heavy vehicles were swept along wadis and newly formed crevasses, that had opened up during the earthquake. They would no longer be participants in this war. In fact most of the combatants were already without heart, after what they had suffered so far - and this without even coming properly face-to-face with their enemy!

The troops were hungry and rapidly getting cold. Being under the tension of battle and uncertainty, they were increasingly demoralised. Many had been stationary for up to three hours. Surely this storm could not go on for much longer? Some had now run out of fuel. Earthquake aftershocks were randomly causing strange vehicular motion.

The persistent downfall of rain was soon causing severe flooding for all those at the foot of valleys. Bridges were collapsing or being swept away with the sheer force of tons of water, completely cutting off both advance and retreat. Within minutes, previously dry wadis suddenly became raging torrents and swirling masses of water, with mud and stones pushing everything away in its path. Maps had become useless. Even when stationary, unless they were refuelled, the vehicle heating systems would not last out overnight. Indeed, if the rapid rise of water continued it would soon engulf the engines and turbines of those who had wisely sought, or just luckily found, higher ground. Worse, their radio calls for help were unheeded. Metaphorically speaking - they were all in the same boat. The satellite navigation systems were still not working. They were lost!

However, Israel's tank Commanders, by rapid re-tuning and by using diverse radio wavelengths and with some contact through the Amos satellite, managed at times to communicate very briefly with their HQ. From time to time they received messages about the weather, the quake and the floods. They were on home ground and better understood the terrain. For much of the time all they could do was report on the extraordinary conditions and hope that their messages were getting through. They were remaining stationary, while preparing to fight if the opportunity or need arose. However, although they had lost some vehicles into floods, they had no way of knowing what the enemy were up to - or even exactly where they were located.

The world's seismic monitors were working overtime and reports of a major earthquake of catastrophic proportions, with its epicentre in the mountainous boundary between Israel, Syria and Lebanon, and along the Dead Sea Valley, were soon flashing around the world. Severe flood and tsunami warnings were being sent out. This was clearly way beyond the scope of anything seen within living memory. Even the aftershocks exceeded normal earthquake levels. The world had seen an increasing numbers of scale 6 or larger quakes in recent years, but only the seismologists and a few others had taken notice that the frequency of larger quakes was increasing.

The predicted large Californian earthquake had not yet occurred. However, quite large quakes had occurred inland in both China and Turkey, but, until today, none had surpassed the most serious quake in China, in 1976. However, most remembered the tsunami, caused by a massive quake under the Indian Ocean, on Boxing Day 2004.

Now, the same was happening again. A massive tidal wave had reportedly commenced movement and was travelling westward along the Eastern Mediterranean Coastlands and Islands. Within the past hour alone, it was assessed to have caused unprecedented loss of life and damage in several low-lying coastal areas in its path. The wave - no respector of national boundaries - was still observed to be six to ten metres high, as it swept past Crete. It was proceeding at a speed of almost thirty kilometres per hour. Within minutes, even those many miles away, who had heard the news, became very frightened. Those closer were in panic.

One CNN reporter, on the spot, said in a very shaky voice, that a major land and sea bed disturbance had occurred in the eastern Mediterranean, with the epicentre in the north of Israel. He could say little more, with any certainty, until stock had been taken at the dozens of affected scenes. The world's telephone and internet communications systems were overloaded within an hour of the first report and Europe's population were reaching towards panic level in several towns and cities.

From hundreds of coastal and low-lying villages - which were further away and could thus heed the warnings in time - people were frantically fleeing to the safety of higher ground. There had been considerable problems in the coastal zones of Egypt, Turkey, Cyprus, Rhodes and Libya. Worryingly, little had been heard from several smaller islands. Apart from this huge tidal effect, their experience told all those living in these lands that there would be after-shocks of considerable strength. These would surely follow such a large quake for several days.

Citizens with cars, having rushed to get away from the sea, were soon to find that the expected series of intense after-shocks had caused tremors strong enough to demolish their escape routes. Buildings collapsed, blocking city streets and roads. Landslides caused earth and stones to pile into valleys. Ancient bridges fragmented into rubble. The Bosphorous Bridge was closed as unsafe, as a travelling shock-wave wave had twisted the structure. The Pope urged prayer and coolness. Few heeded. Nevertheless, men who were a long way from the Middle East trembled for the first time in their lives, such was the force of events. Calls were going out for assistance from many nations.

For many years the earth's structure had been understood to be formed by huge 'plates' that interact along major earth's crust fault lines. One of these fault-lines lies along the Jordan Valley - the line of the valley containing the Dead Sea, the lowest place on earth, and extends southwards right down as far as Africa's Great Rift Valley and northwards into the Lebanon. At this fateful moment it seemed to those located on the fault-line that the plates had somehow 'selected' this precise moment of history, as soon as the battle had commenced, to re-align in a very major way indeed. This, after lying relatively dormant for thousands of years.

Most of the nations of the coalition attacking Israel quickly forgot the war entirely, so as to concentrate on the natural catastrophe that had befallen them. This event was a complete surprise to these nations as they had not been aware that their nations were about to attack Israel in concert. Thus most of the families servicemen suddenly realised that their loved ones were not on exercises but had left to fight a war. They were equally becoming aware that their soldiers were likely to be in the thick of catastrophic trouble,

Almost unbelievably, water from the Red Sea had flowed along a new channel towards the Dead Sea, the lowest point on earth, raising its level and already flooding Ein Ged, Qumran and parts of Jericho. Water levels were still rising.

The nations comprising the UN had not been willing to act when the crisis of war loomed. Now they faced a natural crisis that they could not fail to recognise. The USA and the UN had instituted major disaster aid, but this all took time. The first action was to order troops, already deployed on peace-keeping missions elsewhere, to move to the affected areas. They were still deployed in these diverse locations because the much-heralded 'New World Order', providing 'peace for all', after the Cold War, had still not arrived! The sheer scale of events was such that any aid, that even the strongest nation could provide, would be as a flea-bite compared with what was needed.

Pictures of the events reported were soon being beamed around the world, in near real-time. As they watched, men, women and children, trembled in anticipation of the next event. As they did so, those beyond immediate help, located in the most affected areas, were struggling for life. It was almost every man for himself along the southern Mediterranean coastline as far as Tripoli; and on the northern coastline, as far as Turkish Antalya, and beyond. All the Greek Agean islands with low coastlines suffered losses and in Cyprus entire coastal towns were virtually wiped out. Every ship, every port and all means of road communication near the Mediterranean Sea had been affected in some way. At least the visibility was reasonable in some of these areas and aircraft were soon out on reconnaissance and rescue missions, trying to establish exactly what help would be needed. It soon became obvious that there would never be enough help, for many weeks to come.

Vessels at sea had been swamped, or driven under the pressure of the tidal wave, like giant surf-boards to crash onto beaches, rocks and cliffs. Somewhat ironically, those who did not survive included most that had off-loaded the heavy armour in Syria. They had been making their way back to Libya and the Black Sea ports, with the intention of returning with further military supplies. Other reinforcements, still en-route from Russia, in transit through the Black Sea and Bosphorous, together with follow-up shipments coming along the Mediterranean, from Libya, were all casualties. All having been driven onto rocky coasts or capsized. They had rapidly been forced to forget about the war - only personal survival mattered.

Nothing had been heard from dozens of vessels for hours and, for these, the worst was feared. Wreckage had been reported along many coastlines, but most of the coastal inhabitants were too busy to go looking or had fled to higher ground. What had become of the many passenger ferries which plied between the dozens of mainly Greek and Turkish islands and their mainland ports in the Eastern Mediterranean? Radio operators strove continuously, to try and re-establish contact with them.

The toll on power generating stations was inevitably high. Several that were located at coastal sites had been flooded almost at once and ceased operating, damaged beyond short term repair. They had, of course, been so positioned, to receive regular deliveries of oil and coal directly unloaded from tankers and freighters, via their own bunkering and jetty facilities. Now the supply jetties were damaged by the swamping or had been torn away and gone. Those still generating would only do so while their fuel stocks lasted - there would be no re-supply from the sea for a very long time. Some consumers would not have power again until land-lines and overhead lines were repaired. This would take weeks.

A great number of freight and fishing ports were also damaged. Others would be ports no more. Because of earth movements at land and sea, several were now inland or even on newly formed islands, rather than positioned as they has been for centuries - on the coast. It would be weeks, perhaps months, years, perhaps never, before the fate would be known of all of those who had innocently put to at sea on that fateful day.

As the weather eased, portable satellite dishes were the sole source of reliable communication into the worst affected areas. Communication masts that were located on higher ground, away from the coast, were another surviving means of communicating and broadcasting. Their main problem was the lack of electrical mains power. Those with standby generators, located on site, would only last for as long as their fuel supplies.

For those that could still operate, they suffered from a surfeit of widely speculative and inaccurate news. Had more nuclear weapons caused this or not? Had a large meteorite collided with earth? Had there been more than one earthquake? Those who were near to the disaster area were looking for reassurance, but they were getting confusing information. They could barely comprehend what was happening, even on the spot.

Far away from the worst-affected areas, many were permanently transfixed before their television sets or beside their radios; listening and watching by day and by night. But they were powerless to help and fearful of the next stage. This disaster, as an insurance risk was classified as a natural occurrence, or an 'Act of God' - for which most citizens would not be covered. Not that there was any time to worry about recompense at the moment. Basic survival, for so many, was their prime hope. The perceptive realised that the world's oil supplies were bound to be immediately affected. Hoarding commenced, even before some governments could act to bring in emergency powers and rationing.

In contrast, the nuclear damage that so many had feared - not so many days earlier - was as nothing compared with what had now befallen so many. Any nuclear fall out health hazards, being a longer term effect, was for the moment, forgotten. The entire world's population were acutely aware of the events happening in the Middle East.

Reuben and the others in the National Command Bunker knew little more than had been put out on the news. Several military families had attempted to make contact by phone during lulls in the activities. About half of those manning the bunker, Reuben included, had no idea of the fate of their own loved ones, their homes, or of their colleagues on the front line.

Warnings and advice messages were frequently broadcast. Attempts were made to re-assure those at the western end of the Mediterranean, in southern Europe, in North Africa and in the Gulf of Iran that help was on its way.

At the battle-front the Israeli armoured formations could only see ahead intermittently, as the rain slashed and the hail rattled down. Lightning - flash on flash and rumble on rumble, thunder clap and yet another thunder clap, continued almost without respite. This, as one Islamic Coalition Commander said, was, thus far, 'not the Mother of all Battles' - a term coined by Saddam Hussein before the first Gulf War, almost ten years ago, but the 'Storm of all Storms and Calamities'! The battle crews, many young and inexperienced, huddled in their vehicles, wide-eyed in fear and trembling.

In the last few hours, apart from those who had deserted their vehicles earlier, several had now gone berserk and leapt out, ignoring commands and pointing their rifles at the vehicle commander, in an attempt to fend for themselves. For the moment the odds were that most would have stood more chance of survival by remaining where they were. Others had already suffered a miserable fate in the flash floods, while stumbling around, cold and wet, with no sense of direction and unable to find the relative safety of high ground.

The northern coalition leaders in Moscow, Teheran, Ryadh, Moscow, Tripoli, Damascus and Baghdad were in disarray. Most had no idea of what was actually happening to their forces on the ground. They were receiving only fragmentary, inaccurate, or conflicting reports. Some were already too busy trying to handle the after-effects of the earthquake to bother any further. Even if those in far-away Teheran or Russia had received up to date reports, they could barely have described the awfulness of the situation on the ground. Jordan, Iraq, the Lebanon, Saudi Arabia and even parts of Iran and the Gulf States, were all affected by the quakes.

The perpetrators knew something catastrophic had happened, or, indeed, was still happening to their glorious forces. As in previous wars with Israel, they did not wish to believe it. The Sword of Islam - or at least the force fighting under that banner and spearheaded by Russia - was clearly in serious trouble, mainly, it seemed, through unprecedented 'natural causes'.

The Sword, in which had so trusted their instincts, as they had deviously plotted their concerted surprise attack on Israel, had somehow failed. The final - yes, even their so carefully planned final solution - to their long running 'Jewish problem', had failed again. Where had they gone wrong this time? Why had they failed again?

It was incredible! Unbelievable! Surely they had not failed! As they waited for further news, Ahmed Pavli refused to believe the evidence thus far. His resolve would not fail. He awaited more reliable news from the battle-front. At home, apart from some problems on the shores of the Gulf, Iran itself was not affected inland by the quake.

Ahmed Pavli finally began receiving accurate reports. In summary, they indicated that his coalition forces had indeed been rendered impotent by the combination of earthquake and weather - and this after advancing only a few kilometres into Israel's northern territory.

The reports spoke of appalling conditions. Those who had been rapidly following up behind, to reinforce the forward armour, had found themselves trapped by huge boulders and rock-falls, both behind and ahead. They could neither advance or retreat. Newly-formed crevasses had appeared before them. The full horror of the fate of those present would not be known for days. In reality, some had tipped into these crevasses, with much grinding and tearing of metal. It was the same from Sidon on the Mediterranean coast, right across to the Golan.

It was also reported that, so far, air power had not been used in the actual battle against armour, although Israel had flown some limited helicopter operations - principally for reconnaissance and rescue. The earthquake and weather had dictated the outcome of the battle thus far - not the contestants. Weather had often affected wars before, but never to this extent - and certainly not an earthquake. Nevertheless, as far as Ahmed Pavli was concerned, it was not over yet!

Based on the very limited meteorological data available, the forecasters were predicting weather improvements and Israel hoped that fixed-wing air operations could soon start.

Meanwhile, a rapid coalition dialogue had reluctantly decided upon the implementation of a second phase. Reports could not establish the extent or current status of the armour that had been caught up in the earthquake and weather. They did not have a clear idea of the position of most of the forces on the ground, including logistic reinforcements at sea. For some reason communications at sea had been cut. They had no idea that this was because their supply forces at sea had been irretrievably lost in the tidal wave.

The coalition forces committed so far had not been the whole Sword of Islam. On paper many more had been planned to follow up, by sea and by air. Ahmed Pavli, ignorant of the detailed situation, issued the orders for the second phase to commence. For this phase his manned aircraft, cruise missiles and ballistic missiles would be used. Weather conditions must surely improve in the target area before long. No one had ever known a storm to last for so long. The earthquake aftershocks would surely diminish or become more widely spaced.

Next, his aircraft and cruise missiles would be sent against Israel's airfields. Ballistic missiles would be ranged against her cities and command centres. Shorter-ranged, tactical ballistic missiles would be brought forward as quickly as possible, on their mobile launchers. They would be fired against Israeli units on the forward edge of the battle area. It was time for the big strike. There would be nothing to lose! This would most certainly finish off Israel once and for all. While the more distant parts of the world were mainly mesmerised by the war, all those bordering on the Mediterranean Sea were pre-occupied with the natural disaster. The forces were to be urged onwards, at all costs. Further attacks by Iran and her partners would be the last thing that Israel would expect at this stage. Ahmed Pavli sent out his orders.

A concerted ballistic missile attack on Israel would soon begin. Each of the coalition forces opposed to Israel had been issued with target information and given priority orders to their ballistic missile forces. Forthwith, they were to load the pre-planned target data into the missile memories, to re-fuel them and report launch readiness when they reached their launch positions. To avoid air attack, the final mobile launch positions were not to be communicated by radio. They were in sealed secret orders. A pre-planned launch time would be issued as a coded broadcast, when it was time to co-ordinate the firings.

Iran would again provide the ballistic missile attacks against Israel's northernmost cities, such as Haifa, and also against troops and armour in the Galilee area facing Syrian troops on the Golan. Syrian shorter-ranged missiles would go against selected military hardened targets and airfields, in central Israel, and against the coastal Jewish cities of Netanya and Hertzlia.

Saudi Arabian and Libyan longer ranged weapons would provide the Sword to be used against Israel's more southern coastal towns and against Israel's largest city, Tel Aviv, and also to provide some overlapping cover against Haifa. The targets in this set would include Rehovot, Rishon-le-Zion, Ashdod and Ashkelon.

Jerusalem was not a target, as Islam could not risk an accidental hit on the Mosque of Omar, on Jerusalem's Temple Mount. Thus the entire 'Sword' would fall as one co-ordinated blow. Ahmed had decided that Israel would thus capitulate in Jerusalem, once they saw what had happened to their other towns and cities!

Saudi Arabia would also concentrate her attack on the nuclear facility at Dimona in the Israeli Negev Desert, together with some airfields, principally Ben Gurion Airport, which was also a military air-base. No action was needed against Eilat, in the far South of Israel. Its function as a seaport had been reportedly as largely negated by the effects of the big earthquake. Most of Eilat's buildings, including the airport, had been flooded or shaken by the severe after shocks which had continued for some hours after the main event. The airport was only still useable by small aircraft, due to a wide crevasse, half-way along the runway. There had been loss of civilian life when three of the older hotels had collapsed.

The coalition also readied their cruise missiles. These were not of the popularly reported type, like the US Tomahawk, used in the Gulf War. These had been developed from small air-breathing propeller-driven aircraft, that Iran and Saudi Arabia had procured in the last few months from China and the West - including European Countries - who should have known better. The USA would surely be regretting their sales of the small unmanned aircraft, which they had erroneously been led to believe were to have been used as innocuous drones for target practice and for agricultural use. Iraq still had a few indigenously designed drones that had not been destroyed under the UN resolutions in 2002.

The drones were intended to carry devastating warheads against both civilian and military targets. Israel, if Ahmed's wishes were fulfilled, would soon not be there any more to complain to the UN or the USA. The Sword was primed once again! Ahmed was even more confident!

A SHOT IN THE DARK

Iyad Abed Aziz had left his place of work and driven hurriedly into town. He was in high spirits. Iyad enjoyed his work. It included important responsibilities. Of course, moving around the country, usually in convoy, was not as much fun as flying. Nevertheless, he had promised himself an exceptionally good time today. Proud of his heritage, explained so often by his father Talal Aziz, he felt more than entitled to hold the position of Major in his nation's armed forces. This had brought him to today's situation - a point where he was responsible for preparing the weapons for exercise, in the Missile Battery that he commanded. Perhaps, one day, he would be called to prepare them for actual use against the enemy!

So often had he carried out the classroom drills in practice, that he considered that there was no longer any need to use reference manuals. These were the operational instructions that the Chinese Machinery Company had so conveniently supplied - written in English. This was understandable, since so many of the technical words did not exist in his native Arabic tongue - and who, in Saudi Arabia, understood Chinese?

The influence of Britain and the USA, in so many parts of the Middle and Far East, had resulted in the widespread use of English as a working language for technologies; in much the same way that English had been used for as long as anyone could remember for air traffic control. Many of his fellow flyers and ground technicians had therefore been trained in the West. To undertake their part effectively, in the Royal Saudi Arabian Air Force, their English had to be good. Hence, the current ground-tour, essential for Ayad's career advancement, posed no language or technical problems.

Before leaving for town he had set up the ballistic missile targeting memories, ready for the coming night's exercise. The responsibility entailed enormous trust. He was the new warrior of the future - in the line of Abdul Aziz, proudly counted as one of his own ancestors! Until war came, every exercise was treated as though it was 'for real'. Earlier, using the flimsy exercise targeting sheet, it had been an easy task to dial in the co-ordinate numbers. The only problem had been that the information had arrived by hand of the Defence Headquarters courier, an hour late. The actual target positions were always kept secret. Already delayed, he had done this task swiftly and not bothered to re-check them - plenty of time to do that when he returned tonight, just before the convoy set off!

He had been keener than ever to get away but could not do so until he had hurriedly moved from launcher to launcher, repeating the setting procedures of the entire Battery of four ballistic missiles. As he rapidly departed the missile compound he was confident that nothing was amiss. Of course, it was always possible, although unlikely, that a surprise check would be made by his Regimental Commander, before Iyad returned. Following the preparations, Iyad and the rest of the staff had been stood down until the exercise time. The Duty Officer and the guards remained on site, should an official visitor arrive.

He reflected on the many changes afoot in his country in the last few months. Towards the end of the millennium Saudi Arabia's rulers, were in turmoil. One of the world's last absolute monarchies, with more than 20 million citizens, there was a dilemma in deciding who should succeed to the throne. For some time the old King had ruled in name only, with day-to-day affairs in the hands of a Regent - Prince Abdullah Ibn Abdul Aziz - a distant relative. A power struggle, among the no less than 23 of the 5000 princes, had ensued. Some even wanted one of Abdul Aziz's great-grandsons to take power - but they were barely of age. Clashes of mainly Western-educated liberals with the many Sharia fundamentalists had added to the furore. This had reached a peak soon after the turn of the millennium. It was still not resolved - and the King lived on. Serious changes were just around the corner!

Finally the US and British forces, which had been stationed on Saudi Arabian soil for nearly fifteen years had been reduced. Now, following the second Gulf War, only those necessary for the support of the continuation temporary occupation of Iraq remained. Many were concerned that Weapons of Mass Destruction would eventually find their way into the hands of terrorists and be used around the world. In such a large country the search for these had lasted for many months. It seemed likely that Saddam had moved them across an adjacent border, or hidden them in remote locations. As time went on more and more members of Saddam's regime had been captured, killed, or surrendered. A new government had taken over complete control during 2005. Every Iraqi citizen had a free vote.

Saudi spending on arms had continued to rise, despite the nation's own economic problems. The complexity of the newly purchased weaponry was beyond the capability of most of the available manpower. Therefore, very large numbers of foreign technicians had been imported to maintain the weaponry and train the locals. This was despite the violent objections of the fundamentalists - who did not want a single foreigner on Islamic soil. When the pressures finally reached explosive levels, the Saudi Arabian National Guard, commanded by the Crown Prince could not contain the internal unrest. The entire Royal Family attempted to flee. However, not all survived the raging mobs.

Despite the end of the monarchy, Iyad's father, by narrow consent of the new Islamic Ruling Council, had remained the Oil Minister. Just recently he had been away again, with several oil meetings at short notice. Iyad's father had not explained to his family why the sudden meetings were called, or even where they had been held. His father seemed quite worried the last time they had spoken, but did not say why.

It even seemed likely to Iyad that, with the fall of the House of Saud and the recent take-over by the fundamentalists, that the very name of the country might be changed. The dust kicked up by Iyad's rapid driving across the desert was not the only dust - metaphorically speaking - that had yet to settle in the country!

Iyad rehearsed in his mind all the exercise activities that had been planned for much later that evening. The exercise deployment site for his missile battery would take place deep in the desert, near Buralydah. At some point during the evening exercise, two other officers would arrive to finally authorise the procedure for exercise weapon arming. In war, when the real time came, the same 'key officers', permanently assigned to his unit from headquarters, would provide the final launch authorisation. At that point they would insert the firing keys together. Every effort was made to avoid any incidents or accidents with these ballistic missiles, as they could be loaded to carry weapons of mass destruction.

Having borrowed his father's car, away yet again on another of his oil trips, the distinctly coloured number plates were ensuring an uninterrupted journey. No one would dare interrupt the progress of a Minister's vehicle, or even attempt to overtake. With its tinted glass windows no one could see that it was the son and not the father driving. Nevertheless, he would have to park the recognisable car well-away from his friend's house, so as not to alert suspicion.

His waiting host was the wife of his father's aide, conveniently confirmed to be away on the same oil meeting with his father!

Tonight's exercise was apparently a special one. Perhaps it would last longer than normal, maybe even for several days. He would remember to warn his very special lady friend that she may not see him for a few days. He reckoned she owed him special favours. Life was good, despite all the changes going on. Iyad didn't know much about the Air Force's future plans - but it was treating him all right. He had only recently been promoted to Major, having successfully completed the missile course. Now he had money, position and wealth and lived from day to day. He parked the car and hurried to the distant apartment block. She was eagerly waiting. Two hours later, with his expectations more than satisfied, he fell asleep - exhausted.

During Ayad's absence from base, unexpected orders arrived. They were to bring forward the march hour from 2100 to 1800 hours. Iyad's deputy, the Duty Officer and his Transport Officer, all unable to contact their Commander when he failed to return on time, had to make a crucial decision. Together they decided that the best course of action was to leave adequate information so that he could catch up. They left orders with the permanent guard and the convoy of mobile missile launchers, reload and support vehicles set off, on time, without him. The day was still hot. They had expected to travel later, in the cool of the evening.

Soon, the officers were bitterly complaining about aircrew - like Iyad - doing ground tours and taking liberties, when they were now hard at work. The four huge missile transporters and their support vehicles rumbled off, on the long drive across the desert to their distant deployment location. As one of the other officers remarked - this was not the first time their Major had been 'late on parade' and was probably not the last. No doubt Major Iyad Aziz would be catching them up in that expensive car of his father - and getting away with being absent yet again! He had, the Deputy Battery Commander recalled, done this once before - but not in the middle of an important exercise. Feeling a little guilty of having inwardly criticised his Commander, he turned to view the desert road ahead. His was the lead vehicle and the few desert shadows had already started to lengthen. He concentrated on the navigation.

When, after two hours travelling, they stopped for a break and raised the long-range radio mast to report their progress to Headquarters they received a coded message. The Deputy, still bemoaning his Commander's absence, decoded the signal. It contained yet another change of plan. There would be two deployment positions that night, one almost one hundred kilometres further to the east, followed by yet another, much further north. At the next road junction the convoy turned and lumbered towards the new easterly location. Altogether it would take almost a further six hours, before they were operational for the exercise.

After some time it suddenly dawned on them that they should not have covered up for Iyad's absence. He would not know where they had gone after all! But surely, they surmised - he would know of the possibility of changes anyway - from his earlier secret orders, when he had set up the missiles against their exercise targets. Radio silence was being maintained. The crews had no idea of the chaos going on in the far north, of the huge earthquake, or even that they were also part of a coalition already attempting to attack Israel.

Reuben surveyed the situation map. They were running on standby power and there were cracks in the walls of the operations room. The whole structure mounted on a supposedly nuclear-proof concrete raft, had rocked like a boat at the peak of the earthquake. The national water carrier had been ruptured in four places and teams were busy deciding on the next moves, both civil and militarily.

One of Israel's power stations, located along the coast, at Hadera, was still operating, but with reduced output. Not that they needed to pump or preserve water immediately, as the valleys to the north were flooded and this would seep through and thus add to the underground aquifers, where the water reserves were already adequate. However, precautions would be advisable to avoid water-borne diseases or chemical contamination within a day or two, assuming that the reports of widespread loss of human and animal life were correct.

He was still very concerned about his family, having been unable to raise anyone on the telephone - which he had attempted to do as soon as he had the opportunity after the quake. Maybe, he kept telling himself, the lines were down or flooded or perhaps there was a power failure. Apart from isolated reports on the civil activities, most of his responsibility was military. It was, of course, the nature of their job to stay at their posts as military officers, whatever happened. He tried to put the family out of his mind and focus on the task in hand. Hard though it was, it was the only way to handle the situation.

The adverse weather had kept all attack aircraft on the ground and Reuben and the crisis team were holding back use of Israel's own nuclear-tipped Jericho II ballistic missiles, until absolutely necessary. This would only be used finally, in ultimatum, against the coalition's cities, with Baghdad taking the first 'basket of sunshine' as an example. Reuben's Commander was still not absolutely sure who had taken the lead in attacking his country. Reports were conflicting. It would be a disaster to retaliate against a nation that did not deserve retribution. Reuben naturally hoped this would not be necessary - but Israel's back was against the wall. Again he asked himself, as so many had done for 2000 years - why won't they leave the Jews alone? If the situation became desperate the weapon was ready. The fortress - Masada - would certainly not fall again! Their very right to exist was again being threatened. Apart from the face-to-face confrontation in the north, the military situation was of less immediate concern to the population at large than some of the environmental ones. The teams out searching for the first ballistic missile impact point had found nuclear radiation on the ground. This had resulted in some evacuations and the temporary imposition of a fan-shaped sterile area. Some of the roads in the north of the country were closed, making communications and transport more difficult when travelling towards the Galilee.

The situation was not helped by the fact that military planners had most certainly never anticipated a ground attack by a nation as far away as Russia. The 'Daughter of Zion' had no means of bringing nuclear leverage to bear on Russia to stop their part in hostilities. This was simply because Jericho II could not, through the lack of flying range, reach any Russian fixed target.

Perhaps, reasoned Reuben, the severe Russian ground-force losses would be enough to stop any further advance. Also, surely world opinion would bring pressure to bear on the Russian population. After all, the first democratic government in Russia had already fallen - principally over economics and the human loss of life in their own military adventures in the former Southern Republics, including Chetznya, soon after the start of the 21st Century. Perhaps it would be necessary for Israel to give a nuclear demonstration first, against one of their nearer neighbours.

From the reports received, Reuben was now aware of four startling facts. First, that Israel was facing a huge coalition army, having been deployed in almost complete secrecy. It was almost certainly led by Russia, who had joined together with forces from several of the traditionally hostile nations to the North. Secondly, that these enormous armies - at least for the moment - had somehow been totally stopped by the abnormal weather and the earthquake. Thirdly, that if ballistic missiles were used next, and they came in multiple attacks or from diverse directions at the same time, then Israel's deployed ballistic missile defence system would simply not be able to prevent some leakage. Finally, Reuben was aware that no less than five of the likely aggressors possessed ballistic missiles of varying capability. Some had cruise missiles as well!

He prayed that, if they came, there would be no serious penetration of Israel's barely adequate air defences. They were in this tight situation as a result of Western pressure for what had been called 'peace'.

Reuben concentrated on tasking his ground attack and air reconnaissance squadrons in preparation for imminent air sorties against the armour and massed hordes, now facing the comparatively limited Israeli Defence Forces, in the northern mountains and hills. As a practical soldier he wished he was with them instead of sitting here!

About two hours later the dreaded missile alert sounded. An imminent short range ballistic missile attack had been detected by satellite and was approaching from Syria. The time left was already measured in tens of seconds. The severe thunder clouds had made long range radar detection intermittent and any impact-point prediction might be quite unreliable. Nevertheless, possible longer ranged launches had also been detected when climbing near to their apogee and then had disappeared. It was not clear where these had been launched from.

Another torrential downpour was taking place along the missile's presumed route. This was now blocking the radar sight-line. High wind-shears were present in the atmosphere, as the hub of the storm had drifted in the prevailing wind, in the direction of Syria. Before any defensive weapons could be fired against the incoming SCUD missile variants - for this was almost certainly what Syria would have fired - a series of intense flashes were reported in the northern sky. It was concluded, when no ground impacts were reported after fifteen minutes, that the fast incoming missiles must have malfunctioned in some way. Presumably they had exploded or just broken-up in the sky. Those in the know breathed a thankful sigh of relief.

Now, reports were coming in thick and fast. Within minutes the worst had happened - there were reports of a bi-directional ballistic attack, apparently from Saudi Arabia and simultaneously another coming from the a westerly direction, presumably from Libya. Some minutes later an observer atop the Shalom Tower, reported the flash of a small explosion. It was well to his south, along the Israeli coastline, towards Gaza. This was assumed, from the timing, to be the first Libyan missile, probably carrying a high explosive warhead.

Within minutes it was confirmed that it had fallen on an uninhabited part of coastline, north of Gaza. No intercept had been attempted and there were, thankfully, no casualties reported. However, it was known that Libya had dabbled with chemical weapons - so no one could be sure until this was checked-out. If the weapon was carrying conventional explosives, there would be no other contamination to deal with. Reuben could only guess that the intended target was probably Tel Aviv and that the high level winds in the area, or some other factor, had diverted the missile southwards. A thought next came to mind that he was probably currently sitting in the very building that had been the target. He suddenly offered up a prayer of thanks. Pull yourself together he thought! Reuben - a secular Jew praying - whatever next - and more than once today already! Many others had unexpectedly found themselves doing exactly the same thing in the past few hours.

In the north the forward Israeli armour was still both battened down and bogged down on the hillsides. They were facing what could fleetingly be seen of the enemy armour through the darkness, rain and swirling mists. Just as well they had not moved far forward, under the circumstances, as ahead an enormous explosion and flash was sensed rather than seen through their vehicle periscopes, as it diffused and propagated through the gloom. A huge wind-blast followed and some of their vehicles were literally pushed along a few metres in the mud. Almost at once a second flash occurred, lighting up the murk to their left and followed in turn by a third, though of less intensity, to their right.

Shortly after, yet another explosion occurred, closer but at ground level, probably from a forward enemy ammunition re-supply vehicle. Sulphurous fumes were choking the forces opposite as a huge fireball boiled up. Fortunately, few of the crews had been looking through their rain and mud-spattered periscopes at the exact time or they would have been temporarily blinded at the very least. Something had clearly gone wrong up ahead with enemy targeting.

Suddenly it was clear that at least one, if not all three, of the detonations they had just sensed, must have been nuclear. The tank crews, although provided with radiation detectors did not individually have enough information to evaluate what had happened in detail. The nuclear flash detectors on board had indeed activated and some radiation was already being indicated. The vehicle protective systems had indeed tripped in. Thankfully, they were now breathing using overpressure conditions to keep out radiated particles.

Back in Command HQ, Reuben was reviewing the reports that several more ballistic missiles had recently been fired at Israel from long distances. Some had failed to fire their second stage rockets. Those that had reached their apogee had mainly gone towards the northernmost edge of the forward battle area.

For the coalition attacking Israel it was clear that something had gone terribly wrong. It seemed, from all reports, that the mighty Ballistic Sword of Islam had fallen, literally and physically in the wrong place. The fearsome missile warheads had landed on the leading forces of the mighty Sword of Islam on the ground, and had not reached their enemy!

Within the hour a final blow was to fall on the coalition troops. They were still largely trapped, following the floods, the storm, the earthquake, and the effects of high explosive and drifting nuclear fallout.

Eight ballistic missiles carrying biological warheads and chemical warheads had also been despatched from Iran. Biological and chemical warheads had been substituted for conventional warheads, after Iran realised that something had gone seriously wrong with their earlier ballistic raids. They were not going to launch another nuclear warhead which might not get to the right place. It did not occur to them that these follow-on weapons might similarly be affected by the exceptional weather conditions during the ballistic descent. Daylight was fast approaching and if the sun did break through the murk it would soon degrade their biological agents - the latter being more likely to be effective at night.

Surely nothing could go wrong with simple chemical warheads? They were right - once the weapon reached the ground! However, the combined effect of the unprecedented storms, the extreme electrical charging of the atmosphere caused by the lightning, together with the earlier partial nuclear explosions, had left severely ionised and sterated atmospheric layers at both medium and high altitude. The heating had caused wind shears and extreme turbulence to persist for many hours and the ionosphere itself was much more heavily ionised than normal. All of this combined to disrupt the ballistic re-entry vehicles of all eight Iranian weapons, launched in rapid succession towards Israel. They began to nose-down and dive at an early stage.

Only a small change in flight path angle was required at the enormous speed at which they travelled in order to make a significant difference, when compared with their originally intended trajectories - and hence to their impact points. One tumbled and broke up almost immediately - just like Saddam's badly-modified SCUDS in the Gulf War. The warhead contents would be no longer lethal from this high altitude release, as the chemicals scattered, mixed and diluted, in the atmosphere, while falling tens of kilometres towards the ground. Some of the biological contents would be neutralised by the extreme radiation and ionisation in the upper atmosphere.

On the ground, Israeli detection equipment nevertheless flagged up an initial chemical and biological warning and their forces immediately re-checked their battened-down states. From now on they all operated with vehicle internal air over-pressure conditions to prevent contamination ingress by whatever might be out there from reaching into their cramped cabins. Even, if as claimed, biological materials degraded when exposed to sunlight, they were taking no chances. They had no idea of what was in store and, with this murky weather, there had been no sunlight for the past few days and this state of affairs seemed to be continuing.

Israel, of all the world's nations had been the most alerted to the likelihood of chemical and biological warfare. After all they had regularly been threatened with all manner of such attacks in the past, by most of their near neighbours. Caution, suspicion and abhorrence of these weapons was bred into their national consciousness, following the gas chambers used in Hitler's Holocaust, in World War Two. Now, as well as chemicals, one hundred countries had been credited with a potential biological warfare capability. Further, Israel were well aware - and hence prepared - that their near-neighbour, Syria, with others, may be ready to use these terrible weapons. Like some other enemies of Israel they had not been signatories to the International Biological Weapons Convention.

Although the immediate problem was to detect exactly what had been introduced into the battle zone, many realised that those facing the greatest danger may be the unprotected cities downwind of any invisible and lethal mists. Was this latest attack chemical warfare - the nerve gases similar to pesticides or was it a biological attack? The latter included the feared anthrax spores and the plague. Even worse it could be one of the so-called 'designer bugs'.

Anthrax - highly infectious in low concentrations could have a mortality rate of ninety per cent. Far less would be needed weight-for-weight, compared to chemicals. Only in the past two years had reliable detection equipment been developed. Biological agents had always been most difficult to distinguish from organic matter, occurring naturally. Now the Israeli breathing apparatus and over-garments would protect - since both inhalation and ingestion must be prevented. The over-garments were necessary for nerve gas, since this can enter the system through skin contact.

At the time when the war started few were aware of the development or potential of 'designer bugs'. These can be produced in the laboratory, then cunningly hidden in a harmless 'carrier' bug. Reuben's soldiers could not beat a rapid retreat and they feared the worst if these bugs had been used.

After the 'Desert Storm' War in the Gulf, in 1991, a crash programme was instituted to develop a method of automating the prediction of down-wind chemical and biological threat hazards. Once it had been realised that the ingredients needed for the chemical nerve agents Tabun, Sarin and Soman had been disclosed on the Internet, these efforts had intensified - but the 'cat was out of the bag'. The United Nations inspectors had found that the Iraqi programme had been larger and more advanced than expected.

The West's knowledge of some of Iraq's weapons programme had been enhanced by the defection of Saddam Hussein's son-in-law and his brother, and a host of other relatives in a dash across the desert to Jordan, earlier in the decade. No doubt the rest of Israel's enemies had been similarly busy. General Hussein Kamel Al Majid had, reputedly, been the brains behind Iraq's weapon plans. Very foolishly, Kamel and his brother returned to Iraq, where they were both executed! Reportedly, there was even a particularly nasty virus he was trying to develop, called camel pox! Now, following the second Gulf War Saddam Hussein and his followers were either captured, or had fled. A brief UN inspection had failed to find all the weapons. The advancing US and British troops had found various items connected with weapons of mass destruction. No one knew exactly what might have been hidden, and whether it was still useable.

Reuben, asked to report on likely chemical attacks, could not forget that in the mid 1990s Russia were assessed to have no less than 40,000 tons of the stuff - supposedly awaiting destruction. Now Russia was leading the attack!

Despite the advances in protection, the new predictive algorithms were already in trouble. This came about because the unprecedented wind-speeds, humid atmosphere and turbulence in this battle area, exceeded the equipment design limits and all but negated the effectiveness of the laser radar - 'lidar' and other predictors installed in some of the vehicles. It had been developed for much more benign atmospheric scenarios - indeed for the normally expected weather conditions.

Reliable reports confirmed that the contents of the seven other missiles had indeed plunged well short of Israel's cities and plummeted onto Israel's enemies - the coalition troops. Within minutes the first of these poorly protected soldiers were in serious trouble. As if more needed to be added to the indignities they had already suffered thus far - principally from the main earthquake, the aftershocks, and the weather, rather than from Israeli action. Wind and floods further distributed the biological viruses and the toxic chemicals. Within hours the whole area ahead of Israel's troops would be affected. Within days, even those who had abandoned their units in the hope of escaping on foot with their lives, would perish. Meantime, those that tried to communicate were heard speaking in muffled and shaky voices. The Russian-supplied protection masks were clearly only partially effective.

Ironically, the Soman, Sarin and Tabun group of nerve chemicals had all originated from German scientists, researching during World War 2 for the 'final solution' against the Jews. Now they were, amazingly reversed against the enemies of the Jews. The wheel, as they say, had come full circle. Even a microscopic quantity of some of these on exposed skin could kill - mercifully relatively quickly. Others would suffer for longer, from the effects of the plague virus and the mutations which followed.

Ayad's missile unit was deployed without Ayad's presence. Captain Sa'id Gshem had been surprised to receive an actual launch command - was this a training firing? Had the weapons been programmed to fly along a training range? The reality of the situation was confirmed when the two firing key officers arrived out of the blackness, to authorise the launches. Having been on the road for several hours, they knew little of what had been going on in detail, apart from reports of a large earthquake far to their North.

It was Sa'id Gshem, the Missile Battery's Deputy Commander, who turned the final key and whose finger pressed the missile launch button at the first launch position at the ordered time. He was proud of the way his crew performed. It just showed that the absence of the Major made little difference to their effectiveness. The missile lifted off perfectly - a sight to behold in the night sky. Unknown to the Captain, the missile was not on its way down the test firing route, after which it would have impacted harmlessly in the sea. It had been intended, by his Headquarters, as a shot for Allah.

Within minutes, as they had been taught for survivability reasons, the transporters rolled on their dusty way to the next new launch-position, some thirty kilometres to the North.

There was still no sign of their Commander, Major Iyad Aziz. Little did Sa'id know, but his Commander had slept on for almost five hours and then frantically tried to find his Battalion, but they were at neither of the exercise deployment positions. He was at a loss where to look next and his own vehicle was low on fuel. By then the transporters had travelled many kilometres away, steadily moving towards their new deployment positions. To ring HQ on his mobile phone, so as to discover where his Missile Battery had moved to would, of course, disclose his absence. HQ would realise that the missiles had been sent on a war deployment without their Commander. He would be in real trouble.

Of course, Iyad was not to know that they were now in a state of war or that a second set of deployment orders had been issued, or he would have been even more worried. He had unknowingly committed an offence tantamount to desertion and punishable by death - absence from his unit in war! Further, his responsibility was not only for all the men under his command, but he had been personally responsible for the missile target settings. These he had hurriedly set and failed to re-check. He despaired of finding his unit in this blackness. In the far distance the sky glowed with a rapidly diminishing light - a rocket launch! Presumably a practice firing. It may have come from his own troops or from another Battery out on exercise. It would splash down somewhere far out to sea.

However, as he drove at speed in the direction of the recent, but now extinguished glow, it suddenly occurred to Ayad that his missiles had been programmed to fly from the initial positions he had loaded into their memories earlier in the day. Not from the new positions that they had clearly moved to! The missile that he just seen would end up nowhere near its intended impact area, because it had not been fired from its expected launch position. Realising the seriousness of the situation, he trembled at the possible consequences.

Although some in the forward battlefield areas had sensed the earlier diffused flashes and may have had their suspicions, the overall picture was now coming into perspective. Unknown to the forward armour crews, reports were coming from world-wide sources, including new measurements from satellite sources. Soon the news media broadcast that there had been 'a number of ballistic missile launch detections, followed by tactical nuclear detonations, centred in the Middle East'. It was believed that, due to the intense electromagnetic pulses created by the nuclear detonations, no radio or telephone contact could be made with either Damascus or Baghdad, where, incredibly, a nuclear detonation had been noted at or very near both locations. Surely, said the media reporters, Israel would not have launched Jericho against these cities.

There was continuous media speculation. Could these weapons have exploded accidentally, as soon they had been launched? Surely not! If so it would be proof that both nations had obtained nuclear devices. This was indeed likely, despite all previous denials, in the case of Damascus, but unlikely in the case of Baghdad. Although it was difficult to connect this with Saudi Arabia, there had been rumours that they may have purchased a few nuclear warheads - but this had never been reliably confirmed. Had they transferred them to Syria? Whatever warheads were available to any of these nations, their launchers were mobile and would surely be deployed, with their dangerous warheads, well out in the country. They would be well-clear of their respective capitals when launching took place. Nuclear explosions at Damascus and near Baghdad did not make sense!

Something fundamental, catastrophic and unprecedented was going on. The world's commentators and military experts could not be certain of events. To take stock - first they had started to report yet another Middle East War, surprisingly led by Russia. Then it had turned into a major storm, earthquake and tidal wave story and now there were unexplained missile launches and nuclear events.

The earthquake and storms had triggered floods and aggravated communications difficulties for people far along the Mediterranean. Much of the confirmed world's news in the last few hours, had been about tidal floods, lost shipping and swept-away bridges. However, because of the abnormal atmospheric and ionospheric ionisation, little news had been heard of the state of the original battlefield. Now there were these extra and unaccountable explosions in the most unlikely and apparently disconnected places - far from the location of the battling armies! Had Israel either dropped or fired ballistic nuclear weapons at both the capital cities of her near-neighbours? This seemed unlikely, but nevertheless possible. Those who were anti-Israel - and there were plenty of anti-Semites in the media - immediately accused Israel anyway. Even if they were wrong it would not matter. They had never been forced to retract, correct or even apologise, for any of their blatantly wrong reporting in the past.

The USA soon reported that their ever watchful infra-red satellite-borne sensors, had not spotted any rocket motor hot-spots which would have signified missile launches from within Israeli-held territory. Neither had they spotted any ballistic launches leaving the vicinity of either Baghdad or Damascus.

Apart from the occasional minor hot-spot in the battle area caused by conventional fires and battle-weapons, the only larger events recorded within Israel's boundaries, had co-ordinated to two areas. Firstly at a point north of Gaza. It was the recent impact and detonation of the mis-directed Libyan missile, originally aimed at Tel Aviv. Secondly, with what were perceived as several detonations in the worst weather area along the Islamic coalition battlefield front line, just to Israel's north. These were almost at the forward edge of the battle area - the FEBA, in NATO terminology.

What was happening? The answer, in reality, lay elsewhere, although, inevitably, Israel's enemies had immediately jumped to the wrong conclusion. They refused to believe that these weapons could have originated from anywhere else, other than from Israel. The USA had noted the launch hot-spots in Saudi Arabia, but were seeking confirmation, before drawing any conclusions, or making any announcements.

Confirmed reports an hour later, stated that missile launch hot-spots across the entire Middle East had been noted by the satellites. They had been correlated to launch sites in Syria, Iran, Iraq, Saudi Arabia, and Libya. It was again repeated that no launch hot spots could be determined from near Damascus. The analysts were still checking the vicinity of Baghdad.

It was conjectured that Syria could hardly be firing at Baghdad by mistake, but it was possible that the reverse may have occurred, since weapons launched in Iraq might pass over Syria en-route to Israel and could therefore have possibly fallen short, onto Damascus. Similarly, it was just about possible that Saudi Arabian missiles could fall on Damascus if something had gone seriously wrong with their targeting; causing their missiles to overshoot Israel.

Libya, it was assumed, might have taken the risk of hitting one of the newly independent and autonomous parts of the State of Palestine in an irrational attempt to hit Israel, especially Tel Aviv, at all costs. They might have also risked 'overshooting' into Jordan. After all when viewed from Libya, Israel is a long and narrow strip to hit with their ageing systems.

The Libyans had inaugurated a new chemical warfare plant at Rabta in 1995, following the mysterious catastrophic fire at the previous factory, some years before. Apart from being credited with the production of these horrible materials and possibly poison gas, it had been rumoured within recent months that Libya had somehow obtained a few small nuclear weapons. However, this had not been confirmed by the Gaza explosion, which was clearly TNT. Perhaps the rumours were wrong! At any rate the embargoes on Libya had been lifted in 2003, after their leader accepted responsibility for the terror attack in the Pan Am aircraft that fell on Lockerbie.

New reports were coming in. A nuclear weapon capability had indeed been demonstrated - but in an alarming way for Ahmed Pavli and his band of plotters. They could hardly believe the sad news. The Sword of Islam had, metaphorically speaking, buckled and plunged into its owner's heart! Were the surrounding nations ever going to be rid of Israel in their midst? Would Syria and Baghdad ever forgive Saudi Arabia and Iran for the loss of their capital cities? This was just all quite unbelievable. Surely Allah did not wish this?

THE JUSTICE

"I raise my voice to all mankind. You who are simple, gain prudence. You who are foolish - understanding."

The events in the Middle East had dominated the world news for weeks. Reports had followed hourly, punctuated by dozens of documentaries on the subject. The recovery work after both the earthquake and the battle had gathered pace. Documentaries continued well beyond period of the coverage given to the twin Trade Towers and Pentagon attacks in the USA

As more information became available, it was reported, yet again, that, 'Both north and south coasts of the Mediterranean Sea had suffered from severe devastating floods, never experienced before in human history'. There had been considerable loss of life along a swath that stretched for hundreds of kilometres. It had occurred just as a coalition of many nations, mainly to Israel's north, had simultaneously attacked and failed. The attackers claimed that they had failed due to unprecedented weather effects. An earthquake had brought an unexpected end to the war, amongst massive loss of human life.

Further, Damascus had virtually vanished, in a nuclear weapon attack. Despite preliminary investigations, it was not yet clear how this had occurred. In addition, Southern Baghdad had suffered over fifty per cent devastation. Scenes were shown indicating that, in at least some areas, things were slowly recovering. Once again, several fortunate survivors who lived in the disaster zones were interviewed. Not until they returned home, and listened to the wider world news, had the full force of the tragedies become clear.

Those far from the Middle East war and earthquake zone, both realised that there had been an enormous earthquake, that had been responsible for a major catastrophe. Unaffected nations had suddenly realised that this was a disaster that could have happened to them. Calls on the international community for urgent help were continuing. It was a community already stretched for aid funds and human resources. Additional to the natural disaster had come the catastrophe of a war that clearly involved several nations, including Russia. All that had come against Israel had suffered calamitous results for themselves. The massive earthquake, the formidable weather conditions and what looked like inept ballistic missile targeting, had all combined in a massive loss of life. This had been borne by the concentration of largely Russian coalition forces, as they prepared to attack Israel, on the northern hills.

Of course, the war was over. The coalition advance had been stopped by a combination of the natural catastrophes and the mis-directed coalition ballistic weapons. Current reports indicated that the latter were certainly carrying warheads of mass destruction. However, the results of missile attacks would cause repercussions for many years to come. The perpetrators still insisted that the missiles had been correctly targeted against Israel. They claimed that the weapons had somehow gone widely astray, due to 'technical reasons', and, unfortunately, in a virtual sea of wilderness, had somehow devastated the wrong locations.

The nations behind these attacks, though still stunned from the loss of life, could not come to terms with the unprecedented sequence of events. How could these terrible failures possibly have happened? How could they possibly have killed their own allies by mistake?

The world had become used to many years of uncertainty in the Middle East. There had been years of negotiation to reach the Middle East Peace Agreements, most of which had failed. Now, another war had suddenly erupted, apparently without reason. The man in the street could not grasp quite why all this should have happened. Further, the outcome was barely believable. Wars were bad enough.

Disruption of the West's fuel supplies was considered by many of the distant citizens affected as even worse. They had yet to understand that the world had just passed a major milestone in its long history. Few aspects of life would be the same again! How strange it was that this war had coincided with the largest earthquake ever known!

With the confusion of all that had gone on, the final casualty figures were still not known. Indeed, they might never be known. As suspected, it had gradually become clear that the greatest loss of life had been among the Russians. They had lost virtually their entire force in the front line, totalling several thousands of their best professional soldiers; and most of their equipment. Russian Generals in Moscow were in disarray. Several had not wished their forces to take part, right from the start. Now it was too late!

The force, of which they had become so proud, had been re-built after the cut-backs that had been inflicted on the armies of the former Soviet Union, after the Cold War. It was ironic that, in the first place, the Conventional Arms Reduction Treaty had done them a favour, by insisting on arms destruction. They had made sure that any ageing kit was scrapped, leaving them with nothing but the best. Now, even that was destroyed.

'Lost' was an appropriate word because many hundreds of men had, apparently, come out of their armoured vehicles and personnel carriers to seek safety. They had blundered around, not knowing which way to move, so as to survive. They had soon perished in the swirl of mud, water, sludge, cold and the cocktail of biological and chemical effects. No one even knew where all their bodies were.

UN inspection teams had arrived and surveyed the devastated, but now less-flooded battle areas, both from the air, and, very briefly, on the ground. They reported that it would take years to find the dead and many months to cleanse the land. Just how long was impossible to estimate. For example, no one knew exactly how persistent the diseases or chemical effects would prove to be. How long would it be before the area could confidently be entered? How could they hope to recruit teams to commence the disagreeable and dangerous work? During both Gulf Wars, now fading in people's memories, it was known that Iraq, had obtained both anthrax and botulism toxin. Ten years on, and with Russia involved as well, who knew what lurked in this forbidden area? What was in those deadly missiles? It was not a rescue mission. Any who had survived had long since left the affected area. Some had brought woesome personal reports of the fateful events they had gone through.

The UN took charge of the massive 'clean-up' required. Failure to do so would have resulted in the whole area being declared a forbidden zone for many years. Had the perpetrators experimented with, or had access to Western 'designer bugs' - genetically engineered? Clearly, all who entered the zone would have to proceed very carefully.

As the plans proceeded, all team members were provided with the latest protective equipment. There were gloves with chemically absorbent liners, special decontaminable boots in case of splashing, and personally moulded face masks. A fourth generation charcoal woven under-overall, embedded with carbon spheres, was worn next to the skin. All team members in the first inspection carried vapour sensors and bio-sensors and chemically reactive papers. No chances could be taken!

In addition, in case of any residual nuclear effects, they carried hand-held and wrist mounted radiation detectors, which would provide an immediate audio and visual warning if they stumbled into a nuclear contaminated zone.

Wildlife and many water-courses had been affected. It had long been predicted that the use of these agents as weapons was likely to lead to an unquantifiable land area being contaminated. The forecasts had now occurred. There was considerable argument, in the UN, as to when the work should start.

Plenty of military software existed to carry out the task of estimating the hazard zone. However, at this stage, there was insufficient data to make anything but approximate assessments of the extent of the affected area. During the conflict the winds and storms had been totally unprecedented and went off the measurement scale of most of the instruments anyway.

Many were concerned that the pestilence would spread further, through the migration and natural movement of partially affected animals and birds. International decontamination teams would be trained and ready to commence work, as soon as it was considered safe. For the moment it was a 'no-go' area. The entire area was sealed off. No unauthorised aircraft were allowed to fly over the area.

The greatest civilian loss of life was the almost total loss of Damascus, and the southern part of Baghdad, upon which the coalition's own mis-aimed missiles had fallen. After all the initial rhetoric, the coalition nations had withdrawn into their shells in a mixture of shame and disgrace.

As the various investigations and inquiries took place, it became clear whose missiles had added to the damage that had so cruelly been wrought by the weather and earthquakes. Saudi Arabia was deeply embarrassed. Allah had apparently willed that they should accidentally destroy part of Baghdad. Iran were ashamed that one of their missiles had somehow 'diverted' and just as mysteriously devastated Damascus.

Baghdad's misfortune was, of course, due to one Talal Aziz, who had been absent without leave from his unit during war. Three of Iran's leaders had already been executed for failing Islam. The State of Russia and her collaborating Southern States, were all in a state of shock and mourning.

In the less-directly affected areas of the world, that had escaped the tidal wave and earthquakes, there were already massive oil restrictions and economic chaos. Comfortable lives in the west had been shattered. The rest of the world had not yet come to terms with events. Why, for instance, was Russia involved?. The Soviet Empire had fallen and they had been finally making advances in building a Western-style economy. Why had they been part of this mainly northern coalition, in the first place?

The misdeeds of Iyad Aziz on that fateful day were soon discovered. He was arrested. As nothing could be proved about the targeting errors, for public consumption it was convenient to save face. 'No errors had been committed!' The blame was placed on ballistic missile 'failures'. Clearly this must be the fault of the missile supplier! Nevertheless Iyad was sentenced to public execution. Iyad's father, shamed beyond belief, was last seen fleeing the country.

Years of watching horrendous wars in Africa, the Balkans, Somalia and others, often accompanied by disease, were as nothing compared with this compilation of horrors. There was a growing underlying realisation that the forces unleashed were greater than man could handle. The public had become hardened to seeing wars, almost as they happened, in their front rooms - courtesy of television - but this was something quite different.

There were many personal and national repercussions and an inevitable search for scapegoats, many wild accusations and a general feeling of helplessness. Why hadn't the UN acted to stop this war? This, despite the fact that it had often been shown impotent anyway, throughout most of its history. Why hadn't NATO done something earlier? Again the question - what of the incredulity of Russia's participation? Why was it that the West had allowed these weapons of mass destruction to proliferate? Most forgot that the USA had been attempting to stop the original disaster by mounting their ill-fated Quicksilver attack, weeks earlier.

Those who watched the latest TV reports could not be told much more than they had seen earlier. More a review of the recent, terrible events, than a new investigative report became the norm. Many interviewed were still partially shocked, especially those who had been close to the extraordinary events. The inevitable interviews with the TV pundits, and so-called experts, took place. The air waves were filled with speculation. Through satellite links there seemed to be an 'expert' on hand to be questioned on most aspects. The debates swung from earthquakes to diseases and from nuclear effects to the extremes of weather. None shed any real light on how such a catastrophe could have happened or why there seemed to be so many co-incidences. Each event in isolation would have been bad enough. In the end, the amazing coincidences were, probably, just a 'natural' fact.

Back in Britain, Keith sadly noted the plight of the people who remained at the heart of the aftermath, and their leaders who had hardly known which way to turn or what to do next. No one, armed with however much disaster planning, could have ever developed plans that could cope with such extreme events.

It took nearly three months to assemble and provide the special equipment for the clearance teams and to find volunteers to form the cleansing teams. They would commence at the Western edge of the affected area. The teams found that they had an unenviable task. First, the human remains were to be found and removed from the ground or vehicles and individually identified, if possible, and then sealed.

Topographical features of the area had changed significantly, following the great earthquake. Most of the upheavals had been wrought along the great valley fault line and these extended to about 15 km to either side of it. Once work started, the first phase took no less than seven months of continuous searching. They looked for the most obvious remains and carried out the first cleansing. The area set aside for the burial of the dead, which would surely run to many thousands by the time the task was finished, was rough and rocky. A burial valley was chosen just to the east of the Jordan Valley.

Each of the teams covered an allocated sector and they were divided into two groups. First, the detection group, who used ground-probing equipment. They set up a marker each time a grisly find occurred. Secondly, they were followed by a group who handled the bodies and sealed them to prevent any further spread of disease, or of chemical or biological contamination.

Equipment was set up in special decontamination compounds, and the teams, with such an appalling task, worked two weeks on and one week off to ease the burden. Military vehicles of all descriptions had been involved in the war and caught in the damage zone. Some were burnt-out, while others were partially buried or in water or mud, with or without their previous occupants. The heavy armour, after the removal of bodies, was taken on low-loaders, down to the Mediterranean coast for transportation to demolition centres away from Israel, mostly in freighters across the sea to Russia.

Russian explosive demolition experts were engaged to make each vehicle safe before the retrieval teams could operate. Each safe vehicle was then flagged. Some had to literally be dug out and hauled upright before the teams could enter. This entailed the use of the heavy lifting equipment in the most difficult of conditions and was clearly a long-term task in itself. Other vehicles had been completely buried. The area of devastation was huge and the whereabouts of buried vehicles and individual soldiers could only found by metal detection teams, assuming they had been carrying their personal-arms at the time disaster struck. Others would never be accounted for.

There were weapons of all sorts, many in a dangerous condition, including the air defence rockets. Of course, there were very large quantities of shells and many thousands of small-arms. Their condition was already starting to become dangerous, after months in the open. These had all been expected to provide the defensive shield over the coalition forces as their armour advanced.

The mobile surface-to-air defences had not been required in the early stages, because no aircraft and only a few helicopters could be used in the weather in the contact battle area. Apart from the explosives, substantial quantities of fuel remained in the great variety of front line and supply back-up vehicles that had not caught fire. Altogether, this amounted to thousands of tons of combustible material.

Some had illegally entered the prohibited area and looting had taken place. The diesel fuel in mobile storage tanks alone would clearly last the local population for many years. Hence, it was not long before a few enterprising villagers, with the help of the Israeli Army engineers, found that many of the salvageable vehicles, carried an independent turbine-driven electrical power generation system. Since there was ample diesel fuel around, these vehicles were hosed down and either driven or towed to remote settlements and used to produce electrical supplies. Some of these, with careful use, would run on for about seven years. This was an unexpected windfall, since no one could rely on oil supplies, and the deliveries of coal to Israel's remaining power stations had been severely curtailed by the loss of shipping and the destruction of ports and jetties, along the Mediterranean coast.

After the main phase of the removal of the most accessible and visible human remains, new UN Teams, funded mainly by Russia, had also come in to regularly sweep the area for any further remains. This had to be done to ensure that the risk, which was suspected to include anthrax and various toxic chemicals, was minimised. No one knew, with any certainty, exactly which weapons had been used. Some are persistent, others less so. The effects of VX would have only lasted about three days in summer conditions. What cocktails had been formed? As time went on there was no sign of human, animal or even insect life, over much of the area. Radiation, chemical and biological monitoring equipment was all in use at the same time. It was hard going. The teams sometimes only progressed a few yards in a day.

The speed-up in the western development of a universal chemical and biological laser photonic detector equipment had come just in time. It had been spurred-on by the poison-gas incident in the Japanese subway, several years earlier. Early warning of the presence of antigens was essential. Even low biological concentrations could be highly infectious. During the cleansing process it was also possible to use unmanned aircraft to scan ahead, before the next area was entered. This supplemented the satellite imagery that mapped out the extent and severity of the problem in the areas to be tackled next.

Until the whole site had been thoroughly cleansed it could neither be used for habitation, as a water source, or for the flocks that had traditionally grazed here for millennia. The floods had gradually subsided and the mud had turned to dust as the heat of summer approached. Work was abandoned for a few weeks, as the temperature soared to forty degrees Centigrade. A further search was then instituted, but, after six months it was admitted that the location of several hundred of Russia's front line troops remained unknown.

In the cleansing season the work went on relentlessly. The discovery of a single human bone was sufficient for a marker to be set up. Diggers would then excavate until any other nearby human remains were uncovered. The now well-exercised sealing and transportation teams then came in to take the majority of the remains to the burial valley. The world, through the media coverage, could not forget this gruesome and seemingly endless aspect of the aftermath.

Amazing scenes of violence were screened in the streets of Moscow as some of the dead heroes bodies were returned. NATO, worried by another possible escalation took the precautionary measure, of going onto nuclear alert. It was the first time since the Cold War. It was feared that a violent revolution might take place and that Russia's many remaining long ranged ballistic missiles might fall into the wrong hands. After a while the demonstrations subsided.

The burial valley was renamed the 'Valley of Hamon Gog', since Gog was the local name for the Russian Leader and Hamon means hordes - which indeed there had been. So many, in fact, that it was thought, despite the careful sealing, a most prudent and sensible precaution to close the Valley of Hamon Gog to all travellers. Families could not come to the burial ground for the present. The location would be reopened later, when chemical and virus experts could declare the area to be absolutely safe, with all traces of plague and virus eliminated. So the road to Hamon Gog Valley was blocked to normal traffic and only used by the UN teams going about their funereal task.

A small town - aptly named Hamonah - was built to house the biological and chemical, medical, burial and cleansing specialists. The teams at their peak, including a large number of biologists, chemists, forensic experts, explosives and weapon specialists, and all their support infrastructure, numbered well over a thousand. Many of the rear-based support staff were permanent. Their presence was not rotated, as the front-line 'searchers' and 'sealers' were thankfully allowed to do.

One of the main concerns of the weapon-biologists was that the combination of damp and warm conditions may have possibly caused the virus to cross breed a new bacteriological strain in some unknown way, where swamps had formed. Enormous care was therefore paramount. There was no precedent on which to base experience. Progress was inevitably slow. The earthquake had caused considerable infrastructure problems in both Israel and Jordan. Power lines had come down, water carriers ruptured, roads had been blocked permanently by bridge and rock-falls.

Whole stretches of highway had simply disappeared into crevasses. An enormous amount of repair work was needed. Severe damage had been done to the Haifa road tunnel, under Mount Carmel. Goods and personnel were being ferried across a very low level of water that remained in the Galilee. A long jetty had been constructed to enable goods and people to reach the new water level.

The dam across the southern end of the Sea of Galilee and the Allenby bridge had been breached at a time when the lake was completely full. As a result water had rushed down the Jordan Valley, washing away parts of the valley road and destroying kibbutzim and settlements as it went. Two new bridges that had been built to link Israel and Jordan, following the peace agreement, had been completely destroyed.

The world continued to watch with horror - none more than the citizens of Russia and her Commonwealth of Independent States. First they had suffered 70 years of communism and got absolutely nowhere, then a period in which they failed to generate a viable market economy - and now this! Plunged into a war which should not have been theirs and the almost total loss of the soldiers sent to help, indeed mainly to enhance the Sword of Islam. They had, of course, expected to benefit from oil supplies from grateful Arab nations, far into the future. Indeed this had been their main reason for participating. Even after all this, Russia's future oil supply was still not certain. Like most of the world, they were on fuel rationing.

The world was in no doubt, and indeed the seismologist's had confirmed, that this was the most cataclysmic earthquake ever experienced. While most of mankind imagined that the combination of the earthquake, the terrible storm, and the war, with its almost unbelievable outcome, was indeed purely a coincidence, some were beginning to think that there was more to this scenario than was apparent at first sight.

For example, in the early 1990s several commentators had noted that unique situations had occurred in this part of the world before. It did not take expert analysis to realise that Israel had survived no less than five previous wars, quite apart from continuous internal terrorism since 1948. Israel seemed to have an uncanny knack of surviving, despite being grossly outnumbered in both arms and personnel.

In the wider world it also seemed that major, and apparently unconnected events could, have completely unexpected consequences. For example, the international community, so closely linked in economic dealings, was especially vulnerable. Many had previously supposed that the crash of a major bank, with holdings worth billions of dollars, had been caused by 'natural' causes. Initially it was supposed that mishandling and inadequate safeguards were to blame. When investigated, it was found to have been finally sent 'over the top', not by human factors alone, but by the knock-on impact and losses of a large earthquake in Japan. Perhaps things were not as controlled by man as man had come to accept! Further scientific investigations were started.

In another example, the effects of other planets upon the earth's gravitational field had long been recognised. Around the year 2000 no less than five planets of the solar system had come into alignment - Neptune, Mercury, Uranus and Mars aligned with earth, on the other side of the sun. Over this event mankind clearly had no control - but few stopped to consider how or why this was destined to happen. Most considered that once the universe had been formed, that it was like a clock, and, having been 'wound up', would more or less go on the same for ever! Perhaps, after all, the whole range of gravitational effects was not understood!

In yet another example, French scientists investigating the feeding and migrations of whole populations in the Middle Ages, taken over long periods, had concluded that their plight could be traced back to 'natural' events. It could be shown that the co-incidence of earthquakes and the onset of unique weather patterns had been responsible. Humankind, it seemed, despite their increasing achievements, were not in complete charge of their own destiny after all!

As a background to the latest TV documentary, the commentator had also noted, that Israel was unique. It was the only nation that had been re-born after an exile of her people lasting almost two thousand years. On the formation of the State of Israel, in 1948, they had been attacked at once. Though small in numbers - and with no military experience, somehow the new nation had survived.

In 1967 they were again fighting for their lives. This time Israel not only survived, but regained Jerusalem as their capital. Again in 1973 - the Yom Kippur War - they had survived against all odds. Now this latest situation had unbelievably led to their survival again - after the largest attack of all time.

To many who viewed the programme the final words of the commentator kept coming back. It was just an unexpected 'natural' combination of events. However, the more perceptive members of the public still had that niggle. Could all this just really have been a co-incidence? Keith switched his TV off that night - not the least surprised at the outcome!

THE SWORD OF THE LORD

The human suffering was almost unbelievable. The after effects of the war and earthquakes had been horrifying and cataclysmic for those directly involved. The legacy of that experience would remain for the bereaved families, and for the survivors trying to readjust their shattered lives, for many years to come.

Unlike the majority of the world's population, Keith had viewed these latest dramatic events in the Middle East not only with a mixture of amazement, but with understanding and even expectation. Keith, and quite a few others, had been expecting something awesome like this to occur. The key question in the sequence of world events was the timing! So how could this be?

Quite a number of 'Middle East Watchers', in the same privileged position, would also be reacting in the same way. The incredible fact was that, terrible as they proved to be, Keith and others had been waiting for these events - both the war and the earthquake - to occur in the Middle East. It was clear that these events would be centred on Israel. However, Keith had no way of knowing whether these catastrophes would happen in his lifetime or not. Nevertheless, taking all other factors into account, by the start of the third millennium they were all absolutely convinced that such events would occur within years, rather than decades.

However, for the enormous battle to occur, certain quite specific indicators must be evident. The trigger necessary for these dreadful hostilities to commence was inextricably entwined with the ongoing dramas that involve the State of Israel. Only three times before, in Keith's lifetime, had these Middle East 'Watchmen' really sat up and taken a very close interest. They had good reason to do so on each occasion.

The first time was in 1948, when the State of Israel was attacked, directly it came into being. At that time the Soviet Union was becoming an established power in the Middle East. They had based thousands of 'advisers' in several nearby nations, all hostile to Israel. The second time was late in 1990, when Saddam Hussein, the Iraqi dictator, invaded Kuwait. His threatening rhetoric against Israel reached ever greater heights. Was this to be the time of the mighty battle? By the beginning of 1991, Saddam was indeed keeping his promises to send ballistic missiles against Israel. He did - but it was not the big attack that, one day, would include other forces from the far north, most probably Russia.

In 1991 Keith and his world-wide group of associates had rapidly reached for their individual 'reference books', in order to re-check the conditions under which the mighty and dramatic battle would commence. On each of these previous occasions there was still one critical fact wrong with the scenario! However, 1991 was not to escalate into the big battle, for very good reasons.

It was inescapable that a mighty battle, accompanied by extreme natural disasters, would indeed take place, but only when a specified scenario in Israel's history had been reached. The condition is that, when the huge battle occurs it is prophesied that Israel will be living in apparent peace, with open borders.

This was clearly not the case in 1948, or in the winter of 1990, at the time the first Gulf War commenced. Therefore, on neither occasion could the mighty battle, of the type described in the chapters of this book, have taken place

Although a great many Jews had moved to the State of Israel by 1991, a large number, in fact almost two thirds of the world's total Jewish population, were still scattered among the nations. Secondly, the nation of Israel, was certainly not living in secure and open borders at the time when Saddam Hussein invaded Kuwait! In fact, Israel was having to guard her borders very carefully, at all times.

This was also the case early in the year 2003, when the USA took the initiative to lead the coalition that finally overthrew Saddam Hussein. There had been much talk of peace, but in 2003, Israel was suffering the 'El Aksa Intafada', a continuing terrorist onslaught that had taken place every day since October 2000. This clearly still involved cross-border terror incursions, as well as internal attacks by those anti-Jewish elements, living within Israel's own borders.

For the purposes of this book, albeit with some 'journalistic licence', the events described have been assigned to the year 2008. The military equipment and the tactics employed, have been assessed as those that will be credible, for such an event to occur at that time.

The demise of the Soviet Union, after seventy years of failure for all its citizens and the adverse effects on so much of the rest of the world, was heralded, by many, as a new era of peace. Keith had spent many years as a 'Soviet Watcher', having flown for most of the Cold War with the RAF, lecturing and analysing Soviet military activities. After the fall of the Soviet Empire, it became even clearer that the hapless citizens of that huge landmass had been totally misled all their lives. There had been a conspiracy to suppress all truth. Most were deluded into believing the myths that their leaders and their land was invincible.

By 1991, with the 'Iron Curtain' gone and the Soviet Union broken up into separate states, it seemed that peace, had finally 'broken out'. Limited peace had also occurred in many other areas of the world. World leaders spent much time proclaiming the dawning of a 'New Age' or a 'New World Order'!

In contrast, the findings of Keith's NATO team, during the early 1990s, had been that the world had actually become a much more unstable place. It was predicted and advised by the team, that terrorist actions might well include an aircraft attack on a nuclear power station of one of the Western Nations. It was warned that the purpose of such an attack might be to release radioactive material, possibly to spread across a continent, with the intention of causing thousands of casualties. The activity would gain world publicity for one lot of extremists or another. It was predicted that a collision attack, as part of a hijack, could be expected, rather than an attack with military weapons. The death toll would come from the radiation - and there would be panic across the nation affected.

The 'wake up' call to the nations, was to come, most tragically, in two forms. Firstly, there was the accidental catastrophic explosion at Chernobyl nuclear power station, then the attacks on the Towers in New York and on the Pentagon in Washington. The former catastrophe occurred because of the poor design of safety engineering. It played into the hands of the anti-nuclear power lobby. Few realised that this had sent a message to the extremists.

Thankfully, at the time of writing this chapter, no extremist activity against a nuclear site has occurred. Nevertheless, short of protecting every nuclear plant in the world with permanent air defences, such an attack by a determined group will be very difficult to prevent. Those who considered the possibility of this terrorist option, realised how dangerous an aircraft attack, or just a large aircraft collision could be. The extent of such an explosion, however caused, at any nuclear power plant in the world, was surely demonstrated by the Chernobyl accident. Thousands suffered the effects of radiation. Even today, there are huge areas of land and water, still contaminated and human life damaged.

The twin towers attack was not only designed to kill a great many, but also to cause world trade economic chaos - which it achieved!

Another possibility, set out in clear detail to NATO, is the use of biological or chemical materials to cause similar death and panic.

What is this 'reference book', to which Keith and others had so avidly referred, and why had the peace, so fondly hoped-for by so many, not held? Where are these 'conditions' laid down for Israel, that must preclude the next mighty battle in the Middle East? What has it got to do with Jews going to live in Israel, or indeed, even what Israel is doing?

Following the influence of organised religion in so many of the world's conflicts of the past and present, some misguided religious leaders have imagined that conflicts might be reduced, simply by combining together the religions in some way. They decided that this might occur by taking the 'bits on which they agree' as a common basis. In effect, they have decided that, having created the universe, God somehow 'just wound it up and left it to run'. Instead of God they have assumed that man is now in control!

The key to future world events is clearly foretold. Unfortunately, the remaining biblical prophesies, still awaiting to be fulfilled, are ignored by most 'religious' leaders. However, it must never be forgotten that, as history progresses, God manipulates events. He gradually sets the world stage so that conditions will exist for His next milestone, when it is time. On occasions, as is clear from scripture, He even uses wars to move ahead His own plans. To put things simply, in the totality of over seven hundred biblical prophecies, there are only a few more prophecies still to come! They will happen. We do not know the precise timing. However, we do know the chronology, i.e. the order in which they will occur. What other religious text, or indeed any text, other than the Holy Bible, contains prophecies that have consistently and demonstrably come true?

The majority of Biblical prophesies have already been fulfilled with amazing accuracy in earlier ages. Some have been fulfilled in the 20th Century. Forgotten, deliberately ignored, or just not known by the general public, is the prophesied scenario that the author has attempted to set out here - in the story you have just read.

It is an irrefutable fact that biblical prophecies have been fulfilled. The most spectacular in the last century was the prophesied return of the Jews to their promised land. Everyone knows about Israel - but how many realise that they are there because of a fulfilled prophecy? It was also prophesied that all nations would know about Israel. Indeed, you can hardly miss it in the current world news!

Since its reformation as a State, in 1948, Israel's position has fluctuated between enormous hope and despair. Hope, by those who believed peace could be easily bought, merely by giving up land and making concessions of all kinds. Despair, during the continuing need to defend the nation during five wars and against the almost continuous daily attacks and loss of life.

While all land belongs to God, who created it all, He stipulated who should be the custodians of the Promised Land. The gift of tenure was made by a promise - or 'covenant'. There are clear biblical statements on this fact, including the extent of the land involved in the promise and a warning not to give any away!

Not many months before he was assassinated, and after much negotiation, Prime Minister Rabbi had said, 'Millions of eyes all over the world are watching us with great relief and great joy. Another nightmare of war might be over'. He also said, hopefully, 'A new future in our region and for all mankind'.

The euphoria was catching. A spokesman from the USA said, 'The walls are coming down in the Middle East'. In Jordan, if not the citizens, at least her King, was ecstatic at that time. He had been granted a 'special role', in over-seeing Muslim Holy Sites in Jerusalem, - a fiercely contested issue and by no means to the agreement of Saudi Arabia!

In 1994, a former Head of Israel's Military Intelligence went so far as to remark, to a newspaper reporter, 'We are today in the pre-Messianic era. The conflict is ending.' The first part of his statement was probably correct. The trouble was that he hadn't sufficiently researched the latter - the details of which are clearly set out in what The West calls the 'Old Testament'. A very major conflict indeed is yet to come. This should not be confused with 'Armageddon'.

How had Keith - and the other Israel 'watchers' - known that this was the case? Recalling his early childhood, Keith could vividly recall the main factors which had shaped his life for the last fifty or so years. His defiance of his mother, in World War Two, in leaving the shelter at the age of eight in order to view the 'doodle-bug', right through to his early service flying days; and following that to his time as an electronics laboratory researcher and designer. Then forward again to the 1970s and the early 1980s when he found himself lecturing for a period of no less than eight years to Military Staff Colleges around the world on the very subject of the Arab-Israeli Wars. Later still, as a Chief Scientist, researching and analysing threats, air defences, and especially defence against ballistic missiles.

As a military specialist, the Middle East Wars were a fascinating topic on which to be ordered to lecture. This was because the outcome of each of the conflicts did not bear out the logically-expected military results. Military Staffs were perplexed. How could little Israel, not just once, but repeatedly, defeat such an enormous opposition, with such limited resources? There were no credible military explanations. It even perplexed the majority of Israeli's themselves!

The military students who attended these Staff Colleges were not young or inexperienced officers, but often very senior in rank and experience. They were the most experienced officers of high rank, from all the NATO nations. Keith, and many others, had tried to find some logical explanations to satisfy the students. It was a daunting prospect to stand on the podium in front of large numbers of very experienced officers from all three services.

Many suggestions had been put forward. To explain events, humans will always look for a rationale that they can understand. In this case explanations were needed for an astounding sequence of events in more than one war!

Keith's understanding had been triggered by a major change in his life that had occurred many years before. At the time he was lecturing on the 'Middle East Wars', at senior military colleges around the world. The plain fact was that the results, when the combined Arab Navies, Armies and Air Forces turned on tiny Israel, did not make any military sense. So there must have been some other explanation for Israel's amazing survival each time.

All sorts of ideas were put forward. Surely, it was the Western equipment that was superior to the Russian equipment! Of course, it must have been the better training! Or, perhaps it would be reasonable to say that it was the better planning and procedures? Surely, the Israelis had more military intelligence! Alternatively, it was the better communications....and so it went on and on. An explanation must be found! But none ever was!

Statistical methods were tried. The statistics only proved that something quite extraordinary had occurred each time.

So perhaps 'non military' reasons could be found? The Israelis were fighting for their lives! Their backs 'were against the wall'! The Arabs always made mistakes! Surely the Arabs didn't really want to fight - their leaders were poor!

Or, they were just 'pushed' into it, against their will. The analysis and conjecture went on and on after each of these wars. Considerable analysis also went on in the question periods at the end of each of Keith's talks.

The reputation of Israel's Forces soared. The incredulous watchers then tried another idea. They decided that it was a psychological 'thing' that had defeated the Arabs! In the end no-one had a really satisfactory solution and gave up trying. Then it happened again! Books were written. People were interviewed, including many who had actually taken part. All to no avail.

Keith had been lecturing on the military lessons to be learnt from a series of wars. These included not only the five Middle East wars, but the major Vietnam conflict. Latterly the Falklands War was added to the list. Soon, Keith encountered another incredible situation. When lecturing in certain (Non NATO) staff colleges, a different script was used for the Middle East lectures. This was not only to remove the actual secret performance values for some weapons that had been used (and were still in use by some NATO nations), but to ensure the wording for the particular audience did not 'upset' their particular sensitivities. In plain terms this meant that it had to be implied that the Arabs had not lost, even if they had not won!

In the winter of 1982, a major milestone had occurred in Keith's life. 'There is a talk in Lincoln tomorrow night. Are you interested in going?' said Keith's wife. 'What about?' asked Keith, looking up from his papers. 'It seems to be about Israel,' she replied.

Although Keith was lecturing on the Middle East wars, and had served for several weeks at a time in various nations in the region, he had never visited Israel. Expecting some sort of general travel talk they decided to go to this meeting to see what it was all about. It would be an evening out! In fact, it turned out to be a major milestone.

This talk changed Keith's outlook completely, from living in a world of normality to living in a world where an almost 'God's Eye' view of events was constantly provided, updated, validated and hugely enjoyed. For some reason it had taken until the age of 47 for Keith to receive this level of understanding of what was really happening in the world.

The event turned out to be a completely unexpected - indeed a life-changing experience. The whole thing suddenly came together like inserting the final pieces of a complicated jigsaw. Keith was suddenly exposed to a lot of new information.

It turned out that it is not an accident that Jews were scattered all over the world. It was not a co-incidence that this, relatively small group of people in Israel were almost constantly in the news. Indeed, there was no excuse for anyone on the planet, where radio, TV and news reached, not to know of the existence of this race of people, or what had happened to them over the years of exile from their own land. It was not an accident that, suddenly, lots of Jews had decided to live in Israel. It was prophesied that they would do so! It was not just co-incidence that so many - some 6 million - were trying to leave the Soviet Union. (They would not be free to do so in really large numbers until several years later). It was prophesied that they would be released from captivity in 'the north'. It was not an accident that the problems of the Middle East seemed so unsolvable to so many otherwise able politicians and their advisers.

A huge battle, perhaps very similar to the next major one which will occur in the Middle East, has been described in the chapters of this book. The major war will be against Israel. Indeed, it may well be the next war that follows the second Gulf War, of Iraq's liberation from Saddam Hussein, in March and April 2003. It may not be many years ahead. Even the prospect of such an awful conflict, coupled with awesome natural events, is something that we would all surely like to ignore - or just simply not wish to happen. But it will!

It may not take the course exactly as Keith has described here - but happen it will - make no mistake about it! The enigma is the timing. It cannot and will not happen until Israel is living in open borders - in apparent peace. For this is precisely what the reference book says. Watch out for that day!

This time is getting nearer as the various peace initiatives are completed. All pressure is on Israel and the pressure will increase to an incredible level following the second Gulf War, with the so-called 'Road Map'. Will this next coming peace be the expected false peace. Will it be the temporary peace where all the players will be in their right positions for such a huge battle to occur - or will there have to be more, perhaps smaller conflicts, before the big one? Most probably a key that will also feature strongly is that of oil - hence the choice of trigger for this book.

The 'reference book' setting out the fundamentals of this event does not set out the exact timing of when this will all happen. Nevertheless, it does describe the essential, chronological, sequence of steps which leads towards those fateful days. Most of those imperative milestones are now in position for the first time in world history. You will, of course have realised that the reference book is the Holy Bible. In numerical terms it is a fact that about 600 of the 720 prophesies have now been fulfilled.

Do not confuse this coming battle with the much spoken-about 'Battle of Armageddon' or 'The Apocalypse'. The coming battle is not the last one. But, it is one where God will once again show his hand, but in a far more dramatic way than in the past. It will, almost certainly, not only bring the Jews - who miraculously survive yet again - back to their own God, as God's Chosen People: but also allow them to see Jesus (Jeshua), as their long unrecognised Messiah.

The outcome of this battle will also indicate, to many of the peoples of the world, that the world is not just set on an uncontrolled wild course of 'evolution', but is following God's plan. It is a plan, in the form of prophetic text. It is set out in the Holy Bible, for anyone who cares to read it.

Significant changes on whole populations have been imposed by man, who has ignored God's pattern for happy living. We have seen man increasingly attempting to act as God. History has shown that various personages have claimed to be the Messiah. They have all been proved false. So called, 'Christians' have lowered their original standards and formed various unions with paganism. This has been going on for so long that most people accept these changes without question. They are not even aware that the original has been changed. We are in a more educated society than ever before but still content to swallow 'religious' traditions and ideas, called 'doctrines', without even questioning whether they are valid or not. An easy way to check is to find out whether they were there from the beginning - or has someone invented them since?

For example, there were to be no images and relics required in the worship of the true God. This is not an option - it is a command of God. Our churches are so full of them to the point where, to many, a building would not rate the title 'church', without all these. How many realise that the title 'church' only applies to the people - it is not the building at all! None of these traditional trappings are necessary - in fact they are expressly forbidden!

In one denomination even one of the original Commandments which its rulers did not like, has been removed and the tenth Commandment has been split into two - so as to preserve the number ten! The fact that the ten commandments were given to Moses for the chosen people, not for the, Gentiles has been ignored. Long before Moses came on the scene the seven Noahide Commands were given to Noah, at the time when all mankind were treated by God as one. There was no separation of Jew and Gentile until the Chosen People had been chosen! After the Jews had been chosen, they alone were given the Ten Commandments.

Other changes have occurred. The Fourth Commandment, which is to set aside the Sabbath - the seventh day of the week - has become the first day of the week - the Western Sunday - the pagan day for worshipping the sun. The first followers of Jesus, who were Jews, naturally kept the seventh day, Saturday, as the Sabbath, or 'Shabbat'.

There are many more such examples of man's intervention and modification of what was originally intended for the order of life - but this is not the place to expound on them.

What is worse is that superstitious and fearful populations have been unknowingly manipulated for many years by their religious leaders. Their descendants today actually still believe in - and accept without question - some of the more peculiar edicts. These ideas were just not present at the beginning. Edicts which have since become so ingrained to the extent that they are actually believed as being scriptural. These edicts mean nothing unless they can be found in original scripture.

Where this was in danger of becoming obvious, as people became more educated, the proponents of these beliefs - almost unbelievably - actually had the temerity to change the scriptures from the original words just to suit their purposes! Little wonder that even those who do not profess to be 'religious' have little time for it all. Who can blame them? All that has gone on has caused the remaining prophecies to be largely forgotten.

We need to return to the basics - and to base our beliefs only on the promises which are real. We must note those prophecies which have already occurred and keenly watch for those that are clearly stated, but are yet to come. For they are the fascinating key to what is really happening now and what is still yet to happen in the world. These are the real factors that will affect everyone. There is no time to waste on any others.

The events described are Keith's attempt to bring this information in a new way to as many people's notice as possible, through the medium of this book. The words used here are an attempt at a modern interpretation of the words given by God and written by the prophet Ezekiel, together with other prophets many hundreds of years ago.

Some of the many prophecies of Ezekiel have already been fulfilled, so there is no logical reason to expect Ezekiel's other, hitherto unfulfilled prophecies, to have any less credibility. Certainly we are not empowered to dismiss them! Or indeed, to doubt the credibility of those written by the other prophets so long ago, of which so many have since been fulfilled.

It may come as a surprise to the secular reader to find that many Christian readers of the Bible pick and choose just the bits they want to hear. Even more amazing is that large numbers of Christians also have no knowledge of these prophecies and have never read these important parts of the Bible. They have no right to pick and choose parts to read, or parts to believe. No part of the contents is included by accident!

Keith hopes you have enjoyed this book - even if it has turned out slightly differently than you might have expected from the title. The key question of course is - can YOU, the reader, afford to ignore its message?

If you still have any doubts - don't just put the book down - why not look at the proof check-list, the clear evidence of what is to come. This list follows in the final chapter.

CHECKLIST

"When you see the Russian Army begin to move southward
and enter Turkey, put on your Sabbath garments and get
ready to welcome the Messiah".
(Rabbi Chaim Valushiner Mid 19th Century)

It is prophesied that events, possibly typical of those described in this book, will happen in some form or other, but only when certain preliminary world scenarios are met. The stage is currently being set and sooner or later a situation will arise which will act as the trigger. These events will then happen - but only to a Land and People that fulfil a number of clearly stated conditions, written in prophecy so many years ago. In each case the reference is given where the prophecy can be found.

The Pre-conditions

The pre-conditions that describe and identify the nation to whom this will happen include the following precise information. It is incredible that they were written well over two thousand years ago:

• 'The People who are to be attacked in the big battle in the future, and who have now returned to their land, are the descendants of those who were scattered all over the world in the first place. They were originally driven away from their land because they disobeyed a set of rules which were provided by God - for their own good.' (Pre-Condition 1 - Exodus 19 and 20, Leviticus 26 & Ezekiel 39)

• The nation to be attacked will be, 'Living in a Land that has recovered from war and whose people were first scattered, then re-gathered from many nations.' (Pre-Condition 2 - Nehemiah 1 & Ezekiel 38)

• The nation to be attacked are 'A People who were, many years before, divided into two, but will, by the time the war occurs, be re-joined into one nation.' *(Pre-Condition 3 - Ezekiel 38)*

• 'The People to which this event applies will have been defeated many years before by the 'Sword of Babylon' (now Iraq)'. This was by King Nebuchadnezzar, of Babylon, in the year BC 606 (Pre-Condition 4 - Ezekiel 32)

• 'The People to whom these events will occur, will be living a comfortable life with good pasture and crops, in contrast to the lifestyle they were forced to endure before they returned to their Land to live.' 'The people will settle in their own land.' 'All the lands are at rest and peace.' (Pre-Condition 5 - Ezekiel 34 & Isaiah 14)

• 'The People who are attacked will have suffered the scorn of the world's nations, but now these nations will be put to scorn themselves.' (Pre-Condition 6 - Ezekiel 36)

• 'When the People returned to their Land originally, they would have arrived there to find it in a barren and run-down condition. They will have planted trees, rebuilt ruins and cultivated the land, by the time the big war occurs.' (Pre-Condition 7 - Ezekiel 36)

The results both in Israel and the wider world, when it happens:
The outcome, when the war occurs, will be that:

• 'Supernatural revenge will be taken against those responsible for the attack on Israel, such that not only will the attackers suffer a huge loss of life on the Northern Hills of Israel, but their home cities will be devastated and lie in ruins.' (Condition 1 - Ezekiel 35)

• 'Listen, a noise on the mountains like a great multitude!' 'Listen, an uproar among the kingdoms, like nations massing together.' (Condition 2 - Isaiah 13)

• 'It is predicted that the Persians (Iranians) will be alongside Russians when they invade Israel.' (Condition 3 - Ezekiel 38:5)

• 'This war will not be like any other war, as it will be accompanied by co-incident and unprecedented natural events that will occur at precisely the same time, with dramatic consequences observed by the people of the world.' There will be a cataclysmic earthquake'. (Condition 4 - Ezekiel 38)

• 'The Lead Nation who come against the People living in peace will be located to the far north of the land that is invaded. 'It is almost certainly Russia, probably almost reluctantly in part, as the prophecy says : 'I will turn you around, put hooks in your jaws and bring you out with your whole army........etc.'. It seems, therefore, that Russia will probably lead some sort of substantial coalition. Apparently, they will be encouraged to do so, and apparently there is nothing laid down in the conditions which suggests that they will have to fight their way across several intervening nations, to reach the point of the battle [on the Northern Hills of Israel]. In other words, as the nations in between are not mentioned, then they most probably offer no objection (and perhaps even encourage or assist) those invading armies, as they travel southwards. Neither do others appear to impede the seaborne route from the Black Sea into the Mediterranean. The big battle then commences. (Condition 5 - Ezekiel 39)

• 'The predicted huge loss of life which, it is clearly stated, will occur significantly on the Northern Hills. A huge loss of life will occur. The loss of life seems to be mainly, judging from the prophetic descriptions given, though not exclusively so, mainly caused by chemical or biological events (rather than nuclear events). This has clearly got out of hand and has somehow backfired on the perpetrators, rather than on those attacked. However, those attacked by no means escape unscathed.' (Condition 6 - Ezekiel 39)

• The city of Damascus (Capital City of present-day Syria) will be 'totally destroyed'. This prophecy has never been fulfilled. It seems likely that this will be the war during which this devastating event may well occur. (Condition 7 - Isaiah 17).

• It is predicted that a time will come when 'all nations who meddle with Jerusalem' will be caused real problems. Jerusalem will be a 'stumbling block' to all those who interfere. Further, God specifically states that His land is neither to be sold or to be divided up. This is precisely what is proposed today, in the ongoing attempt to establish a 'Palestinian' State, by using the US-sponsored 'Road Map' to peace! Would you wish to go directly against God's written commands?

Immediately Afterwards

The clearing-up operations that will be required, following the war, are specified in some detail. It is quite fascinating that at the time the scenario was written, no human anywhere in the world knew of any weapon that could cause this type, or scale, of major disaster to large army. At the time of writing the prophecy the nations were using only swords, chariots, clubs and arrows! There was no gunpowder when the prophecy was written. Nuclear, biological and chemical (NBC) weapons had yet to be invented over 2000 years later. (In those days, the only very small scale action to cause disease was the throwing of animal carcasses over city walls, in the hope of causing diseases, or by placing them in drinking water courses.)

It is indeed fascinating that the prophet wrote that special protective clothing would be necessary for those involved in the clean up. Certainly, no such clothing was needed in his day, or was there any necessity to produce any, as these terrifying weapons did not exist.

Special clothing, for protection against radiation, chemicals and bacteria, was much improved during the Cold War and frequently exercised by NATO troops. NATO troops were first seen in a war using this 'NBC' equipment in the 1991 Gulf War in the Middle East and there was frequent television coverage of the equipment during the second Gulf War, in 2003. Only recently have we become accustomed to seeing our anti-terrorist forces exercising, dressed in these unusual garbs.

Hence, it is prophesied that :

• 'The occurrence will be frightening not only to those directly involved, but also to many others in the world, since events are happening beyond their normal human experience and will be seen around the world'. [That statement was made, of course, long before the invention of all the modern news media!] (Ezekiel 38)

• 'When the clearing up operation starts, after the war is over, special teams will be set up to handle the devastation and, in particular, to avoid the spread of disease from the dead.' Of course, today, we call these 'decontamination teams'. A special area (in a specific valley) is designated as the location where the recovered bodies are to be buried. It is even given a special name [Hamon Gog], linked to the name of the attackers. (Ezekiel 39)

• 'The clearing up operation will take seven months - a major and unenviable task.'

• There will be a lot of combustible material (probably mainly fuel), left from the massive logistical support necessary to support modern warfare and weapon systems and vehicles brought to the war zone, but presumably not used before the natural catastrophes occurred that stopped the war. 'This material will be recovered and used by the people in the region as fuel, lasting for seven years afterwards.'

• The fact that the clearing-up operation itself takes seven months probably confirms that chemical or biological contaminants are the main concern in the immediate area where the battle took place, rather than the longer term effects expected from nuclear events. This long cleaning-up period is not unreasonable, as the reader might be interested to note that clean-up operations and restrictions due to water table contamination still apply today at Chernobyl, following the nuclear power station explosion, now twenty years on. (Ezekiel 39)

• 'Phenomenal changes will occur to the landscape and buildings, presumably and mainly as a result of the massive earthquakes. The land upheaval and weather conditions will be such that those drawn up to the front-line battle will not be able to distinguish friend from foe. They will end up in such confusion that they will inflict what, since the 1991 Gulf War, has become known as, 'Friendly Fire', with devastating consequences to one's own troops.' (Ezekiel 38)

Soon Afterwards

• 'As a direct result of this calamitous war, the nation attacked [i.e. Israel], will recognise where they had gone wrong and a new era as God's Chosen People will begin.' (Zechariah 12)

• 'From this time onwards the surviving remnant of the People who were attacked, will be able to explain to the world why this has come about. This is not unexpected as they are prophesied to 'become a blessing to all nations'. They won't have any trouble doing this, since they will have a changed attitude within themselves.' (Genesis 18)

• 'During these unprecedented events the world will have seen an enormous visual and emotional demonstration of a power which they have not understood in the past. The Jews, having been brought from most of the world's the nations, have all the diverse language skills necessary to explain to any who are still unconvinced as to what has been going on, in their own languages; and, more importantly - WHY!' (Ezekiel 39)

• During the aftermath many will still just consider this to have been another war - but - 'At some point in time, after re-settling in the Land, the People, although their unique circumstances and calling will already have been made clear to many, and to many others in the world, many more thousands will suddenly wake up to their unacceptable conduct'. This will happen because the people will realise that their survival was no coincidence. It was not achieved by their own strength but by God's intervention in man's affairs through a massive and unprecedented demonstration of His power. At this point they will all realise that they were chosen as a people apart. They will also realise why a remnant have always survived despite being the most reviled and attacked race, by so many. (Zechariah 13 & Ezekiel 39).

• The prophecy will be fulfilled - 'And I will pour out on the House of David (i.e. Israel) and all the inhabitants of Jerusalem the spirit of grace and supplication, so that they will look on me who they pierced and they will mourn for Him as one mourns for an only son.' (Zechariah 12:10). This prophecy was written 500 years before Jesus, their returning Messiah, first walked in The Land!

Conclusion

The national awakening, yet to come to the People of the Land of Israel, will probably be triggered by events of the type similar to those described in this book. One can only speculate on the possible trigger that will set off the sequence of events, when the time is right. It will also be an awakening for the whole world. Undoubtedly, the catalyst that sets things off will have to be either something that impacts on the whole world very quickly, or a set of unforseen circumstances, where an initial incident spreads rapidly. However, such an attack takes some premeditation and significant logistical preparation. (One might consider a coalition that includes some or all of the nations using, of course, their modern national names, that are mentioned in Psalm 83)

Apparently it will draw in nations who would not otherwise have got themselves involved. Nevertheless the human activities necessary for such an attack will be brought about by ordinary people like you and me. Members of the armed forces of several nations will clearly be involved, together with those in various governments. Once the conflict starts, others, going about their daily lives will suddenly find themselves plunged into this supernatural scenario.

At that time, the nations involved will have re-armed, following the lifting of embargoes, even during economic crisis, with political turmoil and rivalries. Scenarios will escalate either over natural resources such as oil or over territory. Spiritual forces will continue to be involved, certainly driven by evil intentions. Some scenario will occur which finally brings nation against nation again - or, more correctly in this case, many nations against this one key nation, located in the Middle East.

THE ONLY NATION ON THE FACE OF THE EARTH THAT FULFiLS THE CONDITIONS LISTED ABOVE IS THE NATION OF ISRAEL. THIS NATION WAS RE-BORN AS A NATION IN 1948, AFTER YEARS OF DISPERSION ALL OVER THE WORLD. THIS RACE OF PEOPLE HAD UNDERGONE, FOR THE MOST PART, UNPRECEDENTED HARDSHIP DOWN THE GENERATIONS.

It is not surprising that the outcome of wars against Israel have unexpected endings. 'No weapon forged against you will prosper'.......(Isaiah 54). Who, among the nations has still failed to grasp that fact? Is this amazing fact understood in the nation where you live today?

Moses first wrote 3500 years ago that the Jews would be scattered if they did not follow their God. They did not obey and indeed, they were scattered, world-wide.

Is it not amazing that Ezekiel, in the 9th Century BC (about 2900 years ago), could write with such accuracy that this war would happen in the distant future?

Since 1948, the Jews have been moving to Israel in large numbers, from many nations. However, apart from those who had reached the USA, descendants of those who mainly arrived there at beginning of the 20th Century, the majority of the Jewish race, who had survived the holocaust, had ended up trapped behind the 'Iron Curtain'. Almost all of those living mainly in the former Eastern Bloc of the old Warsaw Pact nations and those nations that comprised the Former Soviet Union, were held captive, during the Communist regime, for 70 years. Only a few had managed to leave. However, over one million have moved to Israel from these lands alone, since the Cold War ended.

There are still more to come from several other nations, for example, from the USA, South Africa, France, Argentina and the UK. These include the descendants of families who fled Europe, just before Hitler's holocaust. Many were rejected by other nations, but the descendants who reached the USA now number several million. Probably many in the USA wish to stay there. Nevertheless, in the year 2003 a point was reached, for the first time, when the number of Jews in the land of Israel exceeded the number in the USA.

After the conflict the People of Israel will not only undergo a national renewal, returning fully to their roots as God's Chosen People, but will recognise their Messiah. To the great surprise of so many, He will turn out to be the Messiah their ancestors rejected some 2000 years earlier - Jeshua, Ben Joseph - known in the West (due to the Greek translation) as Jesus of Nazareth!

All this is of no surprise to those who really understand the Bible. It is very clearly prophesied that this will occur, and it was Jewish prophets that made the prophesies. Not Gentiles! 'For I will take you from the nations, gather you from all the lands, and bring you into your own land. Then I will sprinkle clean water on you; and you will be clean: I will cleanse you from all your idols.' (Ezekiel 36)

The reader should note that the first half of this prophecy is actually happening today! This very week, even as you read these words, aircraft and ships will arrive in Israel bringing Jews coming to live there for the first time in their lives. All this is not a pipe dream or fantasy. Ask yourself why Israel (with a population and land area of insignificant size, compared with the majority of nations), is constantly in the news.

This war, that is yet to come, will be seen afterwards by the entire world, as an example of God's power. Many will only then be convinced for the first time that God exists. However, amazingly, despite all that occurs, there will still be some who are unsure.

Importantly, this war will confirm that many other prophesies (i.e. promises) that were made to all mankind and written down thousand of years ago, will indeed also come true at their appointed time.

It is easy to write a conclusion to a situation when the answer is known! One key factor is the prophecy that, 'once Israel is reborn as a nation it will never be destroyed again, or removed from the land.' (Ezekiel 36 verses 22-36, 38 verses 8-16, and 39 verses 23-29). So we already know the end result! All who wish to destroy Israel take note! In blunt terms ' You cannot beat God - He will have the last word!'

World leaders - both those who are currently either support or oppose Israel, would do well to heed these prophecies. Some need to decide whose side they should really take! Especially as it is also prophesied that all the nations will be judged one day, and classified as either 'goat' or 'sheep' nations - and, finally, take the consequences of their actions.

Those who have always thought that natural events are just random, and that uncontrolled disasters are 'a coincidence', will have to reconsider the overwhelming evidence that shows otherwise. University studies into combined natural events have pin-pointed quite amazing changes which have changed the face of history. The experts are finally noting that climatic changes can completely change man's actions and the course of history. For example, in the past, whole empires have been caused to decline by the onset of drought. Torrential rain at the Battle of Waterloo bogged down Napoleon's guns for many hours. Hitler made the disastrous decision to attack Russia in World War 2 and was probably defeated by the weather as much as by the Russian troops Elsewhere, volcano eruptions have lowered temperatures by blocking the sun, changing agriculture and causing famine. Climatic effects on agriculture, with failed harvests, certainly contributed to the problems in the former Soviet Union, forcing on the Communist leaders major economic and social decisions. Some experts have concluded 'History is not man-made - it is the planet itself that controls our destiny.' In that case, one may therefore reasonably ask, 'Who controls this planet?'

Those that are prudent, will take note of what is promised. When the events described in this book eventually occur - or events which are very similar, the majority of the world will be spectators. Many others, sadly, will be very unwilling participants. Due to the modern news and communication media the spread of news, in near real-time, is already commonplace. The technology exists today to do this. Nearly everyone on this planet will be aware of what is going on, more or less as it happens, and many will be very frightened. Knowledge of these awful events, more or less as they occur, will be inescapable. Everyone will know about them! In those coming days, because of what will happen in the Middle East, they will have no excuse at that time to say that they have not heard of the most important fact of all. The proof will be before their eyes - indeed most of it is already available to those that care to look. We all have the opportunity to believe in what was said by One who has unlimited power - and will have demonstrated this power for all to see - and to accept Him as our King.

Although events, of the nature described will be truly horrific, both for those involved and those who hear and see through the news reports, this is not the end. An even greater event will occur when Israel's Messiah returns to earth, but first will come the 'anti-Christ' (meaning 'in place' of Christ). This person will be an impostor, claiming to do good to all. He will be revered and even worshipped by many. Indeed he will even demand to be worshipped. After quite a short time it will become obvious that he is an evil being, driven by pure evil. At that time the world will indeed see further shattering occurrences taking place in Israel's capital, Jerusalem.

Finally, what happened to the key participants of this story? The personalities that I have used as a method of illustrating the likely events, emotions, and outcomes, in the coming war in the Middle East? Some of these participants in my narrative are fictitious. Others are based on personalities known by the author.

EPILOGUE

The character of Keith Perham is based on a real person - the author. He flew in the Royal Air Force, took part in the British 'H Bomb' nuclear tests on Christmas Island and flew on many covert operations from Cyprus, the Gulf and Teheran in the Cold War, He lectured on guided weapons and on the Middle East Wars for many years, lead the NATO Threat Team and was Senior Adviser for several NATO Industrial Advisory Group Studies. He was twice honoured by HM The Queen.

The revelation to Keith of what was really going on in the world - and still is - happened, as described, one night in Lincoln. From that moment onwards, the newspaper reports on what occurs in Israel and in the surrounding nations has been watched with growing fascination and compared with what the Bible says will happen. It became clear, from the evidence, that biblical prophecies have increasingly been fulfilled during his lifetime.

What point have we reached today? What is the next milestone? Where are we now in God's time clock? Clairvoyants and fortune tellers are of no use. The world's future was mapped out thousands of years ago.

During the 1980s and 90s Keith took a leading part in the international strategic and theatre missile defence studies. Firstly, there was the so-called 'Star Wars' programme and then - after the world was woken up again, by the Iraqi ballistic missile attacks against Saudi Arabia and Israel, in 1991 - Keith participated in both the NATO and UK studies into this difficult problem. By this time he was a Chief Scientist (Systems) for the nation's leading electronic company.

Keith has no way of knowing whether the events, or ones very similar to those described, will occur in his lifetime. It is a fact, however, that the pieces of jigsaw are falling into place with ever increasing regularity, and all the technology is present and available to all the potential protagonists. Most of the other necessities, such as the procurement of certain weapons and their delivery systems, the return of a large number of Jews to Israel, the antagonism of her near neighbours and other key factors are visibly coming into line to satisfy the prophesied pre-conditions. Even the anti-biological/anti-chemical protective clothing required, as prophesied all those years ago, is now becoming commonplace.

Even, as Keith writes these words the 'Palestinian' scenario is once again reaching crisis point in the Middle East. According to prophecy it is a pre-condition that Israel must be living in secure and open borders when the big conflict occurs. Will this be the case soon? Most probably it will, if some sort of agreement is almost forced upon Israel? At that point there will certainly be the appearance of secure borders.

The character of Isador was chosen to typify many highly qualified and extremely talented Jewish scientists. Keith met many after the Cold War ended. They had been trapped for so many years behind the 'Iron Curtain'. Large numbers, instead of going to the USA - as so many had done after World War 2 - suddenly found that it was possible to obey the unseen, but very compelling pull, towards the ancient land of their ancestors. The land in which all Jews are entitled to live under the Law of Return.

In Isador's case he might have been able to obtain a temporary visa from the Russian State during the Cold War. If granted, this would have been for a special purpose, for example, for a scientific conference - but always alone. This was the way the USSR made sure their valuable people returned to the Soviet Union. Their families were in reality - hostages, while they were away attending any meetings beyond the surrounding 'iron curtain'.

The barriers came down after the demise of the Soviet Union and Isador and his family were eventually allowed to make 'Aliyah' - immigration - a little over one hundred years after the first Russian Jews had gone back in the 1880s.

It was King Hussein of Jordan, several years before his death, who announced the seriousness of this new Aliyah (from the Arab viewpoint), when he noted this hundredth anniversary in the early 1990s. At that time there was a period when over 10,000 Jews were arriving in the land of their ancestors every month. Thousands more have followed since. More recently this migration has continued at a reduced, but fairly steady rate, even during the most recent Arab Intafada.

In the narrative, the disposition of forces and growing unrest in the area, after Israel had found a sort of peace, reached a point where the prophesied conditions were reached. When the time really comes, something will suddenly trigger the action. The author chose oil. The war could, for example, be triggered by an accidental nuclear event, by a massive terrorist attack, international economics, an assassination or even by a catastrophic natural occurrence. There are many gullible people in that part of the world - take for instance a recent claim by one group that Israel was responsible for the earthquake-induced, 2004 Boxing day tsunami, far from Israel in the Indian Ocean! Hence, there are several possible 'bubbles' that can burst and trigger things off - once all the other players and preconditions are in place. God will certainly orchestrate the conditions in His own perfect timing.

In Israel, Isador and his family survived the battle and the earthquake, but their eldest son perished, apparently when his armoured vehicle was swept into a torrent. It was later found empty. As a boy in Russia he had never had the opportunity to learn to swim.

Afterwards, mourning the loss of his son, the enormity of the events were such that Isador was only just coming to terms with the fact that it was his own fuel invention that had caused the bubble to burst.

Isador himself became a temporary casualty during the war, having set off early one morning to the university, where he had been moved into a team, hurriedly set up to provide advice to the Staff, in the Tel Aviv War bunker. He involuntarily observed one of the intense nuclear flashes high in the sky to the north, when the Iranian premature bursts occurred. It was several weeks before he fully recovered his sight.

The revelation of what God can do came to Isador while he was still partially blinded - he got Sarah to read portions of the scriptures. Three months after the war he accepted Jeshua Ben Joseph as the Messiah and became one of thousands who became Messianic Jews when their eyes were opened after the Ezekiel prophecies and others were shown to be true. It is of course prophesied, that God will reveal the true Messiah to the Jewish people and fill them with the Holy Spirit at that time.

As a scientist Isador particularly appreciated the science of probability mathematics - that of the 700 plus (about 718) prophecies in the Holy Bible, over 580 had already occurred, when this recent batch were so dramatically also fulfilled!

Reuben's character is based on a combination of two real persons, with whom the author is well acquainted and whose lives have encompassed many of the events described, including the past Arab-Israel Wars - though obviously not the actual war described here - yet. Reuben's mother and father had survived the German extermination camps - as children, they were both pushed into an icy fast-flowing stream by their parents, as they passed over a bridge - literally on their way to be murdered by the Nazi Regime. After a traumatic time hiding with farm animals, they escaped to freedom, reaching Israel to live on the kibbutz where Reuben was born. Both of Reuben's grandparents perished in Hitler's Holocaust, and Reuben's mother therefore owed her life to her own mother's quick thinking, at a point where there was nothing to lose.

Reuben's wife and children survived the big war and earthquake by living in one sealed room after the family home was first seriously damaged by falling debris and then partially flooded. They live not far inland, along the Mediterranean coastal strip. Before this war, Reuben, a secular Jew, had nevertheless recognised the main Jewish festivals, such as Yom Kippur. One day he came across the Rabbi's prophecy (that is written at the start of Chapter 25), that he had never seen before. He now knows that the coming of Messiah is near, but has still not yet taken the final step of recognising Him. The Messiah is, of course, Jeshua Ben Joseph, who was born, lived, was brought up and died as a Jew; known in the West as Jesus, son of Joseph.

Hank Keen, who carried out the Quicksilver aircraft mission planning, returned to the USA, from Spain, soon after the abortive attack on the Iranian missile sites. Hank attempted to keep a low profile, after the raid, but was sorely affected by the failure of the mission and the loss of life and aircraft; even though he bore no personal responsibility for the tragic losses. Later, much of the background inevitably become public knowledge. Hank's mother, in Huntsville Alabama, had long understood the biblical prophecies. She had considered that Hank, the product of a God-fearing family, had gone off the rails, when he rejected God in his teens. To his Mother's delight, once Hank saw what had gone on, he returned to the Church of his upbringing. As a serviceman he was reluctant to say much about the planning part that he had played in the abortive raid on Iran's missile sites. Of course, this was as nothing compared to what was to follow in the big battle!

Brett Foreman, the Quicksilver Squadron Commander, remained in the Air Force for one further tour of duty, then retired to the US Mid-West. He felt that he had been made a scapegoat as the Squadron Commander of the failed attack mission to Iran, that had brought so much trouble to the USA. There would be no further promotion, even though none of the failures during that fateful mission were his direct fault. Such is life sometimes in the armed services!

The fate of Iyad Aziz, who wrongly programmed his nation's ballistic missiles and then was absent from duty at the critical time when he could have corrected the situation, was public execution. This was also the fate of the Iranian fanatical leader Ahmed Pavli. It was true that a boy, with similar ambitions, had followed and spoken with Keith Perham in the souks of Teheran, one evening in the late 1950s at the height of the Cold War. Who knows where this person is today? In reality did he achieve his ambition?

The world gradually came to terms with the events which had taken place - but things would never be the same again. God had shown his hand in a way that had spiritually affected many and in a way that frightened even more. Thousands of Israel's secular and religious citizens came to recognise both their God and their long-awaited Messiah. This had an unprecedented impact, not only in Israel, but throughout the world. Jews actually went out to tell people about Jesus - the first time in any large numbers since the first Jewish believers (the followers, or disciples of Jesus - who were later to be dubbed 'Christians'), immediately after the time Jesus was on earth Himself.

Since Jews had returned to Israel from all over the world there was, in Israel, a complete complement of foreign language speakers. An Indian Jew could visit India to encourage Indians. A South African Jew could do the same in South Africa, a Chines Jew could go to speak in China.... and so on for some 100 nations.

The generation alive who see this, when it eventually happens, will marvel and say... 'how convenient it is that this is the case'. Even at that stage many will still not realise or even acknowledge that the 'Master Planner' Himself, has had all this sort of thing well in hand, since time began! In fact He planned it all from the start.

Importantly, these events left a chasm to fill in the huge swathe of the Islamic World. Many had suffered the consequences of their leader's folly for so many years. Thousands would suffer the aftermath of the radiation fall-out for the rest of their lives. Critically, the events had forced most humans world-wide to ask new questions. Millions then took the same route as the Jews and recognised the true God. God's son, Jesus, recognised only as a prophet for so long in Islam, was now given His rightful place in their lives too.

Hundreds of millions of citizens from every nation were affected - right across the world. Apart from Isador, whose invention acted as the trigger, others who took part as characters in this book observed but did not actually influence events, once the conflict commenced. The detail of the events and the timings were all orchestrated by a far greater power than man.

There remains, however, a key event to come. The return of the Messiah Himself. No one, except God, knows exactly when this will be. However, rather like the big battle, described in this book, the chronological conditions which must exist for the Messiah's return are foretold in the Holy Bible. They are being fulfilled in this chronological order, and the majority of the biblical prophecies have already been fulfilled.

You will recall that, for the big battle, the Jews had to be in the Land (having returned from all over the world). This is why biblical 'Middle East watchers', who study the prophecies, knew that Saddam Hussein's war, in 1991, despite many other pointers, was not the big one. That future conflict - and it will be so cruel for so many - is still to come. Unless, of course, God changes His mind!

The conditions for Jesus to return were clearly indicated by His own words. He said, 'I tell You (i.e. the Jews), You will not see me again until You say "Blessed is he that comes in the Name of The Lord."' In other words, Jesus himself said that the conditions would be such that until the Jews recognise Jesus as God's Messiah he would not be coming back. (Matthew 23). After the big war the Jews will increasingly recognise Him.

Meanwhile, as this is written, in the year 2005, it is of great significance today that more and more Jews, including large numbers of Ethiopian (Falasha returnees) and Russian Jews are recognising Jesus as their Messiah. It is even reported that some Rabbis are doing so. For the moment they are, reportedly, keeping a low profile. In the United Kingdom, as increasingly across the world, there are already a number of Messianic Synagogues - a few years ago there were none!

Dr Ron Haddow

Due to family pressure on his birth mother, Keith Perham was sent away and adopted into a Christian family at the age of six months and given a new name, only to loose his adopted father within three years. Even in the mid-twentieth century he underwent a strict Victorian upbringing by his widowed mother. In the early 1950s he went briefly into laboratory testing and research and then left home before the age of 18 to fly with the Royal Air Force. Among many other tasks, while flying in both propeller and jet aircraft, he took part in the first form of radar airborne early warning, long range maritime patrol, search and rescue, the H-bomb tests on Christmas Island and flew 150 special duties missions during the dangerous days of the Cold War. At this time he received the Air Force Medal. His initial tenure in the RAF was to last much longer than originally intended. However, it was briefly broken by a return to civilian electronic research, where he participated [over thirty years ago] in the design and flight testing of the first airborne digital equipment to enter RAF service.

On returning to the RAF a period was spent teaching aircrew and apprentices about flight simulators, radar, electrical and other aircraft systems, radio communications and both computer hardware and computer programming. This was followed by eight years on the staff of the Royal Air Force College, Cranwell, lecturing also world-wide at National Military Staff Colleges. His specialisation continued in Radar, Electronic Warfare, Air Defence and Guided Weapons and, of particular relevance to the future, lecturing on the Middle East Wars.

It was not until 1970s, while lecturing to Senior NATO Officers on the topic of the Middle East Wars, did the current and future significance of Israel and in particular, of Jerusalem, quite suddenly become apparent. During this turbulent period in world affairs he obtained Doctorate and Masters degrees respectively in Radar and Computer Design and also received the OBE.

Returning to research and design, Dr Haddow initially worked on the future airspace control and air defences of the NATO nations. Next came the daunting task of national technical co ordinator for Industry, for sensors aspects of the well-publicised 'Star Wars' ballistic missile defence programme. Later he became Team Leader and eventually a Senior Advisor to a NATO Industrial Advisory Group working on future defences and specifically led the team investigating the future threat perceived to The West. Rising to the task of Chief Scientist for Systems, for the premier electronics company in the UK, for the whole of this period he was also a consultant-analyst to a department in the Ministry of Defence, travelling extensively for NATO, for industry and for the government, including many visits to the Middle East.

After moving home no less than nineteen times and settling finally in Norfolk, Ron Haddow continued consulting for government departments and lecturing for Industry. He was an external examiner for several years and then became Visiting Professor for the Military Electronics Systems MSc courses at the Royal Military College of Science. Dr Haddow was one of just two scientists invited to speak by the International Christian Embassy at the Feast of Tabernacles in Jerusalem, in the year 2000.

Dr Haddow is married with three children and seven grandchildren